Mac's India
by

Susie Baggaley

Copyright

Mac's India
(In The Face of Resistance)
Copyright Susie Baggaley 2021

Published by
Baggatelle Publishers Ltd
ISBN: 9780993212185

Licence Notes

MAC's Trilogy
Book 2
Mac's India

The story so far ...

W hen Doctor Elizabeth Stuart-MacKenzie (Mac to her friends) boarded the ss Narkunda at Tilbury Docks on a grey October morning in 1929, she didn't know a soul. By the time she disembarked in India twenty-five days later, she had administered medical help to numerous sick passengers in a gale crossing the Bay of Biscay, reversed a potential miscarriage of a Rajputan Princess in Port Said, been showered with expensive gifts by a Prince of Jhalanpur, met His Majesty's British Resident and wife in Aden and appeared at the ship's fancy-dress Gala Ball dressed as Scheherazade. She had also acquired two new girlfriends, enjoyed the sexual advances of the ship's surgeon, sustained numerous injuries in a shipboard fire and attended the funeral at sea of a close fellow passenger. All in all, it had been a very eventful voyage.

Once ashore, her plan had been to depart by train for Calcutta to begin a research post at the Calcutta School of Tropical Medicine, but the offer of seven romantic nights at the luxurious Taj Mahal Hotel was too appealing, so she delayed, only to board the Imperial India Mail seven days later in a state of complete mental turmoil, having been deceived by her lover.

On arrival at the CSTM, she was equally humiliated. The misogynistic Board of Governors, having assumed she was a man, were horrified at the idea of inviting a female clinician into the ranks of their 'all male' profession, no matter how well qualified she might be, and made their feelings very clear.

Mac was suddenly faced with the ignominy of returning home to Northumbria as a failure and loose woman, unless something was done to reverse this desperate situation.

Luck and a series of unexpected coincidences saved the day, and by the start of the new decade, Mac was able to put her chaotic life behind her and get on with her career.

Or so she thought. There was just one problem. Bouts of sickness were playing havoc with her days and if food poisoning was not the cause, then life was about to get a lot more complicated and her medical research post would again be in jeopardy.

Mac's story continues . . .

(Book 1: CALL ME MAC – PORT OUT
is available in both paperback and ebook on digital book sites such as
Amazon Kindle and Barnes & Noble, or by ordering the paperback
through High Street booksellers.)

Book Two

MAC's India

(In the Face of Resistance)

Table of Contents

COPYRIGHT	2
BOOK TWO	5
TABLE OF CONTENTS	6
PROLOGUE	8
CHAPTER ONE	10
CHAPTER TWO	19
CHAPTER THREE	27
CHAPTER FOUR	43
CHAPTER FIVE	56
CHAPTER SIX	66
CHAPTER SEVEN	81
CHAPTER EIGHT	85
CHAPTER NINE	101
CHAPTER TEN	113
CHAPTER ELEVEN	127
CHAPTER TWELVE	140
CHAPTER THIRTEEN.	161
CHAPTER FOURTEEN	173
CHAPTER FIFTEEN	191
CHAPTER SIXTEEN	203
CHAPTER SEVENTEEN	216
CHAPTER EIGHTEEN	230
CHAPTER NINETEEN	243
CHAPTER TWENTY	256
CHAPTER TWENTY-ONE	273
CHAPTER TWENTY-TWO	291
CHAPTER TWENTY-THREE	318
CHAPTER TWENTY-FOUR	330
CHAPTER TWENTY-FIVE	349
CHAPTER TWENTY-SIX	364
CHAPTER TWENTY-SEVEN	377
CHAPTER TWENTY-EIGHT	386
CHAPTER TWENTY-NINE	396
CHAPTER THIRTY	404
ACKNOWLEDGEMENTS	408

ABOUT THE AUTHOR   409
REVIEW THIS NOVEL   411
AUTHOR'S BOOKS   412

Prologue

Proof, if I needed it, was staring me in the face. Enlarged ovaries of an immature female mouse confirmed my worst fears. I was carrying Dr Tom Wallace's child.

I was in India and about to begin a three-year scientific research project at the Calcutta School of Tropical Medicine, and the last thing I needed was to be pregnant. I now had a life-changing decision to make.

Elsie and Arthur Thornton, who had welcomed me into their home on my arrival, were away in the Nilgiri Hills on vacation, leaving me alone in their cantonment bungalow. This enabled me to carry out the latest Aschheim and Zondek pregnancy test away from prying eyes.

The technique was straightforward and ninety-eight percent accurate. All I had to do was subcutaneously inject an immature female mouse with my urine, for five days, then dissect it, remove its ovaries, place them under a microscope and see if they were enlarged. If they were, the mouse was prematurely on heat, and I was pregnant.

'Simple,' I announced to fresh air, having dissected many small rodents during my training to be a doctor at Edinburgh University. But there was just one problem. I didn't have a mouse.

The thought of crawling around the Thornton's backyard in the middle of the night didn't fill me with euphoria. There had to be another way.

Walking into the Medical College's science laboratory the following lunchtime, dressed in my white laboratory coat and carrying a specimen jar, I approached a young lab technician and tapped him on the arm.

'Excuse me. Do you have a five-to-ten-week-old female mouse that I can use for one of my hormonal experiments?'

Twenty minutes later, I was cycling back to the bungalow with the mouse hidden in my wicker basket, intent on confirming my worst fears.

Well, five days has duly passed and here it was for all to see. My womb was housing a living foetus which was about to wreck my future career prospects and about as welcome as a cholera outbreak in the overcrowded back streets of Newcastle.

To add to my dilemma, I was single, the child's father was a married man, and my father, a Presbyterian Minister, if told, would struggle to understand why his eldest daughter was seriously considering an abortion.

It was a mess. I was a mess, and I had no idea what to do about it, short of throwing myself off the Calcutta Hooghly Bridge.

Chapter One

I cycled out to the Rabindra Sarovar Lake south of Calcutta looking for peace and tranquillity while I mulled over my options.

Ten days earlier, at the start of the decade, I had been thrilled to accept a Ph.D research post investigating the effects of sub-tropical diseases on female and infant mortality rates throughout India, a position which the Board of Governors at the college had offered me against their better judgement. If it had not been for the Governor of Bengal's covert and underhand shenanigans on my behalf, my application would have been rejected out of hand and I would have been left high and dry.

I cringed at the thought of telling Lord Cottesmore of my present condition after all he had done to overcome the Board's prejudice and loathed the very idea of giving these fellow clinicians justifiable cause to reject me joining their ranks.

'You can't allow this to ruin your life, Mac.' I said, talking to fresh air as I walked the lake's foreshore. 'The foetus has to be aborted.'

Fine, I thought. But abortion was an anathema to me and made my skin crawl.

I dropped onto a grassy knoll and watched a group of bar-headed geese take flight from the surface of the lake, the arrowhead formation heading towards the Hooghly River. This distraction was only transitory, however, my mind refusing to be side-tracked. The issues were obvious. A foetal termination without medical grounds was illegal and dangerous, especially in India. Even if this was not the case, I had only been in the country for ten weeks and had no idea who could carry it out. As to the psychological effect of an abortion, I wasn't sure that I could live with the consequences of killing an embryo. Being agnostic was all very well, but I was also a doctor and taking a human life would mean violating my Hippocratic Oath.

Then there was the problem of the baby's father, Tom Wallace. He knew nothing about the pregnancy and could never be around to help, yet this was his only biological child. Did he have a right to know? Without his agreement, the abortion would be doubly unethical, yet telling him would bring its own problems and, no doubt, the news would devastate his wife.

'Right. That puts paid to that option, Mac.' My hand smacked down hard on a pesky fly and missed, leaving a weal mark on my wrist. I rubbed it as I considered the next option. To face the pregnancy alone and put the child up for adoption.

I now faced three further problems. By allowing the pregnancy to go full term I would have to delay my Ph.D for at least nine months and disappear from Calcutta in the process. But, I argued, I had absolutely no idea what excuse I could give for my sudden absence, or where I would go, or how I would survive without an income? More to the point, where would I find someone to adopt the baby, and could I abandon it to a stranger?

'NO! Absolutely not.' I looked around hoping no-one was in earshot and lobbed a pebble into the water in frustrated anger, watching the surface ripple outwards in ever increasing concentric circles, replicating the effect this pregnancy was having on my life.

'Well then, that only leaves option three,' I muttered, my fingernails now chewed to the core. 'You'll have to give up your post at the CSTM, board a P&O ship bound for England and arrive back home at Riveldene Vicarage heavily pregnant and minus a husband.'

I could imagine the horrendous effect this action would have on my family. Ma would have apoplexy, Pa's respect for me would be severely tested, his parishioners would treat me as a wanton woman and Aunt Karr would write me off as a lost cause. I screwed up my eyes and decided that jumping off the Hooghly Bridge wasn't such a bad idea after all.

'Jesus, Mac, what the hell are you going to do?' I dropped my head onto my knees and whimpered like an animal in pain. Having turned my back on my home, my family and my GP practise in Northumbria to travel halfway across the world to follow my dream, 'being with child', as my mother would say, was nothing short of insane.

'You blithering idiot, Mac.' I sobbed. 'Why on earth did you stay at the Taj Mahal Hotel in Bombay with Tom when you should have been on your way to Calcutta?'

There was no acceptable answer, of course, and wishing it had never happened was absurd. Staring into the abyss, I imagined Aunt Karr's castigating remarks reverberating around my head and I shuddered. This was not the first time she had been called upon to sort me out and I winced at the thought of another lesson in realism.

'Elizabeth Stuart-MacKenzie, when will you ever learn? You nearly failed your medical degree because you were pining over some Irish veterinary surgeon with an ego the size of Mount Everest, and now you're

throwing away the chance of a lifetime because you copulated with a ship's doctor who turned out to be married and would never leave his wife. Lust is all very well, dear, but having unprotected sex is shear insanity. Whatever happened to contraception?'

Karr, tight lipped, steely eyed, annoyingly blunt and with a talent for weeding out miscreants after years lecturing psychology at St Andrew's University, didn't suffer fools easily, and her analysis of my shortcomings was damning in the extreme. Nor had she finished lecturing me.

'Cowering in a corner licking your wounds like some pathetic victim is not going to help you either, Elizabeth. You've made your bed and now you must lie in it. No-one else is to blame but yourself, so stop whining, get some MacKenzie backbone and sort yourself out.'

Her realism was all very well, but what I really needed was a glass of her Harvey's Bristol Cream sherry and a slab of her home-made Dundee cake. In comparison, Elsie Thornton's herbal tea and bite-sized Indian sweetmeats simply wouldn't cut it!

I stretched out my legs and watched the sun as it slid behind a clump of trees, the rays illuminating the bare branches in a fiery amber glow as flocks of birds chirruped in the tops and dusk settled at the edges of my periphery. My head ached from constantly going around in circles and my joints creaked from being too long in one position. I staggered to my feet, picked up my bicycle and headed back to the safety of the Thornton's bungalow, my mind still in a quandary.

Aunt Karr was right, I thought. This pregnancy was my fault and waiting around for some miraculous intervention was neither logical nor sane. I gently rubbed my abdomen and tried to strengthen my resolve. What was needed was a plan. Drowning my sorrows in a large G&T, I crossed my fingers and hoped that one would present itself sooner rather than later.

Dawn brought little clarity, just mental exhaustion and another bout of sickness. It was in this state that I arrived at Dr Chakramachari's office in the Calcutta School of Tropical Medicine to hear what arrangements had been made by the Board of Governors for my research project. Suffice to say, the Deputy Head of Physiology did not welcome me with open arms.

'Good Morning, Doctor Stuart-MacKenzie, please take a seat. We have much to get through and I have a lecture in fifteen minutes.'

The timbre of his voice was devoid of warmth and I had to cross my legs to stop my knees shaking.

'Your research proposal is extremely unusual. Not only does it concentrate on the cause and effect of sub-tropical diseases rather than a cure, but it has a strong prophylactic bias towards sanitation and health. This normally falls under the remit of India's Public Health Department.'

He had grasped the essence of my proposal perfectly, so I remained silent, knowing that the Public Health Department had no interest whatsoever in female and infant mortality, which was why I had been given the funding in the first place. I waited patiently for him to continue.

'Be that as it may, as you have the financial backing to undertake this research, it is our opinion that it cannot be accomplished by you sitting here at the CSTM doing scientific analysis and experiments.' He cleared his throat, sniffed, and continued. 'Therefore, having discussed the project with Doctor Agnes Scott and Surgeon-General Sir Peter Bonham-Cavendish we have settled on a compromise plan.'

I began to fidget in my chair wishing he would get on with it as I was getting desperate to empty my bladder.

'Your dissertation will take three years to complete, but the Women's Medical Service here in India need your clinical skills straight away. So, you will spend three days each week working in various Women's Hospitals around the country acting as a locum doctor. In this way, you will obtain in-depth experience of your subject and the WMS will gain an additional medical practitioner.'

Well, I thought, clenching my buttocks, at least I won't have to see this man's miserable features very often. He drawled on.

'The remaining two days will be taken up with laboratory research and scientific analysis, liaising closely with associates from the Public Health Department and the India Civil Service.'

He looked up to check that I understood. My bladder was seriously under pressure making it nigh impossible to concentrate.

'Of your two supervisors, Doctor Agnes Scott will determine your work schedule and monitor your clinical progress and Sir Peter Bonham-Cavendish will act as a liaison officer between yourself, the Public Health Department and the ICS. He will also mentor your scientific research and subsequent analysis.'

I gritted my teeth and prayed his diatribe would reach a conclusion before I puddled the floor beneath my seat.

'Your initial salary will be £584 per year which will include hospital accommodation and food. This will be provided by the WMS and paid for by the Countess of Dufferin's Fund. Travel expenses, off-site accommodation and any medical and scientific expenses will be financed by the India Research Fund and you will be given a £50 rolling float. Receipts will be required for all such expenditure.' He ripped a pink slip from a carbon-papered receipt book and thrust it at me. 'You can obtain the first tranche of this money from the college's cashier.'

I took the slip, screwing it up in my clenched fist as I chewed the inside of my mouth.

'As to a Government pension? There isn't one for women.' His smirk was pure reptilian. 'But a ten-percent deduction from your salary will be credited to the Women's Provident Fund for use in your old age. Should you choose to leave the employ of the WMS before then, a part-refund may be negotiated.'

Typical, I thought, as he looked at his watch and stood. 'Finally, I will arrange an annual meeting with you to assess your progress and to discuss necessary changes to any of the matters raised today. Are you in agreement?'

It was a race to see who could get to the door first. I won, shook his hand and headed for the lavatory, the pink slip going soggy in my sweaty hand.

My bladder emptied like an opened sluice gate as I mulled over Dr Chakramachari's plan. It all made perfect sense, of course, but I couldn't help thinking that the arrogant and pompous

Governors had been hell-bent on keeping me away from Calcutta for as much of the three years as possible.

Well, I thought, as I washed my hands and pushed a stray strand of hair back into place, at least I now knew what the plan was and mentally prepared myself for a rapid departure to Delhi to join Dr Agnes Scott and her team at the Lady Hardinge Women's Medical College where she was the Principal.

Thoughts of Delhi brought my friend Ruby Tavener to mind. During my twenty-five-day passage on the ss Narkunda from Tilbury to Bombay she had been my cabin companion and was now living in the lap of luxury as an upper-class mistress somewhere in the capital. I had no idea who her secret lover was, but the chauffeur driven Rolls-Royce limousine which had collected her from Ballard Pier on our arrival indicated that he was probably some Colonial British aristocrat whose wife, no doubt, had remained behind in the Shires while he did whatever aristocratic gentlemen did in the Raj and enjoyed the benefits of cavorting with Ruby.

Unlike him, my cabin companion was anything but aristocratic. Born in the back streets of Streatham, Ruby had experienced a disparate upbringing culminating in a career as a *tableaux vivant* at the Windmill Theatre in Soho. She was also well versed in the seedier side of London life. Our paths had crossed because she had been fired by the strip-club's owner, Mrs Laura Henderson, for fraternising with one of its customers which was strictly against the rules. No doubt, I thought, the customer was the same aristocrat who was now financing her lifestyle in return for services rendered.

Nevertheless, she was well placed to advise me on what to do about my pregnancy and would have a plan in place within days.

Tucking the pink slip into my pocket, I walked out into the fug of Calcutta's traffic and checked the time. I was running late, and Sir Peter Bonham-Cavendish would be waiting impatiently in his office. I headed for the college railings where my bicycle was waiting and dug around in my handbag for the padlock-key. To my horror, it wasn't there.

'Bloody hell, I must have dropped it in the ladies' lavatory,' I groaned, as a college lecturer passed by, tutting loudly.

There was nothing for it, I had to abandon my self-propelled transport and find a rickshaw. Flustered, panicking and waving my arms around like some demented lunatic, I stepped straight into the path of a vacant rickshaw, causing its cyclist to make an emergency stop, which nearly catapulted him over the handlebars. I jumped onto the canopied bench-seat turning puce with embarrassment, looked at my watch and asked to be taken to the India Medical Service headquarters in Fort William without delay. All I could hope was that the cyclist understood my accent and that the Surgeon-General of Immunology was running late.

Chapter Two

Three days later I was standing under the Delhi Junction railway clock at four-fifteen in the afternoon feeling abandoned, my baggage stacked by the exit. The building's red and white brick frontage, with its myriad of pointed arches and soaring towers, dominated the skyline and resembled some grand old lady long past her prime.

I was tired, hot and irritable, having spent thirty-three hours on the East India Mail from Calcutta, which had been delayed in Mughalsarai Junction in the middle of the night due to some re-scheduled troop movements. Sleep in my second-class carriage had been impossible due to all the shouting, door banging and general pandemonium going on outside and I was now fractious and angry because no-one was here to meet me.

'If I had decided to go straight to the Lady Hardinge College,' I muttered, 'instead of spending the weekend with Ruby, I wouldn't be standing here kicking my heels.' Patience was not a MacKenzie virtue.

After a further fifteen minutes in the fetid air, a dark green, soft-topped limousine with white-walled tyres cruised across the forecourt and came to rest at the main entrance. I wandered over as a uniformed chauffeur slowly uncurled himself from the vehicle and looked around. As all the other train passengers had long gone, I assumed this man was here to collect me so I raised my hand.

'Excuse me. Are you here to collect Doctor Stuart-MacKenzie?'

The tall middle-aged Indian dressed in matching dark-green livery, his pock-marked face, deep-set ebony eyes and thick, wiry, coal-black beard producing a rather menacing air, turned, bowed and exposed a set of pure white, perfectly aligned teeth.

'You be doctor, Memsahib?' he asked, his head rocking from side-to-side.

'I am, and my luggage is over there.' I pointed to a well-worn, flat-bed trailer with two metal-rimmed wheels, parked by the entrance. 'Please be especially careful with the leather monogrammed trunk and medical bag.'

'Yes, Memsahib Doctor. I not drop, Memsahib Doctor.'

He opened the rear passenger door of the imposing Lincoln Sedan and waited as I stepped onto the wide running-board and climbed inside, settling myself onto the pristine cream leather upholstery as I watched him load my bags into the boot through the driver's rear-view mirror.

'The journey not long. Memsahib Doctor,' he announced, starting the engine and engaging the gears.

We gently pulled away from the curb and as the railway station faded from view, I relaxed back into the opulence of the interior and enjoyed being driven towards New Delhi and the Lutyens's Bungalow Zone. A welcome breeze blew through the open-sided, canvas canopy, tossing my damp, dishevelled, auburn hair in all directions and I stretched my neck to capture the sensation around my perspiring neckline as my stress levels began to decrease.

New Delhi was impressive, the wide landscaped boulevards and grand Lutyens's architecture being in stark contrast to the crowded, narrow Calcutta streets which had become so familiar. The area oozed money and was so typically Ruby, I thought, as the soft suspension of the limousine eased my aching muscles. Never one for doing things by half, my cabin companion appeared to have fallen on her feet yet again, and I was looking forward to a night of sheer luxury in her well-appointed, all expenses paid villa. I closed my eyes and let the convertible take the strain as I analysed our friendship.

Ruby and I were an unlikely match. For a start, her height, Clara Bow looks, sex appeal and worldly experience had always put me at a disadvantage, despite her working-class Streatham background. My father was a Presbyterian Minister, hers was an out-of-work drunkard and gambler. My mother was a tee-total, respectable, life-long member of the WI. Hers was a victim of domestic violence and had died of cirrhosis of the liver from too much gin. While I was being nurtured and educated to the highest standard, where blasphemy was deemed to be a sin, Ruby was surviving on her wits in the backstreets of London with a mouth like a fishwife and a command of Cockney slang second to none.

I smiled as the car coasted on through the leafy boulevards recalling my friend's main talent, which overcame any lack of social standing. Ruby could imitate anyone. At the drop of a hat, she could impersonate a British Countess as if she were born to the role. I was in no doubt that this skill had now placed her at the very centre of Delhi's aristocratic society.

The ladies of the Shires, I mused, were probably under the illusion that she was a young widow who had lost her husband at Passchendaele and had become a model for Dior in Paris, after being discovered at the Folies Bergère by a Madame Du

Lac. All this seemed highly unlikely, of course, but I had witnessed, first-hand, Ruby brazenly repeating her fictious story to any first-class passenger who had happened to enquire, as we cruised towards Bombay. Much to my amazement, they had believed every word and showed genuine sympathy for her plight!

A sudden jolt of the car brought me back to reality and, as we turned into a wide entrance flanked by ornate wrought-iron gates and continued along an immaculately maintained tree-lined drive, my jaw dropped open.

'Jesus,' I whispered, staring at a gabled, sandstone two-story mansion with massive windows and extensive verandas as the limousine cruised to a halt and the engine died. 'This is bigger than Lord and Lady Cottesmore's family seat in Calcutta!'

I nervously stepped from the car recalling the magnificence of Benningtons, situated in the Rabindra Sarovar Lake area of Calcutta, and wondered who on earth could afford a pile bigger than the Governor of Bengal's home just for a mistress. I examined my crumpled linen suit nervously, which now resembled a dishcloth from the galley of the East India Mail train. My sweaty palms, ironing out the creases, did nothing to improve it. I gave up, sighed, shook my hair into a semblance of order and ascended the cream marble steps towards an imposing canopied portico.

Ruby was standing at the entrance, framed by two deep red hibiscus bushes encased in sandstone amphoras, and, as expected, she looked every inch the Dior model. Her tailored white, wide-bottomed silk slacks emphasised her long legs, while her deep-russet, V-necked silk blouse, drawn in at the waist with extending ties, accentuated her slim figure and wasp-like waist. She looked stunning and knew it.

'Well, Mac, how is India treating my very own personal physician?' She walked forward and bent to give me a theatrical peck on both cheeks, her emerald and diamond bracelet sparkling in the late afternoon sunlight.

'Obviously, not as well as you, Ruby.'

'Oh, I don't know about that. I imagine the Lady Hardinge Medical College for Women will compare very favourably with this.' Her arms spread wide taking in the magnificence of the tall Doric pillars.

'Ever the comedian, Ruby,' I replied, chuckling at the absurdity of the remark, and followed her into an imposing marble hall, only slightly smaller than that at the Taj Mahal Hotel in Bombay.

Her attention moved to the butler hovering by the stairs, dressed in a white dhoti with dark green accessories and matching open-toed leather sandals, 'Doctor Stuart-Mackenzie's cases should go to the Peacock Room, Sanjay,' she instructed in a very plumb upper-class English voice.

The Indian took my luggage from the chauffeur and began carrying the smaller pieces up the curved marble staircase. He looked familiar but I had no idea why.

'Nice trunk,' commented Ruby as we passed my gold monogrammed leather case, her eagle eyes missing nothing when it came to quality.

'Umm,' was all I said as I was led out onto a wide rear terracotta terrace, its glorious views over the extensive landscaped grounds oozing class. Ruby looked at her Cartier watch and dropped onto an ochre-coloured sofa, pointing to an identical one to her right.

'It's nearly cocktail hour, Mac. What do you fancy?'

I sank back into deep feathered cushions and threw my bag onto a pouffe close by. 'A very large, very cold Pimms and a full body massage. I don't care which one comes first.'

Her laughter rattled through the wood and tiled rafters. 'Was the journey that bad?'

'Worse,' I replied, kicking off my low-heeled shoes and wriggling my toes to bring back the circulation whilst relaying the reason for our unscheduled middle of the night delay. 'The Indian Army wouldn't know how to do quiet, even if stealth meant the difference between life or death.'

'I wouldn't know,' quipped Ruby, ordering drinks. 'I always travel first class.'

'Lucky old you.' I scanned the grounds wondering again who on earth could afford such luxury. Even Edward VII's mistress, Lily Langtree, I thought, hadn't warranted this level of opulence.

'Do I sense a touch of jealousy, Doctor Stuart-MacKenzie?'

'What do you think, Mistress Tavener?'

'Shame on you, Mac. May I remind you that being a mistress is not all a bed of roses.'

I ran both hands through my hair, feeling crotchety and inwardly chided myself for being so irritated. I wouldn't have wanted Ruby's life any more than she would want mine and we both knew it. Equally, it wasn't her fault that I was battling with a personal problem which also had sexual connotations. I lifted my Pimm's from the silver salver and had a twinge of déjà vu.

The butler's face was very familiar to me, but try as I may, I couldn't place him.

'Exhaustion is making me hallucinate,' I mumbled, as I felt the chilled liquid fizz on my tongue.

'What?' Ruby opened a lacquered box on the coffee-table and placed a cigarette into a long ivory cigarette-holder and waited for the butler to light it. She then nodded and dismissed him with her eyes.

'Nothing.' I replied, watching the cigarette smoke travel in an upward direction, drawn to the rafters by the six-bladed electric fan. 'I was just reprimanding myself for being so tetchy when I should be grateful for the opportunity to stay in your amazing home.'

Ruby brushed my statement away with her hand. 'It's not mine, Mac. I'm afraid my provider isn't that generous.'

'Well, whatever his faults, he certainly knows how to treat a woman.'

My hostess smiled. 'It does have its down-side, you know. When I'm not satisfying his sexual desires, I spend my time rattling around this gilded mausoleum talking to the walls. Frankly, Mac, I'm in need of some scintillating conversation,' she paused and dragged on her cigarette, 'and you are just the tonic I need. So, stop acting like Cinderella and tell me what your plans are here in Delhi?'

I blew her a kiss and relaxed back enjoying the grandeur of my surroundings. 'Other than staying here for the rest of my life?'

'You couldn't afford the rent.'

I choked on my Pimm's. 'Now that, Ruby Tavener, is an understatement.' I unbuttoned the neck of my blouse, blew cool air into my cleavage, and considered my reply. 'My plan is simple. After a bath in ass's milk, I shall dine on Delhi's finest cuisine, prepared by your European cook.' I paused, eyebrows raised, looking at Ruby who I knew hated anything with curry in the title. She winked and went back to her dry martini. 'Then, after a long catch-up on your news, I am going to imitate Sleeping Beauty and hope to be woken up by a frog.'

I closed my eyes and let the peace of the terrace wash over me. 'Tomorrow, I will rise refreshed, ready to meet my mentor, Doctor Agnes Scott, and begin my work as a doctor of obstetrics examining the vaginas and wombs of Indian women who are, have been, or hope to become pregnant.' Ruby's nose wrinkled. 'Of course, I won't feel hard done by knowing that you are whiling away your hours talking to the walls in total luxury while I get up-close and personal to abject poverty, but I will enjoy returning here next weekend when I will bore the pants off you with all things gynaecological.' I raised my Pimm's glass in salute. 'How does that sound?'

'Messy,' announced Ruby, blowing smoke rings in my direction.

'Don't do that,' I coughed, wafting my hand in front of my face, 'you know I hate it.' I stretched my legs out and rested my feet on the edge of the coffee table. 'So, Miss Tavener, what exotic dishes have you got planned for my delectation this evening? And don't say pie and mash.'

Chapter Three

We had just finished a mouth-watering tropical fruit and coconut syllabub when the telephone rang. Ruby got up from the dining table and moved to the hall, pointing her finger at the wine bottle and my glass as she went. I refilled both crystal goblets and sat quietly sipping the smooth French Burgundy while listening to Ruby's dulcet tones.

'Hello. Oh, hi darling. Yes, she's here . . . No, she can't, she has to stay at the Lady Hardinge College for waifs and strays . . .'

I chuckled. Ruby always managed to bring the most prestigious organisation down to street level.

'. . . She will be back at the weekend and you can see her then.'

Crikey, I thought, hoping this rich British aristocrat didn't turn out to be the head of the India Medical Service.

'. . .Of course, I'll pass on your regards. Now, what time are you likely to turn up, so I can tell cook?'

My eyebrows crossed. Having never met Ruby's lover, his '*regards*' seemed rather presumptuous. I shrugged thinking it was due to his typical English upper-class manners and swallowed more Burgundy.

'Right, bye.' Ruby returned and sat, stretching for her goblet. 'Vijay sends his regards.'

I spat red wine all over the tablecloth.

'VIJAY,' I stammered trying vainly to dab the spilled liquid with a table napkin, my mind revolving in ever decreasing circles. 'Vijay Kumar Singh?

She nodded.

'Prince Vijay Kumar Sing II.'

'The very same.' Ruby was now chuckling at my discomfort.

'Vijay Kumar Singh II, son of the Maharaja of Jhalanpur and heir to the Jhalanpur fortune?'

'For God sake, Mac. YES! Who the hell else do you think could afford all this?'

'You're lying.' My hands were at eye level, palms out, questions flying around my head like a plague of locusts. 'You have to be.'

'Why?' Ruby's expression was more angelic than the cherubs in the Sistine Chapel.

'Because . . .' I was floundering, disbelief barring my ability to accept reality as images of our time on the ss Narkunda gutted my innards as efficiently as a fish-knife on sardines. I glared at the cause of my distress.

'Answer me this, Ruby Tavener.' I took a deep breath and countered off questions using my fingers. 'Was it Vijay who bought you that Cartier watch?' She nodded.

'Who got you fired from the Windmill Theatre?' She nodded again.

'And paid for your passage on the ss Narkunda?' She shrugged.

'Who then arranged your private transportation to Delhi from Bombay in a Rolls Royce?'

Ruby's expression was pure Mona Lisa. 'Don't look so horrified, Mac. Even a country bumpkin like you should have figured it out by now.'

'Figured it out! What the hell do you mean, figured it out?' I was shouting at her from across the dining table, anger, disgust and downright shock at her nonchalant attitude shattering any respect I had for this Soho showgirl. 'Have you any idea what your lover did?' If Prince Vijay Kumar Singh II had entered the dining room at that moment, I would have willingly throttled him to death. Ruby froze, her lips tightening as I left my chair and paced the marble tiles, reliving the day Ruby left the ship for a sightseeing tour of Giza and Cairo while I stayed behind in the Jhalanpur Suite attended to the Prince's wife, Princess Dashwanabai.

'Of course,' I suddenly yelled, coming to an abrupt stop. 'That's were I've seen him.'

'Who?'

I pointed to the butler as he hovered by the door awaiting instructions. 'You were the chaprassi in the Jhalanpur Suite, on the ss Narkunda, weren't you?' The butler bowed and slowly backed away.

'Mac, what the hell has got into you?' Ruby circled the table, grabbed my elbow and waltzed me into the lounge where coffee and chocolates were sitting on a glass-topped table supported by four alabaster elephants.

'Now, calm down, sit down, and cut the holier than thou act.' Her hand pressed down hard on my right shoulder and I sank onto the gold, regency-striped settee and watched this larger-than-life East-End stripper chassé across the Persian carpet and lower her very expensive butt onto a matching gold wing-backed chair. She crossed her legs and rested her elbows on the chair arms, her fingertips and thumbs touching. 'Now, explain your problem regarding Vijay and me?'

'How could you, Ruby?' I stammered. 'How could he? How could you both do something like that?' My forefinger was now stabbing the air between us.

'Mac, I think we should begin this conversation again because I've got absolutely no idea what you're talking about.'

I was turning purple. 'Are you telling me, Ruby Tavener, that you had no idea when you and Vijay breezed off to Cairo, that Vijay's wife was suffering a miscarriage on board ship and that the only medic who could give her any assistance at all was ME!' My finger was now puncturing my breastbone.

Ruby was wide-eyed, head cocked, like some puppy waiting for a treat.

'Don't look so bloody innocent. Why do you think Vijay got you to buy me that ludicrously large bottle of expensive perfume in Cairo? What possible reason would he have had to spend that amount of money on someone he didn't even know? Come on, figure it out for yourself.' I gritted my teeth and waited as the penny dropped. 'Did you tell him you were sharing a cabin with a female doctor?'

Ruby nodded.

'Is that why his physician remained by his side instead of returning to the ship? God alive! Ruby. What sort of husband would prefer to bed you rather than save the life of his only son and heir?' I was livid.

'That's out of order. I didn't . . . I mean . . . how could I know any of this. I asked you why you failed to join the shore-party when we got back to Suez, but you were so full of your own importance, you refused to tell me.'

Ruby had a point. Patient confidentiality had stopped me from telling the truth and now she was furiously rubbing her forehead trying to take in my words, their meaning completely wrecking the atmosphere of the evening. Finally, she looked up, her features icy. 'How dare you judge me. Who the fuck do you think I am?'

Gone was the plumb voice, the Swiss finishing-school demeanour, the Hollywood starlet pose. This was Ruby in the raw and it was not a pretty sight. In the stony silence that ensued, our glares fused across the coffee table.

'So, Doctor Stuart-MacKenzie, did you manage to save the child?' Sarcasm oozed from every syllable.

'Yes, Miss Tavener, I did, and I'll remind you that I forfeited my own delights of Giza and Cairo in the process.'

My anger at learning of Vijay's decision to remain ashore even knowing about his wife's dire condition had only been slightly assuaged by Tom Wallace when I questioned him about it some hours after the event.

'Prince Vijay Kumar Singh II lives in a very different world to ours, Mac. The future Maharaja of Jhalanpur would never interfere in matters of the Zenana. You must understand, child mortality is very common in India, that's one reason why these Princes take so many wives. It's their way of ensuring that there is a family bloodline.'

My laugh sounded hard, bitter and full of venom. 'Sadly, my efforts were not enough in the end. The child died after the ship's fire, although you wouldn't know anything about that either, would you?'

Ruby stared at me, her skin the colour of the alabaster elephants, her lower lip turning white between her teeth. 'Well, are you going to fill me in on what happened, or leave me in blissful ignorance yet again?'

It was torture watching what I was doing to her, but I couldn't stop. 'Princess Dashwanabai's fear of burning to death caused her to abort the child while you lay in the ship's sickbay with your ribs strapped up.'

'Jesus Christ!'

'Christ had nothing to do with it, Ruby. Vijay's wife was terrified of fire after being badly burned when she was a child.' I shook my head, trying to escape the images exploding before my eyes. 'Her brother died of asphyxiation in the same fire.' My hands cupped together, and I stared at the empty space within, my words glacial. 'I was the one who held that little dead foetus, Ruby. I was the one who had the Princess's blood dripping from my hands as Vijay's son and heir lay, inert, in the palm of my hand.'

Ruby was now chewing on her fist, her eyelids blinking away tears, as my own pregnancy, a surfeit of alcohol and a need to vent my spleen drove me on.

'Have you any idea how I now feel knowing that you two were making love at the Shepheard's Hotel while she lay abandoned and alone in her marital bed, desperately wanting to give the man she loved a son and heir after three long barren years of trying, and all she had was me to rely on.' I lay back against the deep sofa cushion, closed my eyes and sighed deeply. 'And, in the end, I failed her too.'

The Ormolu gold clock ticked away on the mantlepiece, and we sat in silence, both in a world of our own. It was Ruby who spoke first, her voice now cracked and abraded.

'How old is she?'

An image of kohl-blacked eyes, a delicate frame, small-veined hands and first-degree burns disfiguring her thighs were vivid. 'How old do you think she is?'

'About mid-thirties, possibly older.' Ruby paused. 'Older than me, anyway.'

I opened my eyes and stared at the gold-leaf ceiling cornice, my stomach churning. 'You're way off beam, Ruby. Princess Dashwanabai is nineteen years old. She's a beautiful Hindu girl with long, shining black hair, delicate features and a submissive, sensitive demeanour. Everything you are not.' I heard Ruby's sharp intake of breath. 'She was sixteen years old on her wedding day and that was the first time she had ever set eyes on Vijay.'

'God alive!' Ruby pinched the top of her nose. 'I was under the impression that she was much older, probably rather plain and only there as a token wife to give Vijay an heir.'

'Is that what he told you?'

Ruby's furrowed brow deepened 'No, he didn't . . . well, not exactly. He's a very private person when it comes to his family. He never says much.' She coughed to clear her throat. 'I guess I just imagined it to justify my own existence.'

I scanned the lounge with its exotic furniture and classy décor and wondered what she would do once she was replaced by a younger version. As for Vijay, my opinion hadn't changed. He was self-centred and a law unto himself, living the playboy lifestyle in his very expensive bubble without a care in the world. Ruby was just another notch on his belt, but I couldn't tell her that any more than I could act as a sanctimonious bystander. My Presbyterian upbringing would never allow me to condone Vijay's philandering, but Ruby was right, who was I to judge her? Who was I to judge anyone under my present circumstances?

My hand shot to my stomach and my chest jerked as I took an involuntary gasp of breath.

'What's wrong.' Ruby was half out of her seat.

'Nothing.' My attention majored on my tropical fruit and coconut sorbet which was about to make an appearance. 'Well . . . actually, everything.'

Ruby didn't know whether to sit or stand so she hovered. 'Is there something else I should know about Vijay?'

I could feel my stomach begin to churn and a cold sweat break out on my forehead. 'No,' I muttered, 'not from me. I shouldn't have said what I did. If you need to know any more, you will have to ask him.'

'So why do you look as if you are going to be sick?'

'Because, believe it or not, Ruby, I'm pregnant, and suffering from morning-sickness.'

'Don't be ridiculous. It's nine-thirty in the evening.'

My hand shot to my mouth. 'Bugger the time. Where's the nearest lavatory?'

I lay with my head over the toilet pan feeling wretched. I had no idea why I had blurted out my condition, especially when I knew full well that Ruby was incapable of keeping a secret. By telling her, I now ran the risk that she would inform Vijay, he would pass it on to his close friend, Sir Peter Bonham-Cavendish, and Sir Peter would inform the CSTM Governors.

I could only assume that the shock of learning of Ruby's affair with Vijay had scrambled my brain along with my innards. My hostess was waiting as I came out of the cloakroom.

'This is all nonsense, Mac.' Ruby was pacing. 'You're probably suffering from food poisoning and Vijay's chef is about to get his marching orders.'

I leant against the door-frame, bile bitter in my mouth. 'Ruby, watch my lips move. I'M PREGNANT. Why won't you believe me?'

'Because you're a doctor for Christ's sake. A respectable, moral, boring, studious doctor, and a Vicar's daughter to boot. You would NEVER get yourself banged up, not in a million years.' As usual, Ruby didn't mince her words.

'Thank you for that character assassination, it really helps.'

'Don't mention it.'

I returned to the lounge and flopped onto the sofa. 'As impossible as it may seem to you, Miss Tavener, someone actually found my moral, boring, studious side attractive enough to want my body, and I can assure you that I am well and truly, banged up, as you said.'

'OK. OK.' Ruby dropped down beside me. 'So, were you raped?'

"No.'

'Drunk?'

'No, I was stone cold sober. Although my behaviour on the night in question was certainly out of character.'

'You can say that again. How far gone are you?'

'Eleven weeks.' Ruby was busily counting dates. 'Eleven weeks would put you seven days after we arrived in Bombay and, if you weren't raped, I assume Doctor Tom Wallace has put a bun in your oven.'

'Very graphic, Ruby, but sadly correct.'

She wandered off to the drinks trolley, tutting as she went and poured herself a very large scotch, lifting the decanter and looking my way. I shook my head.

'I still don't understand why two professional physicians would even go there. Was it beneath you to use a condom or was the foreplay so intense you both forgot?'

I slammed my hand down on the settee arm. 'Damn you, Ruby, you make us sound like a pair of rutting tomcats.'

'Good pun, under the circumstances. Well, did you, or didn't you?'

'What?'

'Use a condom.'

'Of-course we did. Lots of them.'

'Then how come you're pregnant, and please don't tell me it's another immaculate conception.' She downed her scotch in one go.

I scratched my forehead, breathed deeply and tried to put the record straight.

'Look, Tom was really careful both onboard and during our stay in Bombay.' I was gritting my teeth. 'That is, until our last day . . .'

'At the Taj Mahal Hotel.'

'How did you know that?'

'Vijay told me.'

'Oh, of course he did.' My beautiful, monogrammed leather travelling case and matching medical bag sprang to mind. A parting gift as he and his entourage left the hotel for his private train to Jhalanpur. 'Can I finish?'

'Sorry.' Ruby refilled her crystal tumbler.

'As I was saying, we were fine until our picnic in the hills above the Bhor Pass. It was one hell of a romantic setting and I was convinced Tom was going to ask me to marry him. I spent the lunch trying to think of a way of letting him down gently.'

'Being seen as one of the Fishing Fleet is not your style, then?'

'Shut up, or I am going to bed right now.'

'Temper, temper.'

I bared my teeth and carried on. 'Well, while I was wondering how to decline his proposal, he announced that he was already married.'

Ruby rotated on the spot. 'Bloody hell! TOM WALLACE?'

I nodded. 'Hard to believe, isn't it?' I rubbed my temples and continued. 'I was spitting bullets as you can imagine, but I was not going to let him see that.' My chin came up and my lips puckered. 'So, I took a leaf out of your book and played the whore, giving him the night of his life using that damned rose camisole YOU gave me as a gift from Cairo.' My forefinger was punching the air again.

'Minus a condom?'

'Minus a condom.' I glared at Ruby daring her to comment. She had other things on her mind.

'Just to put the record straight, Doctor Stuart-MacKenzie, I'm not a whore, I'm a mistress.'

'What's the difference?'

'Touché, Mon amie.'

There was a pause in proceedings while I went in search of an icepack to aid a raging headache. On my return, Ruby was curled up in one corner of the sofa with a bottle of chilled champagne in one hand and crystal glasses in the other.

'Welcome to the club, Mac. This calls for a celebration.'

I was not amused. 'What the hell do I have to celebrate, Ruby?'

As I curled up in the other corner and placed the icepack by my right temple, she handed me a full champagne flute. 'You, dear, have just fallen off your tight-arsed pedestal and joined the ranks of us fallen women. So, welcome to the real world, Doctor. Cheers.'

The champagne bubbles tickled my nose and I sneezed.

'Bless you.'

'Thank you, but I need more than a blessing right now.'

'What are you going to do?'

'I have absolutely no idea. Over to you, Oracle.'

'Does Tom Wallace know?'

My hand shook. 'No, he doesn't, and he is not going to, unless you open your big mouth.'

'Mum's the word, Mac. You know me.'

'Only too well.' My words were peppered with bile. 'I mean it, Ruby. Tom would only complicate the situation right now, so no pillow talk.'

A white line edged Ruby's lip and the timbre of her voice chilled the air between us. 'Mac, you may not believe this, but I am quite capable of taking certain secrets to the grave.' She sat, jaw rigid, her expression cold and calculating and thick with foreboding, except it didn't seem to be directed at me. 'You may think you know me, but frankly, Madam, you wouldn't have a clue.'

The hairs on the back of my neck stood up and my stomach muscles clenched. I had obviously touched a nerve and I didn't know what to do about it. She was right, of course. I didn't know her at all, and I was skating on thin ice thinking I did. I chose my words very carefully.

'If I've misjudged you, Ruby, I'm terribly sorry and have no excuse.' My hand hovered above the cushion, wanting to give her comfort but not knowing if it would be rejected. 'Ours is an unlikely friendship, but we're both a long way from home and I really need to rely on you, so please, take me into your confidence and make me understand.' I watched in horror as Ruby's well-structured, constantly honed, tough veneer began to crumble before my eyes, peeling away like some aging plaster from a damp wall, leaving behind a vulnerable, lonely, deeply scarred, insecure and damaged woman whose good looks and sexual appeal would only dim with age. I held my breath, hoping she would not disappear back into her shell.

'Mac,' she whispered, her words hesitating. 'You think you have problems now you're pregnant. Well, pal, from where I'm sitting, your problems don't even come close compared to mine.'

'Then, all I can say is you must have been through hell in your time.'

Her eyes watered and her lips quivered. 'If being the victim of incest by a drunken father from the age of eight and being put through a back-street abortion at fourteen by your own mother is hell, then yes, I have been through hell.'

She curled into a ball, her arms clasped around her body, holding on tightly to her sanity as the gut-wrenching horror of her words turned my innards to mush. Her experience of growing up in a shabby two-up, two-down terrace in Streatham with a slobbering, gin-soaked mother and a father with domestic violence on his mind and a leather belt in his hand was way beyond my comprehension. I had taken Ruby back to a place no-one should be made to revisit, and I inwardly screamed at my selfish stupidity.

'Dear God, Ruby, how do you survive something like that?'

'You don't.'

'What?' I was still contemplating the back-street abortion.

'You don't survive. Not mentally, anyway.'

'Couldn't the local police help you?' I sounded like a child psychologist.

'The local police would never have believed me, Mac. What happened behind closed doors, stayed behind closed doors in Streatham and any complaint by a child was treated with derision. I grew to hate the world I lived in and became aggressive, unruly and difficult to handle. I played truant from school until I was expelled and ended up in the Juvenile Court for stabbing my Dad with his Swiss army knife during a violent argument after Mam died.' Her sneer was that of a hyena. 'He survived, sadly, and had me sectioned. I ended up in a mental institute in Kennington.'

'How long were you there?' I hated the question, but innate curiosity kept me going.

'Until I was sixteen when I escaped and got a job as a maid in a big house in Regents Park for a man with questionable ethics.'

'What happened to your father?'

'As far as I know he was dropped into the Thames wearing concrete boots, over some gambling debt. You could say he got his just desserts.'

'And you?'

'I survived and went on to work at the Windmill Theatre in Soho and never looked back.' She turned, her smile now that of the old Ruby. 'The rest, as they say, is history.'

Our coffee had gone cold, and the Ormolu clock chimed midnight.

'The witching hour,' I said, realising that I had to be at the Lady Hardinge Medical College at nine o'clock with a clear head. 'Time for bed,' I announced, lifting my aching body off the sofa and walking towards the hall. I began to climb the stairs, mental and physical exhaustion making my feet drag.

'The time has come the walrus said, to talk of many things: Of shoes and ships – and sealing wax – of cabbages and kings.'

'What are you whispering, Mac?' Ruby was right behind me.

'Oh, I'm just quoting a Lewis Carroll nursery rhyme my Ma used to recite to me when it was time for me to go to bed.'

'I wish I had had a mother like yours. Mine couldn't even read.'

It was no wonder Ruby had turned out to be the person she was, I thought, my heart breaking. I paused at the top of the staircase desperately wanting to give her a hug but knowing that she would pull away immediately. Physical contact with others was abhorrent to her and now I understood why.

'We've both said things tonight that should probably never have been divulged, but I promise you this, I will never judge you again. You deserve all the pleasure you can get in life and I, for one, have learnt a very salutary lesson. Sleep tight, Ruby, and know that I will always be there for you, whatever the circumstances. Goodnight.'

Chapter Four

The morning dawned clear and sunny with a faint scent of roses. As I appeared from the guest bathroom, having emptied my stomach yet again, Ruby was coming through the door wearing a beautiful deep blue and pale green kaftan and carrying a breakfast tray.

'The hair of the dog,' she announced, placing a bucks-fizz in my hand.

'Ugh, do I really have to drink that.'

'Take it from Auntie Ruby, it will do wonders for your complexion.'

I looked in the dressing-table mirror and groaned.

'OK, what time do you have to be at the college?'

'Nine o'clock.'

'Ghalib will drive you there so we have time for a leisurely breakfast and to make some plans.' She passed me my cream linen suit which had been laundered and pressed overnight and began buttering some toast. 'Now, I have decided to tell Vijay to stay away next weekend.'

'Why, do you think I'll murder him in his sleep?'

'Probably, but I might get there first.' She handed me the buttered toast. I nibbled on it, praying it wouldn't reappear all over Dr Agnes Scott's desk during our meeting. 'However, that's beside the point. We need to discuss what you are going to do about the baby and there is no better place to do that than here.'

Her words were like manna from heaven and exactly what I had hoped for in Calcutta. I really needed Ruby's input and experience and I was confident that nothing would ever leave these four walls.

'OK, I will be back Friday evening, late.'

'Good. Meanwhile, if an abortion is on the cards, keep an eye out for an experienced female doctor at the college who might not be averse to some financial persuasion.'

'Ruby, I'm flat broke until I get my WMS salary.'

'You might be, but I'm not.'

'That's very generous, but I can't take Vijay's money, not after the things I've said about him.'

'It won't be his money, Mac, it will be mine and don't argue. If you hadn't saved my life during the fire on board ship, I would now be fish food at the bottom of the India Ocean alongside Major Stokes's charred remains. This is the least I can do to repay you.'

I had finished the toast and found myself buttering more. 'I don't know if I can go through with an abortion, Ruby. My Hippocratic Oath and all that.'

She poured some strong black coffee. 'All I'm saying, luv, is check on the doctors at the college while you are getting acquainted with their work and if one of them meets with your professional approval, we can discuss that and your other options next Saturday.'

I sat back and looked at my hostess. Her tough, exterior shell was back in place and she appeared to be on a mission. 'Thanks, Ruby. I'm not sure what I would do without you right now.'

'Don't mention it. Go show all those WMS physicians a thing or two and come back here ready to sort out your life.'

I stepped from the Lincoln sedan with fifteen minutes to spare, looking like a respectable GP from Berwick-on-Tweed, feeling surprisingly fresh and confident. As I stood on the entrance steps of the Lady Hardinge College for Obstetrics and Gynaecology and took in the imposing façade, I wondered why I needed to do any research at all. Looking at the extensive buildings and grounds, covering over fifty-four acres, India already seemed to be well served for female medical facilities. Perhaps, I thought, Ruby was correct in her assumption. The Lady Hardinge did indeed compare favourably with Vijay's luxury Delhi residence.

Back in Calcutta, I had read that this complex was both a college and hospital and had only been open for fourteen years. Its administrative and teaching block was second to none, with lecture halls, museum, library and laboratories, residential accommodation for doctors and nurses and hostels for the student graduates. Several kitchens catered for every religious cuisine and the hospital, with its state-of-the-art operating theatres, dealt with over two-hundred-and-twenty in-patients at any one time and had been modelled on St Thomas's Hospital in London.

If that was not enough, the large recreation ground to one side of the complex provided off-duty students with pitches and courts for hockey, rounders, tennis and badminton, while inter-class tournaments and matches between staff and students were a regular pastime. A myriad of languages was catered for, from Hindi to Urdu, and everything in between. It was impressive and I couldn't wait to get started by meeting the clinicians, surgeons and midwives, who all worked under the professional guidance of Doctor Agnes Scott, my supervisor and WMS boss.

She met me on the first-floor landing of the administration building and could have been Aunt Karr's twin. In her mid-sixties with short curly white hair, broad shoulders, ample bosom, hazel eyes, and a strong mouth, with her half-rimmed gold spectacles giving her a superior air, she was every child's idea of a fearsome granny.

I imagined that she ran the college with an iron fist and couldn't help smiling, recalling Sir Peter jokingly telling me over dinner back in Calcutta that he rather fancied her.

She held out her hand and shook mine with a grip suited to long hours clamping arteries or umbilical cords in various operating theatres around India. When she spoke, her voice commanded immediate attention, although I caught the faintest note of a Cumbrian accent which seemed to soften the hard edges of her words.

'Good Morning, Doctor Stuart-MacKenzie. We finally meet and I must say it is a great pleasure to have you join us here in Delhi.'

'Believe me Doctor Scott, the pleasure is all mine.' I could feel myself beaming at this highly qualified woman and knew instantly that we would get along.

'Please come to my office and let's get acquainted.'

We walked into an orderly, utilitarian office with its well-used metal-framed desk, chipped cream metal filing cabinet and marble-designed linoleum floor the only adornments. Agnes Scott appeared not to do luxury. We were on first-name terms within minutes, and it became clear from the outset that my supervisor was not only a highly qualified and experienced surgeon but was a mine of useful information which I was to benefit from. She lifted a file from the top of a pile of papers and handed it over.

'This is for you to read and digest. Hopefully, you will find the contents concise and to your liking.'

I opened the folder and scanned a list of daily timings, places and events for the week ahead, none of which made much sense to my brain.

'Don't worry, Elizabeth, all will become clear.' She pulled her copy of the sheet from the same pile. 'Firstly, I am allocating one of our undergraduates to assist you as an interpreter for the month that you are here. I assume you haven't had time to grasp any of the languages?'

'Sadly not,' I confirmed. 'I did appoint a retired language professor from Calcutta University to give me one-on-one tutoring, but Sir Peter had me out of the city before I could even learn the Hindi word for goodbye.'

Agnes smiled at my light-hearted quip. 'Sir Peter has never been one to let the grass grown from under his feet.'

'Exactly. However, I did manage to learn one word during my passage to India which might come in useful. *Garbhāśaya*,' I said, my head tilted, my chest puffed-out awaiting praise.

Agnes chuckled. 'Very commendable, Elizabeth. I'm sure the Hindi word for uterus will be a major part of your medical vocabulary in the future, so it is certainly a great place to start, but I can't imagine that the ship's lascars or stewards had any use for it in their line of work. However did you come by it?'

'Oh gosh, that's a very long story. Perhaps I should leave that until lunchtime.'

'Very well.' Agnes returned to the matter at hand. 'As I was saying, you will have your own interpreter who will speak both Hindi and Urdu, although Hindi is the predominant language here in the college. Which brings me onto our medical work here in India. Before delving into the vagaries of sub-tropical obstetrics, you need to be fully conversant with all the cultural and religious differences between the races as they are many and varied and will affect any decisions you will make or problems you may encounter over the next three years. Professor Panday is our expert on all things racial here at the college, and I have asked him to keep this afternoon free to cover this topic in detail. You will find it fascinating and, as he speaks perfect English, having completed his doctorate at Oxford, you will have no problem understanding him . . .'

The minutes ticked by as Agnes systematically explain her plan, detailing the schedule with precision and clarity while I became more and more enthusiastic about the work ahead.

' . . . Finally, Elizabeth, I understand that you have friends here in Delhi. If you would prefer to reside with them rather than here in our accommodation block, that is fine by me.'

I quickly butted in. 'Certainly not, Agnes. If I am to get my feet under the table, I will need to be here as much as possible. One month is not very long and there seems to be a great deal to take in before you send me off into the field.' I lifted the long list to emphasise my point. 'That said, I would like to spend Saturday and Sunday off campus, if that is alright.'

'Of course. Then I suggest you now get settled into your accommodation and I will meet you in the Surgeons' Common Room at twelve-forty-five when I can introduce you to your fellow physicians.' She rang a small hand bell and led me to the door.

'My sub-assistant surgeon will show you to your quarters and then show you around the college and hospital.' The door opened and a middle-aged, grey-haired, slight-framed, pint-pot of a lady stood, in full ochre-coloured sari, her hands making a namaste.

'Doctor Stuart-MacKenzie, this is Doctor Kahlima Joshi.'

'Namaste,' I replied, my hands in prayer by my forehead. 'It is a pleasure to meet you, Doctor Joshi.'

'Until lunchtime then, Elizabeth. Enjoy the grand tour.'

Kahlima Joshi led me out of the administration block and across the quadrangle, pointing out the various departments as she went. Like my abandoned language teacher, she floated across the campus as if on air and I wondered if it was an indigenous technique or the effect of the soft flowing silk material of the sari.

My case and medical bag were already in my small room on arrival, so I unpacked my toiletries in the adjoining shower-room, relieved to know I didn't have to share it with others and re-joined Doctor Joshi for the Lady Hardinge tour.

What I saw was a hospital equipped with state-of-the art operating theatres, all of which would have made any visiting British surgeon green with envy. The lecture halls, with their terraced seating and excellent acoustics, could have competed with any at Oxford or Cambridge and the library was a revelation, stacked from floor to ceiling with medical books in every possible Indian language as well as English. Studying at the Lady Hardinge, I decided, would be a joy for the medical student.

At lunch, I was introduced to any number of doctors and lecturers from all walks of life until my memory bank overflowed, while Agnes explained each person's role and their length of service. Throughout, it became obvious that my supervisor was loved and respected by all her staff and her management skills were second to none. Over coffee, I returned to my explanation for knowing the Hindi word for uterus, beginning with Tom Wallace asking me to attend to a Jhalanpur Princess in distress, realising that she was about to miscarry, obtaining Black Haw from the souk in Port Said and teaching her aunt how to give light uterine massages, which is how the matter of the uterus came up.

'Did the Black Haw work?' Agnes was fascinated.

'It did, along with camomile tea and a complete ban on all spices and caffeine.'

'Perhaps we should get you to give a lecture to the students on this case. It would certainly broaden their knowledge.'

'I would be delighted.' I lowered my voice. 'Even the Prince's physician seemed to be lost for words when he returned to the ship to find the foetus happily surviving in its amniotic sac.'

'Excellent, and don't forget to include the event in your report, Elizabeth. It will all go towards your Ph.D. qualification.'

My afternoon session was another revelation. Professor Panday was exactly how I had imagined him in Agnes's office, with his heavily bearded aging features topped by a wine-red circular pill-box hat, which looked rather fetching and so different from the usual Indian pleated turban. His white thigh-length, fully buttoned angarkha jacket with its stand-up collar, covered a broad chest and slim hips, while loose fitting trousers, gathered in at the ankles, exposed open-toed leather sandals and well-manicured nails. When he spoke, his bushy eyebrows constantly twitched, and his ebony eyes never left my face for over three hours.

The professor, I learned, was a Parsi, whose Zoroastrian ancestors had arrived in India from Persia way back in the eighth century. His people had been traditionally sought after as doctors, lawyers, engineers and teachers, and now formed a large proportion of the professional middle-class in Indian society. I also learned that Parsis had no caste-system, which made them very popular with His Majesty's Indian Civil Services as they had no problem dealing with each other, unlike Hindus. Likewise, their procedures for dealing with their dead were unlike any other Indian religion. Cremation or burial for the Parsi was prohibited, the Parsi culture believing that earth, fire and water were sacred elements that should not be defiled. Their funeral practise therefore was to take their deceased loved ones to the "Tower of Silence" to be consumed by vultures. I had to hang on to my stomach on hearing this, gripping my abdomen with both hands and inwardly praying that my lunch would stay put.

And so it went on, through Hindu, Muslim, Buddhist, Jain, Sikh and Christian cultures and religions until my eyes crossed and my brain was as saturated with knowledge as a blood-soaked theatre swab during an operation. It was both absorbing and mind-blowing.

'Are there any agnostics or atheists in India?' I finally asked, exhausted.

Professor Panday's white teeth contrasted sharply with his dense black beard as he smiled. 'Doctor, be assured, every spiritual or scientific belief, no matter how obscure will be practised somewhere in this sub-continent.'

I liked Professor Pandy, and his cheeky sense of humour behind his earnest demeanour made him very approachable and less austere.

On returning to the administration block, I had only one question on my mind.

'Agnes, why is the Countess of Dufferin's Fund and the WMS so desperate for my research? The Lady Hardinge already has enormous experience in obstetrics and gynaecology, and assuming this is replicated throughout India, pregnant mothers and infants in this country appear to be very well catered for.'

She sat back in her chair and studied me with interest, a wry smile crossing her lips. 'Elizabeth, Delhi is the capital and the showcase of India, but this continent is huge, as you will find out to your cost. Places like Patiala, Amritsar, Jalandhar and Peshawar are not like Delhi, to say nothing of the villages and small conurbations between.' She pointed to a map of India on the wall behind her where small, coloured pins were sparsely dotted here and there. 'In many of these places female medical practice is still in the dark ages and pregnant mothers only have local *Dais* to assist them during childbirth. These indigenous mid-wives have no education or training and are often no better than witch-doctors.'

'You sound like Doctor Hodgson from the Cama Hospital in Bombay. I met her during my train journey to Calcutta and she told me all about *Dais* and their reputation. I got the impression that she believed they should all be shot.'

'She would,' Agnes nodded, chuckling. 'Gloria has very firm views on the subject and has been instrumental in getting a number of the younger ones enrolled in training courses in all the major cities. We have several of them here.' She checked her diary. 'Actually, you'll be meeting her again shortly.'

I must have looked confused.

'She regularly lectures at the college on new obstetric techniques and is very popular with the students.'

I could imagine them hanging onto her every word, just as I had done.

'As I was saying, Elizabeth, once you go out into the field hospitals you will quickly realise how little we really know of the true situation with female and infant mortality because no-one keeps any records. The attitude of the Civil Surgeons from the India Medical Service is no help either. They see no benefit at all in allocating scarce resources to improve the plight of mothers and babies in a nation which, in their eyes, is already overpopulated. Believe me, dear, you will have a real fight on your hands to make any headway with our august male superiors on this subject. I know because I have been doing battle with them for years.'

'Their intransigence was made very clear to me at my CSTM interview, Agnes. If it hadn't been for Lord Cottesmore, I doubt I would be sitting here now.'

'I agree. You owe the Governor of Bengal a huge debt. He played his hand very well indeed.'

She peered at me from under her eyelashes, her eyes sparkling with mirth. Obviously, I thought, Lord Cottesmore had not fooled Dr Agnes Scott one jot during his covert antics on my behalf.

'Then forewarned is forearmed, Agnes. I had better polish my chainmail and practice my own covert tactics, seeing as I am not the first female clinician in India to go up against the establishment.' I returned her knowing stare.

'No, you certainly are not. Over the years my chainmail has become rather battered and worn from sparring with members of the IMS.'

'The question is, did you win?'

'That's for me to know and you to find out, dear. Now, let's get back to the matter in hand.' She swivelled in her chair and pointed again to the wall map. Her finger landed on an isolated red pin north of Lahore. 'Peshawar Province is where you are going next month, Elizabeth, so I suggest you equip yourself with some warm clothes whilst you're here in Delhi.' She turned back and shuffled some papers on her desk until she extracted one that she wanted. 'Doctor Anna Bramsen at the Danish Mission's Zenana Hospital in Mardan has agreed to take you under her wing. Her hospital caters solely for women in purdah which will give you invaluable experience of Muslim obstetrics.'

I recalled the luxurious Jhalanpur suite and zenana aboard ship and wondered how different things would be in Mardan. Agnes was still talking.

'As well as working at the Mission Hospital, part of your job will be to hold community clinics at the local army bases, for officer's wives and children.'

'And the soldiers?'

Agnes's eyebrows met. 'Are you familiar with the latest techniques in the treatment of VD?'

'After years as a GP treating the testosterone-fuelled farmhands around Berwick, Agnes, you happen to be looking at a venereal disease expert.'

'Very good, but let us hope the Mardan army medics have that little matter well under control.'

I hoped so too. After three weeks treating Lord Cottesmore's niece for syphilis, the idea of administering arsphenamine anti-syphilitic injections to the buttocks of the Indian Frontier Forces didn't fill me with enthusiasm.

'The foothills of the Himalayas are bitter at this time of year, dear, so I recommend lots of layers, plenty of chaffing powder and definitely a hot-water bottle.'

I bit my lip and crossed my fingers. 'Are there any other useful skills I will need in the Peshawar Province?'

Agnes gathered her papers together and placed them in the desk drawer. 'Can you shoot?'

I wasn't sure if she was pulling my leg or being depressingly serious. I nodded, turning queasy.

'What about riding a mule?'

Chapter Five

As the days went by, I settled into life at the Lady Hardinge and was amazed to see the female doctors within the Women's Medical Service undertaking all manner of operations from fibroids to cataracts, amputations to hysterectomies, without any interference from the male surgeons of the IMS.

An enlarged fibroid problem had brought me to operating theatre 'C' on my third morning where I was to assist in a full abdominal hysterectomy on a Muslim woman who had arrived at the hospital the day before from Ludhiana.

She was in purdah which was why she had come to the Lady Hardinge Hospital in the first place, and the lead surgeon was non-other than Agnes herself, who I found surrounded by graduate trainees as I entered the theatre, all dressed in full operating attire.

This was my first official surgical procedure since leaving England and I prayed I would not mess it up in front of an audience of students. Agnes nodded as I took my position on the opposite side of the operating table, only her eyes visible above her mask. She lowered the scalpel onto the patient's belly and made a vertical abdominal incision below the umbilicus whilst giving a running commentary to the trainees. I clamped back the skin and assisted as instructed while Agnes removed the patient's uterus, fallopian tubes and ovaries, placing each item in a surgical bowl which the theatre nurse removed to be cleaned and inspected.

The air was hot and fetid causing one student to faint. The last I saw of her were her theatre boots disappearing through the swing doors as Agnes continued undeterred, suturing the cervix while I crossed to the sink where the uterus was now lying on a surgical tray dripping with water. I gently removed a grapefruit-sized fibroid from the mass and immediately realised that there was a complication.

'Doctor Scott?'

Agnes looked up.

'We have a lesion on the uterus wall. It was hidden behind the enlarged fibroid.'

'Has it penetrated the membrane?'

Using the forceps, I turned the uterus over and inspected the underside. 'It's difficult to say.'

'What do you recommend, Doctor Stuart-MacKenzie?'

Agnes knew only too well what she should do, but for the benefit of the students she allowed me to make that decision. I didn't hesitate knowing the danger that this woman might be in.

'The pelvic lymph nodes need to be removed to protect the patient from the possible spread of cancerous metastasis.'

Agnes looked over to Khalima Joshi who was acting as her anaesthetist. 'How is our patient doing?'

'Vital signs good, Memsahib Doctor, breathing deep and regular.'

'Then we can proceed,' announced Agnes, waiting for me to return. 'Watch very carefully girls, I will be asking questions on this procedure during our afternoon lecture. Now Doctor

Stuart-MacKenzie, standby to drain if you please. Sister, the scalpel'.

The operation took over three hours but, thankfully, our patient survived, and I left her under the supervisory care of the theatre nurse and took the uterus and lymph nodes to the laboratory for post-operative investigation. By the time I returned it was lunchtime and Agnes had left a note requesting my presence at two o'clock in the training college where she would be lecturing on our morning's work.

I retired to the refectory and was discussing the patient's chances of survival with Khalima Joshi when someone tapped me on the shoulder.

'I thought it was you, Mac. What are you doing here at the Lady Hardinge?'

'Hello Gloria, Dr Scott told me you would be visiting. How the devil are you?'

'I'm fine, Mac, and delighted to see you in Delhi.'

Gloria Hodgson was an American, from Charleston, West Virginia and had qualified as a doctor in Pennsylvania before coming to India. She appeared to know Khalima well, so I invited her to join us as I answered her questions.

'Agnes Scott has been appointed as my Ph.D supervisor by the CSTM, so I'm here familiarising myself with all things gynaecological at the start of my research project on maternal and infant mortality.'

'Great. So, you took my advice? Well done you.' She placed her lunch tray on the table and plonked her backside on the available wooden chair opposite. 'How's she doing, Khalima?'

'Oh, the Doctor Mac, she doing very well, Doctor Hodgson. Very well indeed.'

'Excellent. How long are you here for, Mac?'

'A month,' I replied, tucking into my lamb curry, 'and its already flying by.'

'Quite a place, isn't it?' Gloria looked around the refectory filled with chattering students of every colour and creed.

'I tell you, Gloria, it puts Edinburgh University to shame.'

'Pennsylvania too.' She put down her fork. 'If you have some free time this afternoon, why don't you attend my lecture?'

'I'll need to ask Agnes. What is it about?'

'The latest Manual Vacuum Aspiration techniques for early-stage abortion,' she announced casually.

Suddenly, both women were furiously thumping my back as my face turned blue and a piece of lamb dislodged itself from my throat.

'Good Lord, Mac, what did I say?'

I swallowed a whole tumbler of water before I could answer. 'Nothing, Gloria, . . . nothing at all. What time is the lecture?' Fate had a weird way of throwing me off balance, I thought, regaining my composure.

'Four-thirty, straight after Agnes.'

'OK, I'll see if I can make it.'

As Gloria had brought up the subject of abortion and with Ruby's comments in mind, I thought I would keep the conversation going and see where it led. 'Do you carry out many abortions here, Doctor Joshi?'

'Only when Dr Scott she think it dangerous to continue pregnancy. No many during the first twelve weeks though.'

'So, why the lecture?'

'Please to understand, Doctor Mac, many women in countryside, they suffer from other diseases which can harm baby . . .'

'Like leprosy or syphilis,' butted-in Gloria between mouthfuls.

'. . . so, better to terminate for mother,' continued Khalima, 'providing it done safely. That is why we have training course for community midwives.'

'Instead of leaving it to the uneducated *Dai* to kill both the mother and the child,' added Gloria, back on her favourite soap box.

I recalled the reason for Gloria's journey to Calcutta when we first met on the Great Indian Peninsular Mail train. She was going to attend a Maternity and Welfare Conference to give a lecture on whether indigenous birth attendants, otherwise known as *Dais*, were worth training. In her opinion, they were not.

'Doctor Hodgson, they not all bad,' argued Khalima. 'We have young *Dais* here. They are students too. They all happy to learn safe medical techniques.' Her head was rocking in true Indian style.

'Unlike their murdering mothers and grandmothers.' Gloria was spitting bullets.

I chuckled. 'Anyone would think you had a thing about indigenous *Dais*, Gloria.'

'Doctor Mac, please you not listen to Doctor Hodgson. The mothers, they now trust the young *Dias* from the college, and many babies are saved.'

Gloria screwed up her face and finished her lunch.

'So, Doctor Hodgson, you are about to demonstrate the procedure for MVA to such student midwives this afternoon,' I commented, changing the subject.

'That I am, Mac. It's not commonly used outside our main women's hospitals yet, but it should be. The procedure is simple, cheap and very effective.'

I gently rubbed my abdomen, thinking back to my training for MVA.

'And the mothers, they live without problems,' emphasised Khalima.

If only it were that simple, I thought. 'So, you reckon a well-trained *Dai* can carry out this procedure without being supervised by a doctor?'

'Definitely,' said Gloria emphatically. 'Apart from anything else, she will have been trained properly, have a certificate of competence and have studied biology as part of her course. Any resemblance to their witch doctor mothers, out there in the backcountry, is purely cosmetic.'

'That's all very well, but who supplies her with the equipment?' I was picturing a manual aspirator.

'We do, at the WMS. As you know, all it takes is a local anaesthetic, a cervical dilator and a manual pump, all of which are quite cheap. The patient is on her feet and getting on with her day within hours and the procedure avoids the danger of puncturing the uterus with a curette or sharp stick.' My stomach flipped.

Khalima cut in. 'We have number of nearly-qualified midwives in the college, and they now work in the community on their days off to get experience and,' she paused trying to find the words, 'how do you say, Doctor Hodgson?'

'Earn money to help pay their college fees?'

'Exactly.'

'Goodness,' I exclaimed. 'I had no idea early terminations were so popular in these parts. How much do the girls earn?' Ruby would have been proud of me.

'That depends on the client, Mac, and her circumstances of course.' Gloria seemed to be a mine of useful information. 'For example, your promiscuous colonial wives and daughters, who seem to have difficulty keeping their legs crossed, are desperate to terminate their unwanted pregnancies without causing a scandal and will pay royally for the privilege. Our hospital midwives can name their price.'

'Really?' I countered, as my cheeks burned. 'I'm sorry Gloria, we will have to continue this conversation some other time. Right now, I must attend Agnes's lecture on uterine fibroids. Perhaps I will see you later.'

'Why don't we meet for dinner? I don't leave Delhi until tomorrow afternoon as my next stop is the Lady Lyall Hospital in Agra which is a mere four hours away.'

'Good idea,' I yelled, half-way out of the refectory door.

I arrived late to Gloria's lecture and found a seat at the back of the hall. The auditorium was full of students all sitting in total silence as Gloria, in her West Virginia drawl, explained the benefits of MVA while a young Indian woman in sari and surgical gown demonstrated the abortion technique on a wax, life-sized dummy.

I leant sideways and whispered into my student translator's ear. 'Who is it doing the demonstration?'

'Fatima Patel, Memsahib Doctor. She is Gujarati and is qualified as top midwife in college. You like?'

I like very much, I thought, and locked the name away in my memory bank for later. 'I am very impressed, Aesha, her family must be very proud.'

'You want she meet you, Memsahib Doctor?'

'No thank you, dear, that's alright, and Aesha, please call me Doctor Mac.'

'Yes, Memsahib, Doctor Mac.'

I gave up and watched with interest. At some point Gloria caught sight of me at the back of audience and nodded. Funny, I thought, as I smiled back, this was the second time in three months that this American doctor had provided me with an opportunity to change my life. The question was, did I want it?

In the staff dining room that evening we continued our conversation from lunchtime.

'Where are you off to next, Mac?'

'Peshawar Province,' I replied. 'Mardan to be precise. The Danish Mission Hospital there. Do you know it?'

'Once seen, never forgotten, Mac.' I groaned. 'Unlike here, that hospital was built in 1906 and is in need of some serious upgrading. Funds are scarce on the North-West Frontier so the staff have to do the best they can with limited resources.'

'How big is it?'

'About thirty beds. Doctor Anna Bramsen runs it and is a friend of Agnes's. She took over from the founder, Doctor Marie Holst and was in charge last time I was there, but that's some time ago.' She tapped her knuckle against her lips. 'Not the best of postings, Mac, and light years away from the Lady Hardinge, I'm afraid.'

My involuntary shudder rattled the cutlery. 'I guess that's why Agnes is sending me there.'

'Probably. You'll be dealing with Muslim women in purdah, which has its advantages, because you won't have the local Civil Surgeon breathing down your neck every five minutes. No men allowed and all that, so if you were thinking of getting laid in Mardan, Mac, think again.'

I nearly dropped my teacup and quickly changed the subject. 'Is there anything else I should know?'

She screwed up her bottom lip. 'I don't think so, except that February is not the best time of year for you to be working in that region. It can be bone-chillingly cold at night in the foothills of the Himalayas.'

'I know, Agnes warned me. Don't they have any internal heating system in the hospital?'

'Hardly. They make do with paraffin-heaters which stink and are murder for anyone with asthma.' She paused. 'You don't suffer with asthma, do you?'

'No.'

'Good, but the posting will still be a baptism of fire, Mac.'

'Thanks a million, Gloria. I need that like a hole in the head.'

'You're welcome, Doctor Stuart-MacKenzie.' She went back to her dinner then had an after-thought. 'Anyway, from what I've been told, if you can survive a Scottish Highland winter, you can survive anything, so the North-West Frontier should be a walk in the park for you!'

'I think I'd rather stick with the Highland winter if you don't mind, even though I've lived in Northumbria for years.'

'And forgo the panoramic vistas of snow-capped peaks around the Khyber Pass. I don't think so. Anyway, your Mackenzie ancestors would turn in their graves at you bottling out.'

'Maybe, but Glencoe is a far cry from the Khyber Pass, Gloria.'

She looked about her, leant towards me and lowered her voice. 'It's not the Khyber Pass you need to worry about, Mac. Take my advice. Stay well clear of Colonel Philpott. I have it on good authority that Peshawar's Civil Surgeon has wandering hands and a habit of writing scathing reports to his superiors if he doesn't get his own way.'

This time I did spill my tea.

Chapter Six

Ruby was waiting in the lounge, cigarette holder in hand, smoke fogging the air as I arrived back at the Jhalanpur residence around ten-thirty on the following Friday evening.

'Have you eaten?'

I placed my medical bag on the marble-topped armoire and dropped into a chair, undoing the tortoiseshell clip holding my hair securely against the nape of my neck. As I shook my head, my brown crinkled tresses spread like an opened fan across my weary shoulders.

'Yes, I ate with Aesha, my translator, after the evening ward round and debrief.'

'You look done-in,' commented Ruby. 'How about a snifter to revive your spirits?'

'I thought you'd never ask. G&T please, with lots of ice.'

Ruby moved towards the bar. 'So, spill the beans. How was your first week at the Lady Hardinge workhouse?'

I kicked off my shoes and massaged my toes against the Persian rug as ice cubes clinked into a tumbler. 'Fascinating, exhausting, intimidating and awe-inspiring, in that order,' I replied, enjoying the sensation of silk thread under the soles of my feet.

'How many lives have you saved on your first week at the coalface?'

'Three. A Muslim woman with a cancerous uterus, a Jain with an ectopic pregnancy and a Belgian lady with a twisted gut.'

'Ugh! It all sounds positively hideous.'

She handed over my snifter which tasted like nectar after a week of nothing but black tea, green tea, jasmine tea and every other tea grown in Asia. 'What about you, Miss Tavener? How many expensive emporiums have you frequented in my absence?'

'Six, not including Old Delhi's Chandni Chowk.'

My head couldn't take in any more Indian place names, so I passed on asking what Chandni Chowk was, but imagined tightly packed bazaar stalls overflowing with stacks of pashminas, bolts of silks and trays overflowing with jewels. This image brought my Ma and Pa in Riveldene Vicarage sharply into focus.

'Somewhere in my work schedule at the Lady Hardinge, Ruby, I need to find the time to buy some belated Christmas gifts for my family prior to leaving Delhi. I never found the time in Calcutta.'

Ruby snapped to attention like a dilatory medical student found wanting. 'Now that's the best thing you've said since arriving in the capital, Mac. Pick a day and I will be delighted to act as your guide. What sort of presents do you have in mind?'

The very thought of shopping with Ruby set my teeth on edge after my experience in Port Said. All I had wanted then was a topi and flyswat for my excursion into the Sahara Desert, and had planned to visit Simon Arzt Department Store for this purpose before treating myself to a birthday lunch at the Casino Palace Hotel. Ruby had somehow gotten wind of my plan, muscled-in and completely took over. I returned to the ss Narkunda with a headache the size of Mount Olympus, the store's delivery boy bringing up the rear with only his fez visible behind a stack of boxes containing half of the women's clothing department, and a bank balance that was firmly in the red.

'I have only one thing to say to that suggestion, Ruby Tavener, so watch my lips move. Never again after Simon Arzt.'

She tapped her cigarette against her crystal ashtray and ignored my sarcasm. 'How about tomorrow?'

'NO! Ruby. NO! NO! NO!'

'You can be quite cutting when you want to be, Miss MacKenzie.'

'With good reason. You might be interested to know that half the stuff I bought that day has never been out of the box and the other half got me pregnant.'

'Sticks and stones, Doctor. Sticks and stones.'

'Maybe, but my bank account has never been the same since. Now, can we get back to my present predicament?'

Ruby pouted and sat.

'You wanted to know if there was anyone at the Lady Hardinge who would fit the bill, assuming I opted for an abortion.'

'And is there?'

I explained who Fatima Patel was and how I had watched her assisting Gloria Hodgson during her lecture.

'Do you know where this what's-her-name lives?'

'Sort of.' I went in search of my bag and pulled out a piece of paper with my own scribbled handwriting on it. 'Her personal details were listed in the midwifery register, but it was all in Hindi so I couldn't understand anything other than Kashmiri Gate, wherever that is.'

'Part of the old city wall,' replied Ruby, taking the note out of my hand. 'Sanjay.' Her summons nearly burst my eardrums. The Jhalanpur chaprassi appeared from nowhere and bowed low. 'I need you to find out where a midwife called . . .' She looked down, then at me. 'Your writing is appalling, Mac. What does this say?' She wafted the note under my nose.

'Shrimati Fatima Patel.'

'If you say so. As I was saying, Sanjay, I need you to find out where this Fatima Patel lives. She studies at the Lady Hardinge training college and her family address is near the Kashmiri Gate.'

'Yes, Memsahib. I go look tomorrow, Memsahib.' He bowed again and backed out of the lounge.

My pulse rate was off the scale as I leapt from my chair. 'Ruby, what the hell are you doing? I haven't decided what to do yet.'

'Fine, but under the circumstances it wouldn't do any harm to find out if she is willing to undertake private work and what she charges, so stop getting hysterical.'

My shoulders dropped. Ruby was right, of course. Time was of the essence as I would be twelve weeks pregnant by the following Monday.

'I suggest we call it a day, Mac. You're obviously feeling tetchy and definitely incapable of thinking logically, so let's delay any further discussion until breakfast.'

I didn't need telling twice. After a long, hot bath, I crawled into my heavily carved teak king-sized bed with its cream silk sheets and vintage Kantha Quilt bedspread and spent the rest of the night dreaming of arriving at the Mardan Women's Mission on a donkey, clad in long-johns and woolly hat, with a hot-water bottle stuffed down my front.

By morning, my energy levels were back to normal and for once I didn't spew up into the toilet. Walking out onto the bedroom terrace, I breathed in the cool winter air scented with jasmine, roses and chrysanthemums, all growing in profusion around the villa walls, and took in the magnificence of Vijay's private grounds. I stretched, releasing the tension in my back and shoulders after a week of bending over operating tables, laboratory worktops and ward beds and thought back over my time in India.

It had been a series of absurd contrasts, between five-star luxury one minute and potential bankruptcy the next, or sexual Bombay nights in the arms of a lover to the threat of losing my career, my reputation and my sanity in Calcutta. I seemed to be in a constant vortex of depression, guilt and self-recrimination over the pregnancy and I wished the world would stop spinning so I could get off and try to make sense of it all.

Ruby breezed through the bedroom door looking as if she was on her way to a health spa, a tape measure strung around her neck.

'Morning, Mac. Come inside. I need to measure you for a corset before you get dressed.'

'A what?'

'A corset.'

I was already losing the plot and it was only eighty-thirty.

'If you are going to have this baby instead of aborting it, you will need an expandable body corset which will hide the bump from prying eyes in the short and mid-term and support it while you charge about the country in the latter stages.'

The thought of a boned and laced corset made my eyes water.

'I have the perfect tailor to make one to measure, so take off that kaftan and hold this notepad and pencil.'

I was lost for words but acquiesced as it was easier to comply than argue when Ruby was in this mood. She went to work, forming a tight ligature around my hips, waist and chest with the measuring-tape and calling out various statistics at each stage.

'You would never make an orthopaedic nurse,' I spluttered, my ribcage in danger of chest trauma.

'Shut up and turn around.' She was now measuring me from neck to coccyx, underarm to pelvic bone. I felt like a cadaver being sized-up for a coffin.

While I dressed, Ruby continued in a world of her own, muttering as she sketched designs onto the notepad, tutting, crossing out and redrawing.

'What you need, Mac, is something lightweight, elasticated and shaped around the womb, yet strong enough to keep your shape for as long as possible.' She looked up from the end of the bed where she was sitting. 'How'd you fancy an all-in-one, with fastenings between your legs? That way there is no need for laces.'

'Great,' I replied, imagining large metal press-studs chaffing my inner thighs. 'It sounds like a straight-jacket by any other name. Will it have strings attached to the arms to tie them across my bosom?'

Ruby's glare was in danger of scorching my forehead. 'Titter if you must, Miss MacKenzie, but innovation is the mother of all creation and your corset could well be the design to elevate maternity fashion to a higher plain.'

'It will be my voice that's on a higher plain if I wear that thing.' I pointed to her sketch of a bodystocking with a central bulge. 'Could I have some breakfast before making history on the pre-natal catwalks of Paris?'

It was mid-morning, and we were still at it, walking around the grounds in a pleasant sixty-eight-degree temperature as a light breeze cooled my fevered brow and I continued to vacillate between options.

'We seem to be going round in circles, Mac,' announced Ruby, sounding like Aunt Karr. 'You don't want to terminate the baby, but you can't imagine bringing up a child on your own. You want to be free to follow your career, yet you hate the thought of putting your baby up for adoption. Have you any other suggestion before we disappear up our own jacksies.'

I sighed, deeply. 'Perhaps I could fall off a horse and break my neck. The problem would then be solved once and for all.' Even I knew I sounded pathetic.

'Typical of a Scot. Selfish to the end. What do you suggest I do with an unused corset after your demise?'

'You could always get yourself pregnant,' I countered. 'I'm sure Vijay would be delighted to have you produce a son and heir.'

'That's below the belt, Stuart-MacKenzie.' She sniffed.
'Anyway, Prince Archibald FITZ-Kumar Singh II doesn't really
trip off the tongue, now does it?'

'Archibald?'

'My Dad's name.'

We paused by the fish-pond; the white waterlilies edged in
soft pink reminding me of my rose camisole.'

'Penny for them?' Her fingers rippled the water.

'I was wondering what Tom Wallace was doing right now.'

Ruby's teeth ground together. 'Well, he's certainly not
worrying about fatherhood, is he? Or you, for that matter, so
don't let's go there.'

Ruby's comment cut me to the quick, which was her
intention. She had never rated men highly and her frustration at
my constant dithering was beginning to pall. I changed the
subject.

'What reason did you give Vijay for not wanting him
around this weekend?'

'None. I simply said I was otherwise engaged. He knows
not to try and control me, that's what keeps him coming back
for more. He gets enough bowing and scraping from his family
and subjects back in Jhalanpur without me doffing my cap.'

We were making our way back towards the terrace.

'Look, Mac, you can't go on like this. At some point you
must make a decision. I respect you for trying to do the right
thing, it shows that you care, but time is not on your side.'

'Damn it, Ruby, don't you think I know that? I stormed
ahead of her, climbing the terrace steps two at a time, torn

between anger and anguish. I crossed to the balustrade and looked out across the lawn.

Ruby followed, ignoring my pique. 'Face the facts, Mac. You didn't get pregnant because you wanted Tom's child, but because you were hurt, revengeful and feeling used and abused.'

I nodded.

'Equally, Tom didn't protect you because he hoped to be a father, but because you were rutting like animals in what can only be described as mutual rape and he didn't have time. And don't say, how do you know?'

My sneer was straight from a Frankenstein movie. 'Don't bother to mince your words, Ruby.'

'Bloody hell, Mac. Sugar-coating your predicament is not going to solve this, and, whether you like it or not, getting pregnant under these circumstances is no way to bring a child into the world, and you know it.' She left me gripping the cap-rail, the finality of her words and the slamming of the patio door bringing any further discussion on the subject to a sudden halt.

I was sitting on the top terrace step when Ruby finally made an appearance twenty minutes later. She handed me cup of coffee and sat alongside.

'Look, Mac, I'm sorry. I've never been good at all this counselling stuff. I . . .'

My hand grabbed her arm. 'It's OK, Ruby. What you said wasn't pretty, and it was certainly graphic, but it was spot on and what I needed to hear.' My smile didn't reach my eyes. 'Aunt Karr would be proud of you.'

'Who's Aunt Karr?'

'Someone else who doesn't believe in sugar-coating the truth.' I sipped my coffee.

'So, have you decided what you're going to do?'

'Yes, I have. If nature won't terminate my mistake, Ruby, then I must. All I can hope is that my maker understands.'

'And is this your final word?'

I clenched my jaw. 'Yes, Ruby, it is.'

'Fine. So, when do you want to do it?'

A great weight seemed to have lifted from my shoulders. 'Next Friday evening would be ideal. It would give me the weekend to fully recover.'

'How many weeks will you be by then?'

'Thirteen, and outside the recommended time frame.' My hands were clenched in my lap, my bottom lip trapped between my teeth.

'Is that dangerous, Mac?'

'It's not ideal.'

Ruby looked at her watch. 'On that basis, it has to be today if that's possible. If not, then tomorrow.' She was on her feet walking towards the lounge.

I crossed my fingers as the gravity of my decision hit home, fearing all the dire complications to an MVA procedure.

'Ruby, if anything goes wrong, I need to find a credible reason to report in sick and hope that Doctor Agnes Scott doesn't become suspicious.'

'That's your problem,' shouted Ruby, already on a mission. 'Mine is to persuade this Fatima Patel that you need her services, yesterday.'

Sanjay returned with Fatima Patel's address written in Hindi on the palm of his hand and confirmation that she did private work in her spare time.

The mansion suddenly exploded in a hive of activity and I was left to have lunch alone while Ruby departed for Old Delhi dressed in a rather plain day-dress, a mid-length brown wig, tortoiseshell spectacles and low-heeled shoes, all evidence of nail-polish or lipstick wiped clean. She resembled Ma on one of her Saturday morning shopping excursions to Berwick-upon-Tweed as I watched her drive from the villa in a small cream Hillman saloon.

When she returned three hours later, I was ushered onto the terrace for a briefing while the maid disappeared with an arm full of parcels.

'It's all arranged, Mac. Fatima Patel has agreed to carry out an abortion on Miss Laura Henderson at the Metropolitan Hotel this evening.'

'Does Laura Henderson know?' I had to smile, even though I felt like death. Mrs Henderson had been Ruby's boss at the Windmill Theatre in Soho and had fired her the previous autumn.

Her hand flicked away my interruption. 'Don't be ridiculous, Mac, she's four-thousand miles away. Now, Miss Henderson's room has already been reserved and paid for,' she dug in her bag and pulled out a large brass ball with a door key hanging from a chain, 'and the hotel staff are expecting her and a nurse between six and seven o'clock. They think she is suffering from Crohn's Disease.'

'Do they know what Crohn's Disease is?'

'No, and nor do I, but it sounds serious. By the way, what does MVA stand for?'

'It's short for Manual Vacuum Aspiration.'

'Ugh!'

'Where is this hotel?' I enquired, seriously impressed with Ruby's covert skills.

'In Central Delhi. It's one of the top hotels in the city and all the best people stay there.'

'Really? So, how much is all this costing me?' Bankruptcy loomed once more.

'Not your problem, Mac, leave the finances to me. Your job is to spread your legs and think of England. By tomorrow, this will all be history and you can get on with your life while I get back to being a high-ranking Rajputana mistress.'

'But what if Fatima Patel recognises me at the Lady Hardinge next week?'

'Believe me, Mac, she won't, not after I've finished with you.'

My features sagged at the thought of what lay ahead.

'Stop looking so sceptical. If you can fool the passengers on the ss Narkunda in your Sheeri outfit, you can certainly fool a young Hindi midwife from the back streets of Old Delhi in a Laura Henderson disguise.'

Ruby was referring to the ship's fancy-dress Gala Ball during our passage to India. At the time, I had nothing suitable to wear so was going to give the event a miss, but Princess Darshwanabai and her relatives found out and insisted on recreating me as Scheherazade. When I emerged from the Jhalanpur zenana weighed down in armbands, ankle bangles, gold drooping earrings, nose chains and Mehndi henna tattoos, all being essential accoutrements to this disguise, even I didn't recognise me.

'As a matter of interest, what does Mrs Laura Henderson actually look like?'

Ruby dropped her brown wig onto the sofa, pulled out a compact from her handbag and dug around for her lipstick. 'Fat, brassy and over-dressed. She's an ex-music-hall flapper with big breasts and a backside that you could balance a tray on,' she sniped, her lips turning a shade of vermillion.

I looked down at my slight frame and flattish chest. 'Then you've got some work to do, haven't you?'

'Elizabeth, Delhi's Laura Henderson will be straight out of the top-colonial-drawer and oozing class. Now, where's my lunch? I'm starving.'

Sanjay arrived on cue with a tray of Danish open-sandwiches and a jug of iced Pimms then retreated, leaving Ruby and me to spend the rest of the hour creating my disguise.

With so much talent at her fingertips Ruby had no difficulty in turning me from a staid, conservative minister's daughter into a femme fatale who would be the talk of the town. My hair was crimped and curled then piled high on the top of my head. My eyebrows were shaped and darkened, my eyelashes mascaraed, my cheeks blushed with a soft shade of pink and a small beauty spot was carefully placed above my lip. She chose a rose-pink lipstick outlined using a deeper pink lip-brush and to finish the effect, soft brown freckles were dotted across the bridge of my nose. I resembled a Hollywood starlet.

'Now for your outfit.' She produced a stylish day-dress in cream and white linen from a large box, matching silk undergarments and suspenders from another and a pair of beige suede shoes with two-inch heels from a third. All were exactly my size.

'Voila,' she cried and produced a pair of silk, seamed stockings from her pocket.

I was made to dress and stand in front of the full-length bedroom mirror as a soft beige and blue cashmere pashmina was casually wrapped around my shoulders. I looked all set for a tea-dance at the Ritz.

'You'll need some jewellery.' Ruby disappeared into her dressing-room and returned with a box full of costume accessories. Pulling out two clip-on, imitation pearl and diamond earrings and a matching bracelet she handed them over. 'Try these on.'

I had no idea how long I would have to wear them but agreed that they gave Laura Henderson a definite air of class. 'Anything else?' I asked, rather pleased with my disguise.

'No, I think you'll do. Now, you need to pack your kaftan, slippers, toiletries and a nightgown for a one-night stay and I will be on hand in the adjoining bedroom in case something goes wrong after Fatima Patel leaves. It would be helpful, therefore, if I knew what the hell could go wrong.'

My stomach did a Highland fling as I reacted negatively to Ruby accompanying me to the hotel. Any sight of blood sent my hostess into a fainting fit which I could well do without, but there was no way I could stop her once she had made up her mind, and the thought of being alone in a strange hotel having aborted my child, gave me the jitters.

'OK, while I pack, I'll explain the possible pitfalls.' We moved to my bedroom. 'In an emergency, particularly if I am haemorrhaging or have fainted, you'll need to get me to the Lady Hardinge pretty damn quick.' I grabbed my hand to stop it shaking.

'How will I know if you're haemorrhaging?'

'I'll have a clammy skin, rapid heart-rate, nausea and there'll be blood all over the sheets.'

'God alive!' Ruby was going green around the gills.

'At the hospital, you must tell the medics the truth, the whole truth and nothing but the truth, do you understand?' Knowing Ruby's talent for subterfuge I needed her to be under no illusions. 'If you lie, Ruby, it's an odds-on certainty that I will be going six foot under along with the foetus.'

'Christ, Mac, do you have to be so specific?'

'Well, you did ask.'

Chapter Seven

T he hotel, with its brilliant white façade and arched, stuccoed windows, looked like an oversized wedding cake as the sedan cruised to a halt under a huge porticoed entrance. In an attempt to keep us both from panicking on the journey, Ruby had given me a running commentary about its history, so I had learned that during the 1903 Coronation Durbar, when Edward VII was crowned the Emperor of India, the Metropolitan Hotel had been the most coveted hotel in Delhi. If I was supposed to be impressed, I wasn't, any interest in the aristocracy was overshadowed by the events of the forthcoming evening.

Ruby breezed into the marble and stained glass reception hall, her wig and spectacles in place, a fox-fur hat and stole adding an air of elegance, her gloved hand waving nonchalantly at the receptionist as she headed straight for the lift.

I followed, eyes down, knees knocking, mouth dry and trying not to trip over my feet in my high-heeled shoes as I attempted to enact my role with a modicum of credibility. I collapsed against the lift's smoked glass mirrored interior holding onto my overnight bag as if my life depended on it, thankful, as we rose to the first floor, that we were not sharing it with others.

Minutes later, I was unpacked and sitting by the bedroom window, tapping my fingers on the occasional table and breathing deeply trying to keep my pulse-rate normal.

'We need a drink,' announced Ruby, appearing from the adjoining bedroom and picking up the bedside telephone.

'Not for me, I need a clear head.' My stress levels were now in danger of causing a heart attack.

'Right . . . Oh, hello, yes, this is Room 52. I would like a Whisky Mac and a jug of iced water. Very well . . . Thank you.' She turned, her top lip trapped between her teeth, her face lacking colour. 'I think I've got first-night nerves.'

'Deep breaths, Ruby. Deep breaths.' She rushed into the bathroom, groaning.

A gentle tap on the bedroom door quickened my pulse and, as I passed the bathroom, I could hear Ruby retching into the toilet pan.

Fatima Patel stood in the corridor dressed in her nurse's uniform and carrying a small case. She bowed her head, showing no signs of recognition and I responded, my thumbs touching my forehead. 'Namaste.'

'Namaste, Memsahib. My name, it is Fatima Patel.' Her voice was hardly above a whisper. 'I am midwife.'

'Yes, I imagine you are.' I tried to keep my voice low. 'I am Laura Henderson. Please, come in.'

She walked past me and laid her case on the chair then turned. 'I get everything ready now. The instruments, they are already sterilized so please, not to worry.'

Fatima had obviously done this before in such surroundings and, relieved, I let her take the lead.

She removed the bedspread and blankets folding them neatly into a pile then spread a rubberised sheet and white towel across the mattress.

'We not want to stain the sheets,' she explained, looking up as Ruby reappeared from the bathroom, dabbing her lips on a damp facecloth. Another tap on the door cut short any introductions.

'Just a minute,' Ruby shouted, indicating with her hands that we should remain well hidden, then blocked the visitors view with her body and returned holding an already half-empty tumbler of whisky in one hand and my jug of water in the other.

'Memsahib Henderson, you undress, please, down here,' instructed Fatima, pointing to her abdomen, then began unpacking her case.

I grabbed my kaftan and headed for the bathroom. On my return, Ruby was conspicuous by her absence. Fatima's eyes stared at the adjoining bedroom door and I nodded, realising that the appearance of the aspirator and dilator would have been too much for my companion.

While Fatima busied herself closing the bedroom curtains, I furtively examined the instruments laid out on a metal tray and checked for errors. Thankfully there were none, confirming the excellence of her Lady Hardinge training.

'What is that?' I asked, pointing to the aspirator and trying to appear ignorant.

'It take all away, Memsahib. Please, not to worry, you no feel anything, I make sure.'

'And my baby, what will happen to it?'

'It go with me in aspirator, Memsahib.'

'NO!' Suddenly I began to panic realising what she meant and was about to cancel the abortion when Prince Kapoor

Dhawan's gentle words drifted into my head following the loss of the Jhalanpur foetus on the ss Narkunda.

'Hindus believe that babies, children and saints are all pure and unattached to their bodies, Doctor Stuart-MacKenzie, so they are buried not cremated.'

'No,' I repeated in a whisper. 'I would like to bury the child myself.'

Fatima's smile was angelic as she nodded. 'Very well, Memsahib. Now, please to lie here.' She pointed to the bed. 'It not take long and I explain everything. I go wash my hands.'

I sat on the edge of the mattress and waited. Well, this was it, I thought. Weeks of constant anxiety and soul-searching were about to come to an end. I ran my hand slowly over my abdomen then lifted my kaftan to expose my naked groin and lay back on the towels, the vivid memory of Gloria Hodgson's lecture revolving in my head with Fatima demonstrating the procedure on a wax dummy.

I closed my eyes, crossed my fingers and succumbed to my fate, feeling warm tears slowly trickling into my hairline.

Chapter Eight

I stood under a mature Hibiscus Tiliaceus tree holding an ornate, miniature metal box, the only sounds around me being the heart-shaped silver-grey leaves rustling in the breeze and the far-off splash from the fountain onto the rippled pond-water below.

I placed the box to my lips, experiencing a depth of feeling much stronger than anything I had ever experienced before and sank to my knees, placing the foetus, encased in its intricately jewelled coffin, into the deep ground amongst the roots of this beautiful tree. I scattered soil over the lid and mouthed the Lord's Prayer then filled in the grave, pressing the damp earth with my hands as my chest heaved and my vision became pooled again in saline tears.

When I rose, Ruby placed her arm around my shoulders and held on tight, an action so human and yet, for her, so out of character. 'This will always be a sacred place, Mac and one you can return to whenever you want.'

We stood for a few quiet minutes then made our way to the house where Sanjay was waiting with a chilled bottle of champagne.

'Rather appropriate,' I murmured, through a watery smile.

'Would you prefer tea, Mac?' Ruby's concern was touching.

'No, Ruby, Veuve Clicquot is fine. It just happens to be the champagne which Tom Wallace chose on my twenty-ninth birthday. Under the circumstances, you couldn't have made a better choice.'

We stood watching the sun's burnt-orange orb bathe the trees in an amber glow as it set across this serene, peaceful, subtropical garden, and even though it was not a holy site, its natural beauty acted as an analgesic on my inner remorse.

It had all been a harrowing experience and I knew I would live with the consequences for the rest of my life. Raising my champagne flute to the sunset I made a promise to my rejected child. Never again would I allow my heart to rule my head.

With hourly changes of sanitary pads, regular doses of laudanum and constant bedrest throughout Sunday, my physical well-being was stable enough for me to tackle my week at the Lady Hardinge College with a modicum of confidence. My mental health, however, was going to take longer to repair so I decided that a complete break from Ruby and Vijay's mansion was probably the best option, rather than be constantly reminded of the previous twenty-four hours. Naturally, Ruby argued strongly against the decision.

'That's crazy, Mac. You have two more weekends to go before leaving for the North-West Frontier, and at least here you won't be disturbed by anyone.'

'Except you and Vijay,' I countered. 'Look, Ruby, right now I need to bury myself in work and put some distance between myself and yesterday.'

'But . . .'

'No buts, Ruby. I'll be forever in your debt and once I have got a handle on my life, we can enjoy whatever India has to offer without a shadow following me around. Meanwhile, I will be much better off staying at the college. You do understand, don't you?'

Reluctantly, Ruby gave in. 'Then promise me you will join me in Simla in June.'

I hesitated, not knowing what Agnes Scott had in store for me during the summer, but Ruby had been through a lot on my behalf and honesty at this juncture would have been insensitive. 'Try keeping me away,' I said, and handed my medical bag over to the chauffeur.

Ghalib dropped me off at the college at nine-fifteen and I watched the Lincoln glide out of the grounds with a certain trepidation, realising that I no longer had Ruby's support if I stumbled. Holding my head high and tensing my muscles, I walked into the building to face whatever the day had to throw at me. Fate had always been wide awake and active in my life and as I entered Agnes's office fifteen minutes later, it proved it in no uncertain terms.

'Ah, there you are, Elizabeth. A change of plan. I want you to spend this week out in the community getting to know how Indian women survive beyond the college walls.'

'Fine,' I acknowledged enthusiastically, looking forward to meeting mothers in their own homes rather than in the sanitised atmosphere of the college hospital.

'This work is complex and varied and I'm afraid Aesha is not yet qualified to undertake such visits. So,' she announced, tapping her pencil on the desk, 'I have decided to partner you with Shrimati Fatima Patel instead . . .'

My heart stopped.

'. . . She is our top graduate in midwifery, and speaks English, Hindi and Urdu.' You will learn a great deal by her side.'

The door opened and in walked my abortionist. I instantly froze and my equilibrium nose-dived into the floor. I was gripped with fear and kept my eyes firmly on Agnes.

'Allow me to introduce you both,' she announced, oblivious to what she was doing to my sanity. Doctor Stuart-MacKenzie, this is Fatima Patel.'

'Namaste, Doctor . . .?'

'MacKenzie, I choked, daring myself to meet her gaze and praying there was no recognition in her eyes. 'Namaste, Miss Patel.'

She smiled, looking at me as if I were some deity on a pedestal. 'Doctor Scott, she say you are a blessing to my country and will do great things for mothers and babies who are sick.' She bowed from the waist with great ceremony. 'I am experienced midwife in community and work often outside hospital.'

You can say that again, I thought, as my heart started up again and I eased myself back onto my chair, severe cramp suddenly reminding me of our intimate association and my need for more laudanum.

'Your first case,' explained Agnes, pushing a street map of Old Delhi across the desk, 'is here in the Dariba Kalan district of Chandni Chowk.' Her finger pointed to the centre of the walled city alongside the word Jama Masjid Mosque. 'Your patient is a young Muslim girl who was married at thirteen to a man three times her age and we suspect she is suffering from severe osteomalacia and stunted growth. Her husband refuses to allow her to come to the Lady Hardinge for an examination, but her mother is pleading for our help. Her daughter, you see, is reaching puberty and pregnancy could be a problem.' Agnes looked to Fatima for confirmation who nodded enthusiastically. 'If this happened without our intervention, both the mother and infant would likely die in childbirth.'

It all sounded horrendous, but I failed to see what help I could be short of whisking the child away from under the nose of her husband in the dead of night. I was about to voice my concern when Agnes cut in.

'Having examined her thoroughly, you must decide what the best course of action should be. If she is pregnant, she will need a termination.' Agnes looked up, finally registering my shocked expression, though misinterpreting its cause. 'Don't look so worried, Elizabeth, I will back you to the hilt if the husband or local Mullah object and Fatima will be there to keep the peace and translate your instructions to the patient while assisting you with the examination.'

'I see.' All I could do was rely on my MacKenzie backbone to keep me functioning as my brain had now shut down at the thought of what lay ahead.

'Fatima, perhaps you would take Doctor Stuart-MacKenzie to see the dispensary and let her check through the medical instruments and drugs you will be taking with you this morning.'

'Of course, Doctor Scott.' She moved to the door.

'And Elizabeth?'

I paused, half-out of my chair.

'I suggest you include a flashlight in your medical kit, so you can see what you're doing.'

My day was becoming more bizarre by the minute. 'A flashlight?' I repeated, wondering if the patient lived in a cave. 'How about a paraffin lamp as well?' I was joking.

'Good idea, but a flashlight is less cumbersome.' Agnes obviously wasn't!

Goodness knows how I got out into the corridor, but I did, then excused myself for fifteen minutes on the pretext of some unfinished business in the hospital, headed for my quarters and prescribed more laudanum and a change of sanitary pad. I joined Fatima patiently waiting for me in the general concourse and headed for the dispensary with my bag stuffed with spare supplies and my fingers crossed.

The back streets of Old Delhi were no better than those in Calcutta and I was thankful that all my inoculations were up to date as I covered my nose with a hankie and entered the house of Jusuf Abbas, the pungent smells of curry and sewage pervading my senses. My navy-blue linen full-length skirt dragged against my legs, my laboratory coat, buttoned at the neck, restricted my breathing and my two-tone blue silk headscarf plastered my hair against my head. I felt hot and sticky in the fetid air and reluctantly followed Fatima into the interior like some matronly aunt.

'*Assalamualaikum*,' muttered a wizen old hag standing in the corner of the open atrium, devoid of teeth and covered in a black cloak and hijab, her face the only visible feature.

'*Mualaikumsalam*,' we both repeated and bowed. Fatima stepped forward and spoke to the woman in Urdu then beckoned me to follow. We crossed the threshold into an inner rectangular room spread with dirty Kashmiri rugs over a stone floor, the long concrete benches attached to the walls topped with equally dirty, large, embroidered cushions. It appeared to be the Abbas reception room, but it was empty other than a mangy-grey cat which lay on the nearest cushion, one leg in the air, actively licking its backside. I shuddered as Fatima turned to whisper something in my ear.

'The woman, she is mother-in-law of patient. She very strange and not caring what we do here. It is all very sad.'

'Where is the husband?'

'Out in bazaar, smoking hashish.' Fatima screwed up her nose. 'He no interested in patient as well. She is number three wife.'

'Where are the other two?'

'They die, Doctor.' She pointed to an opening at the far end of the room and turned. 'That is zenana. Please, we see patient there.'

She pulled an oily rag of a curtain from across an entrance, and we stepped into a dismal windowless box of a room. At first, I could see nothing, but as my irises gradually dilated, I just made out the shape of a young girl sitting on a heavily soiled mattress on the floor, a strong smell of ordure emanating from her person and the only ventilation coming from slits in the walls above her head.

'Dear Lord!' I groaned. If I had not seen it with my own eyes, I would never have believed it and was instantly incandescent with rage. How any man could leave his wife in such squalid conditions was beyond me. As for the mother-in-law, she needed horsewhipping for standing by and allowing such inhumanity. I could feel my hackles rising at the injustice of it all and was thankful that my Urdu was non-existent, or this family would have been told their fortune in no uncertain terms.

'What is her name?' I asked, trying to regain my composure.

'Lamis, Doctor MacKenzie. It mean soft to touch.'

'Then please tell Lamis I am here to help her and not to be frightened. I will be gentle.'

Fatima smiled, then spoke softly to the child, her calm, caring voice pacifying our patient before helping her undress. She cast the tattered clothes aside and redressed her in a clean, fresh hospital gown. Throughout, Lamis remained silent but compliant, like a child's rag doll rather than a human being, and the thought of examining her in this flea-ridden, fetid, dark room made my skin crawl.

As my eyes continued to adjust to the darkness, I could see that she was far too thin, her skeleton frame stunted, her skin covered in fleabites and sores and her pelvic structure so narrow that if she carried a child to full term, it would never be born naturally. Equally, being devoid of nutritious food, abundant sunlight and fresh air, or any regular physical exercise, her health had been severely impacted to the point where, if she had been an animal, a vet would have considered putting her out of her misery.

Fatima worked diligently, producing a freshly laundered, cotton sheet from her bag which I helped stretch across the mattress, before topping it with a well-used and often-laundered towel, the faded bloodstains from past procedures only just visible. I remembered her spreading a towel on the bed in Room 52 of the Metropolitan Hotel and needed a distraction. Quickly picking up the discarded clothes by my fingertips, I walked back into the atrium, throwing the offensive items at the old nag's filthy feet.

'These need a good wash,' I insisted, knowing she hadn't understood a word. I rubbed my hands together in mime, then pointed to the door. Her look of indifference made my blood boil, but she bent to gather the clothes and shuffled off into the street, slobbering as she went. I could only hope that there was a standpipe and some clean water somewhere in the locality.

On my return Fatima was helping the child to lie down, every movement slow and excruciating.

I searched for my medical bag and sanitised my hands in alcohol. 'Really, Fatima, this is hopeless, I can't see a hand in front of me. Can you bring me the flashlight?'

The sudden illumination added a further level of depravity to the appalling conditions. There were rat droppings on the floor, the walls were dank, pitted and crumbling and what appeared to constitute a washbowl was a grimy, cracked earthenware pot which should have been condemned years before. This was not poverty, I thought, this was abject penury and could have been a good contender for the 'Blackhole of Calcutta'. I chewed the inside of my cheek realising that this would not be the last time I would find myself in such surroundings then steeled myself to get on with my work.

I began my examination at Lamis's head and worked my way down, confirming Agnes's worst fears as I went. The child was suffering from osteomalacia due a lack of calcium and Vitamin D, which had caused her bones to soften and deform. Signs of anaemia were obvious as I gently pulled her lower eyelids down, the colour of her inner skin creamy-white from a lack of red blood cells, rather than the dark pink of a healthy human, and the sores on her skin were red and raw. It was not only the cat that had mange, I thought. Her condition was truly appalling for one so young, but it was not until I reached her genital area that I was in danger of throwing up. Rocking back onto my heels, I waited for my nausea to settle and studied the sight before me.

Although there were no signs of penetration into her vagina, her anus entrance resembled a pulverised plum.

'Fatima, we'll need some warm water, clean rags and ethyl-chloride.'

While I waited, I leant over and stroked the child's arm in female solidarity, feeling her trauma and pain, but got no reaction. Her wounded expression, however, encompassed a catalogue of abuse and neglect, like some abandoned, starved and injured dog, found cowering in a storm-drain.

During my years as a GP around Riveldene, I thought I had seen everything, but this child's trauma was on a level beyond my comprehension. She had been penetrated into her back passage habitually, viciously and with rapacious intent, causing her sphincter muscles to tear, probably beyond repair, leaving her with no control what-so-ever over her bowel movements and she was now totally incontinent. Her anal skin was torn and suppurating pus, while the swollen, faeces-stained rectal orifice was shattered and bruised from continuous pounding by a depraved madman demanding self-gratification.

God alive, I thought, imagining the horrific scenes that these four walls had witnessed. It was no wonder she appeared to be lost to the world, her eyes vacant as if no-one was home, and why she couldn't straighten her spine, the very action creating immense pain. How she had survived so far was a miracle.

I was baying for blood and knew I wouldn't rest until the perpetrator was brought to justice, but first, I needed to conclude my examination then give the child some urgent pain relief.

Fatima reappeared with a small bowl of heated water and we spent the next thirty minutes gently cleaning and sterilising the wounds, anaesthetising the surrounding skin when the pain became too much for Lamis to bare.

Concentrating my mind firmly on my work, I engaged Fatima in some question-and-answer dialogue.

'Have you seen this type of damage before, Fatima?'

'Yes, Doctor, but not with girl this young.'

'So, you have seen it in older girls?'

'Sometimes, Doctor, and young boys too, but not so bad.'

'What happens when you report it to the police?'

Fatima shrugged.

'Are you telling me nothing happens?' My question was reflexive. I already knew the answer.

'The police, they no interested, Doctor MacKenzie.' Fatima's wet eyes glistened in the flashlight.

'Well, rest assured, they will be interested when I have finished with them.' My words sounded cold and calculating and were spoken through gritted teeth. 'Now, can you ask Lamis if she has started her courses yet?'

The question in Urdu was met with silence. 'I sorry, Doctor, but she too young to know what are courses.'

'I guess no-one in her family has ever bothered to explain puberty to her,' I acknowledged, 'and the bleeding from her rear passage would have masked it anyway.'

Malnutrition had probably delayed the onset of puberty, I concluded, and her under-developed breasts went some way to confirming this.

'Very well, I think it is highly unlikely that she is pregnant, but she urgently needs a full internal examination and X-ray, so she will be going to the Lady Hardinge without delay.'

Fatima's face lit up at this news.

'Does she have anything warm to wear?' I asked. I wasn't optimistic.

Fatima reached in her cloth-bag and, much to my surprise, pulled out a clean, worn bodice and a long-length of material for a sari. 'Excellent,' I exclaimed, wondering where the clothes had come from.

'I give Lamis good news, Doctor, then we get her dressed quickly before man comes back.'

'Better still, Fatima, I will dress her while you go and hire a tonga to take us to the hospital. If you can, send someone with a message to her mother. She should meet us at the Lady Hardinge without delay. Does she live locally?'

'Yes, Doctor. Very close.'

'Good.' I pulled some nickel annas from my pocket and held them out. Fatima shook her head.

'I have, Doctor. Please, no worry.'

With unpractised hands, I dressed Lamis in the bodice and sari then covered her shoulders with the white towel for extra warmth. She was given a medical dosage of laudanum to help lessen the pain, then I gathered up the sheet, my medical bag and flashlight and assisted the child out of the zenana.

We progressed slowly through the atrium, passing the mother-in-law, sitting on a rickety metal chair, scratching her face with jagged nails and wailing loudly. She was obviously not right in the head, I thought, which did not bode well for the mental capacity of her son, but I was devoid of any sympathy. My priority was to get Lamis away from this hovel and I was relieved to see Fatima reappear at the entrance, take Lamis's other arm, and lead us both out into the dank, rat-infested alleyway.

A commotion up ahead caught my attention and, seconds later, our path was blocked by a rotund, middle-aged Muslim in a grubby jubbah, his head covered in a frayed red and white keffiyeh, his teeth reddened from chewing beetle-nut. He barred our way, shouting Urdu obscenities, while a woman in full black burqa, only her eyes peering out from a small black slit, tried to drag him out of the way by tugging on his clothing.

Fatima grabbed my arm. 'Doctor, these are parents. The father, he very angry you take Lamis away.' Fatima's head was rocking frantically from side-to-side. 'Please, you not listen. You tell him Lamis, she must go to hospital. You show him you are boss.'

I was flabbergasted. 'But he won't understand me, Fatima.'

'He no have to. You are authority here and he frightened of authority. I translate for you. He not argue if you are strong.'

Right, I decided, if I am to be a blessing to Indian women then I will start as I mean to go on. I eyeballed him across the passage and raised my voice. '*As salamu alaykum*,' I said, sounding like a judge announcing the death penalty. He reluctantly returned the greeting, never taking his eyes off me. 'Your daughter is critically ill and without my medical assistance she will die.' I waited for Fatima to translate. 'She is starving and suffering from osteomalacia and anaemia.' The father shook his head and raised his fist. I stepped forward aggressively, waving my stethoscope in the air and glaring into his bearded face. 'Your daughter has been mentally and physically abused by her husband and you have done nothing to stop it. Now get out of my way before I have you arrested for obstruction and aiding and abetting a criminal.' There was a pause then he suddenly cowered before my eyes. I turned to the mother. 'Your daughter is going to the Lady Hardinge Women's Hospital for an operation, and I expect you to be there within the hour. Do you understand?'

Fatima finished translating and placed a coin in her hand. 'That is for bus-fare,' she explained, and repeated it in Urdu then elbowed the father out of the way, holding her ground like a centurion as I moved ahead with Lamis's shoulders cradled under my arm.

The silent, trembling child was eased onto the tonga as a growing, baying crowd gathered behind me. Once aboard, I turned and looked down on the group of bearded male antagonists, chanting and waving their hands in the air, like Newcastle football supporters shouting at the referee after a goal was disallowed. From my elevated position I treated the

Muslim men to a mouthful of Ruby's choice cockney expletives at the top of my voice. They fell on deaf ears, but it made me feel better and, seconds later, the tonga juddered into motion as the driver whipped the horses rear-end and we moved away from danger at a trot.

'Why did the father suddenly fall back, Fatima?' I asked, as we progressed through the traffic, Lamis whimpering at my side.

'He think you place spell on him, Doctor. 'He not argue with British witch-doctor.'

My mouth dropped open. 'Fatima Patel, did you tell him that I use white magic?'

Her smile held devious intent. 'Yes, Doctor, the father he understand magic better than anything.'

Miss Patel, I decided, had the same underhand tendencies as Ruby Tavener, and as I looked into her twinkling eyes through the dust of Old Delhi I could see why she was so popular with Agnes. As for Pa's reaction to his daughter being a white witch doctor, that didn't bear thinking about and the knowledge would likely put him in his grave. Better not mention it in my next letter home, I thought, trying to counter a giggling fit. Well, not to Pa, anyway. 'And the clothes? Where did they come from?' I stroked the emerald-green cotton sari.

'I buy from local charity with money from rich ladies with problems. My mother, she then wash and repair clothes and I give free to patients in need.'

I would have hugged her if Lamis hadn't been in the way, and felt an inner glow warm my heart at this revelation. The money she had received from Ruby was not only going towards her studies at the Lady Hardinge, but to providing clothing for the abject poor of Old Delhi. Wonders would never cease!

Chapter Nine

There was a real buzz in the air when we arrived at the out-patients department. Staff appeared from everywhere and Lamis was helped onto a gurney and whisked away to the gynaecology ward.

I, meanwhile, veered off to my room for some overdue attention to my own personal hygiene. In the excitement of the past hours, pain from my abdomen had been masked by tension. It now returned like a lightning bolt, turning my lips white and driving me towards the laudanum bottle like an alcoholic to whisky.

I sat on the edge of the bed waiting for the opioid to work then rummaged through my leather trunk looking for my camera. Aunt Karr had handed it to me as I boarded the overnight sleeper from Newcastle to London months before, and I found the compact, retractable Ensign E20 tucked between my bed-socks and brushed-cotton nightie; the Kodak film cartridges pushed into the toes of my bedroom slippers. I hadn't used the camera since arriving in Delhi because I hadn't had the time, but now it would prove invaluable in recording Lamis's injuries. I checked all was in working order and headed back to the hospital. Agnes met me as I walked through the ward door.

'You appear to have had an interesting morning, Elizabeth?'

'A slight understatement, Agnes, and thanks for the tip on the flashlight. I couldn't have managed Lamis's examination without it.' I held up my camera. 'With your permission, I intend to record her injuries for posterity, and include them with my report to the local Police Department. Her husband should not be allowed to get away with this.'

'Then don't waste one minute. Speed is of the essence here, and, as I said earlier, I will back you wholeheartedly. Sodomy is a vile crime and all too common in this country. Our chauvinistic police-force should have been shaken out of their lethargy towards Indian women years ago, but it hasn't happened yet, so be prepared for a fight.'

'If it's a fight they want then they've picked the wrong opponent.' Our eyes met with knowing intent.

'Be on your guard, Elizabeth, our District Police Superintendent is adept at finding a weak link in any argument when it doesn't suit his purpose or ambition.'

Icy fingers ran down my spine at Agnes's words. Clearly, she had had history with the Indian Police Department.

'Once you're done with that,' she pointed at the camera, 'meet me in the library. I need to read up on colostomy and sphincteroplasty procedures. It's a while since I have been involved in either of these.'

The college library was an oasis of calm as we sat, toe-to-toe, surrounded by medical books, studying everything the Lady Hardinge had on rectal reconstruction.

'What do you think are Lamis's chances of survival, Agnes?' I asked, examining a diagram of a loop colostomy.

My supervisor removed her reading glasses and stretched her spine. 'Near to zero, I'm afraid. Her physical condition is so fragile, she may never stand a temporary colostomy operation, let alone a full-blown sphincteroplasty. However, we must try and, whatever happens, the child could become a test case for all future legal actions.'

I nodded. 'Fatima is on her way to the developers right now with my camera film. I hope to get the photographs back tomorrow morning, with or without bribery.'

'Knowing Fatima, you will have them by this evening. That girl can turn water into wine.'

'Pity she doesn't drink alcohol then,' I quipped. 'Getting back to Lamis, what happens now?'

'I have asked Khalima Joshi to personally supervise a nursing team to deal with her superficial injuries and any infection. All the nurses speak fluent Urdu, and her mother will be on hand as much as possible to keep her calm. Lamis will get round-the-clock pain relief, regular nutritious food and much needed mental stimulation to aid her recovery. After that, it is up to her, *Inshallah*.'

'When do you think she will be strong enough for general anaesthetic?'

'One step at a time. I have no intention of putting her under anaesthetic for exploratory surgery until she has a more than even chance of survival. That said, until she has a colostomy bag the nursing staff will have a constant problem with hygiene.' She picked up her spectacles. 'Meanwhile, you should concentrate on the husband.'

I picked up a thick tome on Penal Law. 'Rest assured, Agnes, this book will be my constant companion until that maniac is behind bars.'

'Excellent. Keep me abreast of events.' Suddenly she changed tack.

'By the way, how did you manage to extract Lamis from that evil man's clutches?'

I sat back and shrugged. 'I didn't need to. He never appeared. According to Fatima, he was in the local bazaar smoking hashish.'

'Humph,' was her only reaction.

'However, Lamis's father and a baying crowd of Muslim men did try to block our progress into the street, and it was your wily mid-wife who saved the day. I was instructed to appear very British, very authoritarian and extremely dictatorial, which I did with a modicum of success, sporting my monogrammed CSTM laboratory coat and wafting my stethoscope around like the sword of Damocles.'

'And Fatima?'

'You don't want to know, Agnes?'

'Why, could I be struck off?'

I chuckled. 'Not you, but I'm not so sure about me.' I leant on both elbows and lowered my voice. 'Were you aware, Dr Scott, that you are supervising a Scottish white witch?'

Agnes's eyebrows merged with her hairline. 'No.'

'Well, you do now. Miss Fatima Patel made a unilateral decision, sometime during her translations, to inform the crowd that I had psychic powers and would cast a spell on anyone who got in my way. All I knew was that the father's aggression melted away like ice on a hot day and he visibly shook with fear as Fatima pushed him aside.'

Agnes had to wipe her eyes with her hankie.

'It's all right for you to laugh,' I muttered, trying to sound trite, 'but I could be burned at the stake like the North Berwick witches of the sixteenth century.'

'Heaven forfend,' declared Agnes, blowing her nose.

'And now that the genie is well-and-truly out of the bottle, your Ph.D. researcher could be going to her maker on the back of a horned broomstick.'

'Ooh, painful. How should I approach your father with the news?'

Now my eyebrows shot to my hairline. 'Certainly not by telling him I've been dabbling in some ancient Stuart-MacKenzie clan occult magic. Being a church minister, he would be instantly ex-communicated.'

'Oh, surely not,' argued Agnes, returning her hankie to her pocket. 'Everyone knows pagan traditions are intrinsically embedded in Christianity.'

'Try telling that to the Berwick-on-Tweed Presbyterians.'

She cocked her head like a sheepdog awaiting his master's command. 'Well, just look at the positives, dear. Edinburgh University's Medical Department will be delighted to learn of your metaphysical talents and will, no doubt, have them included in their syllabus. After all, Scottish spells could be an excellent way to deal with intransigent male patients with haemorrhoids?'

'Now that, Doctor Scott, is a damn good idea!'

Agnes was back wiping her eyes when a student ran into the library looking stressed.

'Memsahib Doctor, the lavatory in main building. It blocked again.' Agnes rushed out without a backward glance, leaving me surrounded by medical journals, case-studies and a Morgan & MacPherson copy of the Indian Penal Code of 1860. With only an hour to digest Sections 377 and 375 on sodomy and non-consensual sex with a child, before my next house-call, I had some work to do. Fatima and I would then be off once more into the community to examine a mother in her third month of pregnancy who was suffering from an acute shortage of iron and was nursing a ten-month-old baby with colic.

I was in the staffroom after dinner, reading my mail from home when Fatima dropped into a chair alongside me. She pulled out an envelope and handed it over.

'The photographs?' I asked, opening the flap.

She nodded.

'How much did they cost?'

'Not so much. The man, he owe me for helping his wife.' She dug in her pocket and passed over the change from a one rupee note and a scribbled receipt.

'Fatima, I'm speechless. You are a real asset to this college.'

A pink blush coloured her neck as she fiddled with her sari. 'Doctor, I do what I can. The mothers, they need my help or they die and the men, they not care.'

'I know, Fatima, and I will do my best to help you bring about change.' I held up the sixteen photographs showing graphic images of Lamis's injuries. 'I'll go to the police station in the morning and file charges against Yusuf Abbas. Will I need an interpreter?'

'No, Doctor MacKenzie, the police chief, he is English.'

'Good. Now, go home, you look exhausted.'

'I first go see Lamis.'

'That's not necessary, Fatima. You have done enough for one day and I have already been to check on her. She is heavily drugged, and sleeping peacefully, so there's no need to worry. Go home and get some rest. I'll see you tomorrow.'

'Very well, Doctor MacKenzie. Good night.' She pulled herself out of the chair and glided across the staff-room floor like a swan on water, quietly closing the door behind her. I returned to Ma's letter, keen to learn the news from home.

Pa's back was much better, and Ma hoped I had liked my tartan socks and scarf, which she had knitted. I hadn't the heart to tell her that they had gone missing somewhere between Calcutta and Delhi, so a white lie looked to be in order. My brother was now registered with the Royal Blind Institute after contracting smallpox and becoming partially blind before I left for India and was now learning to read in braille. He had also been given a Labrador puppy which was in training as a guide dog and it was getting under everyone's feet, causing great hilarity with the parishioners as it kept escaping and chasing the ducks on the village pond.

Aunt Karr, meanwhile, was fit and well and enjoying her golf. She had been back to St Andrew's for Hogmanay to meet up with fellow professors who she had worked with before retiring and was delighted to tell me that she had been introduced to a colleague of Doctor Agnes Scott's at a dinner in honour of the University's new Chancellor. I was to pass on a Colonel Murray's regards, and to tell her that he was happily seeing out his days living in Forfar. The Colonel had enthused about Agnes's abilities as a medic and Aunt Karr was now convinced that I was in very capable hands here at the Lady Hardinge.

It was a small world, I thought, as I ripped open the next envelope, and made a mental note to remain silent on all matters of my private life if I was to avoid them getting back to the family via bush telegraph. Practicing Scottish witchcraft being one of them.

I unfolded the letter and checked the signature. It was from Lady Virginia Cottesmore informing me that the trial of Colin Montgomery and Maurice Blackthorn for rape and drug smuggling was to be heard in the Delhi Criminal Assizes within two-weeks, and that I would be hearing from Police Commissioner, Charles Tegart, very shortly.

I dropped my hands onto my lap remembering that I was to be a witness in the case and reflected on her niece's rape aboard the ss Narkunda on the night of the Gala Ball. With so much happening in my life, Henriette's case had gone completely out of my mind since leaving Calcutta three weeks earlier.

Virginia and Henriette had travelled to India on the same P&O passenger-liner as Ruby, Frances and me. Henriette had not been the easiest young woman to like either. I had christened her Miss-High-and-Mighty on our first meeting in Tilbury when she insisted that her 'first-class' status gave her priority over my 'second-class' ranking. Fortunately, Ruby had been on hand and proceeded to put her in her place rather forcefully.

Henriette's father was the acting Governor of Tanganyika who had given into her every whim after his wife died prematurely. By the time she reached puberty, Henriette had become a thoroughly spoiled, pretty, slim, insatiable, and rich brat, who ran rings around her elders, and caused her aunt some embarrassing moments with the other ship's passengers due to her lack of manners and over-inflated ego.

On the night of the Gala Ball, Colin Montgomery, an English tea-planter in India, had drugged and raped her on the hurricane deck of the ship and had infected her with syphilis, leaving her utterly debased. Sadly, there were no witnesses other than Montgomery's travelling companion, Maurice Blackthorn, who, it was thought, had also raped her.

I had successfully cured Henriette of syphilis on arrival in Calcutta and subsequently found evidence to prove her claim of rape. It had been a sordid and grave affair which was further compounded when subsequent evidence proved that both men were operating a lucrative drug cartel between Britain and India and it was hoped that a successful prosecution would put Montgomery and Blackthorn in prison for many years to come.

I decided to ring Benningtons, the Cottesmore's Palladian villa in Calcutta, to find out more before I retired, and went to locate the college house-phone. Lady Cottesmore's dulcet tones answered after three rings.

'Hello, Virginia, Doctor Mac here in Delhi.'

'Elizabeth, how are you?'

'Very well, thank you. How is Henriette?'

'Fine, dear. Ronald is teaching her to drive that sports car of hers and I think he is finding it an uphill battle. Hettie was never one for taking instructions.'

I smiled, imagining the scene as the Cottesmore chauffeur tried to keep his boss's niece on the straight and narrow, while she ignored him and careered around Calcutta's leafy lanes in her Riley Ascot drop-head coupe. 'So, where are we with the court case? I've heard nothing from Charles Tegart, so far.'

'Well, Maurice Blackthorn was arrested at his tea-plantation two weeks ago. A large haul of drugs was uncovered on his estate and he has apparently spilled the beans about Henriette's rape in the hope of being given a lesser sentence.' I could hear Virginia's husband, Lord James Cottesmore, chuckling in the background. 'Charles Tegart made a special journey to Himachal Pradesh to head the interrogation and we assume his infamous and underhand persuasive techniques were the reason Blackthorn buckled so quickly.'

'But why is the case being heard in Delhi and not Calcutta?'

'That was James's suggestion. Any subsequent appeal will have to be heard in the High Court there anyway, and the drug-smuggling charges are a capital offence so have to be heard in the capital's criminal court.'

I was well aware of James Cottesmore's powers of persuasion. They had been instrumental in me obtaining my appointment at the Calcutta School of Tropical Medicine, so I knew that no-one would dare argue with his opinion on Montgomery and Blackthorn. He was the Governor of Bengal after all.

This was all serious stuff and would no doubt get a great deal of national press coverage. I could only hope Henriette's name could be kept out of the public domain, along with my own as her physician and expert witness. 'I assume you will be coming to Delhi with Henriette?'

'We all will, Elizabeth, including Jonathan. He is now seen by Hettie as her knight in shining armour, ever since he came to her rescue at the Calcutta Club on New Year's Eve.'

I liked Jonathan Harrington-Davies. He was Lord and Lady Cottesmore's godson and had become a friend of mine during my stay in Calcutta. We had met at a dinner given by my hosts, Arthur and Elsie Thornbury and was a thoroughly nice young man who was working his way through the ranks of the Sanitary Department of the ICS before moving on to higher things. At the Hogmanay party, he had floored Colin Montgomery with a public-school boxer's kick in the villain's nether regions followed by a powerful right uppercut when he found the blighter dragging Henriette across the lawn and into the bushes. It was not hard to imagine Jonathan and Henriette falling for each other.

'In my opinion, they would make a very attractive couple,' I said.

'My thoughts entirely, Elizabeth, and he would certainly temper Hettie's rather erratic character. But, enough about us, how are you surviving Doctor Agnes Scott and the Lady Hardinge Women's Medical College?'

We talked on for quite a while and, by the time I put the phone down, I felt bolstered by Virginia's interest in my welfare. I had become an honorary member of the Cottesmore family and felt a warm glow inside thinking of them all.

It was getting late, and the quadrangle was in darkness as I crossed from the administration block to my room, wondering whether the Cottesmore family would be staying at the Metropolitan Hotel during the trail. It would be just my luck for Henriette to be allocated Room 52, I thought, closing my bedroom door. Knowing fate, I would likely find myself back in the same upholstered chair by the window, trying hard not to look at the king-sized bed. 'Oh, hell!' I blasphemed and doused the light.

Chapter Ten

T he Delhi police station was packed as I made my way through the double doors at mid-morning. A uniformed Sergeant stood behind a chest-high, mahogany counter trying to decide which of the miscreants gesticulating loudly on the other side should be dealt with first, his deep baritone voice making little headway above the racket.

I elbowed my way to the front, waving my envelope above my head, trying to attract his attention. My one advantage in being on Indian soil, was that the men were no taller than me, making it easy to stand-out in the crowd, and as I appeared to be the only woman there, my presence was conspicuous.

The Sergeant soon caught sight of me from the corner of his eye, did a double take, then sidled over to my end of the counter, leant across, his moustache almost touching my topi and breathed stale curry into my face.

'Now then, Miss. What would you be doing in this den of iniquity on a Tuesday mornin'?'

'I'm here to see District Superintendent Windle, Sergeant. I have an appointment.' Agnes had kindly rung ahead to announce my arrival.

'And what would ya name be then, dear?'

'Elizabeth Stuart-MacKenzie,' I shouted above the cacophony all around. 'Doctor Elizabeth Stuart-MacKenzie from the Lady Hardinge Women's Medical College.'

He scribbled that down on his notepad and pushed his pencil behind his ear. 'Right then, Miss. You need to go through that door over there,' he pointed to a green painted door on the opposite side of the room, 'and keep going till ya gets to the end where you'll find a constable who can 'elp ya.'

He sounded just like Stanley, our ship's purser on the ss Narkunda, and for a minute I was transported back to the Departure Hall at Tilbury Docks and that fracas between Henriette and myself.

'Hello?' The Sergeant was waving his fingers in front of my nose. 'Is anyone in there?'

'Oh, sorry, Sergeant. It's just . . . your accent, you see. I haven't heard one like it for some time.'

His guffaw sprayed spittle all over the varnished mahogany and I had to wipe my nose with the back of my hand surreptitiously, not to cause offence.

'Best accent in the world, Miss, if I may say so.'

'Being from Scotland, Sergeant, I beg to differ.' I pointed to the door, he nodded a confirmation, and I pushed my way back through the throng.

Forty-five minutes later, I was getting grumpy waiting for District Superintendent Windle to condescend to see me. I was supposed to be helping Fatima at a dispensary in the New Town and wanted to get on with my day. Finally, his door opened, and I was ushered inside by his male secretary.

DS Windle made a big show of rising from his leather chair, placing his pen on its stand and straightening his khaki uniform jacket before opening his mouth. When he finally greeted me, his accent was straight out of Sandhurst.

'Doctor, eh . . . Stuart-MacKenzie, I assume?'

My hackles were already rising. 'District Superintendent Windle.' I stretched out my hand and took his in a vice-like grip, determined to make my presence felt.

'Now, I understand you have some sort of complaint.' He indicated for me to sit.

'No, Superintendent, I'm here to file an official statement regarding the illegal crime of sodomy in your district.'

He nearly fell off his chair. I doubt he had ever heard the word 'sodomy' escape from the lips of a woman before, and he obviously didn't know how to react. I decided to press ahead while he was still in shock. 'The criminal's name is Yusuf Abbas, and he has carried out multiple illegal acts of non-consensual, carnal intercourse on his under-aged wife and should be arrested, tried and sent to prison without delay.'

'Now, hold on a moment, Doctor MacKenzie.'

'Doctor Stuart-MacKenzie if you please.'

'Yes, yes, of course, Doctor Stuart- MacKenzie.' He crossed his arms and expanded his chest in a gesture of male dominance. 'As I was about to point out, this is a very serious accusation you are making, and I would like to know what possible evidence you might have to justify such an allegation?'

The man was insufferable, bloated with gratuitous over-confidence and I was going to enjoy deflating him like a lanced boil. I took my time removing my written report and sixteen photographs from the envelope and placed them on his blotter.

'Perhaps you should read my report, Superintendent, and study this photographic evidence, all of which have been signed and dated by me, personally.'

He shuffled in his chair then pushed the offending items to one side and looked at his watch. 'All in good time, Doctor. There are other more important matters which I must attend to right now. I will examine these later and advise you of what action is to be taken.'

'What could possibly be more important than sodomy, DS Windle?' I leant over, pulled the photographs back onto his blotter and fanned them out like a croupier with a pack of cards. 'I'm afraid I must insist that you examine them now.'

His sniffed.

'It is quite simple, Superintendent. You are not a qualified physician and cannot fully appreciate the significance of these images. I, however, am qualified and need to explain, in depth, what it is you are actually looking at.'

My opponent was turning puce at my implied insult.

'Like you, I am very busy, so delaying this matter to another day will be highly inconvenient. Therefore, I will not be leaving here until you have been fully briefed.' I picked up one of the more gruesome close-up shots and held it under his nose. 'Of course, I'm sure you recognise that this is an image of a female's back-passage.'

His eyelids resembled a camera shutter on repeat, and his index-finger pulled on his shirt colour trying to relieve the restriction in his windpipe. I kept going.

'According to the Indian Penal Code, 1860, section 377 covering unnatural offences, it clearly states that - *whoever voluntarily has carnal intercourse against the order of nature with any man, woman or animal, shall be punished with imprisonment for life or with imprisonment of either description for a term which may extend to ten years, and shall also be liable to fine.'* I sat back and waited for a reaction, but voyeurism was keeping him locked onto the photographs, so I continued.

'Equally, Section 375 of the same code now includes the Child Marriage Restraint Act of 1929 *which removes the evil custom of child marriage due to the potentialities of dangers to the life and health of a female child, who could not withstand the stress and strains of married life, thus avoiding the probability of death to such minor mothers.'*

DC Windle's expression was that of a comatose bullfrog.

'You may not be familiar with the Child Marriage Restraint Act, Superintendent, as it only came into effect last year, but I can assure you that it does exist.' I placed a copy of the Act on his desk. 'And as Yusuf Abbas's wife is only thirteen years old and incapable of resisting the unnatural sexual advances of a man three times her age and many stones heavier, she is now in such danger.'

'That is merely your opinion, Doctor. I'm afraid I would not be able to arrest this Yusuf Abbas without a second, more qualified medical opinion from the Civil Surgeon.'

What a pompous fool, I thought. He really believes he is defending the misogynistic high ground by trying to pull rank.

I extracted another sheet of paper from the envelope, clearly signed by Agnes and witnessed by Khalima Joshi. 'I imagine this is what you're looking for?'

DS Windle retreated into his chair as if the opinion was about to infect him with the plague.

'My patient is now at the Lady Hardinge Women's hospital and being constantly monitored. Perhaps you should go and see the injuries for yourself.' I paused, holding my finger in the air.

'Oh, I forgot, being a man, you will not be given access. Let me repeat her injuries as stated in my report.' I dragged my statement from under the photographs and dropped it nonchalantly on top. 'My patient has been so badly damaged from the vicious, continuous and violent penetration of her anus, that she is now suffering from shattered sphincter muscles and rectal incontinence which, with the obvious subsequent infection will probably kill her.' I leant forwards across the divide. 'When this happens, you will be adding a charge of murder to the husband's list of crimes.' I was now staring up his nasal passages.

'That's quite enough, Doctor MacKenzie . . .'

'STUART-MACKENZIE.' If looks could kill I would have been on my way to the morgue.

'. . . Stuart-MacKenzie. You appear to be a very forceful young woman and determined to proceed with this criminal prosecution so let me get this straight.' He picked up a steel-point pen, pulled a clean sheet of paper from his desk drawer, and dipped the nib into the ink pot. 'You are suggesting that there has been an illegal child marriage here in Old Delhi, and you are accusing the husband, one Yusuf Abbas, of subjecting his wife,' he paused and examined my report, 'Lamis Abbas, to an illegal, non-consensual, unnatural, sexual act under the Indian Penal Code of 1860, Sections 377 and 357.'

'Not one sexual act, Superintendent, but consistent sexual acts of sodomy. As the head of the Delhi Imperial Police Department, under the auspices of the ICS, and with such incriminating evidence to the crimes now in your possession, I would hope that you would arrest the perpetrator without delay and have him brought to justice.' I stood up, looking down on this ex-Sandhurst army officer with an inflated opinion of himself. 'Abbas's address is given in my report and if your constables cannot find him there, then I suggest they look in the local bazaar where he is likely to be ingesting illegal opioids. If there is nothing else, I will be on my way. Good day to you, Sir.'

I spun on the spot and waltzed out of the door, adding an extra inducement as I went.

'Just to be clear, I have sent copies of my report and photographs to Lady Irwin, who is the President of the Countess of Dufferin's Fund and, as you know, the wife to our current Viceroy of India.'

I continued my daily work as a locum doctor alongside Fatima, getting first-hand insight into the problems facing the Women's Medical Service. Too often, I witnessed women in purdah who were kept in the shadows of a zenana without any education or stimulation. Childbirth was seen to be unclean in this culture, so the new mother became a practical outcast for anything up to forty days after giving birth, receiving no help other than that of an untrained *Dai*. During this isolation, she remained in the smallest room of the house, unbathed and unchanged, and with little ventilation. These unsanitary conditions caused a complete breakdown in health for both the mother and baby, jeopardising their chances of survival. I now had several visual examples of this shocking and inhumane tradition, my camera working overtime to record the awful scenes discovered on my rounds in the city.

As for my research, this was growing exponentially. Hours spent in the hospital laboratory with faeces and blood samples confirmed the existence of parasites, worms, red cell depletions and, even more worryingly, consumption. Something needed to be done about it, but try as I might, I failed to see any remedy. Local Mullahs used the words of the Qur'an to justify such archaic practices and Indian religions in general held sway over the female population.

It was a relief to be approaching the weekend and I planned to go shopping and visit some of the sights of Delhi to take my mind off this conundrum. On the Friday morning, Charles Tegart's summons arrived at the college and I took it across to Agnes as she would need to re-schedule my trip to Mardan if Henriette's court-case dragged on. She read it then removed her reading glasses and settled back into her chair. 'Do you want the good news or the bad news?'

'Good news. It's been a bad week.'

'Lamis's mother told Fatima that the police have finally located Yusuf Abbas, hiding in the Jama Masjid Mosque for protection.'

'Thank goodness for that, I was beginning to believe he had fled Delhi. And the bad news?'

'The Imam is refusing to allow DS Windle's men to enter the mosque, declaring it a sacred place.'

I felt as if we were walking through treacle. 'So, what's Windle going to do about it?'

'I have no idea, but if I were him, I would tell the ICS Sanitary Department that the mosque was infested with rats.'

'How would that help?'

'The Sanitary Department would want to fumigate it with sulphur dioxide gas to avoid an outbreak of bubonic plague and the building would need to be evacuated beforehand.'

'Clever. Yusuf Abbas would have the choice of going to jail or dying of asphyxiation.'

'Exactly, but I doubt DS Windle has the intelligence to come up with that idea. Our ex-Colonial Army Officers are not famous for their lateral thinking.'

'Should I enlighten him?'

'No need, Elizabeth. I already have.'

'What about Lamis? What will happen to her, if she survives?

'You'll need to ask Professor Panday for the answer to that one. He's the one specialising in Islamic Law, but I imagine the marriage can be dissolved as it is illegal.' Agnes was back reading Charles Tegart's summons. 'Are you able to tell me about this rape case?'

'Certainly.' I relayed the circumstances leading up to the summons while Agnes scribbled some notes on her pad.

'For someone who has only been in India for three months, Elizabeth, you could not be accused of resting on your laurels.'

'Maybe, Agnes, but this rape case is giving me the jitters. I've never been cross-examined in court before so I'm not looking forward to being grilled by Montgomery's defence council. Have you ever been summoned as an expert witness?'

She chewed on the end of her pen. 'Yes, actually I have, although it was a long time ago.'

I pulled my chair closer to the desk. 'Oh, do tell.'

'Well, believe it or not, I was once involved in the theft of a diamond.'

Agnes Scott and diamonds didn't seem natural bedfellows, so I was intrigued.

'Actually, it was a very large yellow diamond. I was working as an assistant surgeon in a hospital in Jind at the time and was called upon to do an autopsy on a cadaver by the local District Magistrate. The Civil Surgeon was away on three months furlough and a replacement from the IMS had yet to arrive, so I pulled the short straw. Anyway, it transpired that the dead man was an English agent for the Maharaja of Panajab, who had been sent to South Africa to buy a large yellow diamond for his fourth wife on the birth of his eighth child.' She paused. 'Are you following me so far?'

'I think so,' I replied, my eyes crossing.

'Well, on the way back, the agent was attacked by thieves and killed. The robbers searched his baggage but couldn't find the diamond, so they buried him in a shallow grave and left.' Agnes refreshed her larynx with her morning coffee. 'When the agent didn't turn up at the Maharaja's Palace, he began to make extensive enquiries, found the thieves, apprehended them and handed them over to the District Magistrate for interrogation.'

I was all ears.

'They all insisted that they had never seen the diamond, so the District Magistrate assumed it was sewn into the agent's clothing and went looking for the grave. When he located it out on the flatlands, he had the unfortunate man dug up and thoroughly searched.'

'Did he find the diamond?'

'No, which left him with only one possible conclusion.'

'The agent had probably swallowed it.'

'Elementary, Dr Watson,' quoted Agnes, obviously enjoying herself. 'That's where I came in. On opening him up, I found the diamond in his stomach along with his last meal.'

'Goodness, what did you do next?' I was now hanging on her every word.

'Well, to be absolutely honest, and never to be repeated outside this office, I did consider pocketing the jewel and telling the District Magistrate that his assumption was groundless.' Agnes looked a tad shamefaced.

'But you didn't. Did you?'

'No, Elizabeth Stuart-MacKenzie, I did not.' Now I looked shamefaced.

'Apart from anything else, I had no idea how to turn the diamond into a nice little nest egg for my old age, and I didn't fancy being hung, drawn and quartered by the Maharaja of Panajab if he found out.'

'So, what did you do?'

'I insisted on handing the diamond back to the Maharaja personally, still smeared in curry, and then had to give evidence at the thieves' murder trial.'

'Good Lord, Agnes, this sounds like something out of the Tales of Scheherazade.'

'Well, it takes some believing, I'll admit, but it's as true as I sit here. Now, where was I?'

'You were pocketing the diamond.' She peered at me from under her wrinkled brow.

'While cutting the cadaver open, I decided to do a full autopsy and discover what had actually killed the poor man. I discovered that he had been tied, hand and foot, to a tree stump; there were traces of wood bark in the ligature scars; and he had been garrotted.'

'Ugh, nasty. And the trial? What was the cross-examination like?' I was now virtually sitting on Agnes's lap.

'Lengthy. The defence lawyer was determined to milk the case for all it was worth. As it involved the Maharaja of Panajab it was making headline news, so he preened about the courtroom trying to forensically pull my statement apart and suggested I had no evidence that his clients were anywhere near the murdered agent that night.'

'How did you prove otherwise?'

'Fortunately for me, his knowledge of forensic science could have been written on the back of a postage stamp and I had one ace up my sleeve. You see, the soil samples taken from the thieves' shoes and those at the scene of the crime matched, with one defining characteristic.'

'They were all splattered with the agent's blood.'

'No. Much more interesting. Both soil samples had traces of bird droppings from the Great Indian Bustard, a very rare, endangered species which only frequents the open grasslands of Jind and Rajputan, and never close to populated areas.'

'You're kidding me? I had no idea you were an expert on ornithology.'

'I'm not. As it happened, our District Collector was an amateur indigenous bird sleuth. He suggested I check it out once he heard where the body had been buried.'

'I imagine the defence lawyer was pretty miffed at the news!'

'Absolutely.'

'What happened to the thieves?'

'They were found guilty and shot.'

'And the diamond?'

'I have it on good authority that it forms the centre piece of one of the Maharani Deepkumar Kaur Sahiba's tiaras.'

'Crikey. I assume they cleaned it first.'

Agnes's expression was that of a disgruntled judge.

'Sorry. So, have I got this straight?' I inflated my lungs as I recalled a poem Ma used to recite after a glass of port and lemon at Christmas.

'You are the one,
who found the diamond,
that was bought by the Maharaja,
and swallowed by his agent,
who was garrotted and died,
then buried in droppings,
then found by a Magistrate,
who brought him to you,
who dissected and discovered it
deep in his gut,
all covered in curry,
but all in one piece
and now sits on the head
of the third wife of Panajab
when she attends state ceremonies and durbars.'

'Correct!'

'Then all I can say, Agnes, is that it beggar's belief.' I intended to send my little ditty to Ma to replace the usual *House that Jack built*. 'Do you think the Great Indian Bustard would come to my rescue as well?'

My supervisor smiled and handed me back my summons. 'Hardly, but you can always try. You never know, Montgomery's defence lawyer may be just as dense as his Jind colleague.'

Time was passing and Fatima was waiting for me in the dispensary. I turned as I reached the door.

'By the way, Agnes, a Colonel Murray from Forfar sends his regards.'

Chapter Eleven

'Please place your hand on the bible and repeat after me. I, Doctor Elizabeth Mary Stuart-MacKenzie do solemnly swear to tell the truth, the whole truth and nothing but the truth, so help me God.'

The courtroom was crowded, the atmosphere tense and sweat from my hairline dripped onto my collar.

The accused, Colin Montgomery and Maurice Blackthorn, both freshly shaven and dressed in dark suits, white shirts and flashy ties, reminded me of Groucho and Harpo Marx as they sat with their counsel on the left-hand side of the court. Police Commissioner Charles Tegart occupied the desk to the right with his counterparts from the Delhi and Bombay Police Departments, each resplendent in their formal white police uniforms and service medals.

Both lawyers were wigged and gowned and the Crown's barrister rose to his feet and adjusted his gown as day two of the trial got underway.

I scanned the room, nodding to the Cottesmores who were sitting in the second row, and caught sight of Ruby's head towering above spectators at the back of the room, her face half-hidden in cream netting from her stylish camel-suede cloche hat.

'Please state your full name and occupation,' announced counsel, bringing my eyes back to the bench.

I gripped the witness box brass rail to stop my hands from shaking, coughed and went through the motions.

'And you are currently employed by the Women's Medical Service as a clinician, whilst undertaking a three-year Ph.D research post on obstetrics for the Calcutta School of Tropical Medicine.'

'I am.' I scanned the jury box and saw a couple of jurors making notes.

The next five minutes were taken up with a series of informative questions which only needed monosyllabic answers.

'Did you treat Miss 'H' at her relative's home in Calcutta?'

'Yes.'

'Was Miss H infected with syphilis at that time?'

'Yes.'

'Were healing lacerations on the inner skin of her vagina conducive with forced entry?'

'Yes.'

'Were you aboard the ss Narkunda on the night of the Gala Ball?'

'Yes.'

'Was this Gala Ball a fancy-dress ball?'

'Yes'

'Did you see Miss 'H' and the first accused, Mr Colin Montgomery on the promenade deck together at eight o'clock that evening?'

'Yes.'

I was in danger of losing concentration when the prosecution barrister hit me with a curved ball.

'What were they both wearing?' I hesitated, staring down the barrel of a gun, knowing that Henriette's belly-dancer's outfit would be seen as provocative.

'Miss H was wearing a beautiful Egyptian costume of blue chiffon and the accused was dressed as a Turkish potentate.'

Counsel paused, raised his voice and aimed his question at the jury. 'And, Doctor Stuart-MacKenzie, was the accused touching Miss H at that time?'

Now I was back on safe ground. 'Yes, he was. He had an arm around her waist.' A female juror in the back row tutted.

'No further questions, Your Honour.' The barrister sat, Tegart nodded approval with his eyelids, the audience shuffled in their seats and I tensed in readiness for the defence counsellor's cross-examination.

I didn't have to wait long. The short, weedy, bespectacled advocate, resembling a puff-ball mushroom, sprang to his feet like a Puma about to pounce on its next meal and went straight for the jugular.

'Miss MacKenzie . . .'

'Doctor Stuart-MacKenzie,' I corrected sharply, puncturing his bloated, self-confident pose.

He cleared his throat, fiddled with his glasses, and started again. 'Doctor Stuart-MacKenzie, what possible qualifications do you have, as a woman, to recognise syphilis in others?'

I slowly breathed out and smiled. 'An M.B.B.S degree in General Practice and an MSc Honours Degree in viral disease control.' Virginia was hiding her amusement behind a hankie. I turned to the judge, ignoring my interrogator. 'During my work as a General Practitioner in Northumbria, particularly amongst the young, promiscuous farmhands of the area, I dealt with all manner of cases of venereal disease, and immediately recognised the bacterium, *Treponema Pallidum* in Miss 'H's smears when I examined them under a laboratory microscope.' I glared at Colin Montgomery who defiantly returned my stare.

'But you cannot possibly know that your patient contracted the disease from the accused on the night of the ship's party?'

'Objection,' shouted the prosecution barrister. 'Counsel is leading the witness.'

'Sustained,' ordered the judge. 'Please strike the question from the record.'

'Let me re-phrase my question.' The lawyer was thick-skinned and playing to the gallery. 'What, in your opinion, was the likelihood of Miss 'H' contracting syphilis on the night of the ship's party?'

I didn't hesitate. 'Highly likely. The presence of newly formed lesions in her vagina and swelling in her glands indicated that the infection of syphilis was less than one month earlier.'

'But can you say exactly when she contracted this disease, other than within a four-week period leading up to this examination?' He turned to the jury, palms outstretched, convinced his point was a *force majeure*.

'It would appear you are not listening,' I countered. Two ladies in the jury giggled. 'What I said was that it takes four weeks for lesions to show and glands to swell. That would put Miss 'H's impregnation one month before the date of my initial examination, placing her aboard the ss Narkunda around the night of the Gala Ball, not before or after that time.' I looked across at Lord Cottesmore, who winked.

My rebuff was short-lived, and the over-bearing lawyer's sneer was that of a hyena. 'That may be so, Doctor, but you have already stated in this court today, that being young and promiscuous leads to venereal disease infection. What possible evidence do you have to prove that Miss H does not fall into this category?'

You could have heard a pin drop in the courtroom, and Virginia looked terrified. I clenched my jaw, inwardly chiding myself for being so stupid and played for time by reading through my notes. If I was to extricate myself from this self-imposed trap, I needed the equivalent of Agnes's Great Indian Bustard droppings to come to my rescue. It arrived in the form of the female anatomy, so I crossed my fingers, raised my chin and spoke with superior authority.

'Are you familiar with the word 'hymen?' The defence barrister nonchalantly shrugged and shuffled with his paperwork, too dense to see where this was going. 'The hymen, is a thin membrane of mucosal tissue, formed at the entrance to a female's vagina. It acts as a barrier against germs, dirt and other external objects penetrating the genitalia, and has always been recognised throughout history as a means to corroborate virginity.'

His head shot up from his papers, sensing danger.

I ploughed on, my voice boringly professional. 'In Miss H's case, the hymen had been recently and severely ruptured and torn indicating violent penetration. In my expert opinion, Miss H was indeed a virgin and, on the night of the Gala Ball, had been raped in a brutal and violent manner by a man, or men, who were themselves infected with syphilis,' I stared at Montgomery and Blackthorn, 'and intent on self-gratification.'

Suddenly the courtroom exploded in a cacophony of sound, the women, led by Ruby, rising as one and applauding for all they were worth.

'Order! Order!,' shouted the judge, banging his gavel.

In the chaos and accepting that he was getting nowhere in his attempt to discredit my evidence, the defence barrister dropped onto his chair shaking his head and appeared to visibly shrink into his gown.

The judge, placing his gavel back onto the bench, waited for the courtroom to settle then directed his next question to the prosecution barrister. 'Counsel, do you have any further questions for the witness?'

'Indeed, I do, Your Honour.' He walked over to the witness box, placed his hand on the wooden surround and turned towards the jury, his voice rattling the window-frames. 'Doctor Stuart-MacKenzie, in the course of your work as a medical clinician, have you ever been made aware of any unusual beliefs for the cure of syphilis?'

'Yes, I have,' I said, about to deliver the hammer-blow on Montgomery and Blackthorn. 'It is common knowledge, both within my profession and beyond, that some men,' I eyeballed the accused, 'believe that they can be cured of syphilis by having intercourse with a virgin.' There was a collective intake of breath.

'And does this astounding belief have any foundation, scientifically speaking?'

'None whatsoever.'

'Thank you, Doctor, No further questions.'

'Doctor Stuart-MacKenzie,' said the judge, leaning in and smiling broadly, 'you may step down.'

As I passed Montgomery and Blackthorn, who refused to meet my gaze, I felt a small glow of malicious pleasure knowing that I had dealt them both a substantial body-blow and took my place alongside Virginia as the court clerk called for Professor Karlsson to take the stand.

It was Saturday night, and the illuminated structure of Viceroy House could be seen from miles around as Agnes and I, dressed in our finery, were driven through the imposing wrought-iron entrance gates to attend a dinner party, at the behest of Lord and Lady Irwin.

The Cottesmore family, much to my relief, had been invited to stay at Viceroy House during the trial and the Viceroy and Vicereine were now hosting a private dinner to honour Lord Cottesmore, in his capacity as the Governor of Bengal.

Bigger than Versailles and more opulent than Buckingham Palace, the building was the epitome of Imperial power and so vast that St Paul's Cathedral could have fitted easily inside.

'It's quite a sight.' I whispered, as our horse-drawn carriage drew to a standstill at the grand entrance.

'It certainly is, Elizabeth,' agreed Agnes, 'but there are many in India who consider it to be an extravagant colonial folly.'

'Really, why's that?'

'It was only completed last year, over seventeen years late, and cost more than double its original budget.'

The door of the landau was opened by a regally uniformed staffer who unfolded the varnished wooden steps and helped Agnes and I to disembark. With my freshly washed auburn hair brushing my bare shoulders in soft cascading waves and my silver chiffon evening dress, newly purchased at Ruby's recommendation, billowing out behind, I walked up the imposing entrance steps feeling like a movie star, my silver-heeled shoes tapping a tattoo on the marble tiles. I checked that my ivory and malachite bracelet from Tom was firmly fastened at my wrist as we progressed across the wide terrace.

'How many staff does it take to run this place?' I asked, feeling dwarfed by the massive arches.

'About four-hundred-and-fifty, including the gardeners,' replied Agnes, walking ahead of me into the entrance hall.

'Good Lord,' I muttered.

'That's nothing.,' she added. 'There are over two-thousand civil servants who work here and, as you would expect, they are all men.'

I was about to respond when one of the Viceroy's minions approached us, asked for sight of our invitations, then handed us on to another pristinely dressed employee. My supervisor turned and raised her eyebrows knowingly at me, then corrected her expression and dutifully followed the young man up the grand staircase to the first floor.

We were ushered into the library where the rest of the guests had congregated. Henriette noticed me immediately and rushed over to my side. I introduced her to Agnes then accepted a pre-dinner drink from the steward dressed in black, gilt-seamed, knee-length, satin trousers, white stockings, buckled shoes and a short white jacket, buttoned to the neck. Agnes kept her eyes on Henriette.

'You were amazing in court today, Mac, and made mincemeat of that horrid defence lawyer. I was so impressed.'

I drew closer and lowered my voice. 'Actually, Henriette, so was I. Any lawyer worth his salt could have torn my evidence to pieces.'

'Rubbish,' countered Jonathan standing in earshot. 'The jury were with you all the way. Defence council's big mistake was treating you like 'the little wife' instead of the highly qualified expert on the subject, which you are.'

'Thank you, Jonathan. Allow me to introduce my boss, Doctor Agnes Scott.'

'Ma'am, your reputation as a superb administrator and highly qualified physician proceeds you. I am delighted to meet you in person.' He bowed.

Agnes had a twinkle in her eye. 'And, young man, who might you have been talking to?'

'Sir Peter Bonham-Cavendish, Doctor Scott. He has nothing but praise for your work at the WMS and as the Secretary of the Countess of Dufferin's Fund.'

'Really.'

On the basis Sir Peter had tried to pull the wool over her eyes about my funding, I quickly changed the subject. 'How's the Calcutta Sanitary Department, Jonathan?'

'Up to its ankles in sewage, Doctor Mac. How about the Lady Hardinge?'

'The same,' replied Agnes, thankfully appearing to be amused at his joke. She warmly shook his outstretched hand.

'Have you met the Viceroy, Mac?' asked Henriette, turning to greet Lord Irwin walking in our direction.

'No, never.'

'Well, here's your chance.'

Jonathan bowed his head, Henriette and Agnes curtsied, and I was left shaking hands with the Viceroy of India.

'Doctor Stuart-MacKenzie, welcome to Viceroy House. I have heard many complimentary things about you from my dear wife, and Doctor Scott, of course.' He nodded to Agnes, a broad grin on his face.

'Then,' chipped in Agnes, 'let us hope your officials at the ICS have heard of them too, Edward.'

I nearly choked on my drink at her implied criticism.

'Agnes, dear, you know only too well that the ICS has a mind of its own,' Lord Irwin appeared to be on very familiar terms with my supervisor, 'but, rest assured, Dorothy will do her utmost to promote your newest recruit.'

As it was me they were discussing, I felt I had to intervene. 'Lady Irwin is most kind, Your Lordship, and I am indebted to her for the support she has given me in her capacity as the President of the Countess of Dufferin's Fund. Sadly, without it, my ambitions here in India would have failed miserably. Perhaps I will have the opportunity this evening to thank her personally?'

'You certainly will. We are a small select group this evening and all celebrating the excellent outcome to poor Henriette's trial.' He turned and kissed Henriette on both cheeks. 'Please excuse me for a moment while I greet our other guests.'

Henriette dug me in the ribs as he walked away. 'Well done, you.'

I swallowed my drink whole and wafted my clutch-bag under my nose as perspiration beaded my forehead. If Ma could see me know, I thought, she would be cock-a-hoop.

True to his word, ten minutes later I was being introduced to the Vicereine who, at the first opportunity, drew me to one side.

'May I call you Elizabeth?'

'I would be honoured, Your Ladyship.'

'Good, and please call me Dorothy when we are alone. So much simpler.'

I had no idea why titled ladies always insisted on me calling them by their first names, but I certainly didn't object.

'I must sincerely thank you, Dorothy, for your intervention on my behalf at the CSTM.'

'Not a problem, Elizabeth. Once I heard that the Indian Research Fund were prepared to provide half the cost of your research project, my committee were easily swayed. How is it going?'

'Slowly. I have only been in the post for a month and about to write my first report on my findings since arriving in Delhi. I hope, on reading it, that you will be able to pressurise the Police Department to treat cases of illegal child-marriage with greater urgency.'

'Ah, that thorny question.'

'Indeed. Until Indian men accept that our laws supersede old religious and cultural traditions, young girls will continue to die in atrocious circumstances.'

'Old habits die hard, Elizabeth, as well you know, but that should not deter us from our cause. I will set up a round-table meeting between the Dufferin Fund, the Police Commissioner and the Heads of Religious Bodies here in Delhi next week to discuss it.'

'That would be wonderful. Sadly, I will not be able to attend as I'm to leave Delhi for Mardan on Monday, but Doctor Scott is already dealing with a specific case in the Lady Hardinge hospital and will be the ideal person to bring weight to the discussions.'

'Very well, then keep up the good work and I look forward to getting a copy of your report before you leave. Now, let's get back to more social matters. I think we are about to be called into dinner.'

I was floating on air as Jonathan lead me into the dining-room and I needed him to fill me in on the final days of the court case, so took the opportunity to ask him to update me as we made our way to our seats.

'Montgomery got 10 years for rape and Blackthorn 5 years for aiding and abetting. In addition, they both got 15 yrs for drug-smuggling and are now facing a murder charge into the bargain.'

I nearly tripped over my feet., 'A murder charge. Why?'

'I have to say, Mac, we were all taken by surprise when a lady by the name of Ruby Tavener came to the stand to give evidence against the tea-planters. Apparently, during her passage to India, she had been assisting a Major Stokes in his covert investigations of the criminals for the British Police Force. One afternoon, while the men were playing cribbage with Major Stokes on deck, she searched Montgomery's and Blackthorn's cabins and found incriminating evidence of their drug shipments to and from Scotland. She then suspected that Montgomery and Blackthorn had got wind of Major Stokes interest in them and decided to bump him off.'

'What?'

'Amazing, isn't it. You knew Miss Tavener and Major Stokes, didn't you?'

I was too choked to answer.

'Well, she stated, under oath, that she had personally seen Major Stokes to his cabin on the night of the Gala Ball and that he was neither drunk nor smoking a cigar. She reported this to the ship's Captain after the fire and they decided to remain quiet on the matter until they could speak to the Bombay police.'

'Good God!'

Chapter Twelve

My feet were frozen, I was frozen, and the carriage was frozen, as the Frontier Mail rattled across the Pothohar Plateau on its way to Rawalpindi, carrying me ever closer to my destination in Mardan.

I had boarded the train in Delhi at the crack of dawn. Eleven hours later, I was huddled in the corner of my second-class compartment, wrapped in a blanket with my India-rubber hot-water bottle tucked inside the folds, trying vainly to keep my body warm.

Mrs Witherspoon, a rather angular, spindly lady with a squint, was my only travelling companion, having originally boarded the train in Bombay. She had been in England caring for her aging mother, who had finally died of tuberculosis and she was on her way back to Rawalpindi to join her husband, an officer in the Indian Army Ordnance Corps and was keen to engage me in conversation.

Hailing from Penzance, with a strong Cornish accent, our conversation was decidedly stunted as I couldn't understand a word she said. Undeterred, she had battled on, usually repeating herself at least twice, all the way to Lahore and beyond. I was now exhausted with the effort and feigning sleep in the hope of some peace and quiet.

My mind kept harking back to Jonathan's revelations regarding Major Stoke's death, and I now recalled how upset Ruby had been at the time. I should have been more sympathetic, but we were all in shock due to the fire and equally horrified at what appeared to be a genuine accident. In

Calcutta, some weeks later, I did wonder if there had been more to the Major's demise than met the eye, but all the chaos of my own life had taken precedence and I had ignored my misgivings.

Now, images of Ruby breezing out of our cabin in her Wimbledon ensemble to play deck-tennis with Blackthorn, and Major Stokes sitting in the second-class dining-room with the tea-planters eating a curry lunch, flashed through my mind and tears formed tramlines down my cheeks as my recollections took on greater significance.

'Wossmarrwiddee, Medhyk?' asked Mrs Witherspoon, stretching out her hand and looking concerned.

I rubbed my eyes and shook my head. 'I'm fine, really,' I responded, wishing the Frontier Mail would get a move on reaching Rawalpindi, and sank deeper into my blanket.

The gentle rocking of the carriage must have lulled me to sleep because the next thing I remembered was waking to screeching brakes, compartment doors banging and the guard's resonant proclamation that we had arrived at our next stop.

Mrs Wetherspoon was busy gathering all her belongings together and putting on her rather bedraggled felt hat. I jumped up to help her depart and held open the carriage door as she staggered out.

'Noze daa tha whye, Medhyk. Benatugana,' she said, as she headed off down the platform, leaving me completely baffled, highly embarrassed and relieved to see the back of her.

Three hours later, it was my turn to clamber off the train at Mardan. A vicious wind whistled around my legs as I stepped onto the platform and threatened to throw me off balance.

Pressing my leather medical bag and purse to my chest, I pulled my own cloche hat firmly over my ears and quickly headed for the exit, hoping someone would be there to meet me.

It was dark, I was lonely and not looking forward to joining the clinicians at the Danish Mission Hospital after hearing Gloria Hodgson's graphic description of cold beds, toxic paraffin heaters, sparce medical facilities and a sad lack of personal comfort.

With my heavy trunk bringing up the rear, I arrived at the station entrance and sighed with relief as a uniformed nurse, her fair hair plaited and wrapped around her ears, stepped out of the shadows and introduced herself.

'Good evening, Doctor. My name is Margreth Rasmussen and I am Doctor Bramsen's Assistant Surgeon.' She stepped aside and a tall, broad-chested young man with long sideburns that merged with his heavily bearded jawline, stepped into the dim light, grinning from ear to ear. 'This is my husband, Jens Christenson.'

He grabbed my hand and shook it enthusiastically. 'Praise be, Doctor, you're a sight for sore eyes.'

I did a double take. His accent was pure American mid-west, and his handshake was that of a Northumbrian navvy.

'And you, Sir, are not quite what I was expecting from a Danish Mission hospital. Do I call you Doctor Christenson?'

'Lordie, Lordie, Ma'am. I wouldn't know a bedpan from a stethoscope. No, I'm out here in this heathen frontier doing God's work amongst all the Pathan sinners.'

'Jens is a Lutheran Missionary, Doctor, and a great asset to our cause.'

'Well, it's a great pleasure to meet you both on this bitterly cold night.' I handed my medical bag to Margreth, my icy knuckles chilling her warm skin.

'Goodness me, you are freezing, Doctor.' She clasped my hands in her palms and rubbed them vigorously. 'Jens, take your coat off.'

'No, really, I'm fine,' I insisted.

'Nonsense. Doctor Bramsen would never forgive me if you caught pneumonia.'

I was suddenly buried in a thick black overcoat, a whiff of masculine odour invading my senses and was led to a horse-drawn tonga, helped onboard and transported out of the station at a canter as sleeting rain perforated my cheeks.

The hospital was difficult to see in the pitch-black of night, most of the building hidden behind a high, red-brick wall. Jens opened the heavily engraved, wooden door within the arched gateway and ushered me through. My mood instantly lifted. Before me, at the end of a long, sandy path stood an imposing two-storey brick building, with colonnaded terracing running the full length of the ground and first floors. Gaslights illuminated the entrance giving it a welcoming glow and the whole structure looked brand new.

On entering, everywhere was freshly painted, there was not a trace of paraffin and the aroma of freshly baked bread caused me to salivate.

A tall woman with deep blue-eyes, mid-brown straight hair, parted at the centre of her crown and swept back in a bun at the nape of her neck and topped with a white starched lace cap, appeared from a door by the central staircase and waited patiently while I removed my hat and shook my hair of raindrops.

She looked almost celestial, dressed in a white, pleated, long-sleeved blouse tucked neatly into a white, commodious, full-length skirt, her starched collar buttoned under her chin and an impeccably ironed, matching linen apron covering her clothing from chest to ankle. The only adornment to break the monotony was a deep-mahogany wooden cross hanging around her neck and a small silver and blue badge replacing her top button.

This, I assumed was Dr Anna Bramsen and I liked what I saw on sight. She came to greet me and instantly put me at ease.

'I understand from Agnes that you like to be called Doctor Mac?'

I nodded, removing Jen's overcoat and pulling a letter from my skirt pocket, penned by Agnes, and handed it over.

She looked at the handwriting and placed it deep in her apron pocket. 'And I am Anna Bramsen. Welcome to our Mission hospital, Doctor. You have no idea how long we have prayed for your arrival.'

Like Margreth, her Danish accent with her scattering of v's instead of w's was charming, and her melodic serene voice belayed her advancing years. Agnes had told me she was in her early-fifties, unmarried and from a farming family in Jutland. What she hadn't said was how pious the Mission hospital's Chief Surgeon was.

'You must be tired after your long journey. I suggest we adjourn to the comfort of my sitting room for some refreshment before I show you to your room.' She nodded to Margreth and Jens then led me to her private quarters where a pot of hot tea and a neatly plaited, freshly baked loaf, drizzled with hot butter and brown sugar lay waiting.

This may not have been Ruby's exotic mansion in Delhi, I thought, as I settled onto a green velvet wing-backed chair in front of a roaring log fire, but it was a far cry from what I had been expecting and I exhaled with a contented sigh.

'Agnes has told me so much about the hospital Anna, and your predecessor's determination to build it, back in 1906. Doctor Marie Holst must have been some lady to create this,' I scanned the contemporary interior, 'and it certainly doesn't look twenty-four years old.'

'She vos and it isn't. You have arrived just at the right time. Four months ago, our new hospital vos a building site.' She handed me a cup of black tea. 'Milk?'

I nodded. 'Goodness, I am not usually that lucky. How was it financed?'

'From the generosity of our Danish Pathan Mission. They have been our source of funds from the beginning.'

'Then, I'm not sure who I should thank more for letting me work here; yourself, The Danish Mission or Agnes.'

'Oh, Agnes,' she said, occupying the other fire-side chair. 'Ve go back many years. She has been invaluable to us in her capacity as Secretary of the WMS. Our hospital may be brand-new, Doctor Mac, but ve are desperately short of female doctors.'

'Then I am at your service, and please call me Mac.' The warm liquid was beginning to defrost my innards and, as I sipped my tea, I thought Anna Bramsen's Danish accent was a great improvement on Mrs Wetherspoon Cornish twang.

'How many staff do you have working here?'

'In total, thirty-six. Three female physicians, fifteen Danish nurses, ten trainee Indian nurses, a Sikh compounder, a housekeeper, two cleaners, two cooks, a gardener and a sweeper.'

'For how many patients?'

'Fifty. Mostly Muslim and Hindu women, but ve also have Sikhs, Jains, Christians and Parsis. Our daily clinics attract a great many patients.'

'Is that where you want me to start?'

'No, Mac.' She pulled a buff-coloured file from her desktop and extracted a Lady Hardinge headed letter. 'I understand your research post requires you to work in both the hospital and the community, with adequate time set aside for scientific research.' She looked up. 'Is that correct.'

'It is.'

'Fine. then, once you have settled in, we can make a plan.'

The weinerbrod was delicious, the fire soporific, and fatigue began to attack my eyelids. 'This is the first Zenana Hospital I have ever visited, Anna. Are any men allowed in the building?'

'No, never,' she hesitated, 'except Jens, of course. As our Lutheran Missionary he takes our Sunday services in the chapel and provides pastoral care for our Danish staff and his Christian flock, but he must restrict his movements to the staff quarters at all times.' Anna's smile was that of a mother referring to her beloved son. 'Jens has been our guardian angel on many occasions since arriving in Mardan. 'He is so practical you see and can repair anything.' She refilled my cup, and hovered, choosing her words carefully. 'Of course, our Civil Surgeon is another matter entirely.'

My eyelids snapped open.

'I'm afraid Colonel Philpott believes he is so important, he can ignore our Zenana rules.'

Gloria's warning voice, back at the Lady Hardinge, rang in my ear.

'Stay well clear of Colonel Philpott. I have it on good authority that Peshawar's Civil Surgeon is pompous, has wandering hands, and a habit of writing scathing reports to his superiors if he doesn't get his own way.'

'He usually visits us once a quarter to carry out an inspection and is timing the next visit to coincide with your arrival. He is expected here tomorrow around lunchtime.'

'Then I hope I won't disappoint him.'

'Life in Mardan, Mac, is very different to that in Delhi. How do you say?' her eyebrows crossed, 'you are now in a colonial backwater?' I nodded, 'and single European women are rare. Colonel Philpott is as susceptible to a pretty face as the next man.'

'Even Colonel Philpott would be preferable to the pompous Government officials in Delhi, Anna.'

'I vould not be too sure. However, enough for now. It is late and you need your sleep. Breakfast is at seven o-clock, although the day here begins at six. If you don't feel up to that, please join us in the refectory after the morning hospital rounds.'

'Never fear, Anna, I will be on duty sharp at six o'clock. As my Great Aunt Karr back in Peebles would say, "*Start as you mean to go on!*"

Colonel Philpott marched through the entrance gate of the hospital punctually at midday looking for all the world like Lord Kitchener on his way to Army Headquarters, his military uniform, thick black drooping handlebar moustache, matching sloping eyebrows and centre-parted, wavy hair, giving him an air of superiority.

I was standing on the second-floor balcony with Anna at the time, looking out at the expansive, verdant landscape of Mardan Province. Peshawar's Civil Surgeon spotted us and waved his peaked cap in the air then strode purposefully around the side of the building and out of sight.

'Where's he going?' I asked, as we made our way towards the external staircase.

'I have finally trained him to enter the building by the side entrance into my office.' She had an impish grin on her face, then quickly removed it as a young Danish nurse passed by.

Anna's small example of female one-upmanship rather appealed to me. 'I'm sure being made to use the tradesman's entrance went down like a lead balloon.'

She peered at me from the corner of eye. 'As I said last night, our Colonel is rather over-bearing I'm afraid and . . . a little handy, but a sharp rebuke now and then vill keep him in his place. Of course, I am too old for such advances, but you are not, so be warned.'

Being goosed by Colonel Philpott was something I fully intended to avoid.

'He is an excellent surgeon, however,' continued Anna, 'and this goes some way to counter his . . .'

'Idiosyncrasies'?' I offered.

'Exactly. Nevertheless, his familiarity can be very irritating, as my young nurses have found to their cost.'

'Colonel Philpott will not be the first man to try and put me in my place,' I said, as Detective Superintendent Windle sprang to mind, 'and he won't be the last. But he will learn that Scottish Highland lassies like myself should never be trifled with. We have a habit of biting back.'

I strode through Anna's office door, stepped forward, held out my hand and raised my chin. 'Colonel Philpott, I assume. Your reputation precedes you, Sir.'

He frowned, taken off-guard and unsure if I was being complimentary or sarcastic. Anna lowered her eyes and walked around her desk.

'Miss MacKenzie, my pleasure.'

My grip was like a tourniquet and my counter-attack to his deliberate refusal to greet me as a fellow professional immediate. I turned to Anna.

'Why is it, Doctor Bramsen, that every officer in the ICS and surgeon in the IMS seems to assume that I am single, unqualified and have a single-barrelled name?' She shrugged.

'I beg your pardon?' responded Philpott, his bushy eyebrows knitting together.

'Granted, Colonel.' Anna squeezed her lips together attempting to staunch a smile, while my eyes locked onto his with intense scrutiny.

'I may be some years junior to yourself, Colonel, but I do expect to be treated with the same respect that you would extend to my male counterparts.'

'I'm sorry?'

'Granted again. I would point out, Sir, that I am a qualified General Practitioner from Edinburgh University Medical College and have a Master's degree in virology from their Ashworth Laboratory, so my nomenclature is Doctor not Miss. Equally my surname is Stuart-MacKenzie not MacKenzie.' The temperature in the room dropped by ten degrees.

Philpott visibly rose three inches from the waist. 'Is that so?' He now ignored me and addressed Anna. 'Our new arrival seems to be a little short-tempered this morning, Doctor Bramsen. Perhaps she is overwrought after her long journey?'

'Hardly, Colonel Philpott,' she replied, looking up from her seated position. 'Although Doctor Stuart-MacKenzie arrived very late last night, she rose, like a cockerel, at five-thirty this morning and vos meeting patients on the ward at six.'

I winked at her from behind the surgeon's back then tapped him on the shoulder. 'Tell me, Colonel, how long have you been the Civil Surgeon in Peshawar Province? I understand from Doctor Hodgson of the Cama Hospital in Bombay, that you transferred here from the Army Medical Corps in Bangalore.'

Philpott crossed to a circular oak occasional table in the corner, pulled out a chair and sat. 'Four years.' His words were rather clipped. 'The Governor General personally invited me to take up this post in '26 after the Rawalpindi riots. The area needed a surgeon with logistical skills, who could re-organise and re-equip the field-hospitals, and raise the standard of surgical skills amongst the IMS clinicians.'

'Then you must be very proud of your achievements,' I said. 'From what Doctor Scott told me in Delhi, the standard of operative care in the Province is second to none.'

The man was lost for words, which was my intention. One minute I was chiding him for his lack of respect and the next applauding his abilities as a Civil Surgeon.

'You are, no doubt, very busy today, Colonel. May I suggest lunch?'

'A splendid idea, Doctor Bramsen.' Anna picked up a brass bell from her desktop and shook it vigorously, the shrill sound reverberating around the walls. 'Perhaps our new Scottish clinician could fill me in on events in Delhi while we wait.'

Touché, I thought as I joined him at the table. He pulled out a chair, his hand resting on my back as I sat. I ignored it.

'Before leaving the capital, I was instrumental in getting the Delhi police force to arrest a Muslim man, for sodomy.' His hand fell away as if electrocuted.

Fortunately, at this juncture, Margreth tapped on the open door and wheeled in a trolley covered in a Belgian-lace-edged-linen tablecloth, giving him time to recover.

'Thank you, Margreth, please ask Jens to join us if he is free.' Lifting the cloth away, Anna exposed a plate of Danish sandwiches on dark ryebread, some fancy Danish pastries and a jug of freshly made lemonade. 'Would you care for a beer, Colonel?'

'That I would,' confirmed Philpott, crossing his legs, leaning his elbow on the curve of his spindle-backed chair and undressing me with his eyes from under those tufted brows. 'We appear to have got off to a bad start, Doctor Stuart-MacKenzie,' he finally admitted. 'Perhaps we should begin again.'

'No need, Colonel. Professional women such as Doctor Bramsen and myself are a minority cohort within the male dominated medical profession of India, so I should make allowances for any lack of manners.' My smile was bevelled. 'Please accept my apology if I seemed rather terse, but, sadly, gaining respect within the IMS seems to be like pulling teeth. I am sure you did not mean to cause offence and I am confident we will get along splendidly as fellow physicians during my stay here in Peshawar Province.'

'Sandwich?' asked Anna, pushing a plate under the Colonel's chin.

The rest of the lunch passed without incident and Jens entertained us with his amusing tales of life as a Lutheran Missionary, while Colonel Philpott added graphic accounts of the Indian Army's constant skirmishes in the Khyber Pass and the horrific injuries and grotesque deaths of captured soldiers by the Afridi and Shinwari tribes.

Hearing of men being skinned alive or being made to eat their own genitals rather put me off my sandwich.

'Colonel,' I declared, as the lunch drew to a close, 'I look forward to witnessing, first-hand, your excellent surgical skills in the field, should the opportunity arise.'

He slowly rubbed his moustache with the side of his forefinger, salacious thoughts evident in his gaze. 'I'm sure we will find an opportunity to meet over an operating table, Doctor Stuart-MacKenzie, never fear.'

'Then, I will make a point of bringing along my camera.'

Walking back from the gate after escorting the Colonel off the premises, Anna burst out laughing.

'Mac, you and I are going to get along, how do you say?'

'Like a house on fire,' I offered.

'Like the house on fire,' repeated my Danish custodian, her ice-blue eyes twinkling in the sunlight. 'You seem very experienced at putting medical men in their place.'

'And not only medical men, Anna.' I relayed my battle royal with DS Windle in the Abbas case. She was intrigued.

'There are too many influential Mullahs, Imams and Gurus in India and too few educated females. We try hard to make a difference here at the hospital, but ve are a small fish in a very large river.'

'Sea,' I said, gently correcting her.

She snapped her fingers. 'Of course, sea. My English, it is very bad. Now you are here, I must practice more.'

'Don't be embarrassed, Anna. If you made me speak Danish, we would resemble a couple of nuns in a silent order.'

Her laughter was infectious.

'Do you speak Urdu?' I asked, entering the building and heading for the wards.

'A little. Margreth is much better than me.'

'Then I would like Margreth to put me through my paces when she has time. My New Year's resolution is to learn Urdu and Hindi fluently by the end of this year.'

'Then I vill set aside one hour each day for Margreth to teach you.'

Over the next three weeks, I took an active role in caring for local women and children both in the hospital and on house-calls, and my hot-water bottle did sterling service keeping my bed warm as the nightly temperature regularly dropped below freezing. Transport was very basic from bicycles, to shanks's pony, giving me plenty of exercise and ruddy cheeks in the chill, winter air.

I was in the laboratory checking for *morbillivirus*, the root cause of measles, after a child had arrived at the clinic coughing, sneezing, and covered in a red rash. I immediately isolated him from everyone and headed for my microscope. It proved my diagnosis was correct and I was about to take extra precautions with the staff when Anna arrived at my side looking worn out and in need of some moral support.

'Problems?'

'I've had a message from Colonel Philpott. There is an outbreak of bubonic plague in Hansi.'

'Where's Hansi?' I asked, removing the slide from my microscope.

'In Punjab Province. Ve are to check that everyone coming into the hospital is vaccinated, and the Sanitary Department are standing by to fumigate if necessary.'

'Do they know where it started?' I recalled my conversation with Tom about the Plague of Bombay in 1896. That outbreak had killed nearly two thousand people a week and had started on rat-infested ships at the docks.

'No,' replied Anna, squeezing the bridge of her nose with her fingers. 'I am holding a staff meeting in the refectory at seven o'clock tonight. Everyone must be vigilant for any signs of the plague to avoid an outbreak here.'

Poor Anna, I thought as she departed. Running a hospital was a massive responsibility and the problems never ended.

I made my way back to the clinic and was in the process of telling the mother, through an interpreter, what was wrong with her son when Nurse Freja, tight-lipped and tense, appeared at the door.

'Doctor Mac, a patient has just told me that Mrs Ahmed is demanding a rupee for her medication.'

Whatever next, I thought, as I called for Mrs Ahmed to explain herself. If the medication's compounder was trying to make money on the side, Anna would have no choice but to fire her and, as lying was endemic in India, I was not surprised when she vehemently denied it.

'Very well, Nurse Freja, I will go and question the patient myself. Mrs Ahmed?'

'Yes, Doctor Memsahib?'

'Follow me.'

The middle-aged Hindu patient was sitting in a bathchair, her varicose-veined right leg, heavily strapped, resting on a cushion.

'Did you give a rupee to this person?' I asked, pointing at the compounder.

'No, Doctor Memsahib,' replied the patient in blank surprise.

A large question mark hovered over Nurse Freja's head. 'But you told me five minutes ago, that Mrs Ahmed refused to make up your medication unless you gave her a rupee?'

'No, Bibiji,' said the patient. 'You thinking of someone else.'

I could see the nurse clenching her fists in the folds of her skirt. This was obviously not the first time the Sikh compounder had come under suspicion, but without proof there was not a lot I could do about it other than report the matter to Anna. Qualified compounders, who mixed the patients' medication on instructions from their doctor, were scarce in the North-West Frontier Province and Mrs Ahmed knew it. Her haughty demeanour as she returned to the dispensary irritated me and I was determined to find a way to bring her down to size.

At lunchtime, I was sitting in Anna's office reporting on my morning's work when there was a knock on the door.

It flew open and the housekeeper, Mrs Larsen, a broad-shouldered Viking of a woman dressed in black, her curly red hair, topped with a white lace mop-cap, strode into the room, her diaphragm puffed-out with indignation.

'Doctor Bramsen, I insist on making a formal complaint about the Sweeper.'

Anna slowly blinked, sighed and picked up her pen. 'Vot has Ali Begum done now, Mrs Larsen?'

'The man is idle and refuses to empty the thunderboxes.' Her forefinger punched the air. 'He must be held responsible if the hospital gets an outbreak of cholera or typhoid.'

'No doubt, Mrs Larsen, to say nothing of bubonic plague,' muttered Anna, recording the complaint in her journal. 'If Sweeper Ali refuses to do his job, then he must go. You have my permission to look for a replacement sweeper.'

The housekeeper stumbled backwards, clutching her chest and I shot out of my chair, convinced she was about to need the kiss of life. 'But, Doctor Bramsen, I cannot find a better sweeper?' Her hands were above her shoulders, seemingly communing with her dead relatives in Valhalla. 'And anyway, Sweeper Ali's mother is my best hospital cleaner, and the poor man cannot work if the Municipal Collectors fail to come and clear away the night-ordure?'

Anna's expression was priceless. 'Then, Mrs Larsen, I suggest you tell the Sanitary Inspector in Mardan that he must get the ordure removed immediately or he vill be held responsible for a plague here at the Mission. Now, is that all?'

'Humph!' muttered the housekeeper and strode out.

'You need to have the patience of Job,' I said, watching Anna rubbing her temples with her fingers and decided that this was not the time to inform her of Mrs Ahmed's suspected unscrupulous earnings.

'I've had a letter from Colonel Philpott,' she said, changing the subject. 'Our Civil Surgeon is short of an Assistant Surgeon and is requesting your attendance at the Royal Artillery hospital in Peshawar next week.' She handed over a piece of hand-written paper with Philpott's signature. As I scanned the contents, I couldn't help thinking he had an ulterior motive.

'Do I have a choice?'

'I'm afraid not, Mac. Agnes has agreed. You are to extend your stay in Peshawar Province for a further two weeks.'

I was in the dispensary keeping a knowing eye on the compounder when a large woman in a light-blue burqa arrived at the clinic, doubled up in pain, her weedy husband standing back, wringing his hands. I took one look at the patient and ordered her to be brought into the examination room while a nurse was instructed to find Anna.

The wife was helped onto a gurney by Sister Eriksson and the husband quickly ushered outside.

Drying my sterilized hands in the air, I stepped up to the gurney and began palpating the patient's abdomen. Her stomach was inflated like a balloon and if I hadn't known better, I would have said she was pregnant with triplets. Through my stethoscope, her intestines were in a constant flux and an anal examination confirmed a probable blockage.

'When did the patient last empty her bowels?' I asked.

Sister Eriksson questioned the patient. 'Many days ago.'

'And has she been vomiting recently?'

'Yes, often.'

'Does she get violent cramps?' I didn't need an answer. The woman suddenly grabbed her stomach and nearly burst my eardrums.

Anna rushed into the room.

'I think we have a blockage of the bowel, Doctor Bramsen. Perhaps you would give me a second opinion.'

Anna repeated my examination then turned and shouted above the howls of pain. 'I agree, and if she isn't operated on immediately, she will probably die. Sister, prepare the patient for surgery.'

I stood, leaning against the red-brick wall by the dispensary as Anna gave the husband the bad news and was astonished when he refused to agree to the operation, insisting that his mother-in-law had to give her consent first.

'Where does the mother live?' I asked, assuming she was just up the road.

'In Campbellpur, Doctor Memsahib,' replied Mrs Ahmed, who had come out from the dispensary to see what all the fuss was about.

'Where's that?' I asked.

'Four days away, up country, Doctor Memsahib.'

'But the wife will be dead by then.'

'I know,' cut in, Anna, glaring at the husband's back, 'but Mustafa Hussein is adamant. I cannot operate unless the mother-in-law is told and agrees.'

'Jesus. The woman is in violent pain and close to losing her life. Doesn't he care about her?'

'No, not really. Mr Hussein is more interested in his own personal reputation. If Mrs Hussein's mother doesn't give consent and then she dies under anaesthetic, his name vill be blackened amongst the men of his village.'

'So, what do we do?' I was beside myself with anger and frustration.

'Use opioids for the pain until she dies of a heart attack or gets blood poisoning from a ruptured bowel.'

'This is insane, Anna.'

'This is India, Mac. It's a brutal country, and Muslims are fatalists. She raised her hands to the sky, and murmured, '*Insh'Allah.*'

Bugger *Insh'Allah,* I thought, wanting to murder the man on the spot. 'So, what would happen if we did have the mother-in-law's consent, and Mrs Hussein still died on the operating table?'

'That is not Mr Hussein's problem.'

'But what about his mother-in-law's reputation?'

'She doesn't have one.'

I walked into the dispensary with a heavy heart, thankful that I was an agnostic and instructed Mrs Ahmed to prepare three vials of opioids. If my patient had to die, then I could only hope that it would be swift and pain-free.

She struggled on through the night and died the following morning. I stood on the balcony watching Anna giving the husband the sad news. As predicted, he raised his hands to heaven and cried, '*Insh'Allah.*'

Chapter Thirteen.

'Over here, Doctor Mac.'

I squeezed through the crowd of khaki-clad bodies filling the station platform trying to keep Jen's raised hand in view while a wave of uniformed passengers surged towards the exit, pulling me along like a riptide.

I arrived at his side, flustered, pummelled, and disorientated, my clothes in disarray and my topi hanging by its leather strap from the back of my head.

'Goodness, Jens,' I shouted, trying to make myself heard above the noise of train doors slamming, whistles blowing, and Army Sergeants blasting out orders with ear-splitting accuracy as platoons of soldiers elbowed their way into line and marched briskly towards the station concourse. 'Who are this lot and where are they going?'

Jens took my arm and led me into the dusty Peshawar day, looking about for a vacant rickshaw. 'They are reinforcements on their way to Minchi Barracks.'

'Where's that?' I asked, flopping onto a canopied rickshaw seat and holding onto my hand-luggage for fear of dropping it between the wheels in our rush to get away from the crowds.

'Landi Kotal,' yelled Jens, grabbing the canopy's rail as our cyclist screamed Urdu obscenities at the crowds and shot away from the curb, dragging my companion twenty yards before he managed to jump aboard and curl his bulky frame onto the rickety seat by my side. 'Up on the Khyber Pass.'

'Crikey. Is there trouble up there?'

'According to a First Lieutenant I was talking to on the train, there's an Afridi tribal rebellion up on the border so British and Indian Armies are being deployed to occupy the Khajuri Plain west of Peshawar to build a garrison stronghold while the North West Frontier is being strengthened to stop any Afghan incursion into the area to form up with the Afridi tribesmen.'

'Then I'm glad I'm staying down here in Peshawar's Military Cantonment working with the civilians for the next two weeks.'

'Mark my words, Doctor, if this snowballs there could be many military casualties coming your way. The Generals and Political Agents have experimented for years in training Pathan tribesmen to help the rank and file of the Indian army. They think this is a good way to promote tribal integration on the North West Frontier.'

'Well,' I said, puffing out my chest, 'that's a good thing, isn't it?'

Jens looked at me sideways. 'In theory, yes, but in practice, these Sunni Muslims are only loyal to their own tribes. Once they are fully trained, they desert back to their villages taking their army issue rifles, military skills and British army tactics with them, then turn on the very guys who taught them.'

The rickshaw was now surrounded by a sea of humanity as it crawled along Peshawar's main street, weaving between overloaded carts, military vehicles, tongas, doolies and pedestrians swathed either in dusty brown blankets, white saris or pale blue burqas, all forming a mosaic of ethnic diversity. 'You seem to know a lot about the military, Jens.'

'I should. My Ma and Pa were keen for me to join the Junior Reserve Officer's Training Corp at high school. Pa wanted me to follow in his footsteps and have a stellar career in the military.'

'So, what happened?' I brushed away the hand of a bedraggled youngster pulling at my sleeve.

'He was sorely tested when he learned that his only son was a pacifist who thought the 2nd Amendment right to bear arms was ludicrous and point blank refused to get involved in bayonet practise.'

'My Pa is a Minister,' I said, grabbing Jen's arm as we careered across a junction, 'and would have been delighted with the news.'

'Why do you think I became a missionary?'

We pulled up outside the Royal Artillery Hospital and Jens accompanied me into the reception area.

'What are your plans now, Jens?'

'Gee, I guess that's up for debate right now. I was going to visit the villages in the Kohat Valley, but I doubt I can get anywhere near it with all these troupe movements.' He turned and spoke to an auxiliary walking passed. 'Doctor Stuart-MacKenzie is here to see the Civil Surgeon, Colonel Philpott. Where will she find him, Officer?'

The chap looked a bit confused, stared me up and down then shrugged his shoulders. 'Try the Officers' mess, across the road,' then marched away.

Jens chuckled. 'Well, that's not a very good start, is it?'

'Let me try.' I wandered over to a glass fronted office with the word "Enquiries" over the door. Knocking, I eased the door and poked my head through the gap. It was empty. Raising my palms in the air I wandered back. 'Perhaps we should try the Mess, after all?'

'Can I help you?' A thin, strangulated voice came from behind a huge pile of boxes dumped, shoulder high, in the corner and a short, cross-eyed, uniformed soldier with prepubescent acne shot up like a jack-in-a-box.

'You sure can, young man,' replied Jens, stepping forward. 'The IMS Civil Surgeon, Colonel Philpott has an office in this building. Can you point us in the right direction?'

He rubbed his nose, squinted, and placed his clipboard and pencil on the top box. 'Down that corridor, turn left, up a flight of stairs to the first floor then find the door marked "General Staff".' He nodded to me, picked up his clipboard and pencil and dropped back into his hole.

Jens made a signum crucis sign over the box with his right hand, winked at me and headed off down the corridor.

We arrived at "General Staff" to find the door ajar and no-one inside.

'I give up,' I said, and plonked my bottom on a chair outside.

'Patience is a virtue, Doctor Mac,' countered Jens, his charcoal grey suit, matching waistcoat, starched collar and khaki pith-helmet giving him a rather Sunday-school teacher demeanour. He strolled down the corridor checking on name-plates.' Ahah!' he announced, beckoning me to his side, pointing to a brass plaque.

'Peshawar Province's Civil Surgeon at your service,' he said and was about to knock when the door flew open and Colonel Philpott filled the frame.

'Missionary Christenson! What brings you to my office?'

'I do,' I announced, stepping into his line of sight.

'So I see.' There was a pregnant pause. 'And your luggage?'

I pointed to my medical bag, hand luggage and Topi lying by the hall chair.

'Right, come in and bring that lot in with you.' He stood back to let us pass. 'Tea?'

Over army issue mugs of strong tea, we learned more about the military manoeuvres and Jens decided that he would be more use to the Christian community in Peshawar's Old Town than trying to travel to outlying villages.

'Very wise,' agreed Philpott. 'I'll get one of the orderlies to drive you over to the Lutheran Mission on the other side of town.' He looked at me. 'You, Doctor Stuart-MacKenzie, have a choice of billet. You can either be housed with one of the IMS clinicians and his wife in the cantonment or stay over at the Women's Hospital. Either way, you will be based here for the next two weeks as my Assistant Surgeon while my own chap is away with the troops.'

Not having a clue which was the better choice I opted for the cantonment bungalow, assuming it would be closer to the hospital.

'That is settled then.' He picked up a Bakelite telephone on his desk and asked for a Doctor Rawlings to come to his office.

I sipped my tea, listening to Jens questioning Philpott further on the Afridi rebellion.

'How did it start?'

'Pathan unrest has been brewing for months along the Afghan border. Abdul Ghaffar Khan got it into his head to call for a *jihad* and the Afridi 'Redshirts' have been openly challenging the British and Indian Armies ever since.' He turned to address me. 'Border skirmishes are now commonplace and British casualties are mounting from Pathan sharpshooters hiding in the crags of the hillsides. Anti-government sentiment is growing throughout the North-West Frontier and this is in danger of spreading throughout the tribes, so our chaps are going on the attack with punitive expeditions to quell the unrest and bring the Afridis into line.'

'Is it proving successful?' I asked, not really knowing what I was talking about.

Philpott's sigh oozed sarcasm. 'About as successful as operating on the wrong body part, Doctor Stuart-MacKenzie.'

Jens coughed, looked at his watch and banged his mug down on the desktop. 'Well, this is all very interesting but, if I'm to get to the Mission before lunch, I reckon I'll be on my way.'

Philpott was about to rise when a knock on the office door made us all turn around. 'Enter.'

A surgeon came through the door, fresh from an operation, his theatre gown blood splattered. 'You wanted to see me, Colonel?'

'Yes, Rawlings. This is Doctor Stuart-MacKenzie from the WMS. She will be billeted at your house for the next two weeks and will be working as my temporary Assistant Surgeon.'

We shook hands as Jens made his apologies and left, indicating in mime for me to ring him at the Mission.

I nodded and waited for Doctor Rawlings to make the next move.

'I'll send a message to my wife straight away, Sir, and when Miss MacKenzie has finished here, a car will be waiting for her outside the entrance.' He acknowledged me with a nod, his superior look not lost on Philpott. 'Marjorie will be delighted to have some female company for a change, women in the cantonment are rather few and far between.'

'You will find, Rawlings,' said Philpott, the timbre of his voice dropping like a stone, 'that Doctor STUART-MacKenzie has probably forgotten more than you will ever learn about surgical procedures and is certainly not here simply to provide your wife with some feminine small talk.'

The vicious remark cut the surgeon down to size as if hit by a cannonball.

'Please have the transport ready in thirty minutes.'

Doctor Rawlings hummed with anger, and rightly so in my opinion. He bowed his head in my direction. 'My apologies, Ma'am, if I caused offence, it was certainly not intended. If there's nothing else, Colonel, I'm wanted back in surgery.'

All this male testosterone was getting me down, and the rising tension needed to be diffused if life at the Royal Artillery Hospital was not going to degenerate into a battle of the sexes.

'What operation are you about to undertake, Doctor Rawlings?' I asked, ignoring Philpott.

He paused at the door. 'Transtibial amputation,' he replied in a staccato voice. 'Second Lieutenant Sharp took a bullet in the right tibiofemoral joint from an Afridi sniper three days ago. By the time they got him to me the wound had turned gangrenous, and the lower leg could not be saved.'

'Then I wish you well, Sir, and the patient a speedy recovery.'

'Most kind, Doctor Stuart-MacKenzie.' With that he departed leaving me alone with my nemesis. I leant in, determined to sort out the matter of my name once and for all.

'There is no need to come to my defence, Colonel. I can fight my own battles.'

'I was merely saving Rawlings from a fate worse than death, Doctor Stuart-MacKenzie.'

I burst out laughing. 'For goodness' sake, Colonel, I may be headstrong, but I'm not an ogre. Just call me Mac, and let's be done with this.'

He hesitated, his brows fusing. 'I'm afraid that is not possible.'

I was flabbergasted. 'Why ever not? If Sir Peter Bonham-Cavendish can refer to me as Mac, I fail to see why you can't follow suit.' I could feel my hackles rising. This was all too ridiculous.

'Young lady, you are dealing with the army now, not the WMS. Familiarity breeds contempt and, in the military, it is a recipe for disaster between the ranks. You would do well to remember that.'

'Fine,' I said, losing my temper. 'Then, between the ranks, call me what the hell you like, but in private my name is Mac, or Elizabeth. Take your pick.' I was obviously trying his patience and the last thing I needed was to be reported to Sir Peter for insubordination to a senior officer of the Indian Medical Service. 'Look, Colonel, Doctor Scott has agreed to send me here to help you and the army with its medical workload. In return I hope to glean valuable insight into how clinicians practice medicine in the Peshawar Province and discover the problems facing indigenous women living in this area. Unlike your other staff, I'm neither employed by the army, the ICS or the IMS and nor do I have any interest in making your life any more difficult than it is already. All I ask is to be treated as a fellow doctor, not a woman. If that is impossible, then perhaps I should return to Mardan.'

I tensed, waiting for my marching orders. Instead, Philpott closed his eyes, gritted his teeth and decided to make the best of a bad job with his pesky female physician.

'There is no need to be quite so dramatic, Doctor Stuart-MacKenzie. You've made your point and for the next two weeks I will endeavour, in private, to call you Mac, if that is your wish. In return, you may call me George. However, I must warn you, that overstepping the mark in front of subordinates will result in you boarding the first train back south.'

'Then I shall watch my step very carefully indeed, George.'

Marjorie Rawlings was a sweet young wife from the Midlands who had arrived in India with the 'Fishing Fleet' in '27. She fussed about me like a mother hen and, when time allowed, we did enjoy comparing notes on our passages to Bombay and the vagaries of colonial life.

Her husband was a little more difficult to win over, but with perseverance and a genuine interest in his career he began to warm to me as a medical professional, and we often burned the midnight oil, over a nightcap or two, discussing all things clinical within the British Army. It was not an uplifting conversation.

Meanwhile, George proved to be a hard taskmaster but a fair one. He was, as Anna had said, a very competent surgeon and impeccably correct in his dealings with me.

Working together in the operating theatre patching up injured soldiers and civilians, or dealing with infections, illnesses, and diseases in the community, taught me a great deal about being a medic in the IMS.

I felt particularly sorry for the army wounded who were subjected to new prophylactic injections of tetanus antitoxins. These had been taken from immunised horses and cattle, the blood purified and then injected into the patient. It seemed to work well, except for the side effects of serum sickness, rashes, fever and polyarthritis.

I was coming to the end of my two weeks in Peshawar and delighted that I had avoided George's infamous wandering hands when information reached the Royal Artillery Hospital that a major confrontation had occurred near Minchi Barracks and the garrison was in dire need of medicines, doctors, ammunition and re-enforcements.

I was on 'B' ward at the Women's Hospital checking on a Sikh mother and her newborn after a complicated breech birth when news reached me that I was wanted urgently back at base. I grabbed my belongings and rushed out of the building where an army vehicle was waiting, its engine running. Five minutes later I was in George's office being asked if I could use a gun.

'Yes, in a fashion. Why?'

'Because,' announced George, carefully monitoring my reaction, 'the Royal Army Medical Corp are short-handed with two medics away in the Khajuri Plain, building and equipping a dispensary and two others who are on a training detail in Lahore. Due to this emergency, the IMS have been asked to help out and I need you up at Landi Kotal dealing with the urgent evacuation of injured soldiers.'

I had images of me rushing down a mountainside holding onto the backend of a doolie while Afridi tribesmen, waving swords and threatening death to the infidel, nipped at my heels. The very idea stunned me into silence.

George took great pleasure in twisting the knife. 'You've been vociferous in demanding to be treated like your male counterparts, Mac, and there's no better place to test a man's metal than in a theatre of war, so here's your chance to put your words into action.'

I had been well and truly hoisted by my own petard and decided to try a rebuttal, in an attempt to remain firmly where I was. 'Surely, I would be more useful at this end preparing the hospital for mass casualties?'

The smirk emerging across George's lips at my apparent cowardice stuck in my gullet. 'That said, I'm as good as the next man when it comes to trauma medicine. In Northumbria, I treated many of the injured soldiers from the Great War who arrived back home limbless, broken and in violent pain, so I'm no stranger to blood and guts all over the hospital floor or their gratuitous deaths.' I kept my gaze firmly fixed on the Civil Surgeon's face. 'I'll admit, hand-to-hand combat could be a problem, but as a medic, my job is to save life, and if the army needs my services, then so be it.' Aunt Karr would have been proud of me. 'When do I leave?'

'At first light.' You'll need warm clothing, strong footwear, and a pistol. You can get these at the Ordnance Depot.'

'Not necessary,' I replied. 'I already have my own.'

George opened a filing cabinet, rifled through some buff-coloured files and pulled out a sheaf of paper. 'Good, then make sure as much of this list is loaded onto the Khyber Pass train by first light. I'll meet you at Fort Jamrud at 06.00 hours, and, Mac, dress like a man.'

Chapter Fourteen

I staggered back to the Rawling's bungalow at midnight, feeling shattered, but buzzing with expectation. Marjorie was waiting for me on the veranda, wrapped in her husband's army greatcoat and a fur hat. It was cold, bone-chillingly cold, and the sight of her was like a rum ration to a sailor.

She warmed me up with a hot toddy then insisted on running a bath while I packed a canvas kitbag, borrowed from the stores, with spare clothing, towel, facecloth, toiletries, writing materials, camera, film, compass and whistle. I had no idea how long I would need to be away, but I had no intention of finding myself halfway up a mountain with only a couple of pairs of knickers so, like a good Girl Guide, I added extras just in case.

My beautiful monogrammed, leather medical bag sat on the dresser waiting to be included, but the thought of losing it on the Frontier made me shudder. I had no intention of allowing some Afridi tribesman to get his grubby hands on it, so I emptied the contents onto the satin eiderdown and placed the bag into the back of the wardrobe, then wrapped my stethoscope, instruments, and spare bandages into one of Marjorie's tea-towels and rammed that into the top of the kitbag before fastening the buckle-straps.

My pistol and spare bullets were squirrelled away deep in the pocket of my thick tweed overcoat which just left my travelling clothes. Wool knee-length socks, long-sleeved cotton shirt, khaki jodhpurs, merino-wool jumper, riding boots, knitted fingerless gloves, MacKenzie tartan scarf and gaberdine topi were left, laid out, on the chair while I headed to the bathroom and lowered myself into a steaming hot tub. Sinking below the waterline I wondered, not for the first time that night, what I should do about my shoulder-length hair.

Sleep was impossible in the remaining hours before my departure, my brain seemingly stuck on repeat, constantly checking the supply lists, item by item, even though I had treble-checked them before leaving the supply depot. I gave up in the end and headed for the Rawlings' kitchen, following the enticing aroma of fried bacon, and tucked into two bacon and egg sandwiches, before washing them down with a large mug of laced tea.

Marjorie waved frantically from the veranda steps as I ran down the drive, slung my rucksack onto the back of an army truck filled with a platoon of Khyber Rifles and jumped in alongside them before being whisked off to Fort Jamrud where the Khyber Pass railway train was preparing to leave on its forty-mile journey to the frontier border post.

I found George directing operations at one of the baggage trailers.

'Colonel Philpott, where do I go now?'

'Carriage D. Throw your bag onto this pile,' he pointed to a mountain of kitbags stacked on the platform. I had forgotten to write my name on the tag and suddenly panicked that my bag would disappear into some platoon barracks and never be seen again.

'No thanks, I'll keep it with me. Is there anything I can do to help?'

'No.' He turned and peered at me through the darkness. 'I take it you can you ride a mule?' He sounded like Agnes, back in Delhi.

'I've no idea, Colonel. I've never tried,' I replied, 'but I can ride a horse, so it can't be that difficult.'

'Very well, make sure that chap over there knows you need a mount.'

I could just make out the head of a tall civilian in a pith-helmet surrounded by livestock at the far end of the train. Tapping my fingers to my forehead in a pathetic salute to George, I slung the strap of my kitbag over my shoulder and headed off down the platform.

As I drew closer, I could see a line of horses and mules being led up ramps into wooden-sided, open-topped wagons and tied by their halters to the side-slats, three abreast. A uniformed junior officer was standing alongside the first wagon with a clipboard, calling out numbers, so I made my way to his side and tapped him on the shoulder.

'Excuse me, Officer,' I said, dropping my voice by an octave, 'I need to be added to your list.'

His excuse for a moustache twitched as he looked up from his board. 'On who's orders?'

'Colonel Philpott, Royal Army Medical Corps.'

He sighed, flicked over a page and held his pencil aloft. 'Name and Rank.'

'Stuart-MacKenzie. Doctor.'

'Right, sign here.'

As I scribbled my signature on the sheet, the officer shouted across to the same broad-shouldered civilian who was now leading a black stallion up the first ramp, the animal's flank muscles twitching, the whites of its eyes showing as it made loud snorting noises.

'Another mount is needed, Captain.'

The civilian stopped in his tracks, stroked the animal's withers and aimed his remark squarely at the officer.

'Jesus, Mary and Joseph, Lieutenant, do the Khyber Rifles think they're the cavalry?'

'No, Sir, and it's not for the Rifles, it's for the Medical Corps.'

'Is it, by God. Well, I suggest you tell the Medical Corps it can feck off. My bloody name's not Merlin, and I don't do miracles!' He grabbed the halter and led the stallion onto the flatbed.

'Right, Sir. Whatever, you say, Sir,' shouted the Lieutenant then shrugged his shoulders at me. 'Sorry, Doctor, no can do.'

The Captain's attitude was not my problem, but my mount was, and I had no intention of being snubbed by some Irish Paddy with an honorary title.

'I'm afraid that's just not good enough, Officer. If the Captain is responsible for providing the British Army with horses and mules, then you must instruct him to do the job he is paid for. I am here to save the lives of your men and I need a mount. If this man hasn't got a spare horse in his stables, then I suggest he commandeers one from the civilian population in the cantonment.'

The young officer was between a rock and a hard place and had no answer. The Captain, however, having overheard my complaint reappeared from behind the stallion's hindquarters and chipped in from his elevated position.

'Getting a bit above your station, are you not, Medic? Tis a good job you're only knee-high to a grasshopper or I might be persuaded to come down there and make you eat your words.'

'And,' I shouted back, my MacKenzie intransigence coursing through my veins, 'it's a good job you are not a real army officer or you'd be stripped of your rank before you could say, Leprechaun.'

I felt a presence at my elbow and heard a quiet voice in my left ear. 'Doctor Stuart-MacKenzie, is there a problem here?' I turned to see George returning the Second Lieutenant's salute.

'Actually, Colonel, there is. This chap,' I stabbed the air towards the Captain, 'is refusing to supply us with an additional mount.'

'Is he indeed. Then what are you doing about it, Second Lieutenant?'

'I . . . I'm about to suggest we obtain a civilian mount for the Doctor, Colonel.'

'Very sensible. Now, be quick about it. The train will be leaving as soon as the Queen's Guides arrived from Mardan Barracks.' At that, he marched off along the platform.

I was wondering what the Guides were doing living in Mardan's army barracks when my opponent strode down the ramp with a swagger that was far too familiar, grabbed me by the shoulder and dragged me to the side of the track, looking much like the stallion he had just loaded onto the train.

I froze, every inch of me rooted to the spot, as my mind went into free-fall. The man glaring down at me with murder in his emerald-green eyes was none other than Duncan Fitzpatrick. The very same Duncan Fitzpatrick who had been the cause of me nearly failing my medical degree back in Edinburgh ten years earlier.

At that time, I had been deeply in love with this arrogant post-graduate Veterinary Surgeon from County Antrim who had wrapped me around his little finger for eighteen months, stolen my virginity then unceremoniously dumped me as he disappeared over the horizon without a backward glance, intent on a three-year sabbatical in India, telling me that if I loved him, I would follow. Being young and inexperienced, I was gutted at being so badly used, and it took months to get him out of my system, which was why I nearly failed my medical degree. In the intervening years, I'd longed for the opportunity to get my revenge on Duncan Fitzpatrick by turning him into a capon, but looking at him now, I realised that this was neither the time nor the place to say so.

'You little runt,' he growled. 'Next time we cross paths, be prepared to fight like a man, instead of hiding behind your Colonel's coat-tails.'

The situation was laughable. Having been told by George to dress like a man, Duncan Fitzpatrick had no idea I was female, and I had no intention of hanging around while he found out. Lowering my voice even further and hiding my face below the brim of my Topi I gave him both barrels.

'The next time we meet, you Irish upstart, I suggest you pray I'm not your surgeon, because I happen to do a very good line in castration. Now, get out of my way.'

I shrugged myself free of the large, callus-free hand that had, a decade before, caressed my naked body, and I stormed off in a state of utter turmoil. How the hell I was going to handle the situation, trapped in some Frontier barracks with a past lover, was beyond me, and all I could think of as I searched for my compartment, was Great Aunt Karr's unadorned reprimand back in Peebles.

'For goodness' sake, Elizabeth, pull yourself together and stop pining over some selfish red-haired Irish vet with an ego the size of Mount Everest. You have a career in medicine to think about and will likely throw it away if you carry on being so pathetic.'

Well, I thought, as I staggered through the compartment door, dumping my kitbag and Topi into the netting above George Philpott's head and flopping onto a vacant seat, perhaps turning Duncan Fitzpatrick into a capon might be a real possibility after all.

We entered the infamous Khyber Pass at seven-thirty and began to climb, winding through arid and broken shale and limestone hills which rose thousands of feet on either side, creating a narrow gorge which had been fought over for centuries. Men through the annals of time, had made the ultimate sacrifice in this wild and desolate place, peppered with crags, pinnacles, crevices, boulders and hilltop forts, as various tribes, armies and countries fought for possession.

I sat, my nose glued to the carriage window as we began to snake through thirty-four tunnels and over ninety-four culverts and bridges of the Spin Ghar Range as the two Vulcan oil-fired steam engines pulled and pushed us ever higher towards Landi Kotal, some three thousand feet above me at the Afghan border.

As I took in the barren, hostile views, each mile steeped in death and destruction, I recalled Pa's words back in Riveldene.

'The Khyber Pass railway is a great feat of engineering, Elizabeth, and many of our sappers died needlessly trying to build it for the British Army, while Pathan sharp-shooters picked them off from their hidden vantage points high-up in the rocks . . .'

It wasn't hard to imagine. I craned my neck to view one such steep cliff-side as we emerged from another black tunnel. You could hide a complete army within those rocks and never know they were there, I thought, and shuddered.

' . . . Alexander the Great's army marched through the Khyber Pass back in the 7th century, as did ancient Persians, Greeks and Mughals before them. It has a long history and is now controlled by the British to protect India from the Russians and Afghans. The Government is determined to hang on to it no matter what.'

Down on the valley floor, I spotted a caravan of camels and tribesmen trudging purposefully along an ancient, well-worn track as it threaded its way around the gorge's contours back towards Peshawar. Like their animals, the tribesmen merged into their surroundings perfectly, their dust-coloured robes, camel-hair blankets and Perahan turbans mirroring the colour of the landscape, making it hard to pick them out.

I could imagine Pa, standing in front of the parlour fire on a cold winter's night, reciting Rudyard Kipling as we now made slow progress up this venerated defile.

*East is East and West is West
and ne'er the twain shall meet,
Till Earth and Sky stand presently
At God's great Judgement Seat;
But there is neither East nor West,
Border, nor Breed, nor Birth,
When two strong men stand face-to-face
Though they come from the ends of the earth!*

'Penny for them, Mac?' asked George.

'I was just recalling Pa telling me about this place before I left Northumbria.'

'Did he include the massacre of Elphinstone's army in 1842, commonly referred to as the Kabul Retreat?'

I frowned. "No . . . I don't think so. What happened?'

'Elphinstone's army of 16,500 Anglo-India troops and their camp followers were constantly attacked and killed by Afghan tribesmen during their retreat from Kabul that year. In the end, only one British Army medic, Doctor William Brydon, lived to tell the tale.'

'No?'

'As true as I sit here, Mac. When he staggered, wounded, into a British sentry post at Jalalabad, the occupants wanted to know where the rest of the army was. His reply was short and to the point. "I am the army," he said, and collapsed.'

'God alive!'

'In total, the Afghans massacred 4,500 soldiers and 12,000 civilians, most of them slain right here in the Khyber Pass.'

My skin was becoming cold and clammy as I stared again at the desolate, rutted caravan track cutting through this harsh, soul-destroying gorge far below the railway line, and tried to imagine the thousands of twisted dead bodies strewn across the valley floor in piles, their fatal wounds turning the parched, bleached earth red with their blood.

'We look as if we're in for some bad weather,' announced George, cutting through my thoughts as he leaned out of the window, eyes skywards. I followed his gaze and caught sight of thick dark clouds blanketing the skyline, the tops of the most westerly ridges painted white against the umber rocks.

Reaching into my overcoat pocket, I pulled out my camera and pointed it at the ever-narrowing gap across the gorge, not more than 600 feet wide at this point and flanked by imposing and precipitous escarpments. I had just managed to capture an impressive shot when we plunged back into darkness, the mountain swallowing the train like a whale gorging on krill.

Retracting the lens, I pocketed the camera in the dim lighting and was about to ask George what time we would arrive at Landi Kotel when a screech of metal on metal caused the carriage to shake violently, the braking force catapulting me into the chest of the officer opposite, his head impacting the carriage bulkhead behind him with a resounding thud. Pinpoints of orange and blue burning sparks flashed passed the window like fireworks on November 5th as the train quickly shuddered to a screaming halt with steam and black smoke choking out the oxygen all around me.

'Shut the bloody window, Colonel,' shouted a Captain of the Queen's Own Corps of Guides, as strong hands pushed me back into a sitting position. The window slammed shut.

'Mac, are you alright?' George's breath was hot on my skin, his drooping moustache brushing my nose as he lifted my chin and tried to focus on my dazed eyes.

I coughed black soot from my lungs. 'Yes, I'm fine. I think?'

'EVERYONE OUT!' bellowed someone from outside the compartment.

I grabbed my coat, scarf and topi, and followed George into the pitch-black corridor, dressing as I went, then staggered off the train looking like a muffled pigmy, the air freezing my extremities.

Adjusting to the darkness, I hung on to George's uniform belt and, with eyes aimed downwards searching for the floor, I lurched forward, my right shoulder brushing the railway carriages and my left, scrapping along the rough convex wall of the tunnel until we reached daylight.

The dull grey vista was something of a shock after the bright conditions on the other side of the mountain and I cast around for the reason as a snowflake dropped onto my eyelash and I blinked it away. The train's engine sat half-in and half-out of the tunnel, spluttering and spitting oil and steam from every orifice. I reached for the footplate, rising on tiptoe trying to get a glimpse of the line up ahead but the hot metal singed my skin and I quickly pulled away. A wall of khaki uniforms blocked my view, and I was in danger of being trampled on by a sea of bodies pushing me from behind.

'Stop pushing,' I yelled, desperately trying to stay on my feet.

'Make way,' shouted George with authority. He grabbed me by my scarf and elbowed his way to the front of the crowd, my nose smacking into his back as he suddenly halted. Peering from under his armpit, I stared along the track and blinked. A hundred yards ahead, a tangled mass of buckled and torn steel embedded with splintered chunks of railway sleepers, rose, like some grotesque cat's cradle, from a crater of shattered rock and shingle.

'Dynamite,' muttered George, crouching as he moved ahead, his comment instantly paralysing me to the spot. My scarf yanked at my neck and I was dragged forwards, fear tensing every muscle. Whether I liked it or not, I was trapped amongst the treacherous mountains of the Hindu Kush, witnessing, first-hand, tribal guerrilla warfare against the British Army. I didn't like it one little bit. Others gathered at my rear as I watched George kick his army boot against the ruptured metal in frustration.

'Thank Christ the driver saw this in time, or we would all now be bleeding to death at the bottom of that gorge.'

With my heart in my mouth, I gingerly peered over the precipice edge and swallowed hard. The escarpment was strewn with jagged boulders, scree, and sparse thorny scrub as it dropped precipitously into the valley below and my eyes snapped shut, realising just how close I had come to never seeing my family again. I jumped back, my knees buckling, when something whipped past my right ear and a sharp crack split the surface of a rock where I had been standing, shards of serrated gneiss flying in all directions. I felt something wet drip from my cheek.

'GET DOWN!'

My nose hit the dirt and my lungs deflated as George landed on top of me while impact thuds pummelled the dirt around my head like hailstones on corrugated iron. I heard army boots crunching the gravel and a volley of counter gunfire from close quarters as soldiers formed into a defensive square, all down on one knee aiming their rifles at the mountainside.

'CRAWL BACK TO THE TUNNEL ON ALL FOURS. NOW!' came an order from somewhere close.

I didn't argue. With elbows and knees acting as pinions, I shuffled like a crab back the way I had come, George at my heels and the soldiers matching my retreat while maintaining covering fire.

The tunnel entrance was only yards away when a cry of pain to my right made me look up. A turbaned rifleman staggered, clutching his chest, and fell backwards. Instinctively, I grabbed at his ankles with both hands as he disappeared over the precipice and held on for dear life, his dead weight and heavy equipment dragging me across the dirt after him. I stared down the wall of death as my toes made tramlines in the gravel, trying but failing to anchor me to the ground as the soldier desperately snatched at fresh air trying to make fast on loose rocks or scrub close by.

'Stop struggling,' I yelled, feeling my grip loosening around his army boots as my fingers went numb, my shoulder tendons screamed in agony and my body slipped ever further over the cliff. 'HELP!' I screamed, 'I can't hold him.'

A rapid salvo of gunfire from behind nearly burst my eardrums and I was dragged backwards by my calves until my hands, still around the wounded soldier's boots, scraped over the escarpment edge. Strong masculine hands reached out, grabbed the soldier by his belt and hauled him to safety.

'RUN!'

I was bodily lifted onto my feet and rushed into the safety of the tunnel as bullets peppered the ground in my wake.

'Make space,' shouted George, taking charge. 'Get him into a carriage, and be careful, the bullet could be lodged in his spine.'

Ignoring muscle burn, I ran ahead, screaming like a banshee, intent only on saving the soldier's life. 'Get out of my way! Open that door. Someone, get my kitbag from compartment D. Don't bloody argue, officer, I'm a doctor. Easy now, keep him horizontal. That's right, slowly does it. Now lie him on that bench. Good, now shift yourselves and get me some light.'

The soldier was groaning in pain as I threw my dust-stained overcoat and scarf onto the opposite bench and lobbed my Topi into the empty netting. 'Where the hell is my kitbag?' I yelled as I turned around.

Five, wide-eyed, open-mouthed squaddies, stood, stock still, in the doorway, one holding a lit paraffin lamp.

'For God's sake, lads, find my kitbag, your mate is dying.' My left hand was rammed down on the soldier's chest and blood was seeping through my fingers while my other hand pushed my shoulder-length hair out of my face, and I suddenly realised why the men were looking so shocked.

'For Christ's sake, haven't you seen a woman before?'

'Not in action, Ma'am,' said one, touching his cap and moving aside to provide access from someone behind.

'Well done, Mac,' said George, entering the compartment holding my kitbag and his medical bag. 'Now let's get this chap undressed and see what we are dealing with.'

While George undid the soldier's ammunition belt, jacket, and shirt, I delved into my rucksack and pulled out Marjorie's tea-towel. In the spluttering light I could see that the bullet-hole was clean and located on his right upper thorax. Wiping my hands in alcohol, I passed the bottle to George, then leant over the soldier with my stethoscope and listened to his chest. His beathing was rapid as was his heartbeat.

'We may have a pneumothorax,' I whispered.

'OK. Let's roll him and see if there's an exit wound first, then we can decide on an emergency thoracostomy.'

The soldier howled as we gently eased him onto his side. I lifted his jacket and shirt and immediately located a jagged hole below his right ribcage and nodded to George. The soldier could have internal injuries from the bullet's trajectory, I thought, running through my anatomy checklist, with fractured or splintered ribs and organ damage being a strong possibility, but he wasn't coughing up blood which was a good sign, and the ejected bullet would not fester inside him. Our main concern now was a possible collapsed lung causing death by suffocation. If air got into the right pleura cavity from the open wounds, pressure would build around the lung stopping it from inflating and seriously restricting his breathing.

George took the lead with me acting as his assistant. Within minutes we had cleaned and closed the rear wound with an antiseptic plug and covered it in a secure bandage before rolling him onto his back once more. The soldier was barely conscious, his lips turning blue from a lack of oxygen and showing intense pain with every breath. Shock was setting in.

'It's alright, soldier, try to breathe slowly,' said George, as I cleaned the entry wound.

'We're going to give you something for the pain,' I added, and watched George stick his finger into the bullet entry wound cavity to block it. 'Officer!' I ordered, diving for the door. 'I want a flask of fresh water and a catheter from one of your field kits.'

'Flask and catheter,' repeated the officer and turned to one of his section. 'Sergeant, you heard the doctor. Flask and fresh water without delay and make that two. I'll get the catheter. What does it look like, Doctor?'

'It's a hollow rubber tube, about sixteen inches long and brick red in colour. It will be curled into a sterile bag and if you can't find it, look in the VD medical kit.'

'Right, Ma'am. VD medical kit.'

I looked back at the patient now gasping for breath. 'And be quick about it, soldier!'

As they disappeared, I leant around the doorframe and shouted down the corridor. 'What's the soldier's name?'

'Second Lieutenant Tariq, Doctor. Salim Tariq,' shouted the Sergeant and jumped from the train.

'Right.' I turned to the other soldiers still hovering by the compartment door. 'I need another paraffin lamp in here and does anyone have any whisky?'

'I do,' came a reply from somewhere further down the carriage. 'Great,' I yelled, 'Then bring it here with a cup and, for God's sake, will someone shut down this howling gale.'

Seconds later a small metal cup and a bottle of whisky were thrust into my hand. I didn't bother looking up but poured some spirit into the cup adding a good measure of laudanum.

'Salim, can you hear me?' The Lieutenant's eyes were firmly shut and his breathing now very laboured, but he squeezed my hand.

'Good. I want you to drink this. It will reduce the pain.' I eased his head off the seat and slowly tipped the cup towards his lips, the whisky causing a violent coughing fit as it went down his esophagus.

'Relax, Tariq,' added George, his finger still in the bullet-hole. 'You have the best two surgeons east of Suez looking after you and, with luck, we'll have you back on duty before you can say knife.'

I crossed my fingers and smiled. The last thing Salim Tariq needed to hear was the word knife, but the laudanum would soon be in his system and looking at his pallid, furrowed features I expected the pain to knock him out cold before we ever needed any ether.

'Doctor, is this it?'

I turned. The officer was holding a small pouch. I took it, opened the retaining strip, and pulled out the catheter. 'Thank you, officer, and the flasks?'

'Here, Doctor,' called the Sergeant and pushed two full water cannisters into my hands.

'OK, empty a third out of each then pass them over.'

'How's he doing. Miss?' asked one of the squaddies, peering over the Sergeant's shoulder.

'Too early to tell, lad,' replied George. 'but we're working on it.'

The officer looked at the bottle of whisky sitting on the floor. 'Excuse me, Doctor, but Lieutenant Tariq is a Muslim.'

'Yes, I know,' I said rather irritably, more interested in Salim's present condition than his religious beliefs.

'It's just that . . . Muslims don't drink alcohol.'

'Oh, bugger!'

Chapter Fifteen

With the catheter sutured into position in the bullet-hole and its outer end inserted into one of the water flasks, all that was left was to sterilize Salim's entry-wound with sulfa-powder, bandage it securely then bind the whole ribcage to avoid further damage. All we could do then was cross our fingers and hope.

He was still out cold, but his skin was less pallid and his breathing less laboured. I checked the flask now hanging from Salim's trouser belt by a looped bootstrap and it was bubbling nicely.

'Not much blood now,' I noted, before checking the Lieutenant's pulse. 'And his heartbeat is less erratic. I think the lung is re-inflating as the pressure drops.'

'Good.' George wiped his bloodied hands on the tea-towel and picked up the whisky bottle from the floor, gulping down a large swig of spirit. 'My God, I needed that.' He wiped the neck and handed it over.

I didn't hesitate and put the bottle to my lips.

'I haven't tasted a Jameson's in a long while,' he added, searching in his own medical bag for sulpha-powder. 'The Irish may have their faults, but they can certainly distil whisky.'

My hand hovered mid-swig and slowly dropped below my chin, as I rotated the bottle to read the label. Unless we had the Royal Irish Fusiliers on board the train, I thought, my mind doing cartwheels, this could only belong to one man.

My pulse-rate doubled in a nano-second as my head lifted and I focused on the corridor. Duncan Fitzpatrick, broad-shouldered, copper hair ruffled, green eyes sparkling and a mocking grin spread across his lips stood, leaning against the train window, his arms crossed against his chest and a very familiar russet curl flopping over his left eyebrow.

I gulped, the pungent spirit burning my throat, and for the third time that day, my knees threatened to give way. He stretched over and pushed open the compartment door.

'Tis the liquid of angels, Colonel.' His eyes never left my face. 'Just the thing for a long ride in a snow blizzard.' A sudden rush of icy air from the tunnel froze my ankles. 'Your mount awaits you, Doctor Stuart-MacKenzie, as you ordered.'

He winked and all my subterfuge on the platform at Jamrud Fort seemed suddenly childish. I dropped onto my overcoat and buried my head in my hands.

'Mac, you must be exhausted, and you have a cut on your cheek?' said George, dabbing the bullet entry-wound with a sulfa-swab.

I ran my finger down my torn skin but the blood had already congealed. 'It's OK. I think it's just a scratch from a shard of rock.'

'Good. Now, help me bind this chap's ribcage then I suggest we get the squaddies to make us a brew, and don't let that Irish bugger outside reclaim the whisky. We need it more than he does.'

Poor George, I thought, as I clutched the Jameson's between my knees, he has no idea what subliminal messages are flying around his head right now. I rammed the cork stopper into the bottle neck with unnecessary force and shoved the whisky into my kitbag. Ignoring Duncan, I crossed to Salim, eased my arms under his armpits, clasped my hands tightly together above his clavicle and lifted my elbows, remaining there, eyes firmly fixed on the patient's head, until his thorax was completely wrapped in a tight white bandage.

'That should do it,' announced George, pulling at the bandage to check it was secure. 'Check his vital signs once more, Mac, while I go and find out what the army are up to. Do you take sugar?'

I shook my head, unable to speak, and stared out of the window into the dark tunnel expecting to see Duncan's reflection in the glass, but he had gone. Sighing with relief, I lifted Salim's eyelids and placed the paraffin lamp closer. His irises contracted in the sudden bright light and I tapped my palm on his shoulder, relieved that he was still alive. At least something was going to plan, I thought.

I was in the middle of changing the water-flasks over when George returned with two steaming mugs of tea. He poured a shot of Jameson's into each then settled into a seat and waited for me to finish.

Tipping the bloodied contents of the first flask out of the compartment window onto the track below, my hair was whipped up by the wind and caught in the hinge. 'Ow!'

'Hold still and let me help.' With surgical precision George released me from the hinge and I slammed the window shut. Rubbing my scalp, I took a mug from George's hand and dropped down beside him. 'Is the weather really bad outside?' The tea warmed my innards, and a rosy glow coloured my numbed cheeks.

'It's not good. Snow now six inches deep by the entrance and the wind is building by the minute.'

'What's the plan?'

'A number of pickets from the Khyber Rifles have been sent out around the mountainside to provide cover, while a caravan of pack-mules is being made ready to attempt the climb to the frontier on foot.'

'Jesus, in this weather. How far is it to the border?'

'About five miles and uphill most of the way. We are to follow on horse-back with a platoon of Queen's Own Guides out front and behind.'

'Then let's hope the Afridis give up and go home in the blizzard.' The whine of a bullet whizzing past my ear replayed in my head.

'Unlikely Mac, Afghan tribesmen never give up, so keep your head down.'

My hand shook. 'What do we do about Salim?'

'I spoke to the platoon Captain. The Rifles are going to rig up a doolie and will take it in turns to carry Second Lieutenant Tariq up the track in teams of five men, one at each corner of the stretcher and one steadying the water-flask.'

'But he'll never survive that journey in his condition.' I was horrified. 'If the jarring on the climb doesn't get him, the snowstorm certainly will.'

George took my empty mug and rubbed his callous-free palm across his moustache. 'I know, but we have no choice. If he stays here, he will freeze to death overnight. All we can do is wrap him up in as many blankets as possible, cover his stretcher in a canvas tarpaulin and hope they don't drop him.

'Dear God.' I checked Salim's pulse once more. It was steady at eighty beats a minute. 'Right,' I announced, straightening my shoulders and stiffening my spine. 'If needs must, I had better start clearing up in here and then go find some army blankets.'

'I'll get the blankets while you stay in the warm.' George hesitated, lifting my chin with his fingers, and examining my damaged cheek in the dim light. 'Mac,' he paused, searching for the right words. 'I'm not one for giving praise as you well know . . .'

I tried not to smile and failed. Lord Kitchener's double was turning puce around the gills.

' . . . but I must say, I'm impressed with the way you have handled yourself today. You have more spunk than all the Khyber Rifles put together, and if I ever question your ability to compete with the men of the IMS again, you have my permission to kick me in the goolies.'

I was flabbergasted and was about to say so when his tall frame vanished from sight, leaving me to wallow in the afterglow all on my own.

Digging my riding-boot heels in the flank of the reluctant piebald gelding under my buttocks, I pushed on, the bit on a tight rein as I fought to keep his nose close to the rear-end of the mount immediately ahead. It was all I could do to stay on. With every step, the animal's body shook, its hooves stamping across the uneven railway sleepers like bicycle wheels on a cobbled street. My coccyx was raw and screaming out in pain, my nose constantly dripped, my eyes were red and weeping, snowflakes whistled under my scarf, turning into icy raindrops as they slithered down my spine, and my toes, fingers and lips were white and numb.

Visibility was down to zero and the wind, buffeting my body with violent gusts, dragged the air from my lungs, only adding to my discomfort. I longed for a hot bath and a soft mattress, but any such luxury was well beyond possibility. So far, we had only managed one-and-a-half miles along the railway track and that had taken two hours.

I heard a whinny from up ahead and shouts of panic. The conga-line halted, and we sat, getting vertically buried in snow, while heavy grunts, expletives, creaking axels and sounds of brute force reached our ears on the squall.

'Pack-mule just lost its footing I imagine,' shouted the officer ahead.

I nodded and disappeared further into my overcoat, wishing I were back in Riveldene's Vicarage enjoying a glass of Ma's hot, sweet grog. Funny the things you think about, I mused, as the conga-line started off again and, within 100 yards, began to traverse a narrow metal railway bridge with, what I imagined to be, a deep ravine below.

I shuddered with fear at the sound of rushing water tumbling over jagged rocks far below and instinctively burrowed my chin into the gelding's mane, whispering endearments in the gelding's ear and promising all manner of treats, if only the animal would get us to the other side in one piece.

The horse responded by shaking its halter to loosen the reins, then lowered its nose to the floor and stepped carefully between the sleepers until it reached terra firma once more.

Obviously, I concluded, releasing the tension in my shoulders, the offer of a bag of carrots did the trick, though where I would find any up on the frontier was quite beyond me.

We reluctantly plodded on, forever upwards, as the freak storm did its utmost to hamper our progress, while Khyber Rifle pickets, somewhere high above me on the mountainside, pressed ahead in the blinding and treacherous blizzard with the ever-present danger of slipping to their deaths or tripping over a hidden Afridi amongst the scrub. It was comforting to realise that I hadn't heard a single gunshot since leaving the tunnel. I was sure that the sound would have ricocheted off the valley walls if an enemy sharpshooter had tried attacking the convoy.

That image brought Salim to mind, and as we attacked another incline, I prayed he was still breathing. He desperately needed to be taken into the garrison hospital and a proper investigation done on his injuries. Army morale would plummet if he died en route, but these mountains were not called the Hindu Kush – *the Hindu Killer* - for nothing, and just the catheter coming loose would be enough to finish him off.

A brief respite in the next tunnel gave me the chance to stretch my legs and remove the knots from my spine.

'Only one more mile, Mac,' announced George, handing over a hip-flask half-full of brandy.

'If I drink any more alcohol, Colonel, I'll fall out of my saddle.'

'Rubbish. You've already proved you're a Highlander, and from what I know, they can fill their boots and still be standing when everyone else is under the table. Now drink up, your adrenalin needs a boost.' He slapped me on the back making me choke and wandered away to talk to the platoon Captain. No wonder he hasn't groped me, I concluded, winding my tartan scarf back across my ears, nose and neck, and ramming my Topi's leather strap under my chin, he's got so used to thinking of me as a man, his libido isn't getting a look-in.

I chuckled, wondering what his droopy moustache would feel like in a clinch and my mind instantly recalled an image of Tom Wallace. I visibly jumped. It had been weeks since Tom had entered my head and the feeling of his soft whiskers brushing my sensitive skin as he made slow, erotic love to me in the Taj Mahal Hotel made me quiver.

'Christ, Mac, pull yourself together.' I clenched my teeth and began adjusting the straps on the gelding's saddle for something to do before grabbing the pummel, placing my foot in the stirrup, bouncing up and down three times and heaving my eight-stone frame skywards, landing, fair and square, on the horse's back to a rousing cheer from a crowd of soldier.

Looking back, I saw the Rifle unit appear carrying a stretcher. 'We've brought Salim Tariq to say hello,' announced the Sergeant holding onto the water-flask and pulling back the tarpaulin.

With hardly a pause, and imitating a circus acrobat, I threw my right leg over the horse's head and slid off the other side of the saddle, rushing round its withers to kneel by the doolie, now lying on the ground.

'Sergeant, you're a star. Pass my kitbag,' my eyes travelled to the saddle, 'there's a spare water-flask in there and a half-full bottle of Jameson's. I'll take the flask while you lot polish off the whisky. COLONEL PHILPOTT!'

The unit didn't need telling twice and deep sighs of approbation could be heard above our heads as George and I checked our patient's vital signs and changed the flask.

'Where am I?' Salim's slurred enquiry reached my ears. 'He's awake,' I announced to all and sundry. 'Our patient is awake.'

Another round of raucous cheers echoed through the tunnel and I bent to Salim and brushed his cheek with my fingers. 'You are halfway up a mountain, Lieutenant, suffering from a gunshot wound and your mates are carrying you to Landi Kotal.' Salim looked horrified. 'Don't panic, everything's under control. All I want you to do, is breathe normally, stay calm and pray that we all make it through the last leg of this journey without further mishap. We only have a mile to go.'

I tucked him back into his cocoon, got a leg-up into the saddle from one of the soldiers, and looked down at two deep brown eyes staring back at me from amongst a pile of khaki blankets. 'By the way, Lieutenant,' I shouted, my finger pointing directly at his sternum. 'You owe me a drink. Now try and get some sleep while this lot take the strain.' I turned in the saddle and looked behind me. 'Sergeant . . .'

'Yes, Doctor,'

'. . . make sure that flask remains below the stretcher or Lieutenant Tariq will explode in his own blood and guts.'

'Nice,' commented the unit's Captain coming to see what was going on. 'Right, men, time to move out. On the count of three.'

It was getting dark as we passed below an ancient, crumbling, circular Buddhist stupa, a few hundred yards below Landi Kotal Bazaar, and never was I so pleased to see a building in my life.

The pickets were standing around smoking, looking like abominable snowmen, but displaying no more strain than having just got back from a cross-country ramble in the sunshine, rather than trekking along three-thousand-foot peaks in a snowstorm. I was desperate to thank them for their efforts on our behalf, but my patient was my priority, and Landi Kotal garrison was only a few hundred yards further on.

Yearning for some warmth, my heels dug into my mount's flank, my frost-bitten ears descended into my shoulders, I clamped my mouth shut to stop my teeth from chattering and we moved on.

It must have been the lack of food or, more likely, hyperthermia setting in which caused my ears to catch the sound of bagpipes coming in on the wind.

'I'm hallucinating,' I shouted to the officer ahead. 'I swear I can hear bagpipes.'

'You can, Doctor. That'll be the Gordon Highlanders giving us a right royal welcome at the garrison. They've been stationed here for the past twelve months.'

'You're kidding me,' I shouted back, my mood immediately lifting as the bellowing melody of *Scotland the Brave* misted my eyes and pulled at my heartstrings.

Fifteen minutes later, a company of pipes and drums, six abreast, emerged from the mist like ghosts, and marched in formation towards us, their Pipe Major swinging his long, gilt mace from side-to-side and throwing it into the air as a crescendo of sound enveloped us in glorious Highland music.

They looked magnificent in their dark blue, green and yellow tartan kilts. Their white and black horse-hair sporrans, brown-belted khaki jackets, matching knee-length socks, leather spats and Tam-o-Shanters, gave them an almost mystical air. On the Pipe Major's command, they wheeled around on a sixpence and led us up to the garrison gate, through the entrance, and out onto the parade ground as if we were entering Horse-guards at the Trooping of the Colour. I half-expected to see the King standing on the garrison steps taking the salute.

By now, I couldn't walk, I couldn't sit, I could barely stand, and my core temperature was hovering around the comatose level, but just seeing them there in this swirling snow-filled storm, miles from home, on a spit of land between India and Afghanistan, made me so proud to be a Scot, and a Highland Scot at that. Any feelings of anxiety or exhaustion since nearly falling over a cliff just faded away on a wave of pipe music.

Sitting on the back of the gelding listening to the rousing chorus of *Heilan Laddie*, I congratulated myself on surviving the journey and reaching my destination. I was a bit battered and bruised but I was still in one piece and it felt good to be alive. There and then, I made myself a promise. No chauvinistic clinician from the India Medical Service or pompous administrator from the Indian Civil Service would ever again be allowed to treat me with disdain. I was Elizabeth Stuart-MacKenzie, a doctor and honorary surgeon with the British Frontier Forces and had earned my stripes saving the life of a British soldier whilst under enemy fire. Any autocratic official who dared to question my authority from now on would simply be put in his place and if he tried to argue, he would be referred to George Edward Philpott, Senior Civil Surgeon of the IMS and Colonel of the British Army Medical Corps in India. As George had so graphically put it back in the Khyber Pass, I'm was a woman who was full of spunk, and had the right to kick men in the goolies!

Chapter Sixteen

T he first test of my newfound confidence came after a
gruelling day in surgery, operating on men from a platoon
of Guides who had been on reconnaissance around Fort
Tamerlane and were ambushed by the Mahsud tribe. They were
suffering from sniper injuries to either their heads, bodies or
legs and, of the six who arrived alive at the frontier garrison,
two had since died from a loss of blood, three were in a critical
condition and one was now minus a left leg which couldn't be
saved. Lieutenant Tariq, on the other hand, was improving by
the hour, his three broken ribs, lacerated liver and bullet
wounds were repairing well.

I was now a celebrity throughout the ranks, bush-telegraph
spreading the word that there was a female doctor in the camp
which caused long queues to build up outside the dispensary
every morning with many squaddies complaining of nothing
more than a cracked fingernail.

They had all taken to calling me Dr Mac without asking,
and it was with some difficulty that I separated the genuine
from the sham cases in order to get through the morning's
clinic in time for lunch.

Fortunately, the blizzard had now moved east, leaving the
North-West Frontier experiencing cold, crisp dawns, deep
amethyst dusks, wide-open skies and amazing views out across
Afghanistan and the plateau. I was woken each day at sunrise
by a piped reveille of *"Hey, Johnnie Cope, Are Ye Waking Yet?"* a
tune that commemorated the Battle of Prestonpans, and in the
evening I watched the sun sink into the west to the sound of a

bugle call announcing the *"Retreat"*, confirming the end of the military day. These traditions never failed to give me goosebumps and the constant Scottish accents resounding around the garrison only heightened my longing for Riveldene, Ma and Pa and the rolling green hills of Berwick.

It was around sunset on my sixth day when an Orderly accosted me as I was on my way back to my room in the Sergeants' Mess.

The Regimental Sergeant Major had allocated me a private room and separate shower-room on the south side of the building, and a large sign now hung on the corridor swing doors informing the NCO's that the area was strictly out-of-bounds. Much groaning was heard on the first night when the men learned that their kit had been relocated elsewhere, but bad feeling soon turned to pride when I appeared at dinner and was introduced to the whole mess as the new medic. Chairs shuffled, elbows dug into ribs and space was made for me at the top table between the RSM and senior non-commissioned officers. The camaraderie between them all was a joy to behold, and I began to understand why men so enjoyed messing together in ranks.

'Where does the word "mess" come from?' I asked, breaking the ice.

'Och, weel, Doctor Mac,' announced a Glaswegian Warrant Officer sitting opposite as a plate of sliced toast topped with tinned sardines was thrust under my nose. 'It stands for the **M**aintenance of **E**qual **S**ocial **S**tatus, though the Frogs would tell ye otherwise.'

I must have looked confused.

'Boney's lot insist it came from their French word *mes*, but we know different, don't we lads?'

'Aye, we do that,' chorused the other Scots around the table.

'By messing in ranks,' he continued, 'we can speak our minds, wi'oot the top brass sending us to the brig.'

'Or Tamerlane Prison,' added a Corporal.

'Where's Tamerlane Prison?' I enquired.

'Between Michni Border Post and Torkum,' chipped in another, 'where the Mahmuds fired on our lads two days ago.'

'Crikey, is that where the Mahmud tribe lives?' I shuddered, realising how close it was to the garrison.'

'No, Doctor Mac,' chipped in the RSM. 'Tamerlane dates back to the fourteenth century. It's an ancient fort built by King Tamerlane, a Mongol-Turk conqueror and butcher.'

'His infamous dungeon is a really nasty affair,' said a Warrant Officer, 'and not strictly a dungeon, but a long vertical tunnel on a steep decline below the fort, fixed with sharp metal blades. The king would throw his enemies in at the top end and what came out at the bottom wasn't worth burying.'

I nearly jettisoned my sardine.

'It's still there, if you're interested, but no-one's allowed inside because it's too dangerous.'

I made a mental note not to go wandering around the Michni Border Post and concentrated on my dinner.

I was standing by the parade ground watching a black vulture circling overhead as the sun dipped towards the west when I was interrupted.

'Hold-up, Doctor Mac.' I turned to see Major Pendleton's batman running towards me. 'Major Pendleton has requested your presence at dinner tonight in the Officer's Mess.'

'Crikey. What time am I expected?'

'Seven-thirty, Doctor Mac, in full mess dress.'

'I've no idea what mess-dress is, Orderly.'

'Sorry, Doctor, what I meant was, formal attire. Best bib and tucker and all that.'

'Oh Lord.' My best bib and tucker were still packed in my trunk at Marjorie Rawlings bungalow in Peshawar, which meant that I was going to have to be creative.

'What should I tell the Major, Ma'am?'

'Eh? . . . tell him I would be delighted, and Orderly,'

'Yes, Ma'am.'

'Should I wear my tiara?'

'Oh, very droll, Doctor. Very droll indeed.' He backed away chuckling to himself as I stood and listened to the bugler calling *Retreat*.

'Right.' I looked at my watch. 'I'd better get a move on or the Major will think I've gone AWOL.'

My reflection in the wall mirror did nothing to impress me and I knew Ruby would have been horrified as I examined my calf-length, cream linen skirt and white appliquéd cotton blouse. But then, I decided, she wasn't on top of a three-thousand-five-hundred-foot mountain being fired on by Afridi tribesmen.

I had tried. My freshly washed hair was pinned up with a tortoiseshell clasp, Ma's cameo brooch sat demurely at the centre of my collarbone and a broad, brown leather belt, pulled in tight around the waist, went some way to emphasising my bustline and feminine curves. It was hardly evening wear, but at least I didn't look like a man. All I could hope was that I would not resemble the poor relation amongst the formal mess-kits of the regiments and rummaged through my toilet bag for my pale-pink lipstick, applied it liberally, rubbed my lips together, shrugged my shoulders, slipped into a pair of flat leather pumps, threw my overcoat around my shoulders, and headed for the exit.

Walking under the Officer's Mess entrance canopy, full of pent-up excitement, I found my way barred by the mess Havildar, a tall Indian soldier resplendent in his thigh-length, khaki jacket, white trousers, knee length black boots and khaki pleated turban, a Khyber Rifles Regimental badge attached front and centre.

'Sorry Ma'am, you no pass. This mess is men only. Women not allowed.'

'Well, Sergeant, on this occasion you will just have to make an exception.' I went to squeeze passed him, but his long-butted rifle blocked my way.

'No possible, Memsahib. We have rules.'

'But, Sergeant, I am here at the invitation of your own Regimental Major.'

'Then you have proper invitation, Doctor Memsahib?'

'No, Sergeant, I do not. The invitation was given to me verbally by his batman only an hour ago.'

'Then I sorry, Doctor Memsahib. Without invitation, you no pass.'

I was beginning to feel my toes turning blue and my hackles rising. 'Havildar, either you go and find Major Pendleton's Adjutant right now, or I will report you to your Commander.'

His black eyebrows knitted together and his bottom lip twitched. 'Please, you wait out here. I go check.'

'No, Sergeant, I have no intention of standing out here freezing to death. I will wait in the lobby.' My neck was beginning to ache trying to keep eye contact with this six-foot staffer, but I refused to give ground.

The Havildar glared down his long, hooked, Muslim nose at me, the very idea of being ordered about by a woman being an anathema to his masculinity. However, it was clear, even to him, that this Scottish Highland Lass was not taking 'no' for an answer, so he reluctantly stepped aside and I marched through the glass doors without a backward glance.

'I go find Major. You not move,' he ordered, striding passed, pointing to the spot I was standing on and disappeared, leaving me steaming with indignation and rage. Seconds later, the Adjutant rushed in looking like a politician who had just been caught fiddling his expenses.

'Doctor Stuart-Mackenzie, I do apologise. There seems to have been a slight cock-up in communications. Havildar, take the doctor's overcoat. We will have words about this later.'

The Pathan resembled a rottweiler being held on a tight leash, but he took my coat as if it were full of fleas, saluted his superior and retreated.

'Obviously got out of bed the wrong side,' I commented, as I was led into a room full of impeccably dressed officers, their red, bottle green or dark blue mess-jackets brimming with gold stars, broad stripes, and chest-bars of shiny medals. Each had a sheathed ceremonial sword at his right thigh, and I could see my face reflected in pairs of highly polished black shoes in the gaslight. My feeble attempt at formal wear would have been better suited to 'below stairs' I thought, but I took a deep breath, raised my chin and eyeballed my audience as if I were the Queen of Sheba.

To my horror, Duncan Fitzpatrick hove into view, standing towards the back of the room, a pewter mug in his hand. I hadn't seen him since the train tunnel and my stomach flipped.

'Doctor Stuart-MacKenzie,' announced Major Pendleton, emerging from the group, his bald head, chubby cheeks, potbelly, sloping shoulders and grey sideburns giving him a rather *John Bull* appearance. He bowed, shook my hand then moved me to the centre of the room. 'On behalf of the Officers' Mess, I would like to welcome you as our guest of honour on this very special occasion.'

'Thank you, Major, I do feel very honoured. I doubt many women have graced these hallowed halls.' The Adjutant had a sudden fit of coughing.

'Indeed not, my dear. Now, what is your tipple?'

'Gin & Tonic,' I replied, having absolutely no idea why the evening was so significant. No doubt it will all become clear as the evening wears on, I thought.

The steward returned with my drink, dripping in condensation, and sporting a sliver of lemon balanced across the rim. We could have been at a soirée in London rather than stuck on a barren plateau at the North-West Frontier, but I wasn't going to complain, the aperitif tasted like nectar.

'Allow me to introduce you to some of my fellow officers.'

I circled the room, acknowledging all and sundry until I came face-to-face with Ireland's answer to Rudolph Valentino, his chin's slight dimple playing havoc with my self-imposed celibacy.

'And this is Captain Duncan Fitzpatrick, a highly qualified veterinary surgeon who has a temporary commission with the Royal Army Veterinary Corps and is an absolute genius with stallions.'

'Really?' I said, wanting to wipe the smirk off Duncan's face.

He lifted my hand and brushed his warm lips across my skin. 'Doctor Stuart-MacKenzie, tis a pleasure to meet you, Ma'am . . .'

Electricity shot up my arm and it took me all my strength not to pull away.

' . . . I've heard nothing but praise from the officer class about you since leaving the station platform at Fort Jamrud.'

'Is that right, Captain? Well, I must say, your reputation proceeds you too. I have it on good authority from the lower ranks that you've proved highly popular in the Peshawar cantonment with the mares.'

Pendleton guffawed at that riposte, assuming it was an innocent quip. Duncan stuck his tongue into his cheek and returned to his beer.

'You'd better watch yourself, Fitzpatrick,' remarked the Major, 'it sounds as if the doctor has your measure.'

'Indeed, she does, Major. Indeed, she does.'

We continued on, and I didn't see Duncan again until dinner. He was seated at the other end of the long table, much to my relief, and far enough away to be ignored. Surreptitiously, I studied him from under my eyelashes and had to acknowledge that he was too damned handsome for his own good. My thumb and forefinger pinched my thigh muscle until it turned blue in an attempt at self-flagellation.

Fortunately, I was distracted by my host who kept me occupied for the next hour with a myriad of questions while I consumed a four-course dinner of onion soup, fish stew, goat curry and lemon posset. By the end, I had given him chapter and verse on my life so far and felt thoroughly bloated and in need of some Andrews Liver Salts. I decided to ask a question of my own while I covertly expanded the notch on my leather belt by two inches.

'Major, why is the large tree in the courtyard held down by a ring of heavy chains?'

'Ah, you've noticed it?'

'One can hardly miss it, Major.'

'Well, Doctor, thereby hangs a tale. Crawford, why don't you enlighten our guest?' Major Pendleton raised his hand at the chief steward whereupon a platter of cheese, a decanter of port and a box of cigars appeared in the centre of the table.

'I have it on good authority, Doctor Stuart-MacKenzie,' explained the Adjutant seated to my left, 'that the old oak tree has been imprisoned in chains since 1898 on the orders of a Captain James Squid.'

I was intrigued.

'The story goes that one Saturday evening, after a typically inebriated regimental dinner, the young Captain left the mess for a late evening stroll. Passing the tree, he noticed that it appeared to be drunk and swaying around wildly. Without further ado, he ordered the mess Sergeant to arrest the tree and chain it down.'

'But that was thirty-two years ago.'

'Quite,' replied the Adjutant, 'but Captain Squid was deployed elsewhere the following day and never came back to counter his order, so the tree has remained chained ever since.'

'That is plain daft,' I announced, turning to the Major for support.

'Maybe, my dear, but, in the army, rules are rules,' argued the Major, chuckling and wiping his eye with his linen napkin.

I was still laughing when he tapped the side of his port glass with a spoon, stood and brought the room to attention. Nodding to his Adjutant, he placed his thumbs under his mess-jacket lapels and waited, reminding me of a Victorian squire preparing to arbitrate on some village dispute.

'Madam, . . .' I returned his smile. ' . . . and fellow officers. We are gathered here this evening for a very special and unusual occasion.'

I looked at George sitting half-way down the table, twiddling his thumbs above his place setting. Catching his eye, I shrugged, hoping for a reaction. He simply nodded and downed a glass of port. Duncan, meanwhile, gently swayed backwards on the rear legs of his chair, rubbing his upper teeth with the tip of his tongue, and undressing me with his eyes. My head shot back to my host so quickly I nearly ricked my neck and my fingers dropped to my right thigh, grabbed some subcutaneous fat and clamped on fast.

'During my long years in the British Army,' announced the Major, 'I have witnessed many instances of great courage and gallantry. Indeed, it has been my privilege to affirm such bravery with the presentation of a number of gallantry medals to the men concerned.' The Adjutant appeared through the dining-room door carrying a long slim box.

'However, Gentlemen, tonight, I have the honour of presenting an equally prestigious award to a civilian in our midst in recognition of her gallantry. Doctor Stuart-Mackenzie . . .'

My mouth dropped open.

'. . . On behalf of the Khyber Rifles Frontier Force, please accept this 1808 Afghan Jezail rifle as a token of the regiment's esteem for your swift action in saving the life of Second Lieutenant Salim Tariq whilst under enemy fire and thereafter assisting in keeping him alive under extreme conditions.'

The Adjutant ceremonially opened the lid of the box as if we were about to hold a duel and the Major lifted out a long-barrelled, curved stock, gilt-damascened tribal rifle, slowly rotating it horizontally, taking care not to knock over the port decanter and solemnly presented it to me with due reverence. A cacophony of clattering cutlery and stamping feet shattered the silence.

'Three cheers for the Doctor,' shouted an officer seated somewhere in the room.

'Hip hip, Hoorah! Hip hip Hoorah! Hip hip Hoorah!'

The officers were all now standing, their glasses raised. 'To one of our own,' announced the Pipe Major of the Gordon Highlanders. 'Doctor Stuart-MacKenzie,' shouted the others and shots of port disappeared down every gullet.

'Speech,' yelled Duncan, thoroughly enjoying my embarrassment. 'Speech!' echoed the others. 'Speech! Speech!'

I gingerly handed the heavy rifle back to the Adjutant, raised my hands, and waited for the racket to die down, trying to gather my thoughts. Addressing a room full of army officers was not a problem after years reading the lessons in Pa's church on a Sunday, but having never received an award for valour, I had absolutely no idea what to say. In for a penny, in for a pound, I thought, and crossed my fingers.

'Major Pendleton, Colonel Philpott, distinguished Officers of the Khyber Rifles, Queen's Own Corps of Guides and our own Gordon Highlanders, I must say, I am overwhelmed by your generosity and rather at a loss to know why I am receiving such an honour when, as a doctor, saving a life is the very essence of my Hippocratic Oath. My action was instinctive, not brave, and I would do it again, enemy fire or not.'

The room erupted with cheers.

'Nevertheless, I am proud to accept this award on behalf of all my colleagues in the Women's Medical Service of India. We may be small in both number and stature, but I can assure you, Gentlemen, we punch well above our weight and we never take prisoners.'

There was a roar of approval at this from the room and I wondered if George was recalling our first meeting in Anna Bramsen's office.

'As an example, the Women's Medical Service never listens to pleas by male patients, who, itching around the nether regions, cry out for their mothers when a catheter, syringe or enema appears.'

The laughter and facial cringes of my audience proved I had struck the right note.

'In the battle of the sexes, there are few occasions when we females get the upper-hand over you men, but in the case of catheters, syringes and enemas we can certainly wield power, so I strongly suggest members of the British Armed Forces adopt the apposite motto of *"Abstinentia est melius remedium."* Take it from one who knows, Gentlemen, abstinence is far better than the cure.'

The place was now in uproar and George had a wry grin on his face. I waited until the room settled.

'As for this wonderful Afghan Jezail Rifle,' I stretched out my hand and placed it on the antique weapon. 'Suffice to say, I shall practice shooting it at the enemy whenever the opportunity arises, remembering at all times to aim low to ensure I hit him where it hurts!' My eyes locked onto Duncan Fitzpatrick as my audience banged their fists on the dining-table with gusto. 'That said, I doubt any Scottish Ghillie would be too impressed if I totally decapitated one of his grouse out on the moors firing the rifle at twenty yards, but be assured, the Jezail will be my constant companion from now on, and all grouse and male combatants should know to stay well out of my way.' With that I sat down, took a gulp of port and lowered my eyes, as I received a standing ovation.

Chapter Seventeen

We retired to the bar where I paid for a round of drinks, praying that my bank balance would stand it. The steward was not known to skimp on measures, but this gesture would cement my relationship with the officers and men, which was a rare thing for any female civilian.

The one dissenting presence in the bar was the Muslim Havildar, who stood in the shadows, rather like Magwitch, hovering ominously in the churchyard in *Great Expectations*. The fact that I was a female and had been honoured for bravery by the British officer-class was insulting enough, but using an antique Afghan Jezail to mark the occasion, probably made by one of his own ancestors here on the North West Frontier, only added insult to injury, and I could feel his animosity across the room. I went cold as we exchanged glances, his dark, brooding countenance marring the thrill of my evening.

'Quite a piece,' commented Duncan, coming up behind me.

My shoulders slumped. I was obviously not going to be left alone by my ex-lover, whose ego refused to be ignored. 'It certainly is.'

He opened the presentation box and read the silver engraved plaque attached to the inside of the lid, caught in the light from above the bar.

1808
Gilt and Mother-of-pearl Afghan Jezail Rifle
Presented to Dr Elizabeth Stuart-MacKenzie
by the Khyber Rifle Frontier Force
In recognition of her gallantry whilst under fire.

'If you had told me back in Edinburgh that I would be awarded a unique military firearm for an act of gallantry, I would have thought you had lost your marbles.'

'Back in Edinburgh, Mac, your mind was on much more salacious activities and I doubt you had time to consider such things.'

'That's enough, Duncan Fitzpatrick. You may believe I still hanker for your attention, but you're wrong. The days of being young, innocent and susceptible to your shallow Gaelic charm have long gone. The sooner you get that into your thick skull the better. Now, if you'll excuse me, I need to speak to Colonel Philpott.' I slammed the lid down on the rifle nearly trapping his fingers, shoved the box under my arm and headed over to the fireplace where George stood propped against the marble fire-surround.

'Would you like me to relieve you of the rifle, Doctor Mac?' asked Major Pendleton's batman, stepping out from behind the bar, arms outstretched.

'I would, Orderly, if you don't mind. It's rather large for a handbag.'

'I'll take it to your quarters right off, Doctor, and Ma'am, I think your mess-kit is just perfect.'

'Thank you, Orderly. Pity about the tiara.'

I watched him depart then joined George. 'Colonel Philpott, would this evening's presentation be anything to do with you?'

'Heaven forbid, Doctor Stuart-MacKenzie.' His hand hit his left breast, and his bushy eyebrows crossed. 'I may be a Colonel, but any influence over the Khyber Rifles would be stretching cred . . . credibility to the limit. However, I do think their decision to present you with an Afghan Jezail was very appropriate seeing as you were shot at by an Afridi sniper, wouldn't you agree?'

'I hardly think the mess's Havildar agrees.'

'That man never agrees to anything the 'ritish Army does, so ignore him.'

'If he's so anti-British, why is he here?'

'Local tribesmen make good scouts and the Goverwent's Political Agent inshists on cultivating them for the good of diplomacy.'

George was beginning to slur his words and his eyes kept wandering to my bust. He leant in and breathed strong whisky fumes into my left ear. 'I muss say, Mac, you look ravishing thish evening. I've never seen you looking sooo . . .'

'Feminine?'

'Curvaceous.'

Alarm bells began to ring in my head.

'I have a liddle secret too, though you dirn't hear it from me.' He swayed and grabbed my shoulder for support as he continued to whisper. 'Pendleton has written to Lord Irwin in despatches, recommendin' an EGM for your mantlepiece.'

'EGM,' I queried, whispering back.

'Empire Gallantry Medal. The King's gong for brawery.'

'Good God, George.' I stepped back as if shot.

'Shhhhh!'

His finger pressed into his lips and his furtive look made me giggle. He sprayed spittle over the front of my blouse as he leant in further.

'You're not shupposed to know about it until King George
V signs on the dotted line. I could be arrested for terring you.'
My voice dropped to a murmur. 'Well, we can't have that,
can we, George? How would I get back to base with you
behind bars?'

'Wiv difficulty.' His hand was now sliding from my
shoulder towards my armpit.

Here we go, I thought, recalling Anna Bramsen's warning.
'Then I'd better call it a night. I have an early start tomorrow.'

'Me too, Mac, me too. I'll shee you safely to your room.'
His mouth appeared to have stopped working and I doubted he
would make it to the door of the mess without assistance.

'Eh . . . that's not necessary, Colonel,' I replied rather
loudly. 'I'm quite capable of finding my own way.'

'I'm shur you are . . . hic . . ., but I don't want you gerring
moleshted by that drunken oak tree outside. Drink up and we'll
be on our way.'

He downed another army measure of whisky, grabbed my
elbow and propelled me across the bar, shouting goodbyes to
the rest of the officers as I was half-dragged into the lobby.

'Havildaaar, Doctor Shuart-MacKenzie's coat, if you
please.'

I gritted my teeth and mentally prepared for the inevitable
as I struggled to get my arms into the sleeves with George
hampering my progress. We then rolled our way across the
parade ground like two ships riding a gale, George muttering
endearments, as I tried to keep him upright until we reached
the Sergeant's mess.

'Thanks, George, I can make my own way from here.' I grabbed the door handle.

Strong hands swung me round, pressed my body against the doorframe and pushed themselves inside my coat, rubbing my breasts and trying to pull at the buttons of my blouse. I savagely resisted without losing my temper, but his alcohol-fuelled and addled brain assumed this was sexual foreplay, and being twice my size, continued with his onslaught.

Getting nowhere with the small buttons, his lips clamped onto mine and he slavered whisky-soaked spittle into my mouth as his tongue coated my tonsils and his moustache hairs blocked my nose. I was having difficulty breathing and his right hand had now reached for my skirt and was attempting to lift the hem above my thighs. I screwed my face sideways, gasped for air and lost my temper.

'George, for God's sake, pull yourself together!'

With the door rammed against my head there was no escape from his sexual advances, and with his mouth now locked once more onto mine and his fingers trying to gain access to my pubic hair, I had no choice but to ram my knee into his groin as hard as I could.

His kiss turned into a strangled choke and he was about to disengage when a force from behind lifted him bodily into the air, threw him against the mess wall and whacked him under the chin. I watched in horror as George slowly sank to the floor, his eyes staring vacantly at his boots with Duncan straddling his legs, his clenched fists poised ready for a second attack.

I saw red. 'What the hell did you do that for?'

'To save you from being raped by a drunken buffoon like him.' He kicked George's thigh.

'That's enough. George Philpott is a well-respected surgeon and, as it happens, I had the situation perfectly under control, so I didn't need you coming to my rescue.'

'Perfectly under control is it? Then why, in the name o' God, is your skirt halfway up your arse?'

I pulled it down below my knees and knelt to slap George on the cheeks to bring him round.

'Don't do that, ya blitherin' eejit.' Duncan pulled my hand away. 'If he wakes up now, you'll become the butt of his venom in the morning.' He pulled me to my feet. 'Just leave him to me and get yourself off to bed.'

The mess door screamed on its hinges and I stomped inside.

'And, Elizabeth . . .'

'What?'

'Next time, say thank you.'

'Oh, FECK OFF!'

Sitting by the entrance gate having a conversation with the duty-guard during a well-earned break the next day, my attention was interrupted by a Gordon Highlander rushing up the road from Landi Kotal with a sapper slung over his shoulder, a platoon Captain following on behind. They had been down on the railway line repairing the broken tracks while pickets patrolled the ground above, and I assumed an Afridi sniper had got through the cordon. I rushed over and asked what had happened.

'Eye-wound, Doctor Mac,' shouted the Captain. 'Sliver of wood buried in his eye-socket. A bullet hit a railway sleeper as his section were lifting a new steel track into position.'

I lifted the sapper's head and examined the grubby field bandage covering his right eye, a jagged piece of blackened hardwood poking out from the middle.

'Bloody sniper copped it though,' continued the Captain as we made our way towards the dispensary. 'Fell face-first onto the track when one of our Rifles picked him off as he made his escape.'

'Aye,' added the Gordon Highlander, 'it was good to see the bastard lying there wee a bullet hole through his forehead.'

'Where is he now?' I asked, running alongside the pair and mentally revisiting procedures for eye injuries.

'Once we'd relieved him of his Jezail and ammo, we kicked him over the cliff-edge and helped him on his way.' The Captain swung the Afghan rifle from his shoulder and brandished it with pride.

'Last I saw,' panted the Highlander, pushing the dispensary door open with his kilted buttock, 'the bastard was doing cartwheels in the air as he continued doon hill, looking like a shot pheasant.

'Right, lie him down here.'

The sapper was stretched out on the examination table, his hands twitching and his head rolling from side-to-side. 'Has he had anything for the pain?'

No, just a large slug of whisky.'

'OK, leave him to me. What's his name?'

'Sapper Jack Collins of the Queen's Own Guides, Doctor. I hope you can save his eye.' The Captain grabbed his hand, pressed hard, then retreated with the Highlander, no doubt to down a large slug of their own.

I carefully peeled the bandage away making sure I didn't knock the thin wooden shard, then gave Collins a dose of opium and a prophylactic injection of anti-tetanus serum to counter any oil, dirt or animal urine which may have impregnated the railway-sleeper. The projectile looked as if it had gone straight through the centre of the lad's eyeball. I doubted it could be saved and squeezed his arm in sympathy. Jack Collins would spend the rest of his life blind in one eye, I thought, and be discharged from the army on medical grounds.

George walked through the door as I was cleaning around the eye-socket and I felt my stomach drop to my knees. I punched a hole through a clean, antiseptic bandage with a scalpel and placed it gently over the injury, nodded to my boss, then patted Collins on the arm once more. 'I won't be a moment, Jack, just try and lie still.'

I walked into the bright sunlight with George at my heels. 'Good afternoon, Colonel,' I said, sheepishly. He looked as if he had been hit by a ten-tonne truck. I gritted my teeth and kept the conversation professional. 'We have a probable evisceration case in there.' I indicated by my thumb back into the casualty room. 'Sapper Collins has a sharp splinter of wood through his cornea from a railway sleeper which was hit by an Afridi bullet as he was bending down.'

George nodded, then winced.

'Have you had an accident, Colonel, your chin is very bruised?' My fingers were crossed inside my laboratory coat pockets.

'A . . . slight mishap as I was going back to my room last night. Woke up this morning with a headache the size of the Taj Mahal and a very tender jawbone.'

Hell, I thought, praying he couldn't remember the circumstances. 'What happened?'

George turned a deep shade of burgundy. 'To be frank, Mac, I haven't a clue. Memory completely gone. Last thing I remember is getting up from the dinner-table after your presentation.'

'The bar steward really knows how to pour his drinks, doesn't he?' My relief was that of a patient being told their tumour was benign. 'I'm sure you're not the only one who is suffering from a hangover today.' I stared at his blood-shot eyes. 'Still, I should check your jawbone, you may have cracked it.'

George grabbed his chin and waggled it. 'No need.' His lips turned white. 'Bloody painful but I can't hear anything grating.'

'Well, that's good, anyway.' I began to breathe normally. 'Now, about Sapper Collins. Is there an ophthalmology surgeon down in Peshawar?'

It took a few seconds for George to get his brain into gear. 'No, the nearest one is in Lahore and I recommend we get him transported there before sympathetic ophthalmia affects the other eye.'

'I'll get a message to his superior immediately.'

'Let's hope they get that railway track mended pretty darn quick or he'll be travelling down the dust trail used by the caravans.'

I cringed at the thought. 'Do we know how they're doing with the damaged track?'

'According to Crawford last night, they hope to be up and running by Thursday.'

'And our replacements?'

'Should be here Friday.'

'So, we could be back in Peshawar by the weekend?'

'If Crawford is right.'

'Great, I'm in need of a change of under . . .' My mouth clamped shut and I held my breath. George, however, seemed more interested in waggling his lower incisor. 'Right, I'd like your opinion on what we should do about Collin's splinter.'

The army was as good as its word, and by Friday lunchtime, two army medics from Rawalpindi were settling into the Sergeant's mess. George asked me to brief them while he organised getting our critical patients back to Peshawar.

It was as I was finishing the briefing and about to go for a shower that Duncan appeared by the entrance door holding onto his right arm and looking as if he was about to faint.

'Mac, for Christ's sake, do something.' My ex-lover staggered in, his right shoulder lying at an odd angle.

I pointed to a chair noting his pallid complexion and felt a certain innate pleasure in seeing him suffering. 'Let go of your arm.'

Hell hath no fury like a woman scorned, I thought, as my hand moved towards his bicep. 'This might hurt.'

Duncan's guttural growl sounded like a male elephant in the throes of coital ejaculation.

'Dislocation,' I announced, turning away and biting the inside of my lip to stop myself smiling. 'Medic, can you help him with his jacket?'

One of the two clinicians stepped forward as if approaching a wounded grizzly.

'What happened?' I asked, watching events through the wall mirror as I removed a triangular bandage from the cupboard.

'Pendleton's stallion . . . Jasus Christ! . . . he got spooked when some . . . Fecking hell! . . . bastard . . . Mudder o' God, weel you leave it to me!'

'It's alright, Medic, I'll take over now. Get yourselves to the mess and freshen up before dinner.' I slid the jacket sleeve from Duncan's good arm and tossed the garment onto the gurney. 'You were saying, Captain Fitzpatrick?' The door banged shut.

'Some stupid bastard decided to take a pot shot at a buzzard while I was checking Samson's fetlock joint for possible swelling . . . Ow! Mac, that hurts.'

'Stop being a baby and drop your arm by your side.' The look I got was pure evil. 'Go on.'

'Well, the damned animal took off like a bat out o' hell after kicking me in the shoulder.'

'Glenohumeral joints are not designed to make contact with stallion's hooves.'

'Gleno what?'

'Shoulder joint,' I explained, kneeling in front of him and taking his right arm in a firm grip. '

'Well, try telling that to Samson.'

I slowly raised the lower half of his arm until it was at a ninety-degree angle and laid across his waist.

'Shite! Do you know what you're doing, Mac?'

'Would you prefer George Philpott to come and deal with it?' Duncan looked suitably chastened. 'Now, close your eyes, count to ten and make sure you keep your elbow exactly where it is.'

Duncan crossed himself, gritted his teeth, snapped his eyelids shut and began to count. 'One, two, tree, four . . .'

Grabbing his clenched fist and keeping the upper arm rigid, I slowly arced the forearm away from his body, while increasing the pressure at his shoulder.

'For feck's sake, Mac, it feels as if me arm's being ripped off.'

'It is. Now, shut up and keep counting.'

'Eight, nine, ten . . . Oooowww!'

I heard the shoulder joint click back into position, killing the pain, at which point Duncan passed out before my eyes. I quickly leant him against the back of the chair and strapped his arm against his chest with the triangular bandage then left him in peaceful oblivion while I organised some painkillers and salicylic acid for the inflammation.

Standing over him a couple of minutes later, I looked down at the familiar tussled curls and tried to feel some compassion for what I had just put him through, but his rejection of me ran deep. I could not forget how he had enticed me into his bed, run roughshod over my emotions, and left me to pick up the pieces of my life without an ounce of guilt. Seeing him there, flopped in the chair, that persistent russet lock falling across his forehead, I felt nostalgia like a smouldering ember which refused to die out and, without thinking, I brushed it back with my fingers, curious to know where he had been and what he had been doing throughout the intervening years.

The sound of the bugle announcing the *Retreat* brought me to my senses and I wafted some ammonia under Duncan's nose to bring him round.

'Here, drink this,' I said, holding out a metal measuring cup. He reminded me of my brother being made to drink a spoon of cod-liver oil back in Riveldene.

'I suppose you don't still have some of that Jameson's whisky, do you?' he asked, coughing and spluttering as the concoction went down.

'Sorry, can't help you there, but the opioid you have just swallowed will kill any residual pain and the salicylic acid will help with any inflammation around the joint. You'll need to rest your shoulder for at least ten days and treat it with due respect in the future. As for the whisky, the Officer's mess is your best bet.'

He stood, gently rotating his shoulder joint inside the bandage then cocked his head at me. 'Well, I'll say this for you, Mac, you're not half-bad as a medic, though I can't say much for your bedside manner.'

'And I'm amazed, Duncan, that a Captain in the British Army doesn't think to check where the firing range is before examining a stallion's fetlock.'

'Humph!'

I helped him into one side of his jacket and placed the other over his shoulder then walked to the door and pulled it open. 'Let's hope Samson isn't halfway to Kabul by now or Major Pendleton will be wanting your testicles served in aspic.'

'Oh, very droll. You always did have an acerbic wit, which was what attracted me to you in the first place.' He invaded my personal space, his piercing green eyes boring into mine. 'That and your passion for Guinness.'

'Actually, these days I prefer Newcastle Brown Ale,' I replied, raising my head and holding his stare. 'Much better for the digestion.'

'You don't give an inch, do you?'

'Not when it comes to Irish Veterinary Surgeons, Captain. No.'

'Then I'll take my leave. God go with you, Cailin.'

'And the devil with you, Buachaill.' I stepped back, as my heart pounded like a Highland drum.

He bent and kissed my cheek then turned and walked away.

'By the way, Duncan,' I shouted down the corridor.

'Yes, darlin'?'

I could hear his boots clicking on the stone floor as his ego pulled him back.

'Next time I realign your dislocated shoulder, say thank you.'

'Oh, FECK OFF!'

Chapter Eighteen

I dropped my bag and jezail rifle-box on the tiled floor of the Rawlings's bungalow and picked up a pile of mail sitting on the hall stand. News from home, a letter from Frances in Poona and a typed letter from the Lady Hardinge were amongst the envelopes.

Flopping onto a chair, I ripped open the one from Agnes Scott, posted four days earlier.

Dear Elizabeth,

I'm not sure where you are right now, but I have received a request from the WMS senior clinician at the Seva Sadan Training Hospital in Poona asking for help. They are short-staffed and have a backlog of cases which need urgent attention. I have said that you would contact her as soon as you were able, with a view to relocating to Poona for your next assignment. Contact details given below.

Let me know what transpires and how you got on in Peshawar Province. Looking forward to your latest report.

Have a good Easter whatever you are doing.

Kind Regards

Agnes

ps: The Frontier Mail to Bombay has a good connection through to Poona so it should be a straightforward journey.

pps: Sir Peter Bonham-Cavendish sends his regards.

With everything that had been happening to me, Easter had never entered my head and I pulled out my diary to check the dates. As I thought, Easter had come and gone the previous weekend and I had promised Frances that I would try to join her at St Saviours School for Young Ladies where she was the resident headmistress. Frances had suggested the visit when she was staying with me in Calcutta at Christmas, and, although no firm arrangements had been made, disappearing of the face of the earth without confirming my plans was neither good manners nor friendly. I tore open the envelope with her familiar cursive writing on the front and sat back to read the contents.

Dear, dear, Mac,

I hope this letter reaches you without delay . . .

I checked the postal date and realised it had left Poona three weeks earlier and had arrived in Peshawar via Delhi and Mardan after I had left for the frontier.

. . . It seems an age since we were together at the Thornton's for Christmas and the New Year and a great deal has happened since. But first, are you free to visit over Easter? The school breaks-up on the 16th April for two weeks, and most of the girls will be off with family or friends for the break, leaving the school premises virtually empty with plenty of room for you to stay in-house. Let me know if this is possible, and I can then get things organised . . .

I checked my watch and banged my fist on the chair-arm. 'Bugger, bugger, bugger!' By going straight to the Military Hospital from Fort Jamrud with the injured soldiers I had missed getting a cable off to Frances letting her know what had happened to me. It was now too late as the Post Office was closed. I sighed and returned to the letter accepting that I could do nothing about it until the morning.

. . . As for my news. Much of it can wait until your arrival, but you will be relieved to know that my Deputy Head has finally departed this

Victorian pile, having been caught with her fingers in the petty-cash box by the school cook during Matins. Long story, but the Governors reluctantly agreed that this matter had to be hushed up or the reputation of the school would be brought into disrepute so 'Beaky' Beckinsale was asked to resign her post without notice. I took great pleasure in waving her off the premises after all her covert attempts at getting me fired, and life here has been much less stressful since her departure. She managed to obtain a teaching post at a girls' school in Madras after I provided a glowing reference about her abilities as a teacher!

Jim is on his way back from Singapore as I write. He has been on secondment to the ss Rawalpindi while their navigator is on compassionate leave and will finally take up his permanent post with the ICS Maritime Division in Bombay at the end of the month. I doubt you will see him during your visit as he is not due back until after Easter, but hopefully we will all be able to get together in Simla during the summer . . .

The mention of Jim Hamilton's name brought Tom Wallace sharply back into focus, and an upsurge of pain and nostalgia for him, my aborted child and what might have been, triggered a sudden and violent panic attack. Having concentrated solely on my work around Peshawar Province and the North-West Frontier, I had suppressed my need to grieve, and the full force of this delayed, pent-up anguish of loss and guilt now hit me like a sledgehammer, binding me in a vice-like grip as violent shakes spread through me in waves of remorse.

My forehead touched my knees and my arms crossed against my abdomen as I rocked like a pendulum, back and forth, trying to control the physical reaction to my intense psychological misery.

'Oh, God, forgive me,' I groaned. Minutes passed with only the sound of my strangulated sobs puncturing the silence.

'Oh, Mac, you're back.' Marjorie Rawlings breezed through the door, then shot to my side.

'In heavens name, what has happened, has someone died?'

I shook my head, stomach cramp gripping my innards, my brain searching for an excuse. 'No,' I choked, 'No. I . . . think . . . it must be reaction . . . having come through unscathed after days at the Frontier.' I shuddered once more, hearing myself lying with impunity.

'Right, what you need is a hot bath, some decent food and a good night's rest. You should never have been up there in the first place.'

I sniffed my armpit and wrinkled my nose. 'I must stink to high heaven, Marjorie.'

'I've smelt worse,' she said, taking off her coat and kicking off her shoes. 'Did you find your mail. I was going to send it up to Landi Kotal, but then I heard about the railway line being blown up. Were you hurt?'

'No.'

'Well, that's a relief. Was there anything urgent in your letters?'

Her comments and questions gave me time to regain some composure. I held up the letter from Frances. 'Actually, yes, I was supposed to be in Poona for Easter, and I've let a close friend down by failing to make contact.' I slowly uncurled and focused on Marjorie's anxious expression.

'Can't you send her a cable?'

'I would, but the Post Office is now closed for the day.'

'But you could send it from the telegraph office at the railway station. They don't close until nine o'clock.

'Why didn't I think of that?' I said, desperate for some air, space and time to deal with my panic attack alone. Organising a cable to Frances would give me all three. 'Marjorie, may I borrow your bike?'

'Of course, but are you sure you're up to it? I could go for you.'

'No, that's OK. It won't take long, then I can have that hot bath.' Grabbing my coat, Agnes's letter, my purse and my address book, I shot out of the house and peddled my way across the cantonment as if the tyres were on fire, the physical effort countering the constant thumping in my chest.

There were two other people ahead of me in the queue at the telegraph office, so I waited in line on the concourse and thought through my plan of action. I may have missed Easter, but there was still a week left before Frances had to start work again and the break would do me good. After cabling Frances with my imminent arrival, I would go to the ticket office and make a reservation on the next Frontier Mail train bound for Bombay then, after dinner, I would pack my baggage and, in the morning, inform George that I was leaving immediately on Agnes's instructions. I could send another cable to Frances with my actual arrival time in Poona before boarding the train, then sit back and enjoy seventy-two hours of peace and tranquillity, catching up on international news and writing my latest report.

I was still mulling over my plan when the telegraph operator caught my attention.

'Can I help you, Memsahib?'

'Oh, yes. Yes, you can. I would like to send a telegram to Poona.'

'Very good, Memsahib. Please to take paper and write name, address and message. Here.' The BB&CIR employee pushed a lead pencil and notepad across the counter and returned to help the chap ahead of me. I dumped my letters and purse on the counter-top and scribbled my message down, keeping it as short as possible.

Frances. In Peshawar. Long Story.
On way to Poona tomorrow. Expect to arrive late Wed night.
Will cable later with timings. Mac x

While my missive to Frances winged its way south, I rushed over to the ticket office before it closed. The uniformed staff member was leaving his seat as I rapped on the window.

'Excuse me,' I shouted through the glass, 'I need to reserve a second-class berth on tomorrow's Frontier Mail to Bombay. It's urgent.'

The ticket officer, sighed, sat back down and raised the box-framed window.

'Sorry, Memsahib, Frontier Mail tomorrow full.'

'No, it can't be.' My well-defined plans of a minute ago were in shreds around my feet. 'You must have something. I must get to Poona. It's life or death.' My head was almost through the window in desperation.

'I sorry, Memsahib,' his head was rocking alarmingly, 'no second-class tickets left. All gone.'

'Then what do you have?'

'I look, Memsahib. You wait.'

'Of course, I'll wait,' I screamed, wanting to shake him until his head fell off, my nerves in tatters.

He opened a wooden drawer and took out a large, frayed ledger, slowly turned the yellowing pages to the appropriate date and ran his fingers down the columns.

'We have one space, Memsahib, in the first-class, with big cost.'

'I'll take it,' I announced, ignoring an image of a tutting Dr Chakramachari at the CSMT. 'I also need an onward ticket to Poona.'

I tapped my fingers on the narrow counter as he rifled through the drawer, peering at the innards like a surgeon checking a patient's haemorrhoids. 'You need speak with guard on train. He arrange ticket to Poona.'

'Fine. How much is it to Bombay?'

'Twelve pounds, Memsahib.' I gulped. 'It include meals. You provide bedding.'

How I was to explain twelve pounds to the accounts department at the CSTM I had no idea, but, undaunted, I extracted the money from my rolling cash reserve, handed it over and took the ticket and the receipt. 'What time does the train leave here?'

'Seven o'clock, Memsahib. Tomorrow evening.'

'Thank you. Do you happen to know how long I will have in Bombay to change trains?'

He scratched his head, pulled a thick, train-timetable compendium from a wooden pigeon-hole by his side and leafed through the well-thumbed sections until he found Bombay. 'Fifteen minutes, Memsahib.'

Good Lord, I thought, imagining myself tearing through Victoria Terminus with my stack of luggage and jezail rifle. 'Let's hope we are not late then,' I commented sarcastically.

'Oh, Frontier Mail never late, Memsahib.' His puffed-out chest and erect head reminded me of Elsie Thornton passing on salacious gossip to her neighbours.

Heading back to the bungalow on Marjorie's rickety bike, I tried to work out what time my train would arrive in Poona. Perhaps I should stay in Bombay overnight, I thought, as I crossed a major intersection without slowing down, recalling the Taj Mahal Hotel, then broke out in a cold sweat and concluded that a delay would only reduce my time enjoying Frances's company. I braked hard by the Rawling's wicket gate and nearly catapulted myself over the handlebars.

The station platform was packed as I searched for my first-class coach and Compartment 4. On entering, I came face-to-face with two rotund gentlemen in suits and a young man with a pockmarked face, all settling in for the duration. I backtracked to the platform and went to find the guard.

'Excuse me, Guard, but would it be possible to find me another berth?'

'What is problem, Memsahib?'

'There are three gentlemen in my compartment?'

'Which compartment is that, Memsahib?'

'First-class, Compartment 4', I shouted over the din of the platform. 'My name is Doctor Stuart-MacKenzie.' I dragged my crumpled ticket from my coat pocket and handed it over.

The guard checked his list and rubbed his nose. 'The gentlemen, they leave train in Delhi tomorrow morning, Doctor Memsahib, then ladies all way to Bombay.'

'But, that's the point, Guard. What do I do about my sleeping arrangements tonight?'

'It no problem, Memsahib. You sleep on top bunk, you not be disturbed.'

The crowds were thinning, and the guard looked at his pocket watch. 'We leave in one minute, Doctor Memsahib. You go now to dining car or you miss dinner.' He looked about him and ushered me away with his hands.

I stood my ground and raised my voice. 'That is not good enough, Guard. I have no intention of spending the night with three strange men.' I followed him along the platform as he slammed closed various coach doors. 'There must be something you can do?'

'Memsahib, I do not have time now to change. I very busy. Please, you go.'

Two hours later, after dining on soup, poached fish, roast duck with rice, a fruit compote and coffee, the train pulled into Rawalpindi station and I was handed a note by the headwaiter.

You please move to Coach B, Compartment 6.

I quickly gathered my bedding and valise from Compartment 4 and returned to the platform.

'Can I help you, Lassie?' offered a Gordon Highlander, grabbing both from my arms.

'I'm off to the Compartment 6,' I replied. 'Seems I've been relocated.'

'Och aye. This will be it then.' He opened the door and let me pass.

I climbed the step and froze as my eyes took in a triangular bandage, a tweed jacket and Duncan's amused expression. 'Good Evening, Cailin, would you be travelling to Bombay by any chance?'

'How the hell . . .'

'Temper, temper, Mac. We wouldn't want you offending Sergeant McBride, now would we?'

The Highlander stood on the platform grinning from ear to ear. 'We didna' lie to the guard, Doctor Mac, all we said was that you were the regiment's medic, and we were best placed to look after you.'

'Bloody hell. Who have I changed with?'

'Our Staff Sergeant. He's getting off in Ambala before breakfast, so he volunteered.'

I turned back to Duncan. 'This is your doing, isn't it?' His smirk said it all.

'Well, you did seem rather exercised on the platform in Peshawar, and with lungs the size of a horse, the world and his mother could hear you complaining. All we did was come to your rescue. Isn't that right, Sergeant?'

'Aye, Captain. We were real vexed for you, Doctor Mac.'

I glowered at Duncan which only made him more amused. 'And, I suppose I'm going to have to put up with YOU all the way to Bombay?

'Correct,' replied Duncan, taking my bedding in his good arm and placing it on a top bunk. 'Admit it, Mac, even I'm a better option than two boring old dodgers with flatulence and a young, spotty-faced ICS staffer.'

Duncan did have a point, but I wasn't going to let him know that. 'Why are you going to Bombay anyway?' I leant against the toilet door as MacBride made himself comfortable in a Queen Anne chair in the spacious first-class carriage.

He rubbed his injured arm and sat back down. 'I've been asked to do some lecturing at the Indian Army Veterinary College while my shoulder heals.'

'What about you, Sergeant?' I removed my coat and hung it on a bulkhead hook.

'Two weeks furlough, Doctor Mac. Pipe-Major Cameron and I thought we'd enjoy the sights and sounds of Bombay while we had the chance. Have to be there anyway to perform at one of Sir Frederick Sykes's official gatherings.'

'Sir Frederick Sykes?' I queried.

'Governor of Bombay. He has some high-flying officials calling in on their way to Australia and needs our pipes and drums to act as the welcoming committee.'

At this juncture the door flew open and another strapping Highlander stepped in carrying my jezail-box.

'Here you go, Doctor Mac. We thought we'd retrieve this from the baggage car afore it got nicked. You can never trust these bleedin' station-wallahs.'

I took the box and stood it on end at the bottom of the lower bunk. 'Good thinking, Pipe-Major . . . ?'

'Cameron, Doctor, but you can call me Hamish.'

'Well, thank you, Hamish.'

The guard's whistle blew once more, and we were on our way to our next stop in Lahore, four-and-a-half hours away. 'OK, Lads,' I said, dropping onto the other Queen Anne chair, 'please call me Mac. Three days of all this doctor stuff will drive me mental.'

'Aye, Mac, and I'll be Fraser.'

'Fraser McBride and Hamish Cameron,' I mused. 'You two couldn't be accused of being Sassenachs with names like that, now could you?'

'Nay, Lassie, and with a name like yours, you'd be hard pressed to pass for one either. Now who's got the bottle?'

Hamish dragged a bottle of 12-year-old Cragganmore malt whisky from his backpack and chucked it in Fraser's direction.

'Where on earth did you find that Hamish?' I asked, peering at the label.

He tapped his nose. 'Let's just say Pendleton's orderly owed me a favour and he thought we'd appreciate it more than his boss. Fraser, would you be getting Mac a glass from the cludgie?'

I caught sight of Duncan from the corner of my eye, grimacing as he moved his shoulder. 'Are you in pain?'

'A bit.'

I dragged my valise across the floor and pulled out my medical bag then measured five drops of laudanum into the glass, topped it with malt whisky and handed it over. 'Here, drink this.' He downed it in one and passed the glass back for another. I added a large shot of malt for myself and tipped back my head. 'Slàinte,' I said, and felt the warm liquid lubricate my larynx. 'So, Gentlemen, own up, who's paid for YOUR first-class tickets?'

Lying in my bunk listening to the heavy snores of my companions, I had to admit, they were a great improvement on those in Compartment 4. Nevertheless, the fact that Duncan and I were to spend the next three days closeted together in this carriage was far from ideal, especially when I knew that his charismatic charm was going to play havoc with my defences, which is exactly what he intended.

I rolled over and faced the wall, conscious that he was lying almost in touching distance from me and questioned how I could even think about his effect on me when only twenty-four hours earlier, I had been in the grip of a panic attack, fighting for my sanity against culpability and shame. I blinked away a tear and realised that, yet again, events had overtaken me.

'Blast you, Duncan,' I murmured into my pillow. 'Why the hell are you here?'

My body ached from all the tension and I knew that if I didn't allow the bereavement process to run its course, I would be at risk of becoming mentality sick. Exhaustion took over and my eyelids became heavy. Perhaps the next few days would provide somewhere quiet where I could give full rein to my emotions, I thought. I gently rubbed my lower abdomen and fell asleep.

Chapter Nineteen

I woke with the sun streaming through the compartment window and loud sounds of anal explosions emanating from the other side of the bulkhead. These were followed by some tuneless humming of '*I Love a Lassie*', as water was swished around in a wash-hand basin. If I had forgotten I was sharing my compartment with two burly Scots and an ex-lover, this was instantly rectified.

'Top o' the mornin' to you, Cailin,' said Duncan, from his half-prone position on the opposite bunk. 'Did you sleep well?'

Rising from my pillow, I shook my hair into a semblance of order and shrugged. 'Yes, if you can call it sleep with a chorus of rampaging, grunting bulls puncturing the peace.'

'Sorry, Mac,' announced Fraser coming in from the adjoining lavatory, 'hope I didn't wake you just now. Too many onions in the mutton curry last night.'

'Not a problem, Fraser. It proves your digestive system is working. What time do we reach Ambala?'

'Seven-fifteen. Half-an-hour stopover for breakfast, then onto Delhi.'

I looked at my watch. It was six-thirty-five.

'Anybody mind if I go next?' I asked, jumping down from the top bunk in my ankle-length brushed-cotton nightie.

'It's all yours, Mac,' announced Hamish from a lower bunk. 'I'll shit and shave after you.'

'Don't mind Hamish, Mac,' said Duncan, 'his barrack-room vernacular is quite normal at this time of the day.'

'Oh, sorry, Doctor. I keep forgetting you're a lassie.'

'I don't know if that's a compliment or an insult, Hamish. Either way, after two weeks up on the frontier with a garrison full of squaddies, I doubt there is much vernacular that I haven't heard.'

'Well said,' commented Fraser, 'The bathroom's all yours, Mac, and the window's wide open.'

'Thanks, I won't be long.' I closed the door behind me and plonked my valise on the toilet seat as fresh air vortexed round the cubicle dragging any lurking miasma out into the countryside racing by.

Ambala was a hive of activity as we made our way along the platform to the dining car. First-class carriages didn't have corridors which made them much larger inside, so our mealtimes were programmed around station stop-overs. Settling in, I ordered my usual porridge followed by eggs and bacon, while the others tucked into copious quantities of sausages and mash.

By the time the guard announced our departure to Delhi the dining car was already being turned into a first-class lounge, with newspapers, books, playing cards, stationery and refreshments, and much to my amazement, a working radio.

I made myself comfortable at the far end and began writing my report. I was still there three hours later as we pulled into Delhi Junction and the headwaiter hovered, hoping I would move so he could re-organise the dining-car for the midday meal.

'Is there a telegraph office on the station?' I asked.

'Yes, Memsahib, by ticket office in main entrance.'

'When do we leave?'

'Eleven-fifteen. Memsahib. Will you want lunch?' He produced a pencil from behind his ear and stood poised by a wall-mounted clipboard.

I shook my head. After my full English breakfast, I was having difficulty fastening my belt. 'No thank you, Steward. I'll wait till dinner.'

Jumping from the train I was struck by how warm it was in the capital compared to the cool temperatures of the Frontier. Removing my jacket and unbuttoning my collar, I headed for the concourse, hoping I could get a cable off to Frances and find a runner to take my report and accompanying letter to Agnes at the Lady Hardinge. With only seconds to spare, I stepped back into Compartment 6 to find Duncan, sitting alone in the corner, reading the Delhi Times.

'Where are Hamish and Fraser?' I asked, perspiration trickling down my neck.

'At lunch.'

Realising the implications of this statement, I turned to leave, only to have the compartment door slammed in my face by a station-guard who raised his green flag with a flourish, and the platform began to move backwards. 'Bugger,' I muttered under my breath and threw my purse into my valise.

'You cut that fine, Mac,' commented Duncan, offering me a handkerchief.

I pulled my own out of my pocket, went to rinse it in cold water then flopped onto the opposite bench, wiping my hairline as the Frontier Mail picked up speed. Facing three hours alone with Duncan didn't appeal to me one little bit, but he must have sensed my unease because he disappeared behind his newspaper and left me to my own devices.

I pulled my writing pad out of my valise, unfolded the drop-down bulkhead table and spent a contented hour writing home with all my news, cherishing the silence and making a mental note to have my camera films processed as soon as I reached Poona so that I could include shots of the Khyber Pass, the Gordon Highlanders pipe band and my Afghan Jezail for the family's delectation.

It was as I was finishing off my letter to Karr that Duncan stretched, made a big thing of neatly folding his paper and placing it in the bulkhead rack, then rising to push the window open to give us more air. I tensed, convinced that this past hour had all been an act to lull me into a false sense of security and I was to be proved correct.

'Well, here we are, alone at last,' he announced, resembling a Bengal Tiger eyeing up an antelope for dinner.

'Are you in pain?' My attempt at changing the subject fell on deaf ears.

'Some of the time but I can manage. Now, Mac, I have a question for you.'

I gritted my teeth and waited.

'Would you mind telling me why, for near on three weeks, you've been avoiding me like the plague?'

'I didn't realise that I had.'

'Don't lie to me, Mac, I know you too well.'

'Duncan, you don't know me at all.'

'Maybe not now, but I did, and intimately.' He tapped the upholstery beside him, but I didn't take up his offer. 'Are we going to talk about this while we have the chance, or will you go to your grave still treating me as if I'm the devil incarnate?'

'Probably the latter,' I said. 'Now do you want some more painkillers or not?'

'Oh, for God's sake, Mac, NO, I don't want more painkillers.'

I shrugged.

'Will you get down off your pedestal and tell me what's bugging you?'

'Why?'

'Because I think you're looking for an explanation from me, that's why.'

'It's a bit late for an explanation, don't you think, Duncan?'

'Jesus, Mary and Joseph!' He pushed his hair back from his forehead in frustration. 'What I think, is that we have some unfinished business here, and whether you like it or not, it needs sorting.'

I could feel pent-up anger bubbling below the surface like magma in a volcano and swivelled on my seat, facing him head on. 'What is your problem, Duncan? If you wanted to say something, you should have said it years ago while I was still too naive to know better. Anything you say today will simply fall on deaf ears because I now see you for what you are.'

'And what would that be?'

'A self-centred bastard with an ego the size of the Titanic.'

'Is that all?'

'Actually, no, but if you don't mind, I'd rather not have this conversation at all?'

He leant forward and touched my knee with his good hand. 'Well, Darlin', that's a pity because I would.'

His acerbic words punctured my carefully constructed defences and I exploded, ripping his hand away from my skirt. 'Don't you dare 'Darlin' me. You gave up that right years ago.'

'OK, OK.' He retreated as if stung. 'But for the love o' God, Mac, even a murderer is given a chance to confess.'

'Well, I'm not a priest and this is not the confessional.'

'Damn your eyes, Elizabeth Stuart MacKenzie, if this is to do with me leaving you in Edinburgh, then I did what I thought was right back in the day, and looking at you now, I'd say I did the right thing.'

'What, by tossing me into the gutter like some discarded cigarette butt, without one word of explanation?'

'I didn't toss you in the gutter.'

'Yes, you did,' I yelled, only the rhythmic grating of metal wheels on metal track obscuring my outburst from reaching the ears of occupants in the next carriage. 'You wound me around your little finger with your Celtic promises and silver tongue while using my body for your own sexual gratification, then, when it suited your purpose, you upped and left without a second's thought. What would you call that if it wasn't tossing me into the gutter?'

'Shhh!, Mac, the whole train can hear you.'

'Frankly, Duncan, I don't care if the whole world can hear me. You insisted on this conversation so stop whinging.' A decade of pent-up anger was pouring out of me like Niagara Falls.

'What the hell did I do that was so bloody awful?'

'Christ Almighty, man, you've got the skin of a rhinoceros.' I was on my feet. 'You not only left me to pick up the pieces while you swanned off to India, but you couldn't even be bothered to write to say you were sorry. Not even a *Dear John* letter rejecting me for someone else.' I found myself standing over him, digging my forefinger into his damaged shoulder, his scapula twitching with each jab.

'For a start, there wasn't anyone else, and I had every intention of keeping in touch with you once I settled into my new life.' His vocal cords dropped an octave as he struggled to keep his temper.

'So, what happened then?' I countered. 'Couldn't you find a pen or did the letters get lost in the post?'

'Oh, for Christ's sake!' He massaged his collarbone where my finger had been. 'Just cut the sarcasm, alright? The letters didn't get lost in the post because they never got written.'

'As I suspected,' I yelled.

'And they didn't get written because I was told, in no uncertain terms, that I was to leave you alone.'

'Oh really? And who would that be then, Santa Claus?' Now it was my words that dripped acid.

'As I recall, it was your bloody University Medical Director.'

I stared at the wide-open countryside racing passed the compartment window and refused to allow his words to penetrate.

'You don't believe me, do you?'

'No, Duncan, I don't.' Peering down at him from the corner of my eye, I felt suddenly liberated from being a victim. 'Spin whatever lies you like if it makes you feel better, but it no longer works on me because that young undergraduate with stars in her eyes, who you manipulated to satisfy your own ego, no longer exists.'

'How dare you say I'm lying, you Eegit.' He had me by the throat, as we stood, noses touching, his teeth bared.

I should have been scared out of my wits, trapped with a man I really didn't know, who was much bigger and stronger than myself and with an obvious score to settle, but I wasn't. Duncan's fingers were not around my neck but around that of all strong women who didn't bend to his control. I stared into his tortured eyes and saw the truth. My ex-lover was afraid of the opposite sex and needed to overcome that fear by manipulating them sexually. That was the reason he had seduced me, that was the way he gained peer group respect and that explained the way he made love. Compared to Tom Wallace, Duncan's sexual prowess was abysmal.

It was like a light going on in my brain. Some deep-seated phobia embedded in his psyche was at play here and it was the height of folly to allow it to continue.

I slowly peeled his fingers off my neck and moved to the other end of the carriage, pressure marks rising to the surface of my skin. He turned his back on me and smashed his right fist into the window glass with frustration. It must have been excruciating but he didn't cry out, instead, he leant his forehead on the hard surface and remained silent, all tension gone in that one act of violence.

'You will listen,' he muttered, after a long pause.

'What?'

'I said, you will listen.'

His words had a sinister edge to them, and warning bells continued to ring in my head. I recalled Duncan once telling me that his mother had been a redhead with a violent temper when crossed. He had inherited her hair and her temper, and I wondered if it had been his mother who had been the root of his neurosis.

I held my breath. All this psychoanalysis was all very well, I thought, but with no means of escape I needed to rapidly diffuse the situation. I exhaled and relaxed back against the bulkhead. 'Fine,' I announced, trying with difficulty to keep sarcasm out of my voice. 'I'm all ears. In fact, I'm fascinated to know what Pa's close friend from university thought he was doing interfering in my personal life.'

Duncan remained where he was, rubbing his injured fist. 'It's not a lie, Mac, as God is my witness. A letter really was waiting for me when I arrived in Bombay. It had come from some Edinburgh University Medical Director who didn't mince his words.'

'Can you remember his name?'

He shook his head. 'I was accused of being a selfish egotist who had enjoyed toying with your emotions while studying at Ashworth Laboratories and, having cast you aside, was now jeopardising your prospects as a doctor by messing with your head. If I continued to dangle you on a string, then the Faculty's most promising medical student would likely fail her degree, kiss goodbye to her medical career and return to her family with her tail between her legs, or something to that effect. In short, Mac, I would be to blame for buggering up your life.'

My grunt was pure warthog. 'And you've still got that letter, I presume?'

'No, dammit. I wish I had, then I could prove I was telling the truth.' He dropped onto his seat and stared at his hands, cupped together against his breastbone, his head lowered like some spoilt brat about to be expelled from school. 'His words were so insulting Mac, so I tore them into shreds and shoved them down the drain.'

'Along with our affair.'

'To be sure. But you did become a doctor and, from all accounts, a bloody good one at that.' His eyes finally found mine. 'Looking at you now Mac, with your feisty character and good looks, your life seems to have turned out just fine, so it has, and I'm glad I paid some part in that.'

Watching him verbally whitewashing his own callous behaviour towards me, any lingering feelings of loss dissipated like water down a plughole. This man wasn't pleased with my success, he was riddled with jealousy because I had succeeded despite him. That was the reason he knocked George Philpott out cold. He was not saving my reputation but blind with anger at another man enjoying something he had lost.

I couldn't resist giving him a round of applause. 'I'm sorry to disillusion you, Duncan, but any success in my life has nothing to do with you. It's true that I was in danger of failing my medical degree. Thinking back, it's a miracle I didn't die of a broken heart, but if anyone deserves the credit for getting me back on track, it was Aunt Karr. She was the one who pointed out that my infatuation for you was momentary, while my medical degree was for life.'

'And you believed her?'

'Of course, I believed her.'

'Then all I can say, Cailin, is that your anger towards me is misguided and your Aunt Karr never experienced true love.'

'But you have, I suppose?' I was again in danger of inciting violence and had to weld my teeth together to stop any further insult seeing the light of day.

'Correction, Mac, we have, and we could again.'

I nearly fell off my chair. Even after all this, Duncan was still trying to manipulate my emotions, and it had to stop. I softened my voice as if giving a eulogy. 'No, Duncan, that was not love, that was an adolescent infatuation which could never have stood the test of time. I moved on, long ago, and all that is left are painful memories and a desire never to make the same mistake again.'

'But, Mac?' his charm offensive was about to be given full reign.

'No, Duncan, we draw a line under this right now and put the whole thing down to experience. If you haven't already, I sincerely hope you find the kind of relationship you are searching for, but it will not be with me. The alchemy is all wrong.' His jaw muscles tightened. 'Friends maybe, but lovers, never. Now, can we leave it at that and change the subject?'

'Only if you get me some of that pain-killer concoction you offered me earlier? My fist hurts like hell.'

He was unbelievable and as slippery as an eel. I produced the laudanum bottle from my medical bag and mixed it with a shot of whisky. 'As your doctor, Duncan, I strongly recommend that you stop using your body as a battering ram if you want to see forty. Here, drink this.' He smiled, downed the concoction in one go and wiped his mouth with the back of his left hand. 'Thank ye kindly, Ma'am, you're a regular angel so you are.' He was like Jekyll and Hyde and I began to believe I was living in a parallel universe where our conversation of just minutes before had never really happened.

Once the laudanum took effect, Duncan's eyelids drooped and he dozed, stretched out on the bench-seat with not a care in the world, while I penned a letter to Ruby. We had twenty minutes to go before reaching our next stop at Mathura, and I was keen to post it before moving on to Sawai Madhopur, but my thoughts kept straying.

The previous hour had been very cathartic for me and certainly very revealing. If there had been one ounce of truth in Duncan's explanation, then that only went to prove how impressed the Faculty had been with my medical ability. It would be a simple matter to prove it as well. All I had to do was ask Pa if Professor Bainbridge had indeed written such a scathing letter to Duncan and if so, on who's instruction.

Although Pa might baulk at using his close friend to rid me of the Irish Veterinary Surgeon with an oversized ego, Aunt Karr certainly would not. She and Bainbridge had been lovers in their university days, and I knew from personal experience that Karr could move heaven and earth if she put her mind to it, and her niece's career prospects, or lack of them, would have definitely exercised her mind. I chuckled under my breath. Professor Bainbridge would have been told in no uncertain terms what he had to do.

'Well, Mac,' I whispered, returning to Ruby's letter. 'You live and learn.'

Chapter Twenty

The rest of the journey passed without further incident and Duncan maintained the air of a perfect travelling companion throughout. On arrival at Bombay's Victoria Station on the evening of the third day, I pecked his cheek and promised to stay in touch, then rushed away with Hamish at my heels carrying my bedding and valise and Fraser bringing up the rear, pushing a flatbed truck with my trunk and rifle-box, having commandeered it from a station porter insisting it was Army orders.

The station's dull lighting made the place feel rather sombre and foreboding as I dashed to the Poona platform gate brandishing my train ticket at the guard.

'What date is the Governor of Bombay's parade?' I shouted over my shoulder, heading for an open carriage door.

'Saturday, 10th May,' bellowed Hamish. 'On the Gateway to India parade ground.

'Right, I'll be there waving the Union flag.'

'See that you do, Lassie. Now up you get and give my best regards to Poona.'

Fraser rattled passed on his way to the baggage truck, his kilt swinging wildly from side-to-side as I jumped aboard grabbing my belongings from Hamish's arms in the process. 'Say goodbye to Fraser for me, Hamish, and both of you, stay away from Kamathipura District.'

'What would be there, then?' quipped the Sergeant, his eyes twinkling.

'Syphilis, Hamish. Syphilis!'

'Then, I promise to keep your Army motto close to my heart.' He stood back, clicked his heels, saluted and bellowed 'ABSTINENTIA EST MELIUS REMEDIUM,' at the top of his voice as the guard's whistle blew.'

'Just make sure you stick to it, or you'll itch your way through the Governor's Official Jamboree!'

Two hours later I was hugging Frances and longing for my bed. As usual she was highly organised, even at short notice, and after a light supper in the school's refectory, I was ushered to 'Beaky' Beckinsale's old room and was asleep before the clock stuck midnight.

During breakfast the following morning, Frances went over our itinerary.

'Now, Mac, we have four glorious days to relax and see the sights of Poona before I welcome my little devils back into the fold for the spring term and you take up your position at the Seva Sadan Hospital and Maternity Home.' She began clearing away the breakfast crockery. 'I want to give you the grand tour of this Victorian pile before our visit to the Aga Khan Palace at eleven o'clock, so drink up and let's get on our way.'

'Which Aga Khan would that be?' I asked, pouring some coffee.

'Sultan Muhammed Shah Aga Khan III.'

'Which century would that be then?' I sounded like Hamish.

She removed the coffee pot before I could take more. 'Born 1877 and spiritual leader of the Nizari Ismaili Muslims who built the palace in an act of charity for the poor of this area who were suffering from famine. To my knowledge he is still alive today and active in politics.'

'Well done, Headmistress, you seem to have done your homework.'

'Needs must, Mac. Year 5's history syllabus starts with it, followed by the obligatory guided tour, which I dread. The little blighters insist on fingering all the objet d'art knowing full well that it is forbidden.'

'Girls will be girls,' I commented, watching my close friend sweep crumbs into her hand from the tablecloth.

'I tell you, Mac, I will swing for them one day. Take our visit last February.' She brushed the crumbs into my porridge bowl. 'My heart was in my mouth when Cynthia Postlethwaite deliberately knocked against a Ming vase from the Tang Dynasty. My dive to the floor to catch the vase in both hands before it smashed to the ground was worthy of a place in the England cricket team and saved the school from bankruptcy.'

I giggled at the thought of Frances sliding across the grand hall fielding this valuable and irreplaceable masterpiece from the sixth century as if she were at Lords. 'What happened to Cynthia?'

'Lady Cynthia, to be precise. Closely related to the Governor of Madras. She was expelled, and not before time.'

'And the Ming vase?'

'It is now safely behind glass.'

'Then I look forward to seeing it.' I put my cup down. 'Right, I'm done. Lead on, Macbeth.'

St Saviours Boarding School for Young Ladies was exactly as Frances had painted it back in Calcutta at Christmas. The red-brick, leaded windowed, gabled and turreted façade oozed Victorian grandeur, while its rather austere presence was partially softened by the one-hundred-and-twenty-acre grounds surrounding it, sporting expansive lawns, tennis courts, hockey, and rounders pitches, a running track, a horse menage and a large open-air swimming pool. Frances was the head of an institution comprising of 32 staff, 185 pupils and the school's mascot piglet. I was impressed.

'How is piglet?' I asked.

'Growing.' We rounded the corner of some outbuildings and Frances pulled open a wooden door. 'See for yourself.'

In four months, piglet had become a ten-stone sow and was fast asleep on a bed of straw.

'The girls love her,' remarked Frances, banging the side of the wooden pen. The sow slowly opened one eye, appeared unimpressed with her visitors, and shut it again, returning to her dreams.

'Did they give her a name?'

'Trotter.' We both burst out laughing, 'And she gets her daily exercise being led around the grounds on this cerise lead.' She held up a long length of bright pink plaited hemp.

At the Calcutta Club New Year's Eve Ball, Frances had accidentally trapped "Trotter" between her feet when it ran under her skirt in fright. The club had a tradition of letting twelve tiny pink piglets loose amongst the inebriated guests at midnight, and if anyone caught one of the baby porkers they were allowed to keep it. This one was destined to become St Saviour's school mascot and as Frances's surname was Trotter, the sow's moniker was a foregone conclusion.

'She's obviously lost her ability to tear about the place,' I observed, counting her tramline row of teats.

'Oh, don't be fooled, Mac, if her snout locks onto the smell of food, she's off like a rocket, usually pulling a fourth former along in her wake.' She looked at her watch. 'Time to go.'

The Aga Khan Palace's cream and white stuccoed exterior with its arched colonnades and spindled balconies was a far cry from St Saviour's unadorned architecture, and the light interior was a joy to walk around after my barren surroundings in the Hindu Kush. We strolled passed ornate fountains, box-hedge borders, and heavily scented rose gardens while I related my experiences up on the Frontier, concluding with the presentation of my Afghan Jezail.

'Wow, this all makes my life in Poona seem very tame. Where is the rifle now?'

'In Beaky Beckinsale's bedroom.'

'Then you MUST give a talk to the sixth-form girls next week, Mac. They will hang on your every word and it will be good for them to have a role-model for inspiration.'

'Frances, are you telling me you want to educate the cream of Imperial debutants into becoming combatants of the Indian Frontier Army?'

'No, of course not, Mac, but most of the time their heads are filled with frippery and fancies. It would be good for them to hear, first-hand, that life is not all lace bonnets and whalebone stays.'

'How do you think they will take to my graphic description of the Tamerlane Prison's 'Death Tunnel' then?'

'I'll be standing by with the smelling salts.' Frances had a wicked grin on her face. 'And I will also invite the Governors to attend. They should find your talk very interesting if they can stay awake long enough.' She turned out of the entrance gate and hailed a rickshaw.

'Where are we off to now?' I asked, climbing in.

'Lunch. My treat.'

The veranda of the Hotel Grand was an oasis of calm as we sat sipping ice-cold punch and watching the world go by. This was colonial elegance at its best and I wallowed in the luxury of the place as an electric fan quietly rotated overhead. It was eighty degrees in the shade and for the first time since leaving the passenger liner the previous October, my soft lemon organza dress had made an appearance and was wafting in the gentle breeze while my heavy linen suit and brushed-cotton blouse were consigned to the bottom of my trunk.

'You had something to tell me in confidence, Mac,' said Frances as she curled her dark hair into a chignon and held it in place with an ivory clasp. 'Gosh, that's better.'

I peered at her over the rim of my cocktail glass as she wiped the back of her neck with a lace-edged hankie.

'How I'm going to get through the next term without expiring I really don't know.'

'What you need is a spell up at Landi Kotal. You could die of exposure up there, to say nothing of the sanitation.'

She grimaced. 'Well?'

I cleared my throat and lowered my voice. 'There is something you need to know before you arrive in Simla this summer.'

She stopped dabbing her neck and cocked her head. 'Spill the beans, Doctor Stuart-MacKenzie.'

'You remember we were musing over who Ruby's wealthy lover was before we left the ship?'

'Indeed. As I recall, we decided it was some titled Government dignitary with a long-suffering wife back in the Shires.'

'Exactly. Well, we couldn't have been further from the truth. Think Rajputan Prince with an eye for the women and an inexhaustible bank account who you socialised with on the deck of the ss Narkunda.'

'NO! Prince Vijay Kumar Singh II?'

'As I live and breathe. Frances, your mouth is hanging open.'

She took a few seconds to let the news sink in then downed half of her punch. 'Of course, it all makes perfect sense now, doesn't it? That trip to Cairo, the expensive clothes, their whispered conversations which stopped the minute we came into view.' She studied my face. 'How did you find out?'

I chuckled. 'While I was staying with Ruby in Delhi. I wrote to you describing her fabulous Romanesque villa.'

She nodded.

'What I didn't tell you was that on arrival I was sure I had seen the butler somewhere before but for the life of me I couldn't place him. Then, that evening during dinner, the telephone rang, and I couldn't help overhearing Ruby asking the caller what time he planned to be at the villa the following weekend. You know what a loud voice she's got.'

Frances nodded again.

'Well, as she returned to the table she nonchalantly said, "Vijay sends his regards." I tell you, Frances, a myocardial infarction couldn't have hit me harder.'

'A what?'

'Sorry, I've been around too many medics recently. A heart attack.'

'But you said Vijay's wife was on board the ship as well?'

'Not only his wife, Frances, but most of her family too.'

'Jesus Christ!'

It was not like Frances to blaspheme, which only went to show how much the news had shocked her.

'Did you see him in Delhi?'

'To be honest, I bottled out. I was busy anyway at the Lady Hardinge and I knew if I met Vijay, I would likely throttle him to death.' Care was now needed as Frances had no idea of either the Princess's miscarriage or my abortion. 'Anyway, the point is, I then realised who the butler was. He was the family's chaprassi in the Jhalanpur Suite.'

'You've rather lost me.'

'I'm not surprised. The chaprassi is a type of butler-com-official messenger in a Maharaja's employ. I met this one when Tom asked me to attend to the Princess suffering from suspected food poisoning. He couldn't examine her because she was in purdah.'

'Is that how you got your Scheherazade outfit?'

'Yes.'

'I did wonder, having seen the limited contents of your trunk on the night of your birthday.'

Her comment took me straight back to Cabin 20 and I would never forget her reaction to my staid selection of Northumbrian evening dresses when Tom Wallace invited me to celebrate my twenty-ninth birthday at the ship's stern with a bottle of Veuve Cliquot, followed by a romantic dinner under the stars on the hurricane deck. If it hadn't been for her shortening my emerald silk, crosscut, strappy gown, which Ruby had insisted on me purchasing in Simon Artz Departmental Store that same day, I doubt Tom and I would have progressed beyond being professional colleagues.'

'You do realise that it is your fault Tom found me so stunningly attractive.'

'Me! What did I do?'

'You turned this Highland ugly duckling into a screen goddess for the night. Tom didn't stand a chance.'

'Rubbish, Mac. All I did was shorten your rather lovely evening gown. Ruby's accessories did the rest, and you must admit, it did put a smile on your face.'

It was not only the heat that was making my colour rise. 'Speaking of Tom, has Jim said anymore about how he is, or even, where he is?'

'No, and he's not likely to until he gets back to Bombay. I imagine his mail has been trying to catch up with him for the past three months as he moved from one P&O ship to another, serving out his notice.'

'When is he back?'

'Around the sixteenth of the month if all goes to plan.'

'Great, because we have a date in Bombay on the eighteenth.'

'Really?'

'The Gordon Highlanders' Pipe Band will be performing for Sir Frederick Sykes and his guests on the parade ground by the Gateway to India. I promised Hamish and Fraser that I would be there waving the Union flag. I thought we could stay over for the weekend, assuming you can get away.'

'Mac, that's terrific, and I know just where we can stay. Jim has signed a six-month lease on a rather nice bungalow in the Civil Lines. We could travel down late on the Friday night and Jim could pick us up at the station. What time is the parade?'

'I'm not sure, but we could always ring Governor's House.'

'Oh, Mac, it is so good to have you here in Poona. There were times in the winter when I felt so isolated, what with Jim off on the high seas and you up in Delhi. When do you have to leave again?'

'Not for at least a month if not longer. I imagine Agnes will want me back in Delhi for a debrief before everyone heads into the mountains for the summer. When do you break up?' The waiter appeared with the lunch menu.

'Late June,' said Frances, taking hers and scanning the contents. 'You mentioned the Lady Reading Hospital in Simla, last night. Is that where you'll be working during the holidays?'

The chef's dish of the day sounded interesting. 'I hope so because they have just opened a brand-new maternity wing.' The waiter returned with his pen and pad. 'I'll have the grilled vegetable salad with mango yoghurt and spiced sautéed potatoes, and we'll have some more punch, please.' The waiter bowed, took Frances's order and departed. 'What's on the itinerary after lunch?'

'A swim in the school pool followed by some serious sunbathing.'

'Now that, Miss Trotter, is an excellent idea.'

The days flew by and come Sunday afternoon, Frances was already welcoming her students back into school and instructing the staff on their responsibilities for the coming week.

I called in to the Seva Sadan Hospital to introduce myself to Doctor Emilie Jackson, a Canadian clinician from Montreal and she gave me a tour of the premises. It was hardly a hospital, more an oversized clinic on three floors of a concrete building in the centre of Poona's Priyadarshani Nagar district, but the operating theatre was well equipped and the Hindu staff well-trained and enthusiastic. I confirmed that I would be staying at St Saviour's for the duration of my assignment as Frances had yet to replace her Deputy Head, so Beaky's room was free. A school bicycle was allocated for my exclusive use and Frances saw me off the premises on the Monday morning rather like my Ma on my first day at Junior school.

The work at the Seva Sadan was certainly varied and by mid-week I was well integrated into the team and enjoying being back in the mainstream of gynaecology and obstetrics within a mainly Hindu community. My only regret was that my knowledge of Hindi was no better than when I had left Delhi, so a staff member had to be present throughout my consultations to translate.

'It's not good enough,' I moaned to Frances over dinner, 'my translator could be better used caring for patients than following me around like a shadow.'

'Leave it to me,' said Frances, and by Thursday, I found myself being schooled in Hindi for two hours every evening by Darsh, a young Hindu student from the local Government College of Civil Engineering. The extra income from St Saviour's supply-teachers' fund helped Darsh supplement his fees and once some of the sixth formers saw this rather tall, good-looking chap wandering around the college after hours, they begged Frances to let them join in.

We had great fun getting our English tongues around Darsh's native language and before long the class had grown to forty students. The fact that most of the syllabus revolved around female issues and medical terms didn't seem to faze the girls, who, by now, had all decided to become doctors anyway!

Like "Trotter", I had become a school mascot, although I avoided being walked around the grounds on a cerise pink lead, and after my talk on my experiences at the North-West Frontier, my standing in the school rose to the giddy heights of celebrity status, while my Afghan Rifle took pride of place for all to see, mounted on the lobby wall opposite the entrance.

Frances insisted on me penning an essay with embedded photographs of my time with the Khyber Rifles to be used in future school lectures on the life of British and Indian Frontier Forces, so extra copies of my photographs were immediately ordered from the local Kodak shop.

At the morning clinic on the following Monday, a highly nervous Hindu mother appeared with her three-month-old baby boy, Kaka, who she insisted belonged to Doctor Emilie Jackson. I was somewhat taken aback by this statement until I learned that the little chap had been seen as a miracle birth by his parents. They had tried for many years to have a child and had spent all their meagre resources on local ineffectual cures, before approaching the Seva Sadan for help. Emilie Jackson had performed a small operation to remove a blockage in the mother's cervix and shortly afterwards Kaka was conceived, and thereafter referred to as Emilie's son.

He was here to be circumcised, much to the consternation of extended family and friends. The thought of a syringe, local anaesthetic and a knife being plunged into Kaka, gave the mother palpitations which was what I now faced being allocated the job as surgeon on duty.

While the theatre nurse prepared the baby, I tried to convince his mother that all would be well. Her rapid breathing and rocketing pulse rate, caused by dire warnings from neighbours, grave doubts by her husband and horror stories from the local *Dai*, were strong counters to my assurances and I hoped I wouldn't have to attend to a sudden cardiac arrest halfway through the operation.

However, all went well and Kaka was placed safely back in his mother's arms within the hour, with instructions to keep the wound covered and free from infection and to make regular visits to the hospital clinic until it healed. Prayers of gratitude to every deity known followed the whole family down the street, the cacophony of sound increased substantially by the baby bellowing at the top of his voice, demanding food.

'How did the circumcision go?' Emilie asked at lunch.

'Fine,' I replied, enjoying a fresh tabbouleh salad. 'I was more worried about losing the mother than the child as it happens, but all concluded without any loss of life, and I am pleased to announce that you have been upstaged. Kaka is now Doctor Mac's child.' Our laughter could be heard three streets away.

As usual that evening, Darsh invited me to relate something that had happened during my day for him to use as the basis for his evening's lesson. He turned puce when I mentioned Kaka's circumcision and the girls were quick to capitalise on his discomfort, insisting that I draw a diagram of a penis and foreskin on the blackboard, and explain why the operation was necessary. I was not known for my artistic skills, but I made a stab at it while questions flew around the room.

'What is the word for circumcise in Hindi, Sir?' asked Cecilia Stamford.

'*Parishuddh karan*,' replied Darsh, slowly disappearing under the lectern.

'Are all men circumcised, Miss?' came a question from the back as Dorothy Wainthrop jumped up and down waving her hand in the air.

'No. Normally it's a cultural or religious thing.'

'So, Miss,' she gasped, 'which cultures and religions do it?'

'Many,' I said, knowing exactly where this conversation was going. 'For instance, the Aztecs and Mayans of South America were believed to practise it in ancient times as were aboriginal Australasians. Juddaism, Islam and the Coptic Orthodox Church continue the practice to this day.'

'Does it hurt?' asked Alice Northwood.

'A little, but we use a local anaesthetic and small babies are far too young to remember it.'

Penelope Abraham, having three brothers and being present at each's *bar mitzvah*, went for the jugular. 'Have you been circumcised, Sir?'

I jumped in as Darsh choked on his own saliva. 'As I am probably the only one who will need "*parishuddh karan*" in the future, I suggest we move on.'

'*Parishuddh karan*,' shouted the girls in unison, as Frances walked through the door. Approaching the blackboard, she raised her right eyebrow and gave me a very old-fashioned look.

'Perhaps, Doctor Stuart-MacKenzie, you would enlighten me on what *parishuddh karan*, actually means.'

'It's the medical term for circumcision, Miss Trotter, at least I believe it is.' I looked at Darsh who's head was swaying loosely above his spine as he visibly shrank by four inches. 'I performed such an operation on a three-month-old Hindu baby today at the Seva Sadan, which is why we have the Hindi word for it.'

'And did the baby survive?' Frances was having trouble keeping a straight face.

'I am pleased to report that he is in the best of health and is now in the bosom of his own family.'

'What's the Hindi word for bosom, Sir?' shouted Dorothy, now on a mission.'

Frances gritted her teeth. 'We will deal with that during our anatomy class, Dorothy,' suggested Frances over her shoulder as she slowly rubbed my pornographic artwork away with the blackboard rubber. 'Meanwhile, I would like to know who will be going on the trip to Bombay this Saturday for the Governor's parade?'

It was now my turn to raise my eyebrows.

'Me, Miss,' shouted all in the class.

'Fine. Then you are to put your names down on the attendees list pinned to the information board before lights-out so that we can organise the train tickets. You will be leaving the school at seven-thirty so breakfast will be at six-fifteen. Hopefully, you can all manage not to miss the school bus.'

'Yes, Miss,' they chorused, and Frances left us to continue our lesson.

We were sitting in her drawing room enjoying an after-dinner coffee when I brought up the subject of the Governor's parade again.

'Don't look so worried, Mac, we will be nowhere near the St Saviour contingent on the day. I have instructed Miss Troutbridge to take charge and I've been in touch with the Girl's Catholic School in Bombay who will be overseeing our group, along with their own during the parade and afterwards at a celebration picnic. The Head has arranged with Governor's House for all private school pupils in the district to stand together in full uniform and for the head girls from each school to present various dignitaries' wives with posies before the parade. Apparently, the Governor's wife thought it a splendid idea. We, meanwhile, will be free to do as we please.'

'Thank goodness for that.' I refilled my cup. 'Sorry about tonight, Frances. Unlike you, I'm not well versed on what not to discuss with sixth-formers.'

'Actually, Mac, I thought it was great. I can use this to talk about female genital mutilation, which, as you know, is rife here in India.'

'I've yet to see it, to be honest, Frances, but I wholeheartedly agree that the girls should know of its existence.'

'How did Darsh manage after I left the room.'

'I moved us on to bathing babies which took up most of the last hour, and I think Darsh was eternally grateful.'

'Poor lamb, what with your medical attitude to all things genital and my Year Six's instinctive interest in all things sexual, the poor lad is completely out of his depth.'

I chuckled at Frances's description of the Hindi language class. 'Well, by the time I leave St Saviour's, you will not only have a well-educated class of biology students, but a young Hindu civil engineer who is conversant with the vagaries of colonial pubescent girls.'

'It's enough to put him off women for life.'

'It certainly puts me off teaching. I don't know how you stand it.'

'With difficulty, but at least 'Beaky' Beckinsale wasn't here to see your graphic drawing on the blackboard. She would have had apoplexy.'

'I'll try to remember to stay well away from appendages in the future, but what shall I do if my next patient is suffering from haemorrhoids?'

'Elizabeth Stuart-MacKenzie, don't push your luck.'

'Yes, Miss.'

Chapter Twenty-One

The Poona to Bombay train was packed as Frances and I settled into our seats that Saturday morning. It was only seven-forty-five, but the temperature was already eighty-five degrees, and my sweat glands were working overtime.

The excitement onboard was palpable, everyone looking forward to the 'Gateway to India' parade and Miss Troutbridge had her work cut out keeping forty-two fifth and sixth-formers in order further down the platform.

'Don't you feel guilty leaving your latest staff member to handle the likes of Dorothy Wainthrop and Penelope Abraham?' I asked, tossing my straw sunhat on top of my weekend bag lying in the rack above my head.

'Not in the least, Mac,' replied Frances, squeezing between two Salvation Army ladies, clad in red uniforms and black hats with red ribbons, whose substantial pelvic structures straddled her seat. They must have been stifling, I thought, and kept a close eye on them in case they both expired before reaching Bombay.

'The art of a good headmistress is to delegate,' continued Frances, shuffling her bottom onto the upholstery opposite me, 'and as it is my free weekend, I see no reason why St Saviour's outing to the Governor's Parade should interfere with my plans.'

I thought how fresh and lovely she looked in her apple green cotton dress edged in white satin, her hair loose across her shoulders instead of the usual formidable bun at the nape of her neck.

Her plans, as I well knew, were to see Jim for the first time in months and to have some private time with her intended in the privacy of his accommodation. His cable had arrived at St Saviours two days earlier, confirming his arrival back in Bombay, and I had every intention of making myself scarce whenever possible to give them the chance to be alone.

I suddenly felt rather envious of my close friend and wondered what I would have been doing this weekend if Tom Wallace had not been married. I shook the thought from my head, straightened my own cream and white ensemble which Ruby had bought for me to wear when pretending to be Miss Laura Henderson at the Metropolitan Hotel in Delhi, and added my two-pennies-worth of knowledge to the general conversation in the compartment.

Frances didn't hold back when telling our travelling companions of my recent work as a doctor on the North-West Frontier, which resulted in me giving a lengthy explanation of how I knew that the Gordon Highlanders' Pipes & Drums would be participating in the parade and what life had been like at the head of the Khyber Pass.

By the time the train pulled into Victoria Station I was hoarse from shouting over the noise of the train rattling along the track and needed a drink to soothe my throat. Frances, spying Jim in the crowds, his brown wavy hair towering above the throng, pushed through the mass of humanity and straight into his welcoming arms. He swung her around and hugged her as if the world was about to end and I smiled. This was so different from their reserved behaviour at the bottom of the ss Narkunda's gangway at Ballard Pier back in October when

Frances departed to take up her new post in Poona. I could only hope that our group of St Saviour's girls were far enough back down the platform not to see this open expression of love and affection, and chuckled imagining 'Beaky' Beckinsale's horrified expression at such behaviour by the school's headmistress.

'Mac, you are a sight for sore eyes,' said Jim, hugging me in like manner, then gathering us both up and waltzing us into the station's hotel café for a cool drink and a late breakfast.

'Here, girls,' he announced as we settled into our chairs, handing over two Union Flags on wooden sticks.

At that moment I would have willingly foregone the parade and remained under the electric ceiling fan to help cool my body temperature and said so.

'There was a chap outside the station selling peacock fans, Mac. Would that help?'

'It certainly would,' I replied, perspiring from every pore.

'Then you order for me, Fran, while I go and barter.' Jim was out of his seat and across the café before she could respond.

He returned minutes later as the Indian waitress, in her lovely cool silk sari, set a platter of pastries and a tray of teacups on the table, followed by a steaming pot of *chai*.

'How about these?' He ceremonially produced two beautiful peacock feather fans on wooden handles from behind his back and wafted them vigorously.

'You'll need some lessons from Ruby if you're thinking of taking up a career as a stripper at the Windmill Theatre, in Soho, Jim.'

He wafted one under my nose and made me sneeze. 'Less of your cheek, young lady. Now, I have a surprise for you both.'

'Not another one, Officer Hamilton,' I said, fanning my drenched collarbone.

'Indeed.'

He sounded so like Frances I couldn't help chuckling.

'As the new Bombay Port Authority's Deputy Conservator, I have commandeered three seats on their grandstand for the parade. We should have a great view of the event sitting just to the right of the Gateway to India Arch.'

'Fantastic, Jim. How did you pull that one off?' Frances had stars in her eyes looking at her man.

'I told them we were entertaining a very important guest who had just returned from serving on the Frontier with members of the Gordon Highlanders and had been presented with an antique Jezail for bravery under fire.'

'I bet you didn't tell them that your guest was a woman.' I said, staring at him from under my fringe, beaming from ear-to-ear.

'They didn't ask so I didn't say, Mac.'

'Just as well, Jim, or you would have been drummed out of the boardroom for casting aspersions on our great military traditions.'

'Well, that's just ridiculous, Mac,' announced Frances, getting on her soapbox. 'What is wrong with women getting awards for bravery. If you ask me, they should all get one for giving birth.'

'Try telling that to the IMS.' I went back to my pastry.

'So, I assume you left them believing that Mac was a man?'

'Let's just say, Fran, I simply said Doctor Stuart-MacKenzie was the VIP guest and left it at that.' He grabbed her peacock fan and disappeared behind the feathers.

'Coward,' remarked Frances and winked at me.

We made ourselves comfortable on the fourth row of the grandstand and scanned the expanse of the parade ground. It looked enormous from our elevated position and was crowded with on-lookers, the perimeter heaving with black-haired heads belonging to every colour, creed and dress.

The schoolgirls were bunched together alongside the adjacent grandstand, one girl at the front of each uniformed group, holding a small posy of flowers. In front of the Gateway to India Arch, a low canopied rostrum had been set up with lines of chairs for the various dignitaries and their ladies, the wooden lectern taking centre stage for the Governor of Bombay to take the salute.

A welcome breeze wafted over us as Frances pulled out a set of binoculars from her bag and brought the promenade into focus. 'Here they come,' she whispered, pointing at the far corner.

Sure enough, the crowd parted, and the Governor's open-topped Rolls Royce appeared, slowly arcing around the perimeter of the parade ground before drawing to a halt at the rostrum. Sir Frederick and Lady Sykes emerged accompanied by the newly appointed Governor-General of New Zealand; one Charles Bathurst, The Right Honourable Viscount Bledisloe, who was on his way to the Antipodes to take up his new post. The crowds enthusiastically waved their Union flags as a procession of cars carrying other ICS and Military VIPs followed in line until all the occupants were safely deposited at the rostrum and had taken their seats.

I took the binoculars from Frances and scanned the people on the rostrum then hovered, staring over their heads at a portly lady in a large, flowery, straw hat, waving her fan madly in our direction from the opposite grandstand.

'Frances, I do believe Sybil is trying to attract our attention.'

'Sybil Wetherington?'

'The very same.' I waved back and saw her dig Lord Wetherington in the ribs. He appeared to be dozing at the time and came to with a start, banging his knees on the bench ahead. I giggled and hid behind my neighbour's back for fear of being seen through Sybil's binoculars.

'Who are you two talking about?' asked Jim, leaning in for a better view.

'My cabin companion, Jim,' confirmed Frances. 'Lady Sybil Wetherington in all her glory. You might remember her more as Queen Victoria, Empress of India at the ship's Gala Ball.'

'How could I forget,' remarked Jim. 'She stood on my toes several times during the Military Two Step and with her weight, my toes have never been the same since. As I recall, she also nearly capsized the jolly-boat when we transferred her to the ss Mulbera after the fire.'

I could see Sybil in my mind's eye, standing in the bow of the tender, waving her hat at us as the small tender swayed alarmingly in the choppy waters between the two ships. 'Perhaps we should keep a low profile?'

'I doubt that is going to be possible, knowing Sybil,' said Frances, giving her a friendly wave across the divide, her attention interrupted by the sound of pipes and drums announcing the Gordon Highlanders' imminent arrival.

Within seconds, Pipe Major Fraser Cameron appeared on the parade ground, his tartan kilt swaying rhythmically, his mace twirling back and forth as he led the pipe band onto the square, their pipes and drums filling the air with the strains of *Black Bear.*

I stood and waved for all I was worth, stamping my feet in time to the music and trying to attract Fraser's attention. The band looked magnificent in the morning sunlight and all thoughts of my Highland roots rose to the surface just as they had on that cold wintry day at Landi Kotal.

Someone tugged on my dress and I turned to find a rather angry gentlemen sitting behind whose view was being completely blocked by my body.

'Oh, I'm so sorry.' I shot back into my seat, wincing and feeling a complete idiot, realising that Fraser was too far away to ever notice my head amongst the crowds. I settled back to enjoy the spectacle as regiment after regiment marched past the grandstand to take the salute.

The 13th Duke of Connaught's Own Bombay Lancers looked magnificent as they appeared on horseback, sitting erect, their blue and scarlet uniforms and striped turbans resplendent, their heads turned towards Sir Frederick and Viscount Bledisloe as they passed by the rostrum, carrying their red and white regimental pennants on tall staffs which fluttered in the breeze, above perfectly groomed steeds, all held on tight reins. I watched, feeling such pride at now being associated with the armed forces, and felt Frances dig me in the ribs. She handed over a note which had been passed along the row. I opened it, read the contents, grimaced and handed it back.

Dear Frances and Doctor Mac,

Archie and I will be having lunch at the Taj after the parade and invite you and your party to join us in the bar for drinks beforehand. It will be lovely to catch up.

Sybil

'Can we refuse?' I asked tensing, as I looked across at Sybil who was staring back.

'Hardly,' replied Frances, nodding in her direction, although I would prefer it if we didn't get roped into lunch as well.

I closed my eyes and gritted my teeth. Entering the portals of the Taj Mahal Hotel was the last thing I wanted to do, and I baulked at being reminded of my week there with Tom and all that it had entailed.

'Are you OK, Mac, you've gone white?'

I nodded, eyeing her sideways. 'Must be the heat, Frances. Do we have any water?'

'Here,' said Jim, handing over a silver hip flask, 'have a shot of brandy, much better than water.'

I drank deeply, closing my mind to the past and covertly checking my pulse rate. It was banging away at one-hundred-and-twenty beats per minute, and I inwardly swore at Sybil for spotting us amongst the crowds.

The hotel's concierge, Mustafa, beamed at me as he swung the hotel entrance door wide and allowed us to walk in. I quickened my pace hoping he hadn't recognised me and followed Jim into the bar, the thumping in my chest like a piston engine on full revs. Sybil and Archie were seated by a bay window and beckoned us over immediately they recognised us.

'My dears, what a lovely surprise. I had no idea you were coming to Bombay today. Why didn't you write, Frances, and tell me?' Sybil gave us her usual bear hug then shook hands with Jim. 'Officer Hamilton, I recall. Shouldn't you be out at sea?'

He would have answered if he could have got a word in edgeways, but Lady Wetherington was already introducing us to her husband, Archie, demanding more drinks from the waiter and relaying to one and all in earshot how I had saved her from a fate worse than death when she contracted food poisoning aboard ship at Port Said. 'She was a marvel, Archie, a real marvel, and as for Frances, well, I doubt there is a better headmistress this side of Tunbridge Wells.'

'Your wife exaggerates, Lord Wetherington,' I countered. 'By the time I arrived at her bedside she was over the worst.'

He chuckled. 'I know my wife well, Doctor Stuart-MacKenzie, and I can assure you that if she thought she was facing a fate worse than death, then I must conclude that she was.' He winked at me and picked up his crystal whisky glass.

Sybil stretched across the table and touched my arm. 'Now where's that nice Doctor Wallace at the moment. Such a charming man, Archie, with such a lovely bedside manner.'

'Will you excuse me a moment,' I said, feeling my knees shaking. 'I must just visit the Ladies' Powder Room.' I rose and headed out, crossing the reception area feeling as if I was going to faint.

'Memsahib Doctor,' shouted Mustafa, sprinting across the marble concourse, intent on gaining my attention.

'Oh hell,' I muttered under my breath and halted by the central flower display. 'Mustafa, how nice to see you again.'

'Memsahib Doctor, you come back.'

'Yes, Mustafa, I come back.'

His pillar-box topped head rocked like a metronome. 'And Doctor Tom, he here too?' He scanned the concourse.

My stomach flipped, I shook my head and continued in the direction of the lavatory at great speed. Locking a cubicle door behind me I dropped onto the toilet seat and chewed on my hankie trying to sob quietly as another panic attack threatened to overtake me. Had it only been five months since I had wandered through the corridors of this famous hotel with my head in the clouds, my arm through my lover's, his adoring looks convincing me that life was set fair and everything under control. How wrong could I have been?

I knew I needed to pull myself together before Frances came looking for me, but no matter how I tried, the same feelings of rejection and self-recrimination had me in a vice-like grip and all I could think about was Tom's confession at being married and my aborted child lying in cold earth in Vijay's garden.

'Mac, are you in there?'

I jumped up, wiped my eyes, flushed the toilet, and stepped out of the cubicle.

'Good God, Mac, you look as if you've seen a ghost.'

I rinsed my face with cool water. 'Sorry, Frances, it's being here at the Taj. Too many memories.'

'Oh, Good Lord!' Frances hit her forehead with the base of her palm. 'I completely forgot that you were here with Tom. I'm so sorry, Mac, I'm so wrapped up in Jim I never even thought about it. We should leave immediately.' She took my hankie and wiped away a stray tear.

I restrained her with my hand, thankful that she had no idea of the true depth of my distress. 'There's no need to make a fuss. We'll finish our drinks then make our escape on some pretext of meeting your girls for the picnic lunch.'

'Very well but let me look at you first.' She pinched my cheeks, suggested more lipstick and we left arm-in-arm, as if on our way to a village fete.

'Ah, there you are, Girls, we thought we had lost you,' announced Sybil as Jim and Archie stood.

'Sorry, Sybil, I think the heat got to me out on the parade ground.' Jim gave me a very dubious look and returned to his beer.

'You should carry a parasol, my dear, I never leave home without one, isn't that right Archie?' persisted Sybil.

'Er . . .'

'Now, I was just saying to our new Port Conservator here, there is a polo match at the Bombay Gymkhana Club tomorrow afternoon, and we would like you all to be our guests. Archie and I insist, don't we, dear?'

Lord Wetherington had long since given up arguing with his wife and smiled his acceptance while looking at his watch.

'That's settled then,' concluded Sybil, brooking no argument. We will leave your invitations at the Club reception. Shall we say two-thirty?'

I gulped my sherry while Frances replied on our behalf.

'We will do our best, Sybil, assuming nothing gets in the way.'

'What can possibly get in the way, Frances?'

'Well, for a start, Sybil, forty-two pubescent girls who have to be returned safely to St Saviours later this afternoon. Assuming I don't lose any of them in this Metropolis, we will be free to join you for polo tomorrow.'

'But surely, dear, you have staff to deal with that?'

'Indeed, I do, but as their headmistress, I will be held responsible if any of the little treasures go missing.'

'Quite right,' announced Lord Wetherington, preparing to depart to the dining-room.

'Now, if you'll excuse us,' concluded Frances, 'we have a Bombay Girls Grammar School celebration picnic to attend, don't we Jim?'

He spluttered into his beer, emptied his tankard, and stood. 'Indeed, Frances. Indeed, we do.'

The peace of the Civil Lines' bungalow garden was a balm to my soul, giving me the opportunity to finally be alone with my thoughts.

Having excused myself after a light lunch, on the premise of catching up on my mail, I had adjourned to the small wooden garden house, set in a thicket of trees at a distance from the bungalow, where I could allow my mind to dwell on my memories without fear of interruption. Frances had tried to object but Jim had placed his hand on her arm, nodded for them both and suggested we gather at dusk for an aperitif. Like me, I thought, as I left the confines of the house, he needed his own quality time with Frances after so many months away at sea.

I settled into an aging wicker swing-chair and took in my surroundings, absorbing the beauty of dappled sunlight casting flaxen rays across the wooden veranda as broad evergreen leaves of the Neem trees gently stirred in the light breeze. I smiled, remembering that Neem trees were commonly known as healing trees because of their medicinal qualities.

'Very apt, Mac,' I muttered, feeling my stress levels diminishing as male cicadas hummed from every tree trunk and myna birds clicked, whistled and squawked as they flitted from branch to branch, their bright yellow heads and jet-black bodies clearly visible against the verdant rich foliage.

I delighted in seeing a lucky black kitten skitter passed the veranda steps playing with a betelnut in the parched earth while a lazy star tortoise, so rare in the wild, plodded through the undergrowth beyond, searching for young, succulent vegetation to chomp.

Gradually, my mixed emotions of the morning rose to the surface and I tried to bring some perspective to my unease by asking myself some questions.

Was I jealous of Frances and Jim?

Yes, of course I was. Being around them only emphasised my self-inflicted isolation and although my mantra of *"Once bitten and twice shy"* was all very well, it didn't stop me yearning for strong masculine arms wrapping themselves around my body.

Was I sexually frustrated?

Absolutely. Tom had introduced me to a world of sexual pleasure which my body continued to crave, and no amount of professional satisfaction could ever replace the feeling of total sexual abandon in the arms of another.

Would I risk another pregnancy?

Categorically not! But that didn't stop me feeling angry at my situation, frustrated at being celibate and envious of other women who didn't have to choose between a career and motherhood.

'You're never satisfied,' I groaned, kicking the wooden balustrade as my seat swung forward on creaking metal rings, causing a black and yellow cloud of shivering wings to rise from the treetops, with loud screeches, before settling again moments later.

'What you need, Elizabeth, is a night of casual, spontaneous debauchery with some handsome lothario who will love you and leave you with no questions asked.' Aunt Karr really did have the most annoying habit of entering my head when least invited.

'And who would you suggest? Duncan Fitzpatrick.'

'Why not, dear?'

'Christ Almighty, Karr, that's rich coming from you.'

'When needs must, Elizabeth.'

'If you think I'm going to climb back into bed with that self-opinionated narcissist, you are sadly mistaken.'

'Who said anything about bed?'

'That's enough, Karr!'

'If you say so, dear, but I guarantee, he wouldn't get you pregnant.'

'Unlike Tom Wallace?'

'Exactly. You have been the one paying the price ever since, but enough is enough. All this self-flagellation isn't solving anything. You made a mistake, a big one, now accept it and get on with your life.'

'That's easier said than done.'

'Maybe, but consider this. You might well have miscarried anyway. Your mother did, twice, before she had you.'

I must have dozed because the next thing I remember was hearing Jim's dulcet tones calling from the house.

'Aperitif time, Mac.'

'Goodness, what time is it?' I called back.

'Half-past six.'

'I'm on my way.' Wandering up to the bungalow I was met by my host holding a bottle of gin in one hand and a cocktail shaker in the other. 'What's on offer?' I asked.

'Martini?'

'Um, sounds good to me.' I joined him by the terrace bar. 'Where did you learn your bartender skills?'

'Oh, in the odd Shanghai brothel over the years.' He grinned as he poured dry vermouth over gin and ice.

'Does Frances know that?' I asked, confident that Jim was pulling my leg.

'If she doesn't, she should, and if she doesn't watch out, other nubile young women will be after my body.'

'Oh, such optimism,' announced my hostess, appearing on the terrace with a tray of small dishes. 'Why do all men think they're God's gift to women, Mac?'

'Search me, Frances. Perhaps it's something to do with their latent desire for rape and pillage.'

'More likely, doting mothers and no discipline. Anyone for a samosa?'

'If you were ten years younger Miss Trotter, I would put you over my knee and give you a good spanking.' Jim was trying unsuccessfully to appear stern.

'Oooh, yes please,' she replied.

'Count me in too,' I added, watching an olive drop into my frosted glass.

'Pity Ruby isn't here,' mused Frances, placing the dishes on the bar. 'Then you'd have three of us to chastise, Officer Hamilton.'

'Major Stokes was right. You three are a coven of witches.' Jim bit into his hot samosa. 'Ow!'

I studied them both from my bar stool, feeling so at home in their company. 'Speaking of Major Stokes, I still think there was something odd about his death.'

'Really?' Frances paused between mouthfuls.

'Yes. Having heard all the evidence against Montgomery and Blackthorn during the trial in Delhi and knowing that the Major was covertly investigating them during the passage, it's not impossible to imagine that they started the fire in his cabin on the night of the Gala Ball.'

'You could be right, Mac. Major Stokes was quite capable of holding his drink. After a career in the Army, I imagine his liver was well pickled. The chances of him falling asleep with a lit cheroot in his hand and burning himself to death seems pretty unlikely to me.' Frances sipped her martini. 'What do you think?' Jim was suddenly very serious.

'I think Montgomery and Blackthorn found out that the Major was working for the British police and decided to silence him.'

'Did any of this come out in the trial? Frances wasn't really sure when I asked her.'

I shook my head and consumed a second samosa then gave a potted history of the court case. 'Don't you think it's odd that neither were in their cabin during the fire?'

Jim recharged our glasses, his mind retracing events of that night. 'Very odd. They were nowhere to be seen when we mustered the second-class passengers on the promenade deck and counted heads. It was Salvatore who found them in one of the bathroom cubicles sharing a bottle of whisky.'

'Didn't you think to report it?' asked Frances.

'At the time, I had my hands full with hysterical passengers all demanding to know what was happening to their personal belongings and it never entered my head.'

'Why should it? None of us knew at that stage that Major Stokes was an undercover agent for the police.' We sat in silence for a few moments.

'I do know Tom questioned Salvatore once we arrived in Bombay and sent him to Calcutta to make a statement to the police,' said Jim.

'I know, I met Salvatore outside the police station as he arrived. The Police Commissioner was investigating the drug cartel and had built up quite a file. Salvatore must have had some evidence regarding the drugs. Commissioner Tegart eventually charged the pair with drug-smuggling, rape and murder, but despite Ruby's evidence, there was not enough proof to bring in a verdict of murder.'

'Pity,' said Frances, folding her napkin. 'They should be hanged for their crimes.'

'Don't worry, Frances, if other prisoners don't kill them then syphilis certainly will.'

Chapter Twenty-Two

I had never been to a polo match, so I questioned Jim about it over coffee the next morning while Frances set to, re-organising the kitchen to her liking.

'I can't say I know much about its history, Mac, having spent most of my time at sea, but from what I recall, there are two teams of four riders, each with long mallets, and the object is to drive a rubber ball down a grass field and between two goal posts from the back of a horse. Each team has a string of very expensive polo ponies and the game is split into six chukkas.

'What's a chukka?'

'It's a period of play. I think it last for seven minutes. During half-time, spectators walk out onto the pitch and press the divots down with their feet.'

'Do you know which teams are playing today?'

'All Lord Wetherington said was that the current home team was the King's Own Royal Hussars. As for the opponents, I've no idea.'

'Well, we'll soon find out.' I could hear all sorts of banging and crashing coming from the kitchen window. 'Does your landlady approve of Frances re-arranging her kitchen?'

'What she doesn't know, she won't miss, Mac. The Arbuthnots are away in England until October, so Fran has plenty of time to re-organise things.'

'Will you get up to Simla in the summer?'

'I expect so, but I'll know more tomorrow. What about you?'

'I'm waiting to hear from my supervisors, Agnes Scott and Sir Peter Bonham-Cavendish. There's a Women's Hospital in Simla called The Lady Reading, so I imagine I will be seconded to them for most of the season.'

'Mac, there is something else I'd like to say.'

Jim's voice sounded tentative and my stomach muscles clench.

'I want you to know that Tom was very genuine in his feelings for you during the passage.'

'That's OK, Jim, there's no need to . . .'

'No, let me finish. I've known Tom for many years, and he is the most loyal and honourable man I have ever met.'

'So I understand. Frances told me at Christmas about his marriage to his sister-in-law. Enid, isn't that her name?'

He nodded but kept his silence, allowing me to continue.

'At the time, I felt badly used and abused. Any woman would, but on reflection, I guess he's not the only man to take on his deceased brother's family in wartime. Come to think of it, here in India, it's a cultural requirement.'

'Maybe, but Muslims take on many wives, including their sisters-in-law. Englishmen don't have that privilege.'

'Are you implying that Tom is hamstrung, being English?'

'I'm afraid so, Mac. This marriage is a sham, but Tom is too loyal to do anything about it and just keeps on trying to make the best of things for the sake of his nephews.'

'Where is he now?'

'Back at sea and probably wondering where it all went wrong.'

I wondered what he would think if he knew I had aborted his child. 'Well, we can't change history, Jim, so I don't dwell on what might have been.'

'Are you happy, Mac?'

'Yes, in a way, and my work keeps me busy.'

Frances's head appeared at the kitchen window. 'More coffee, anyone?'

The interruption was well timed. 'No thanks, or I won't sleep tonight. What about you, Jim?'

'No, I'm done too.'

I carried the cups and saucers to the window and peered in. 'Happy now?'

Frances looked very pleased with herself. 'I must say, Mac, the owner of this establishment obviously never stepped foot in this kitchen. You could write your name in the dirt at the back of the cupboards.'

'Colonial ladies never dream of getting their hands dirty, Frances, they have staff.'

'Then all I can say is, they should be shot.'

'I have the very weapon if you wish to borrow it. It's hanging in the lobby at St Saviours.'

The Bombay Gymkhana Clubhouse, located on the south of the city by the Fort, had the appearance of a huge English cricket pavilion, the two-storey, red-and-white gabled building, stretching forever across the front of a manicured lawn would have put any British county ground to shame. Inaugurated in 1875, this exclusive Gentlemen's Club had become the sport and social centre of Victorian colonial society, where the cream of the ICS and Military could drink, dine and play sport away from prying eyes. The extensive facilities included cricket, rugby, hockey, tennis, badminton, equestrian sports, a gun-club and an Olympic-sized swimming pool in the grounds, whilst inside members could play billiards, snooker and table-tennis or entertain their business colleagues and friends in the restaurant, bar or private meeting rooms. Women, of course, were only tolerated at certain events like their Wednesday evening Ladies' Nights, held in the club gardens. It was a token gesture to the members wives and girlfriends who were expected to know their place. Being seen and not heard was the order of the day for the 'Fishing Fleet' and, as usual, I hated it.

Entering the building in our finery, I couldn't help whispering derogatory comments under my breath about pompous, superior men with high ideals and small appendages.

Frances decided to put a stop to my ranting. 'Now, Mac, keep your temper. We are here to enjoy a game of polo, not to change the world order, so behave.'

I saluted her as the doorman bowed his head in greeting, ignored us completely, asked Jim for his name and checked through his invitation list.

'Officer Hamilton, the invitations, they are here.' He pulled three small white embossed cards from under the members' ledger and handed them to his male guest. Frances dug me in the ribs. 'Welcome, Sahib. Lord Wetherington is on the terrace finishing lunch. Please to follow me.'

We mere women were left to bring up the rear, the snub adding to my angst. Archie Wetherington, thankfully, was better mannered and pulled out a chair for both Frances and me then ordered drinks all round. I sat back, crossed my legs and took in my surroundings, settling on a doubles match taking place on Court 1.

'Do you play tennis, Doctor Stuart-MacKenzie?' asked a chinless wonder sitting alongside who, it would appear from the introductions, was something big in Bombay's Public Works.

'Infrequently, I'm afraid,' I responded. 'My preference is golf, riding and obliterating misogyny.'

Frances kicked me under the table and leant in. 'Doctor Stuart-MacKenzie is researching the effects of tropical diseases on obstetrics and gynaecology at the WMS.'

'Oh, how interesting.' He was about as interested as a sloth in a one-hundred-yard sprint race.

'Yes', I said, too cross to be polite. 'The Public Works Department could eradicate such killer diseases as cholera and typhoid overnight if it paid more attention to improving sanitation for the masses and less playing cricket. Don't you agree?'

He looked as if he was about to have a seizure, mumbled some unintelligible excuse, and the last we saw of him was his backside disappearing through the clubhouse patio doors.

'Mac, you're impossible.'

'And they're a disgrace to the Empire, Frances.'

'Maybe, but this is hardly the time or place to say so.' Jim, standing to her left, decided to occupy the recently vacated chair.

'For the rest of this afternoon, Jim, you do not leave Mac's side and if she dares utter the word *misogyny* once more, you are to waltz her out of the door and take her back to the Civil

Lines. Is that understood?' She turned and smiled at Sybil on the other side of the large circular table.

'Yes, Ma'am. Anything you say, Ma'am,' he replied, doffing his cap. 'But what happens if I mention it?'

'You could be looking for someone else to massage your libido, Officer Hamilton.'

'Ooops!' I said and burst out laughing. Sybil, having no idea what the joke was about, joined in.

'Mac, is that you?'

I froze. A very familiar voice cut through my brain like a scalpel through flesh. Slowly turning my head, I was met with pristinely polished mahogany-brown leather riding boots, long, jodhpur-covered muscular thighs, an open-necked white, monogrammed polo-shirt, a finely chiselled chin, sensuous mouth, kohl-black eyes edged with long thick eyelashes and a mass of tussled Indian locks. My eyes were not deceiving me, standing, towering over me, was none other than Prince Vijay Kumar Singh II, Jhalanpur's future Maharaja, in all his glory.

'Vijay, what a surprise.'

He bent, took my hand in his, brushed my knuckles with his soft lips, then lifted me to my feet. 'Are you here for the polo?'

'Yes, as it happens. I assume you are too?' I nodded to his jodhpurs.

'I hope so, or the Princely States Polo Team will be without their Captain.'

He turned to Frances. 'And how is Florence Nightingale today?' He regally bowed, laughter lines creasing the wrinkles at his temples as he recalled her character at the ship's Gala Ball. 'I trust India compares favourably with the Crimea?'

'Indeed, it does, Your Highness.' Frances was not at all fazed.

'Excellent, though how you managed to get this reprobate through the doors of the Gymkhana Club is quite beyond me.' He chuckled and shook Jim's hand enthusiastically. 'How the devil are you Jim, and where's your ship?'

'I'm extremely well, Sir, and the ship has finally sailed without me.'

'Then that is P&O's loss and India's gain. What is your plan now?'

'I'm about to take up the post of Deputy Conservator for the Bombay Port Trust, responsible for the administration and operation of the port.'

'Rather different from navigating P&O passenger-liners across the world's oceans.'

'Indeed.'

'Well, good luck in your new career, you will probably need it, if the present chaos is anything to go by.' He placed his hand firmly under my elbow. 'If you'll excuse us for five minutes, Mac and I have some outstanding business to discuss.' He looked across to the other guests at our table, smiling particularly at Sybil. 'Lord Wetherington, Ladies and Gentlemen, enjoy the polo.'

Before Archie could get to his feet, I was being gently manoeuvred along the covered terrace to the end of the Pavilion then into a room at the side of the building marked '*private*'. My mind was doing cartwheels as he closed the door and lowered his backside onto a solid oak conference table, allowing his feet to swing in mid-air.

'Mac, Ruby tells me that you were very shocked and disappointed at learning of our relationship. It goes without saying, this genuinely saddens me. Am I really such a disappointment to you?'

I wasn't sure how to react. He didn't need my approval to be unfaithful to his wife, yet he appeared to be asking for just that. 'Vijay, even accepting that you're a polygamist by culture and religion, I cannot condone what you did back in Port Said.'

'What did I do that was so terrible?'

I really didn't want to have this conversation, particularly here at the Bombay Gymkhana Club. 'I prefer not to say.'

'Why?'

'Because it's not my place to criticise you. OK?'

'No, it's not OK. You are Ruby's closest friend here in India and I would not want my actions to cause a problem between you.'

He was obviously not going to let the matter drop so I decided to throw caution to the wind. 'Vijay, you chose to put your own desires before the health of your wife and son, and in my opinion, being an Indian Prince is no justification for running roughshod over those who love you . . .'

He drummed his fingers on the table-top but allowed me to finish.

'Had I been a naive bystander on that ship, such behaviour would have been none of my business, but unfortunately it became my business, didn't it?'

'If you say so.'

His glib reply shocked me. 'I do. While you took your mistress to Cairo's Shepheard's Hotel, I was doing everything I could to save the life of your only son and heir.'

'For which, I am eternally grateful.'

'Not good enough, Vijay, so stop hiding behind fatuous platitudes.' A red mist was forming before my eyes. 'You left your child's destiny in the hands of a stranger, and took your physician along for the ride, apparently ignoring the needs of your pregnant wife, who was left without any medical protection whatsoever.' What did you expect to happen if she haemorrhaged?'

He gulped at my graphic suggestion. 'But you don't understand, Mac.'

'Oh, believe me, I understand only too well, and frankly, I'm sick and tired of witnessing men treating women as vassals and pregnancy with utter contempt. Did you honestly believe that a bottle of perfume would placate my professional opinion of your lack of care? If you did, then you were wrong.'

'I see that, now, Mac, but at the time, I had little understanding of who you were or what was going on.'

'I find that hard to believe, Your Highness. I know that Ruby was oblivious to the situation, but you would have been told that your wife was suffering a miscarriage immediately it became obvious, I could hear my voice rising and paused to count to ten, 'but you did nothing. Why?'

His shoulders lifted as he shook his head, his expression grave.

'Perhaps if you had been the one facing potential death from a spontaneous abortion instead of Princess

Darshwanabai, you would have understood the gravity of the situation better.'

Vijay searched my face for some pity, but I felt only contempt.

'Your wife had been trying for years to give you a son an heir, and her heightened stress-levels at the thought of losing the child didn't make my job any easier. It was a miracle that I managed to save the foetus under the circumstances.' My voice splintered. 'But it was all for nothing in the end.' I leant my head against the wall and closed my eyes, the image of the lifeless bloody embryo lying in my hand merging with that of my own son weeks later, weighing heavily on my heart.

'Shush, Mac, you've said enough.' Vijay placed his broad hands on my shoulders and waited until my personal remorse had dissipated. 'You were my son's angel, fighting against impossible odds to save his life and you were successful. It was not your fault he subsequently died. It wasn't you who killed him, but my wife's fear of fire.'

His hands felt so powerful, his fingers digging into my skin, as if trying to physically drive my guilt away.

'Meanwhile,' he continued, 'I was his devil incarnate and I will live with that for the rest of my life.' He moved to the window and looked out across the cricket pitch almost talking to himself. 'One day, Mac, I will find the right way to compensate you in his memory. Until then, know that the Jhalanpur family are forever in your debt, no matter what the outcome, and I ask you not to walk away from your friendship with either Ruby, the Princess or me. We would all be the poorer without it.

'If I can't respect you, then how can we be friends?' I murmured, feeling utterly drained.

'I must do whatever I can to win back your respect.' He turned, a wry smile crossing his lips. 'Would annihilating the King's Own Royal Hussars at polo today go some way to achieving that goal?' His tentative quip helped ease the tension between us.

'As long as you don't fall off your horse in the process, I replied, sighing.

'If I do, will you be there to patch me up?'

I nodded, relieved that we had cleared the air between us.

'Then I will attack with gusto, confident that I am in good hands.'

He saw me back to my seat, bowed to one and all and strode away across the lawn towards the stables and his string of thoroughbred polo ponies.

Watching him go, I wondered, not for the first time, how odd our friendship was and where it would lead.

The game was riveting. Pounding hooves thundered past, sounding like the Charge of the Light Brigade, the riders digging their heels into the flanks of their powerful steeds to drive them on. With spittle flying and grunts and groans left in their wake, the horses wheeled and turned, foaming at the mouth, as wooden mallets clashed together and a small, hard ball was whipped from the ground and shot across the pitch like a cannonball across a battlefield.

The horsemen in their tight jodhpurs, short-sleeved shirts and khaki pith-helmets lunged from their saddles like circus acrobats as they galloped at full speed towards their opponent's goal, flicking the ball between the posts to a roar of approval from the crowd.

'It's a goal!' I shouted, as Vijay tipped his hat to me and the teams changed ends during a three-minute break. I was so close to the action I could smell the horse's breath and I was enthralled, having never seen anything like it and was hoarse from shouting encouragement to Vijay and his team.

By the third chukka, the pitch looked as if it had been hit by shrapnel, divots lying at all angles from contact with the horses' hooves and I still had no idea who was winning. Half-time was announced with a shrill whistle and I joined the others, in a line of human garden-rollers, stomping down divots across the field of play while the competitors caught their breath, changed their mounts, and gathered their strength for the next chukka.

'Who's winning?' I asked Lord Wetherington as I returned to my seat.

'The Princes, by one goal, dear. Should be a great second half.'

I caught sight of Vijay's syce in the pony lines tightening a thoroughbred's saddle, grabbing the reigns, and leading the animal towards his master, then bending, hands clasped, as Vijay's booted foot stepped onto his rough palms. In one fluid movement the Prince dropped onto his horse's saddle and slid his toes into the metal stirrups as the horse neighed and shook its head. Patting its neck with his leather-gloved hand, Vijay grabbed his mallet, tightened his chinstrap and turned, calling to his fellow princes, then jabbed his heels into his mount's flank and trotted towards the middle of the polo-field.

The audience grew quiet as the eight horses and riders mingled in a disorganised tight-knit pack waiting for the umpire to roll the ball between a mass of equine legs, rather like the scrumhalf in a rugby game, and the fourth chukka was again in play. Back and forth they went, first one side lobbing the ball down-field then the other up-field, horses chasing horses, mallets blocking mallets, riders jarring legs as the seconds counted down.

'Goal!' shouted Jim, and a white flag shot into the air at the bottom-end of the field. The Royal Hussars had scored. I was becoming desperate.

Seconds later the Prince's team were awarded a penalty and Vijay smashed the ball through the goalposts from forty-yards-out.

I crossed my fingers, the teams swopped ends and they gathered once more for the throw-in. Vijay was the first to strike the ball which ripped across the grass to his number two who whacked it on, swerved in a left-hand arc as Vijay tore past, dropped his right hip out of the saddle, placed his mallet head behind the rolling ball, flicked his wrist and drove it between his mount's galloping legs and diagonally across the goal mouth. I held my breath and watched as it bounced off the left-hand post and tumbled into the outfield between the posts.

'YES!' I screamed, jumping for joy. A whistle blew and another three-minute break gave me chance to get my breath back.

'It's a wonder they don't kill each other,' announced Frances, wafting her face with a crumpled programme.

'I'd rather be the rider than the horse,' said Jim. 'At least you have a clue where you're going.'

While we waited, I scanned the field with Frances's binoculars in the hope of seeing someone famous, only to find the lens filled with the tall, dominant frame of Duncan, talking animatedly to the umpire on the other side of the pitch. I wondered what he was doing here as I followed his progress back along the field to where a party of young men stood waiting expectantly. Veterinary students, I concluded, as he explained some point of the game to them then raised his own binoculars, brought me into focus and waved. It was time for the sixth and final chukka.

Within minutes, the Hussars had won a penalty when Vijay's Number 3 blocked an opposing rider's progress at the sixty-yard line, but their Captain missed the goal mouth. With only two minutes left the Princely States Number 4 back-hit the ball down the centre of field and Duncan appeared at my side.

'We meet again, Mac.'

'Shush,' I said, watching Vijay and an opposing Hussar racing after the ball like two greyhounds after a rabbit. Vijay dropped out of sight over the right-side of his saddle, only his backside visible to the spectators, and swung back his mallet as both horses hammered passed me at great speed. The crack of wood on wood rang in my ears and Vijay's mallet flew into the air as the Hussar yanked on his horse's bit and the animal broke to the left.

'NO!' I screamed as the full force of the horse's shoulder smacked into Vijay's mount, driving it sideways and off-balance. The impact catapulted Vijay out of his saddle, his left foot trapped in the stirrup and I watched in horror as the thoroughbred hit the ground with a stomach-clenching thud, Vijay's body disappearing under the flank of his horse as it rolled over his legs.

'DUNCAN!' I yelled and left my seat, racing at top speed for the thirty-yard-line. The mount was on its back screaming in pain, thrashing the air with its hooves and in danger of kicking Vijay in the head. The Prince was out cold, his left leg bent under itself, white bone protruding from the thigh, his throat half-choking from the strap of his pith-helmet which had been dragged back on impact.

Prioritise, I demanded inwardly as the horse flailed around us. Crouching as low as I could I got my fingers under the buckle, snapped it open and dragged the helmet off Vijay's head then began slowly easing his upper torso away from the stallion's dangerous hooves, praying I was not adding to any spinal injury. Mayhem reigned all around me as I checked Vijay's vital signs while the horse's tortuous cries were in danger of bursting my eardrums.

'What can I do?' shouted Jim, diving down beside me, his practical words bringing a semblance of order to the chaos.

'I need splints, bandages, alcohol, a stretcher and a sharp knife. DUNCAN!'

Jim pulled a sheath knife from his trouser pocket. 'Will this do?'

Once a sailor always a sailor, I thought, as I grabbed the instrument and felt fresh air where Jim had just been. Vijay's pulse was erratic, but he wasn't dead yet, so I levered his clenched teeth apart, rammed my fingers down his throat and checked he wasn't swallowing his own tongue.

'Mother of God, will you give me room. Now, shift yourselves before the bloody horse does more damage to itself and the Prince.' That familiar deep Irish voice bellowing orders with such authority helped keep me focused.

'And who are you to give orders around here,' yelled an upper-crust voice to my right.

'A bloody veterinary surgeon. Now get out of my way.'

Leaning my ear against Vijay's mouth I sensed hot breath on my cheek and moved on, lifting his eyelids and closely examining his black pupils. One was dilated, the other not. Vijay was concussed and in need of very careful handling, and for a split second I had no idea how to cope.

In the corner of my eye, I saw the burgeoning crowds of spectators, team members and staff part and a young, uniformed officer charge through with stewards bringing up the rear carrying a stretcher.

'Right men, get the Prince onto the stretcher immediately and let's get him to hospital. Madam, move away please. Your ministrations are probably not helping.' A masculine elbow shoved me out of the way.

The sudden violent crack of a pistol shot reverberated through my brain allowing it to function on all cylinders as a communal gasp of horror punctuated the deathly silence around me. 'What the hell do you think you are doing,' I hollered, grabbing the man by his jacket and pulling him off Vijay. DON''T YOU DARE MOVE HIM, you imbecile.'

'I beg your pardon, Madam. I'm a doctor and you will keep quiet. Now, let go of my jacket.'

'Like hell I will. I'm also a doctor and this man stays exactly where he is until his femur is realigned.'

'Are you deranged, Madam? This pitch is not an operating theatre, and you have no idea what you are talking about.'

I looked about me for support, terrified that Vijay's thigh muscles would spasm before the bone could be reset and saw Jim holding back the stewards with his outstretched arms while Duncan had his hand firmly on the doctor's collar.

'That she does, pal, and if it were me on the ground right now with a shattered thighbone, I wouldn't want a toffee-nosed twat like you giving orders.'

'How dare you insult me!' He pointed to Vijay. 'This man is badly injured and needs a hospital right now!'

'Doctor Stuart-MacKenzie, what do you plan to do?'

The voice, so deep and cultured took me straight back to the Jhalanpur Suite on the ss Narkunda. I looked up and found Prince Kapoor Dhawan staring down at me, his flowing robes, grey beard, deep amber eyes and regal presence commanding order in the chaotic scene around Vijay's body.

'Your Highness, thank goodness you're here. Your nephew has a compound fracture of the femur which needs realigning immediately if he is ever to walk again.'

'Is there no other choice?'

'No, Your Highness, I'm afraid there is not. It will take too long to get to St George's Hospital and by then the muscles will have contracted and shortened. This is his only chance of making a complete recovery.' I could hear a bell clanging somewhere in the distance and bit my lowered lip, drawing blood.

'Then you must proceed.'

'But, Your Highness,' argued the doctor.

'You heard his Lordship,' said Duncan, pushing the young medic to one side. 'Right, Mac, what can I do?'

With lots of tutting and head shaking, the medic stormed back through the crowd, shouting back to me across the divide, 'Be it on your own head, Madam.'

I ignored him and checked again for any deposits of blood appearing in Vijay's mouth, nose or ears. They were clear.

'Help me straighten his left leg, then cut the stitching on his boot so we can get it off.' I grabbed the sheath knife from the ground and exposed the vicious blade. 'Jim, I will need your help too.'

Seconds later, the knife flashed and the stitches sprang apart as if unzipped, exposing more red-stained jodhpur. Duncan eased the wrecked leather boot away from Vijay's heel, then tossed it over his shoulder while I examined the white bone jutting through the skin and cotton twill, like the mast of a sunken yacht, as blood seeped from broken capillaries and veins and puddled around my hand.

'Thank God there is no evidence of a punctured artery,' I muttered and cupped my palm over the injury, as Jim knelt by my side.

'What's next, Cailin?' asked Duncan.

'Slit the jodhpurs to expose his flesh but be careful.' He nodded and raised the knife. 'Jim, can you check Vijay's breathing, and do either of you have any alcohol?'

Jim dug into his breast pocket and handed over a hipflask. I heard the material tear exposing Vijay's thigh and I followed, liberally pouring the contents of the flask over the flesh and wound.

'Let's hope that sterilizes it.' I poured the remainder over my hands.

'You smell like a distillery,' said Duncan, wiping the bloodied blade on the grass and snapping the sheath-knife shut.

'His breathing is rapid and shallow, Mac,' announced Jim as Vijay began to groan.

'Then we must be quick. 'Duncan, you take his calf. Jim, we're going to use traction to try and realign the ends of the femur bone while we still can, so I want you holding his pelvis down. Our actions will be excruciating for the Prince, but we can't do anything about that right now. Hopefully the intense pain will knock him out.' I scanned the crowd. 'Who has the medical box and splints?' Two stewards stepped forward.

I rubbed sweat from my eyes with the back of my hand. 'Whatever you do, Jim, don't let go until I say. Are you ready Duncan?'

'I am that.' He wrapped his hands around Vijay's calf, his muscular arms already taut, his eyes locked onto my face. Then he winked.

I ripped a dressing from its packaging with my teeth and placed it over the fracture-wound. 'Right, slowly. No jerking. On the count of three. One . . . Two . . . Three.'

Time stood still as the lower section of the femur retracted, painstakingly pulling back as the two ends of the bone appeared to move in opposite directions. I could feel them grating against each other under the dressing.

'That's good,' I confirmed, as Duncan heaved, and Jim pressed down on Vijay's pelvis. 'Don't stop.' I lifted the dressing. 'Not much further.'

'Jesus, Mary and Joseph,' groaned Duncan, every sinew straining while Jim gritted his teeth and fought against Vijay who was trembling with pain.

I ignored them both, concentrating on my own job and following the lower bone until I felt it sink. 'Hold Fast!' I shouted, one knee pressing down hard against the thigh, keeping the leg horizontal, and grabbed clean dressings and bandages with my free hand. 'Duncan, when I say, slowly release tension at your end, and Jim, for Christ's sake, don't move. OK, let's do it. NOW.'

Duncan slowly released his grip on Vijay's leg and the powerful quadricep muscles surrounding the femur contracted.

'Right, Duncan, raise his leg off the floor about six inches using his ankle, but don't let the knee bend.'

With the leg slightly elevated and my hand still giving downward pressure onto the fractured bone, I covered the wound with more dressing, then wrapped the thigh in bandages, pulling the knot tight using one hand and my teeth.

'OK, lower his leg and you can both relax.' I pulled the splints along the grass and positioned them either side of the leg and with Duncan's help, strapped them tightly together.

'Jim, Is Vijay still breathing?'

'Yes, Mac, shallow but definitely breathing,' he replied, listening to Vijay's chest.

'Thank the Lord, for that,' I murmured, and checked the Prince's pulse, mouth and ears once more. Sitting back on my heels, my hands shaking, I took stock. 'I have no idea if the Prince has a spinal injury, so we have to be extremely careful when we move him onto the stretcher.'

Concerned spectators were beginning to crowd us again, making it difficult to move.

'For pity's sake, give the doctor some air,' demanded Jim, as I locked onto Prince Kapoor Dhawan's eyes and confirmed all was well with a nod. He smiled at me, then turned to face the crowd and pushed them away with his bejewelled hands. The circle instantly widened.

With sinews taut and arm muscles straining, Vijay was carried at speed across the polo-field towards the clubhouse, Prince Dhawan Kapoor keeping pace at my side as my fingers continued to check Vijay's pulse.

'Doctor Mac, we meet again.' His Rajput voice prompted so many memories.

I nodded, my eyes watering.

'The Prince's physician has gone ahead to the hospital. You will stay with my nephew until we get there?'

'Try keeping me away, Your Highness. The Prince is in shock and unconscious and I have no idea if there are any spinal or brain injuries. The leather strap of his helmet was caught around his neck when he hit the ground which has caused some ligature constriction and could have impacted on his vertebrae.' I handed over the dented pith helmet, grabbed from the field as we left.

'What about the horse?'

'Dead,' gasped Duncan, his knuckles white as they gripped the stretcher. 'Shot in the temple by me. Right fetlock and cannon bone shattered, ribs crushed and a suspected punctured lung.'

'Who are you, Sahib?'

'Captain Duncan Fitzpatrick of the British Army Veterinary Corp and Doctor of Veterinary Surgery.'

I watched Jim's eyebrows arch from his position on the other side.

'I see,' grunted the Prince.

'Duncan, allow me to introduce you to Prince Dhawan Kapoor, Prince Vijay Kumar Singh's uncle by marriage.' I sounded like a pair of fire bellows. We were now yards from the clubhouse.

'Pleased to meet you, Your Highness, but, if you don't mind, we can discuss the death of the Prince's horse later. Right now, the priority is to get your nephew into an operating theatre.'

We continued through the crowded lobby and out to the ambulance on the other side, its rear doors wide open awaiting the patient. In one smooth movement the stretcher bearers slid the litter inside and the driver revved the engine as Prince Dhawan Kapoor and I jumped aboard, leaving Duncan and Jim to slam the doors shut.

'We'll meet you at the hospital, Mac,' shouted Jim, as the interior darkened and I flopped onto a bench running along the length of the interior, noticing for the first time that my dress was covered in Vijay's blood.

'What are his chances, Doctor Mac?' Pressure lines furrowed Prince Dhawan Kapoor's forehead as he clung on for dear life.

'He'll live, but I'm not sure about his left leg. With luck and careful nursing, it can mend, assuming it does not get infected, but he will need constant physiotherapy which will take weeks and his leg may end up shorter than before which will result in a permanent limp. As for his head and spine, only X-rays can provide the answers.'

'Are you staying in Bombay?'

'No. I came to the city for yesterday's Governor's Parade. I'm working in Poona at the Seva Sadan Women's Hospital, and you can get a message to me there or at St Saviours School for Young Ladies. I'll be remaining in Poona for another few weeks before returning to Delhi.'

'Very well.' His shoulder bounced off the ambulance wall as the vehicle cornered at a steep angle, the bell clanging loudly demanding attention. 'I only wish we didn't keep meeting in such dreadful circumstances.'

'I'm afraid, this time it's my fault.' Pain shot through my chest and I thumped my breastbone. 'I told the Prince not to fall off his horse before the match. How could I have been so stupid.' I looked at Vijay, his head lolled on one side, his lips white.

'You are not to blame, Doctor Mac. Polo is a dangerous sport and accidents happen. The Hussar should never have veered his horse the way he did. There are rules and he ignored them in his determination to stop the Prince from scoring.'

I shook my head, desperate to believe him but convinced I had jinxed Vijay's game.

'Yet again, you have been there in my family's hour of need, and we have no right to expect you to take on such responsibility.'

'I wanted to . . .' The ambulance ground to a standstill and the rear doors flew open. Instantly the medic in me took over.'

'Take great care moving the patient,' I ordered as I climbed down. 'The Prince may have a spinal injury and has lost a lot of blood.' A surgeon in green theatre-gown and trousers walked towards me as nursing staff gently pulled the stretcher onto a gurney.

'Doctor Metcalfe,' said the middle-aged Englishman, his hand outstretched.

'Doctor Stuart-Mackenzie . . .' I shook it and followed the gurney. '. . . pulse faint, breathing shallow, patient unconscious and in shock, potential spinal injury at neck and back, compound fracture of femur, now re-aligned, no pain-relief given . . .' and on I went, relaying Vijay's injuries and treatments like a metronome as we walked through the swing-doors into Casualty. 'He fell from his horse during a polo-match with his foot still caught in the stirrup. The animal rolled across his left leg and his helmet almost throttled him.'

'Very well,' replied Doctor Metcalfe. 'I'll take over from here.' I could feel his breath on my cheek as he leant in and lowered his voice. 'You are also in shock, Doctor Stuart-Mackenzie, and you're covered in blood. Are you injured?'

'No. I'll be fine now I know he is in your professional care. What I need is a stiff drink and a change of clothing.'

'Your Highness,' announced the surgeon, turning to Prince Dhawan Kapoor, please take care of this remarkable young woman, who has my deepest respect. Your nephew, meanwhile, will be my responsibility and I can assure you I will do everything in my power to restore him to full health.' With that, his gave a quick nod of the head and rushed towards the cubicle where Vijay was now surrounded by medical staff and equipment. 'Sister, do we have a pulse?'

'Come, Doctor Mac, let's leave them to their work.'

Broad hands wrapped around the skin of my elbow and I was eased towards the swing doors just as they bounced open and Duncan appeared, giving a good impression of a bull elephant in full charge, a whisky flask held in his palm.

'Here, drink this and don't stop till you get to the bottom.'

The alcohol singed my oesophagus as it flowed to my stomach.

'Perhaps we should adjourn to the waiting room?' suggested the Prince and he released me.

'To be sure, Your Eminence. Mac, come here.'

Duncan led me out of Casualty where Jim and Frances were waiting.

'I will be in touch, Doctor Stuart-MacKenzie,' said the Prince, very formally, 'as soon as I have news. Forgive me, but I must return to my nephew's side. On behalf of the Jhalanpur family, thank you once again. We are forever in your debt.' He made a namaste and I watched as the flowing white and gold-edged robes disappeared into the interior.

'Mac, are you alright? How is Vijay?' Frances's voice was strangely shaky, matching my knees.

'Let go, Darlin', I've got you.' Duncan buried my head into his heaving chest. 'For pity's sake, release the tension or you'll burst.'

His familiar masculine smell filled my nostrils, his voice massaged my pain, and his body penetrated my defences like the Israelites' trumpets at Jericho. I capitulated, all attempts at resistance gone and I sobbed, my whole being basking in the sheer relief of being smothered once more in the embrace of a man who I had once loved. No words were said, there was no need, Duncan's actions spoke louder than words.

Eventually, he raised my chin from his wet shirtfront with his cupped fingers, lowered his forehead to mine and covered my mouth with his. All those years of bitter rejection suddenly lost their relevance and I clung to him like a limpet, desperate for his strength.

'As you gathered,' he said, lifting his head, 'my name is Duncan Fitzpatrick, and I've loved this feisty medic since we met at Edinburgh University back in the day.'

'And as I said in the taxi, I'm Frances Trotter and one of Mac's closest friends,' came the reply. 'It's a real pleasure to meet you, Duncan.'

'Likewise, Frances, and I must say, your man here is as calm as a cucumber in an emergency.'

'Lots of training,' replied Jim, finally shaking Duncan's hand. 'Jim Hamilton, ex-Navigation Officer in the Merchant Navy and soon to be heading Bombay's Port Authority.'

'Well, I'll be.'

It felt good to be encompassed in this triangle of care. Wiping my eyes, I interjected. 'What time's our train?'

'Seven-thirty,' replied Frances, handing me a wet hankie to clean my hands from the blood stains. 'It's the same train you arrived on two weeks ago.'

'What time is it now?'

Jim looked at his watch. 'Four-twenty.'

'Well, there's nothing more I can do here. Vijay is in the capable hands of Surgeon Metcalfe of the IMS and all we can do now is pray.' I pulled my skirt out and examined the mess which was my favourite outfit.

'I suggest we get back to the bungalow and sort you out, then have dinner close to Victoria Railway Terminus.' Frances was back in charge. 'Duncan, would you care to join us, you look as if you could do with a stiff drink yourself.'

I was about to argue but Duncan got their first.

'To be sure, that would be delightful, Frances.' He looked down at me from his great height. 'Wouldn't it, Mac?'

Having just been in a very visible clinch with my Irish ex-lover, it hardly seemed magnanimous to refuse, which was just as well, because Duncan had me in a firm possessive grip and I was being propelled towards to the main hospital entrance with the afternoon sunrays piercing my eyeballs like hot flames.

'By the way, Medic,' Duncan announced as he raised his right arm above his head and hailed a passing taxi. 'You never bothered to ask me about my shoulder, but I'm pleased to tell you that it's as right as rain.'

'Why, what was wrong with it?' asked Frances, being helped into the vehicle by Jim.

'Don't ask, Frances,' I replied, climbing in after her. 'You really don't want to know.'

Chapter Twenty-Three

'Right, Elizabeth Stuart-MacKenzie, I want to know where, when and how you became the apple of Captain Duncan Fitzpatrick's eye, and why you have never mentioned him before . . .'

I stared out of the train compartment window at nothing but the black night, my mind fixated on how the operation was going on Vijay's leg at St George's Hospital.

' . . . He was obviously a serious part of your life in Edinburgh, and you cannot deny he is extremely good looking, highly qualified in the veterinary field and every girl's dream of a husband, so why are you looking as if you have swallowed a surgical swab?'

'It's a long story, Frances, and not one I'm particularly proud of.' An army officer walked past our door and stared in, decided against joining us, and went on his way. 'However, this is neither the time nor place for such a discussion so, if you don't mind, I'll postpone giving you the sordid details until we get back to St Saviours.'

Although we had the carriage to ourselves, I really didn't want to get into my relationship with Duncan until I had sorted out my head. Frances nodded and changed the subject.

'How did Ruby react when you phoned her from the station?'

'Badly. No-one from the Royal household had bothered to ring her, which only emphasises how precarious a position she has as Vijay's mistress. I gave her whatever information I could and told her where he was.'

'What is she going to do now?'

'Head straight down to Bombay and take up residence in the Taj Mahal Hotel. If I know Ruby, she will be investigating the possibility of flying down.'

'But it's pitch-black outside.'

'I know, but that won't stop Ruby. With the amount of money she has at her disposal anything is possible, even flying at night.'

Frances shuddered, the very idea being a total anathema to her. 'She must be completely mad.'

'No, Frances, she's in love.'

That brought Duncan and our earlier embrace back into my mind. It had been warm, soft, and loving, but I couldn't decide if his action had simply satisfied his ego or because his feelings for me were genuine. Either way, my celibacy had well and truly hit the buffers, and I could no longer shy away from the fact that sex with Duncan had been on my mind ever since coming face-to-face with him on Fort Jamrud Station, and it was playing havoc with my head. 'Bugger!' I groaned.

'What?' Frances looked up from her book.

'Nothing.' I leant back against the seat-back, closed my eyes and tried to push Duncan's image into the recesses of my mind. It didn't work, of course. Our erotic nights in Edinburgh flashed across my mind, his athletic, muscular body rubbing against my fair skin, his knee easing my thighs apart and the force of his penis driving into me were so vivid I almost had an orgasm sitting there on the compartment seat.

'*What did I tell you, Elizabeth? Sexual proclivity is embedded in your genes. You were never destined to be a nun, and trying to pretend it's so, is just plain daft.*'

'Oh, get lost, Karr.'

'Mac, will you stop mumbling to yourself and either get some rest or engross me in scintillating conversation.' Frances put down her book.

'What do you want to talk about?' I sounded like a peevish child.

'Oh, I don't know.' She cast around the compartment looking for inspiration. 'What did you think of Jim's bungalow?'

I had lost the ability to be diplomatic. 'It reminded me of Elsie and Arthur Thornton's place in Calcutta. All aspidistras and heavy drapes. What does the landlord do for a living?'

'Something important in the ICS. Procurement or such like.'

'Figures. He probably commandeered all that old-fashioned furniture from Government stock. Still at least the bed was comfy.'

'Humph!' was all Frances said and returned to her book.

On the Wednesday, I received a cable at the school from Prince Dhawan Kapoor.

Operation on femur successful. Now pinned and in plaster cast. Pelvic fracture of ilium. Double vision, some hearing loss and slurred speech after concussion. Prognosis – probable slight loss of left leg-length, speech and hearing problems temporary. Eyesight a concern. Long period of convalescence in Delhi. Miss Taverner to monitor progress. Prince D-K

I immediately wrote to Ruby at the Taj Mahal Hotel asking for the name of the Orthopedic and Ophthalmic surgeons attending to Vijay at St George's hospital, and wandered if Colonel Grafton-Young would turn out to be one of them.

I had met this pompous physician when Tom and I had visited the hospital on our arrival in Bombay. Tom had been seconded to the Colonel's medical team while the ss Narkunda was under repair, and I went along to see what the facilities were like in an Indian hospital. Colonel Grafton-Young turned out to be the Governor of Bombay's private surgeon and in charge of all the clinicians throughout the Maharashtra Province. On meeting me, he made it very clear that he considered female medics to be a complete waste of his time, so I felt a surge of self-righteous one-upmanship on imagining his face when he learned that it was me who had re-aligned Vijay's femur on the polo field.

'Put that in your pipe and smoke it,' I muttered under my breath, licked the envelope, and got Darsh to post it on his way back home.

Jim arrived in Poona the following weekend and filled us in on his new job and what had happened to the Hussar who had caused Vijay's injuries.

'I understand from Lord Wetherington that he was immediately suspended from the team and may never be invited to play polo with them again.'

'Good Lord, all for veering left instead of right.' I was astonished.

'I imagine, Mac, it's because Vijay is from one of the oldest Princely States in India. Must make an example of the chappie,' he mimicked, standing by the fireplace with his thumbs in his shirt lapels and rocking on the balls of his feet.

'All the same,' said Frances. 'Controlling a thoroughbred in those circumstances can't be easy, Jim. Prince or no Prince.'

'My thoughts entirely, Fran, but if he had turned the horse to the right instead of barging into his opponent, Vijay's mount would still be alive, and Vijay wouldn't be facing life-changing injuries. How is he, Mac?'

'The operation was successful, according to Prince Dhawan Kapoor, but you are right, his injuries could be life-changing, particularly if his vision is impaired. The optic nerve is very delicate and a violent smack to the head could have major repercussions, even wearing a helmet.'

'What about his leg?' Frances had read the cable.

'He'll probably have a permanent limp and might even have to use a walking stick for the rest of his life. As for his ability to play sport . . .'

'No chance,' interrupted Jim. 'He'd be handicapped trying to play cricket with one leg shorter than the other and as for polo, without good eyesight his ability to hit the ball would be in question.'

'It doesn't bear thinking about, does it.' Frances had forgotten all about the plight of the Hussar.

'No, Frances, it doesn't, but polo is a contact sport and Vijay knew the risks. They all did.'

'Maybe,' she replied from the sofa. 'But, if that's what can happen playing polo, promise me, Jim, you will never take up the sport.'

He dropped down beside her and took her hands in his. 'Never fear, Fran, unless the horse had a bow and a stern, I wouldn't have the first idea how to steer it.'

Work and nightly lessons in Hindi continued to fill my days, while life at St Saviours went on as normal, and then I received a letter from Agnes.

Dear Mac,

I am in receipt of your latest report from Poona and details of the dreadful accident to Prince Vijay Kumar Singh II. Of course, you should remain at the Seva Sadan hospital until we all decamp to Simla, although I would like you back here at the Lady Hardinge for a couple of days for a debrief before we head off into the mountains for the summer. I have written to the Chief Surgeon at the Lady Reading Hospital who is looking forward to having you join their team. It will be very different to working in Poona, so make the most of your time there and in Bombay.

Once you know your arrival date here, send me a cable and I will ask Sir Peter to join us. That way, there will be no need for you to journey to Calcutta to discuss your proposal for Government funding of free milk for all infants and better training for Public Health Officers. I'm sure you will have a battle royal on your hands with the ICS, but you have a very persuasive argument and Sir Peter will argue your case with great determination. He is not a man to be trifled with and will back you to the hilt, as will I.

As for your recent case in Poona. I am, of course, aware of the phenomenon and, like you, find it incredible. I can't wait to examine the growth in question.

Regards

Agnes

I tucked the letter into my bag and sat quietly, reliving the day a Mrs Banerjee of the shudra caste appeared at the clinic complaining of blurred vision and gnawing pains in her abdomen. She was well into her fifties, had two grown-up sons and was generally fit for her age, albeit, overweight.

The first problem was relatively easy to diagnose. Although rather late in life, she was suffering from what we in the medical profession called deficiency disease or more technically, *Menopause*. Being an only child, whose mother had died in childbirth, no-one had ever told her about a woman's natural loss of oestrogen in middle-age, so she was convinced she was going blind. I checked her for dryness in the corneas and for glaucoma. They were not the cause. I then gave her a full external examination, extracted some blood, and asked her to dress and remain in the waiting room while I went to the hospital's laboratory.

Referring to my medical books, I turned to the section on deficiency disease and checked Mrs Banerjee's symptoms. Unlike Western women, who tendered to suffer from hot flushes, low sexual drive and mood swings, women in Eastern countries seemed to be dogged by severe shoulder pain while Indian women predominately complained of sight blurring and sight loss.

Having confirmed my diagnosis, I was able to put Mrs Banerjee's mind at rest and prescribed a course of Ovariin tablets, made from powdered cow ovaries, to improve her oestrogen imbalance, and suggested she bathed her eyes regularly in fresh water and used some herbal remedies, such as alfalfa and star anise, to help alleviate further discomfort.

It was during my external examination that the matter of her abdominal pain came to light. As my knowledge of Hindi was still far from fluent, one of the Hindu nurses was called upon to translate.

'She say she has pain in belly, Memsahib Doctor. It come and go and it move about.'

'How long has this been going on?' I asked, frowning.

'It start some weeks ago. She had same pain many years ago, but it went away. Now it come again.'

I palpated her abdomen once more and felt a hard lump under my fingers. Maybe it was a hernia, I thought, or a hematoma, or even a cyst? All three could cause intermittent pain, but none had been known to move about. Then there was the possibility of an ovarian tumour. Whatever it was, it needed to be surgically removed and without delay.

'Nurse, I would like you to admit Mrs Banerjee for surgery as soon as possible. The lump may be benign, but if it isn't, the sooner we remove it, the better.

Emily Jackson and I stood on opposite sides of the operating table, gowned, masked and gloved, my hand poised, holding a scalpel, ready to cut through the skin and subcutaneous fat below my patient's belly button. Her breathing was regular and her pulse-rate steady, the ether keeping her in a deep sleep.

Ready?' I asked the others. Emily and the nursing sister both nodded and I drew the blade down the centre of the abdomen then diagonally across to the right groin. Emily swabbed the escaping blood and parted the skin with clamps which exposed the womb and right fallopian tube, lying below the large bowel. My fingers descended into the cavity and gently felt around the area for the lump which I assumed would be in the fallopian tube or ovary. I looked at Emily as my fingers located the growth and my eye sockets widened.

A hard, rough object, the size of a small melon was tangled in Mrs Banerjee's intestines, but was not attached to anything. I managed to manoeuvre the object into the palm of my hand while gently extricating it from the cats-cradle of guts using a blunt-nosed medical probe, then began to retract my fingers, bringing the hard sphere into the light.

'Surgical bowl please, Sister.'

'What is it?' asked Emily, her vision blocked by my arm.

'I've no idea.' The slimy mass cupped between my fingers, was like some alien calcified cannonball. I dropped it into the metal bowl and handed it to Emily while I examined the organs for damage. None were evident.

Checking that all the used swabs were in the kidney-bowl, I sutured and sterilised the wound before dressings and bandages were applied and the patient was wheeled into the recovery room. Emily and I took the growth into the laboratory, cleaned it then slowly began chipping away at the shell.

'Glory be,' gasped Emily, dislodging a convex piece of calcified shell and lifting it away with pincers. There, before our eyes was a fully formed mummified child, curled into a foetal position, looking for all the world like a china doll.

'A Lithopaedion,' I muttered, awestruck. 'The hard shell must have been the placenta.'

Emily nodded. 'A stone-baby.' She looked at me in utter amazement. 'I've read of such a things but I never expected to see one.'

'Me neither. Let's weigh it.' I placed the solid infant on the scales with its shell and checked the dial. 'Seven pounds.'

Emily didn't believe me and checked for herself. 'It's incredible. She must have been carrying this inside her for years.'

'Well, we'll soon find out.' I carefully placed the stone-baby on an antiseptic cloth. 'Once Mrs Banerjee has recovered from the anaesthetic, we can ask her.' I went in search of my camera and photographed the object from all angles, knowing my next report to Agnes would include some very interesting images.

'What should we do with it?' queried Emily, peering more closely at the inside.

'Right now, I've not got a clue,' I said, winding the Kodak film to the end and extracting the cartridge, 'but I'm sure the Lady Hardinge would be delighted to include it with their other medical specimens.'

'No doubt the Cama Hospital and the Calcutta Medical College would too. When this gets out, we're going to have some high-ranking obstetric clinicians knocking on our door.'

'Perhaps I should ask Doctor Scott what we should do with it? I'm sure she'll know.' I closed the camera case and put it in my medical bag. 'Meanwhile, I suggest we keep the existence of this Lithopaedion strictly to ourselves.'

'Agreed. Now, let's go and find out how old this baby is.'

Frances found me in her office that evening writing my report to Agnes.

'Had a good day?'

'Exceptional. Sit down and listen to this. You'll never believe what I'm about to tell you.'

By the time I reached the part where Emily and I went to question the mother, Frances was turning grey.

'What did Mrs Banerjee say?'

'Well, it was rather garbled, but from what I can gather, she became pregnant shortly after giving birth to her first son and carried the foetus for about six months, at which point she went into labour, but the baby never appeared. The village *Dai* . . .'

'The what?'

' . . . the village birthing attendant. An unqualified indigenous midwife who wouldn't know a birthing canal from a tube of surgical lubricant. She and her kind regularly kill both the mother and child out of sheer incompetence.' Frances was clutching her stomach.

'Anyway, according to Mrs Banerjee's *Dai*, it was Aditi, the Hindu Mother of the Gods, who had taken the baby for herself, and being a low-caste Hindu with no education, Mrs Banerjee believed her.'

'You have to be joking?'

'Unfortunately, not. The pains eventually went away, and all she was left with was a distended stomach and a feeling that something was floating around in her tummy. Two years later, she became pregnant again and went the full term. As her next son was born naturally, she thought Aditi had blessed her with this child to replace of the previous one and never questioned it further.'

'But how did this stone-baby get into the abdomen?'

'A possible tear in the wall of the womb, which then healed over.'

'And how long has she been like this?' Frances decided she needed a drink and produced two glasses and a bottle of sherry.

'Thirty-six-years.'

She nearly dropped the bottle.

'If Mrs Banerjee hadn't come to see us about her blurred vision, she would still have been carrying the stone-baby when she died.'

'Enough!' Frances emptied her glass in one gulp. 'Please tell me you didn't discuss this with Darsh and the girls at the Hindi language class tonight.'

'Never fear, Frances, I kept the subject of stone-babies strictly to myself.'

'Thank goodness for that.' She refilled her glass. 'So, what did you talk about?'

'Venereal disease.'

Chapter Twenty-Four

I tapped gently on the ornately panelled, dark teak door of Ruby's bedroom and waited. After a short pause I was staring into the burnished, wrinkled features of Vijay's physician, his dark, rheumy eyes acknowledging me from under his white pagari turban, his long white beard, thigh-length angarkha jacket, white tapered trousers, and brown leather sandals reminding me of a painting in Pa's study of Saint Peter standing at the pearly gates of heaven. The doctor greeted me in the usual Hindu way, then stood back to let me enter.

'The Prince, he is resting. Please, you do not stay long.'

I crossed to the imposing four-poster bed and rolled back the muslin drape masking the Prince from my view. He lay on a bank of feather pillows, his left leg encased in plaster from ankle to hip and elevated in a leather sling suspended from the overhead wooden bedframe.'

'I am in next room if you need me,' said the physician, and with the click of the bedroom door, I found myself alone with Jhalanpur's future Maharajah. I leant over, noting his sallow skin and loss of weight, fingering his carotid artery to get a pulse.

'It's OK, Mac, I'm not dead yet.'

All royal protocol vanished with those few words.

'Well, Vijay, you very nearly were. That horse of yours almost shortened both our lives.'

One eyelid opened, and a faint smile crossed his lips. 'Maybe you'll tell me what the hell happened that day, because no-one else around here seems to know.' The other eyelid opened, and he struggled, trying to raise himself off the pillows. 'Damn it, Mac, how the hell can I hold a conversation with you while I'm lying on my back.'

He sounded like Aunt Karr complaining about her rheumatism. I lifted his shoulders and re-adjusted the mass of pillows until he was propped up at a forty-five-degree angle.

'Is that better?'

'Well, at least I can see you now.'

'How is your vision?'

'Fine. Well, a bit blurred in my left eye.'

'Interesting.' I sat on the intricately embroidered coverlet and decided to keep the conversation light. 'I had a Mrs Banerjee complaining of the same thing back in Poona. It turned out she was suffering from the women's affliction of the *menopause*.'

'Great, so you're telling me I changed sex while I was unconscious.' He coughed and tried to swallow.

I grabbed a glass of water from the bedside table. 'Here, drink this, the cool liquid will ease the dryness in your throat.' The red wheel-mark from the leather helmet strap below his open-necked nightshirt had almost disappeared. 'At least you haven't lost your acerbic wit.

'That's the least of my worries. Now, are you going to tell me what happened that day?'

'Only if you promise not to faint. I don't have any smelling salts handy.'

'I'll remind you, Doctor Stuart-MacKenzie, that I come from a long line of Rajput Warriors. Jhalanpur Princes never faint.' He drank some more water and handed back the glass.

'We'll see.' I cleared my throat, thought back over events and began the explanation at the point where the sixth chukka was about to start.'

'What happened to the Hussar?'

'I've no idea, but he lived to tell the tale because Jim Hamilton told me he's been suspended from the team and may never be invited to play for them again.'

Vijay stared into the distance. 'And what happened to me exactly?'

'Your left foot got caught in the stirrup as your horse fell. It then rolled over your left leg causing a compound fracture of the femur. You were also concussed from smacking your head against the pitch, and your helmet was pushed back on impact, the strap stretched around your neck and about to strangle you.'

My patient was now visibly turning white around the gills. 'Your femur bone was in two parts and poking out of your thigh. Captain Fitzpatrick took one professional look at your horse and shot it with his army pistol, while I sent Jim Hamilton into the clubhouse for the medical box, some splints and a stretcher.' I paused giving him time to digest what I was saying. 'It was essential to re-align the femur before your leg-muscles seized, so, with Jim's strong hold on your pelvis and Fitzpatrick pulling on your calf, I managed to retract the bone back into place then strapped and splintered it before sending you off to St George's Hospital and an orthopaedic surgeon.'

Both eyebrows lifted. 'What did he do to it?'

'He's pinned the fracture. That's the safest way to stabilise the bone while it knits together. Your wound was then stitched, and your leg sheathed in plaster of paris to immobilise the thigh.' I tapped the plaster-cast with my knuckle. 'All you have to worry about now is possible infection in the wound.'

'What would that mean?'

I didn't mince my words. 'Gangrene could set in and your leg would have to be amputated.'

'*MAADHER CHOD!*' He screwed up his eyes trying to bring me into focus.

'Did you just wink at me?' I pulled back his right eyelid and held up my index finger. 'Tell me when my finger comes into focus.' I slowly moved it towards his eyeball.

'Now,' he said, and I repeated the exercise on his left eye. 'You'll live. Now, what were you saying?'

He had the grace to look embarrassed.

'I haven't yet learned swear words in Hindi, but I assume that was one of them.' He didn't answer. 'Well, at least you haven't fainted. Now, I want a complete run-down on how you're feeling.'

We continued the question-and-answer routine for a few minutes more, Vijay confirming what I already knew. He was in constant pain from his fracture, his eyesight was troubling him, and he had a gnawing headache and a dull ache from his pelvis. However, he could wiggle his toes, his circulation seemed fine, and his hearing and speech had returned in full. Exhaustion, from a lack of sleep, and frustration at being made to lie still were making him tetchy and worrying about his future wasn't helping.

'When can I get out of this cast and get back to riding a horse?'

'What did the orthopaedic surgeon say?'

'He didn't. Just mumbled something about me having to remain static while the fracture healed.'

'I assume you want the truth?'

'Yes. I do.'

'Are you sure?'

He paused, scanning my face and biting his bottom lip. 'Yes, I'm sure.'

'Very well. My emergency action on the polo-field means you should have the full use of your left leg, once it's mended, assuming you do as you're told. However, I can't guarantee that it will be the same length as it was before the accident, and you may be left with a permanent limp and possibly have to use a walking stick to get about.'

He grimaced.

'I haven't finished. If you don't let the femur heal properly, you could spend the rest of your life in a wheelchair. In the meantime, being immobile will cause your leg muscles to atrophy and you will need weeks of physiotherapy to get them back into shape, so you're not going anywhere without help any time soon. Mood swings may occur due to your severe concussion, and the headaches and vision impairment are a work in progress. Only time will tell with these. You'll be in plaster for another four weeks, so I suggest you take up chess, and finally . . .'

'You mean there's more?'

I pricked his big toe with a needle.

'Ow!'

'Yes, there's more. Stop taking your frustration out on Ruby. She's not a punchbag.'

He paused, his cheek muscles tensing. 'What about polo?'

'Don't push your luck, Laddie. I told you in the clubhouse not to fall off your horse and at that time I was joking. Falling off again could mean that you are disabled for life and this time, I am not joking. Is that clear?'

The bedroom door opened and the physician stood in the doorway tapping his watch.

'That's enough bad news for one day,' I said, rising. 'I'll be back tomorrow. Meanwhile, I'll leave you to mull over what I've said.' I removed my pen from my pocket and began writing along the length of the plaster-cast.

Rajput Warrior bones break just like every other human being.

'Read that,' I said, moving away, 'whenever you decide to ignore medical advice.'

Ruby was standing by the fishpond when I walked out into the grounds, the reflections from the fountain bouncing off her gold bracelet. My eyes travelled to the tall hibiscus tree at the bottom of the garden, and I swallowed hard.

'How is he?'

'Grumpy,' I said, joining her, 'and wanting to know when he can play polo again.'

'Bloody hell! What am I going to do with him, Mac?'

'You're going to keep him calm, surround him with love and make absolutely sure that every medic who comes near him knows what he's doing.'

'Fine, but what about his foul moods?'

'Ruby, he's in pain, he's frustrated and he's facing an uncertain future. You'd be bad-tempered under those conditions. As I recall, you only suffered two broken ribs on the ss Narkunda and you were a pain in the backside.'

'Don't exaggerate.' She flicked water at the head of a Koi Carp.

'Temper, temper, Miss Tavener.'

'I'm sorry, but Vijay is wearing me down, Mac. I don't think I've got the stamina for all this.'

'Yes, you have, and I'm now around to take some of the strain. Have any of the family been to see him?'

'No, he refuses to have them anywhere near him, especially his father.'

'So, apart from you, he spends his days surrounded by sycophantic staff.'

'I'm afraid so.'

'Then it's no wonder he's tetchy. That physician of his is enough to drive a man to drink. Vijay didn't even know what had actually happened to him on the polo-field.'

'I know, and I couldn't tell him because I wasn't there.'

'Well, he knows now, and I've told him not to use you as a punchbag. Why don't you get some of his polo team to visit?'

'The physician refused them access.'

'Then override him. They were there, they saw what happened and they would boost his confidence. Lying alone day-after-day wallowing in self-pity is the worst thing he could do.'

Ruby's sigh was steeped in tension. She turned towards the house. 'Let's go in.' We settled onto the terrace sofas.

'Look,' I said, 'Sir Peter Bonham-Cavendish is arriving in Delhi tonight. He is one of Vijay's old university friends and I know Sir Peter will be delighted to visit him.'

'Could you arrange it?'

'Of course, I can. I'm meeting with him and Agnes at ten-thirty in the morning. What time would suit Vijay?'

'Late afternoon. Say around four.'

I nodded and smacked my neck. 'These blasted mosquitoes are driving me crazy, to say nothing of the heat. I tell you Ruby, I'll be glad to get out of Delhi. The humidity here is draining me of all my energy.'

'Do you think we could get Vijay up to Simla?' Ruby's hang-dog expression resembled a Basset Hound.

'I don't see any reason why not. His private train can get him comfortably as far as Kalka, and he could then stretch out on the back seat of your Lincoln Sedan for the final sixty miles up to Simla. The cool mountain air will be far better for his recovery than the heat of these damned plains.' I squashed another mosquito and sent it to its maker.

'Why don't you travel up with us. That way, you can keep an eye on him, and your baggage can go up with ours.'

'That's the best idea you've had all afternoon. If Agnes doesn't need me at the Lady Hardinge, we could depart at the end of this week.'

'Great.' Ruby leapt from her seat, the need for something to do galvanising her into action. 'Are you staying tonight?'

'No, but I'll call in every day. Can Ghalib drive me over to the Lady Hardinge? I came straight here from the station and my luggage is stacked in your hall.'

'Of course. Ghalib will be waiting for you out front with the car in five minutes.'

'Thanks, and Ruby, I have another request?'

'Sure. What is it?'

'Could you look after my Afghan Jezail? It's far too cumbersome for me to keep dragging around India.'

'No problem. I'll lock it in Vijay's office. It will be safe there.'

Agnes and Sir Peter were drinking coffee in her office when I walked through the door the following morning. Sir Peter jumped to his feet and hugged me like a long-lost relative.

'Well, it's about time you came back to civilisation Mac. Trying to keep up with your travels is like following Phileas Fogg on his adventures.'

Agnes chuckled and handed me a filled coffee cup. 'You've certainly be in the wars, I'll give you that, and you appear to have won over half the British Indian Army in the process.'

'Hardly,' I said, beaming from ear to ear. 'Although, I agree, it's not all been a bed of roses.'

'How's the Prince?' asked Agnes, pulling my latest report to the top of the pile.

'Structurally on the mend. The femur is pinned and immobilised, his hearing and speech seem to be back to normal, but he's still getting blurred vision and constant headaches. More worryingly, I think he's descending into a deep depression and needs some mental stimulus.'

'Could I visit him?' Sir Peter showed genuine concern.

'I wish you would. He's surrounded by his minions right now and is refusing to see any of the Royal family. What he needs is some straight talking from his own peer group.'

'Then I'll visit later this afternoon.'

'Great, around four o'clock would be good.'

'Then four it is. Now, let's get down to business.'

We spent the next two hours going through my reports since leaving Delhi in February and none of them made good reading. Finally, Sir Peter picked up his pen and asked for my conclusions.

'Firstly,' I said, getting my thoughts into order, 'India's Public Health Department needs complete root and branch reform.'

'Is that all?' His hand hovered over his writing pad.

'Sir Peter, half the men working in Public Health don't know the first thing about obstetrics, gynaecology or child mortality, which is ludicrous when half the population is female. I don't expect them to have a degree in midwifery, but one chap actually had the audacity to suggest that Child Welfare was pointless when the country was already over-populated.' Agnes nodded.

'Then there's the matter of female health visitors. Women doctors, nurses and midwives are all very laudable, but training them is expensive and lengthy, whereas an army of female health workers, spread around the Provinces, trained in the basics of food and health hygiene, would be a quick and cheap way of improving death rates. As an example, they could abolish the medieval practice of feeding babies '*bal-golis*' to keep them quiet . . .'

Sir Peter was writing furiously. '*Bal-golis*?'

'Opium pills,' cut-in Agnes.

Sir Peter visibly gulped.

'. . . and insist on pregnant mothers exercising outside in the fresh air, instead of being trapped like outcasts in windowless, filthy rooms for weeks on end.'

'Anything else?'

'Yes. The Government needs to provide proper baby food for infants instead of the mothers feeding them on *conjee*.'

'I give up, what's *conjee*?'

'Rice gruel. It's about as nutritious as gunpowder, but it's all they have. If clinics were given supplies of dried baby-food and free milk, the mothers would attend post-natal clinics just to get their hands on it. The WMS would then have a better idea of what was going on in the community, records could be kept, and valuable statistics would be available when applying for extra funding.'

'You're not asking for much, are you, Mac?' commented Sir Peter, turning the page of his notebook.

'After seeing how much the Government is spending supplying the Indian Army with uniforms, rifles, ammunition and victuals, Sir Peter, my recommendations would amount to small change.' Agnes had a wry grin on her face.

'Now for the thorny question of sanitation and the Public Works Department. Sanitary conditions are worse in the cities than in the country, but even at the Danish Mission Hospital in Mardan, the Sweeper constantly complained that the Sanitation Department regularly failed to turn up and remove the night-ordure.'

Sir Peter rose from his chair and walked over to the window, his hands in his trouser pockets. 'You do realise, Mac, that our Public Health Commissioner will have about as much interest in this subject as eating a diet of *conjee*.'

'Well, you did ask, and that's before I get onto the matter of tropical disease control, rat infestations and clean water.'

He turned to Agnes and shrugged his shoulders. 'She's only been here for eight months and she's already about to cause mayhem in the corridors of power.'

Agnes gathered my report pages together and placed then back in a buff folder. 'It is nothing less than we at the WMS have been saying for the past ten years, Sir Peter, but our voices have fallen on deaf ears.' She handed the folder over to him. 'Perhaps Elizabeth, representing a new generation, will have better luck. We both know she can be a formidable adversary, particularly when she's wielding her Afghan Jezail.'

'I don't want us to take no for an answer, Sir Peter.' He placed the folder in his case. 'I have a sheaf of case studies and, if these and my Jezail fail, I would like to appear in front of the Public Health Committee with one of these unfortunate mothers and her child to see what effect that has on our great Indian Civil Service. By the way, Agnes, how is Lamis?'

'Who's Lamis?'

'A thirteen-year-old Muslim child bride,' I replied. 'She's about to undergo a full-blown rectal reconstruction due to the damaged she suffered from her husband's vicious acts of sodomy.'

It felt rather strange being back at the Lady Hardinge, and as I crossed the quadrangle to the refectory, I mulled over everything that had happened to me since boarding the Frontier Mail train back in the winter.

'Doctor MacKenzie, you come back.' I turned to see who was calling my name and smiled as a very familiar face came into view.

'Yes, Fatima, I come back. How are you, and how is Lamis?'

'I am good, and Lamis, she now improving. Doctor Scott, she say Lamis will make good nurse one day.' Fatima walked along beside me, her quiet voice and gentle features grounding me after the traumas of the past months.

'What happened to her husband?'

'He arrested and in prison. Lamis, she now free and talks of you all the time.'

'I can't wait to see her.'

'You stay now in Delhi, Memsahib Doctor?'

'No, Fatima, I'm about to leave for the Lady Reading Maternity Hospital in Simla, but in the autumn, I will be back.'

Her smile lit up the quadrangle. 'Then I pleased when summer is over.'

'Fatima, where will I find Lamis?'

She lifted the watch pinned to her left breast and checked the time. 'She eats with Muslim students in Block C. You find her there.'

'Very well. I assume the temporary colostomy has been a success?'

'Yes, Doctor MacKenzie, and now she build strength before next operation. She learning hygiene with Muslim first-year students while she wait.'

'And her mother. Is she happy for her daughter?'

'Oh, very happy. She hope Lamis will make good recovery and prays to Allah he keep her safe from now on. Please we talk later, I go now to help with lecture.'

'Don't let me delay you, Fatima, and please, call me Doctor Mac. After all we have been through together, I think we should be less formal.'

'Thank you, Doctor Mac, I try to remember.'

I watched her climb the huge marble staircase to the college entrance and thanked my lucky stars for bringing this highly qualified midwife to me in my hour of need. Perhaps, I thought, as I headed for Block C, Lamis will achieve the same level of midwifery and go on to help many other Indian girls in their hour of need. Little did I know at that moment, how significant this idea was to become.

It was midnight and I was still sitting at my desk when I heard the college clock strike the witching hour. I stretched and re-read my letter to Frances.

Dear Frances,

Ruby, Vijay and I will be travelling up to Simla next Friday in his private train and I will be staying with them at Mallards, his Jhalanpur mountain retreat, while I find my feet at the Lady Reading. This way I can keep an eye on Vijay's recuperation and not put pressure on the hospital's accommodation . . .

I continued along the same lines until I reached the main topic of my letter.

. . . I caught up with Lamis today, here at the Lady Hardinge. You will be delighted to hear that she has put on weight, her temporary colostomy has been a great success and she will be having her rectal

reconstruction procedure when Agnes and I return to Delhi in the autumn.
Meanwhile, she remains at the hospital and is being given basic training on
hygiene and sanitation which brings me to my next question.

You said yourself that girls such as Lamis deserved better in life and
after all she has been through, I want to help her in any way I can. She
needs to start with a good education and I'm hoping you can recommend a
girls' school who accept Muslim students. I am happy to pay, assuming the
cost is not beyond my means. Let me know what you think.

Mac

x

I posted the letter with others destined for Northumbria the
following morning and went to meet Ruby at Connaught Place
for some overdue retail therapy.

'When did you last have your hair cut, Mac?' The question
reached me across the crowded aisle of the departmental store
as Ruby powered ahead towards 'Women's Wear.'

'Calcutta,' I replied, suddenly embarrassed.

'Then it's high-time you were placed in the capable hands of
my stylist.'

I felt like one of Gloria Swanson's lapdogs as I followed
Ruby along an oak-panelled corridor, and through two highly
polished swing doors into, what can only be described, as an
up-market brothel minus its male customers. We were now in
Delhi's most sought after beauty parlour, and the sole domain
of well-heeled colonial ladies who were there to be pummelled
and preened, at enormous expense, by European masseuses,
hairstylists and make-up artists, and I was about to be their next
victim. It reminded me of the Jhalanpur zenana without the
saris and my reticence was not lost on Ruby.

'How the hell do I afford all this?' My eyes took in the gold velvet couches, crystal chandeliers and wall-to-wall mirrors.

'By opening an account and paying the bills over months or even years, like the rest of British colonial society.'

'Miss MacKenzie,' called out a smartly uniformed woman with a French accent.

'Doctor Stuart-MacKenzie,' corrected Ruby, beating me to my usual response.

'Madame, I dooooo apologise. Please, allow me.' She removed my linen jacket, placed it on a satin covered hanger then led me through to the hair-salon, placed me in a recliner chair against a wash-hand basin, covered my shoulders in a soft fluffy white towel, pushed my head back and lifted my thick unruly tresses with her hands. Her look was one of total disgust at the bird's nest before her, so I closed my eyes and willed myself back to the Khyber Rifle's barracks.

When I surfaced an hour later, most of my locks were lying on the cutting room floor, and I was crimped and teased into a cloned version of Coco Chanel.

'Well?' I asked, as Ruby spun me around in the reception area like some tailor's dummy.

'Much improved, Mac. Now let's find you an outfit to replace the one you ruined on the polo-field in Bombay.'

I had tried to wash my Metropolitan Hotel two-tone cream-linen dress in St Saviours laundry-room, but no amount of scrubbing could get rid of Vijay's blood stains and I felt surprisingly sad when Frances dropped the garment in the school rubbish bin, having no idea why the garment was so significant.

True to her word, Ruby had me in a version of the same dress minutes later and insisted that the cost was to go onto Vijay's account, along with a new pair of matching shoes, because, as she pointed out, 'he bloody well should!'

We arrived back at the villa at midday, and while she was organising lunch, I went to check on our resident patient.

'What happened to Doctor Mac,' quipped Vijay as he shuffled into an upright position to get a better view.

'Don't ask.' I flicked a short, crimped lock from my eyes and checked his vital signs.

'Do I pass muster?'

'That depends on what we are comparing you with. You're definitely not a candidate to scale Mount Everest, but then I wouldn't recommend putting you out of your misery either.'

'Doctor Stuart-MacKenzie, there are times when your Scottish bedside manner leaves a lot to be desired.'

'So people keep telling me.' I pushed Duncan back into his box. 'Which is a shame, because I'll be taking control of your convalescence for the next few weeks up in Simla.'

'Really?'

'Yes.' I placed my finger in front of his right eye. 'You know the routine.'

'Now,' he said, as I moved to the left eye.

'I have to thank you for buying me a new outfit to replace the one you ruined by falling off your horse.'

'Will I like it?'

'I've no idea, but Ruby insisted it would be just the ticket for a garden party at Viceregal Lodge, so I guess it was expensive.'

'It would be.' He blinked as my finger touched his cheek. 'Now.'

'Umm, not so good. Never mind, I have something to cheer you up.' I clapped my hands, the bedroom door flew open, and Ruby appeared from the landing pushing a large wicker bathchair mounted on a four-wheel bogie.'

'What in the world? . . .'

'This, darling,' she announced, making a grand entrance, 'is your new mode of transport which Mac and I have had specially commissioned in the back streets of Chandni Chowk.'

Vijay was speechless, his eyes oscillating between Ruby and myself before bursting into a fit of laughter, his guffaws ricocheting off the bedroom walls and out into the garden beyond.

'Thank God for that,' whispered Ruby as she walked passed.

'OK, Your Highness,' I said, helping her to manoeuvre the bathchair alongside of the bed, 'are we going to help you into your new conveyance, or are you going to lie there all day?'

He paused, searching for some acerbic response. 'What's that expression you often use, Ruby?'

'You mean the one, "do men have egos"?'

'Typical,' he muttered, attempting to lift his plastered leg off the sling. 'I was thinking more about women and expensive outfits.'

It was wonderful to see the instant change in his mood as we all sat on the bedroom veranda, sharing a light lunch, Vijay upright and supported by a pile of feather cushions, his left leg raised on a matching wicker cradle attached to the bathchair frame and us sitting at a wicker table.

'Comfortable?' I asked, as Ruby handed him a plate of hot stuffed samosas and bhajis.

'Never felt better, Mac. When can I go downstairs?'

'Ruby,' I enquired, shaking my head, 'is he ever satisfied?

'Never,' she replied, helping herself to a grilled haloumi salad. 'Perhaps, all things considered, you should have him put down after all.'

'Oh, I think that might be a bit harsh, not to say messy, and disposing of his body could also be a problem. Then there's the matter of the Maharaja of Jhalanpur. How would we explain his son's demise?'

'Oh, that's easy. We just dump our patient in the Yamuna River and tell his father that he went for a swim in his plaster-cast and sank like a stone, never to be seen again.'

'Excellent, so, we have a plan, but can I have my lunch first?' I picked up a lamb kebab and enjoyed the aroma of mixed spices.

'Have you two quite finished?'

'That depends.' Ruby was intent on getting her own back after weeks of aggravation. 'Are you going to thank us for your mechanical thoroughbred, or do I get Ghalib to cart you off to the river-bank right now?'

'I . . . yes . . . no . . . Oh, for the love of Lord Shiva, THANK YOU!'

'Don't mention it,' she quipped, as I bit into my spiced lamb.

Chapter Twenty-Five

T he bells of Christ Church calling the congregation of Simla to prayer echoed across the ridge as I stood overlooking the deep, dark valley below and breathed in the fresh mountain air. After the arid plains of Punjab, it was a relief to be surrounded by jagged, snow-capped peaks, towering pine and cedar trees, crystal clear, babbling streams cascading down rocky ravines, verdant forests and deep icy pools, as lush vegetation spread like a mosaic tapestry across the countryside and a kaleidoscope of rhododendrons, roses and dahlias jostled for sunlight amongst the herbaceous borders of every bungalow, lodge and cottage garden.

It was like home from home; the great and good of British society whiling away their days in what can only be described as Little England in the foothills of the Himalayas. While Lord Irwin and his myriad of ICS staff ran India from Viceregal Lodge, the rest of Simla's colonial residents gossiped in coffee-houses, bowed their heads in prayer, attended afternoon garden parties, played tennis and croquet at their club, enjoyed the latest amateur dramatics at the Gaiety Theatre and sated their appetites long into the night at numerous and ever-more extravagant dinners and soirees. In short, the Shires were alive and well and prospering at seven-thousand feet above sea-level.

I had left Delhi with Ruby and Vijay at first light, five days earlier. Anyone would have thought they were emigrating with the amount of baggage piled high on the railway platform and it took an age for the railway porters to load it all onto Vijay's private train along with Ruby's limousine, the bathchair and a huge block of ice, which was dragged bodily across the compartment floor and dropped into a sunken metal box covered in a gilt metal grid. This was to provide cool air in the carriage during the one-hundred-and-eighty-mile journey to Kalka.

I made Vijay comfortable on the daybed specially set up for the trip, then settled back to enjoy the views as we moved away from the capital and steadily climbed into the undulating hills of Himachal Pradesh.

'Sir Peter told me that you intend to take on the Surgeon-General of the IMS,' stated Vijay, as his eyes appeared above his copy of the Times of India.

'Did he?'

'Yes. I gather you want to persuade this distinguished gentleman that the Public Health Department needs a rank-and-file rethink regarding hygiene and sanitation.'

'Well, there's no doubt it's long overdue, but as I don't know the Surgeon-General from Adam, I hardly think I will be bending his ear anytime soon.' My attention was drawn to a group of young, grubby children playing in the dirt alongside the track. 'Why was Sir Peter discussing my ideas with you anyway?'

Vijay disappeared back behind his newspaper, his blurred vision now much improved. 'I was asking him how you were getting on with your Ph.D. when he called to see me the other day.'

'What did he say?' I was intrigued.

'That you're a feisty wee besom who is likely to rub the SG up the wrong way with your assertive views on female and infant mortality.'

'Well, that's nothing new, and if the Surgeon-General is anything like the rest of the IMS, I'll be wasting my time even trying to bring his Public Health Department into the modern age.'

'You may get your chance to prove that while you're in Simla, Mac.'

'Really, why's that?'

'Sir Charles Ponsonby-Pritchard and his family live just up the Ridge from us.'

'The Surgeon-General?' I could see Vijay's crown nodding. 'And I suppose his eldest son went up to Oxford at the same time as you,' I quipped.

'Actually, it was his second son, William.'

Vijay's contacts never failed to amaze me. 'And will William be just up the Ridge too?'

'Sadly not. He died in Mons during the war, but his elder sister Edith will be there and has always had a soft spot for me.'

Ruby's ears pricked up at this point. 'Is she still single?'

'No, she's married to Lord Henry Postlethwaite, nephew to the Governor of Madras, and has a brood of children, but she might be a good contact for Mac, don't you think?'

Ruby winked in my direction and went back to her magazine. I stared out of the compartment window at some ramshackle houses nestling between a thicket of deodar trees and tried to remember where I had heard that surname before. There could not be many Postlethwaites in India, but I couldn't recall why it was so familiar, until the memory of a Ming vase being deliberately knocked off its plinth at the Aga Khan Palace in Poona caused me to smile. Small world, I thought, and wondered what Frances was going to say when she found out that her ex-pupil, Lady Cynthia Postlethwaite, was staying in Simla for the summer.

There were no vehicles allowed on the Ridge apart from that of the Viceroy and certain other high-ranking dignitaries, including Vijay, so I was able to meander slowly back down the lane to the Lady Reading Hospital with only the odd rickshaw or bicycle to disturb my peace.

My work in the new maternity wing was a joy after Peshawar and Poona, with everything brand new and solely for the care of the indigenous women of the Himachal Pradesh Province. The British and European ladies were highly upset by this ruling and were lobbying the Vicereine constantly to get it changed, arguing that this was colonial discrimination, but the WMS were standing firm and, for the first time since arriving in India, I actually believed that attitudes were beginning to change for the better.

My social calendar was also getting rather booked up. Once we had settled into Mallards, Ruby handed me a 'Who's Who' of Simla's upper-class ladies and posted me off on a bicycle to deliver my calling cards to their various households. One of the first responses was from Lady Edith Postlethwaite, who invited me to take tiffin with her at Wildflower Hall on the following Friday. This imposing building had been the country residence of Lord and Lady Dufferin before being converted into a hotel, and I was intrigued to see it first-hand.

As I approached the hospital entrance, Agnes was stepping down from a rickshaw and beckoned me over.

'How was the journey?' She handed the rickshaw driver a few annas and waited for a second to pull up alongside.

'Luxurious, as you would expect,' I said, delighted to see her. 'We left Vijay's train at Kalka and drove the rest of the way by limousine. The suspension on that car handled the bumps in the road with ease, and with the top down we had panoramic views right across the valleys and up to the Himalayan peaks. I've never seen anything like it. How was your trip?'

'Long and tedious. That small-gauge 'toy-train' from Kalka to Simla is very rickety and takes an age, but I agree, the views are spectacular.' She placed her bag on the ground and went to help a sari-clad occupant step down from the second rickshaw. As they both crossed to where I was standing, I could hear Agnes speaking to her charge in Urdu.

'Elizabeth, say hello to Lamis.'

I peered into the small, familiar, black-lashed, deep-brown eyes of my favourite patient, took her hands in mine and greeted her the only way I knew how.

'*As-Salam-u-Alaikim*, Lamis.'

'*Wa-Alaikum-Assalaam, Umi*,' she replied, placing her hand on her heart, then bending in supplication, lifting the hem of my skirt and holding it to her lips.

I immediately reacted. 'No, Lamis, there is no need for this.' My eyes pleaded with Agnes to concur as I lifted Lamis to her feet and patted her arm.

'Get used to it,' was all Agnes would say as she tipped the second rickshaw driver. 'Lamis believes you are her saviour and insists on referring to you as her mother. She will be forever in your debt and there is nothing you can do about it.'

Dr Iris Crawley, the Assistant Surgeon interrupted us, greeting Agnes like a long-lost friend. I helped Lamis into the lobby, eased her into a chair and waited for them to follow.

'I understand, Mac, that you saved this young lady's life in Delhi.'

'I did Iris, with help from the occult.' I looked across at Agnes and chuckled.

'Take no notice, Iris, the fact that our researcher cast all manner of evil spells on Lamis's father for trying to block their escape has nothing whatsoever to do with saving the child's life.'

'Lordy, Lordy,' replied Iris, crossing herself.

'I do hope having a Sottish white witch on your staff doesn't cause you a problem, Iris, but be assured, I have no intention of practicing such occult mumbo-jumbo here in Simla.'

'Well, that's a relief. Now, what are we going to do with this young lady?' She smiled at Lamis who responded with another Muslim greeting.

'She's to stay in the student nurse's accommodation and help out as an auxiliary for the time being. I thought the mountain air would help build up her strength,' announced Agnes, turning to me. 'I've decided to carry out the sphincteroplasty here at the Lady Reading in a month's time.'

Lamis's fingers wrap themselves around mine in a vice-like grip. She hadn't a clue what we were talking about but must have sensed it was something about herself and was becoming anxious.

'Why,' I replied, rubbing her palm with my thumb in reassurance, 'are the facilities here better than at the Lady Hardinge?'

'Certainly not, but our Surgeon-General is. Throughout the medical profession, he is renowned as an expert in rectal reconstruction, so I'm going to invite him to lead.'

'But surely Sir Charles will be far too busy to agree, Agnes?' argued Iris, picking up a small brass bell from a side table and ringing it vigorously.

'Well, he shouldn't be. Lamis's case is a fine example of why the WMS exists here in India, and I can't think of a better way of demonstrating this than by the Surgeon-General of the IMS personally carry out the operation. I doubt he has ever had to do it on a thirteen-year-old Muslim girl, and it's high-time he did.'

Agnes made me proud. 'Maybe I can help on that score, Agnes. I've been invited to have tea with his daughter tomorrow. Perhaps I could introduce Lamis's case to her and see how she reacts. With luck, I'll be able to commandeer her support and bring pressure to bear on her father when the time comes.'

'Good idea, Elizabeth. I assume this invitation had come about because you are staying at Mallards?'

'Correct. I doubt many addresses here on the Ridge can compete with that of Prince Kumar Singh II, and I intend to use my association with the Jhalanpur Royal Family to open doors wherever possible, starting with the SG and Lamis.'

Iris appeared confused and I was about to explain when an Indian nurse appeared in the lobby in answer to the bell. Iris instructed her to arrange a bed for Lamis in the student block and I agreed to go along to settle her in, which was just as well because my patient refused point blank to release me from her grip. I looked at my watch.

'Perhaps you would fill Iris in, Agnes, and I'll catch up with you later as I have a ward round to do in fifteen minutes.'

The nurse wanted to know all about my charge as we made slow progress to the student block and I noted that she was not at all shocked at Lamis's story. 'Have you seen these types of injuries before, Nurse?'

'Yes, Doctor Mac. We see often in the villages. Boys too.'

My heart sank. 'Do you speak any Urdu?' We walked into the student block.

'A little.'

'Then please explain to Lamis that I want to examine her in the clinic once she has been shown where she will sleep. I'll get my medical bag from my locker and see you both there.'

Lamis gripped my arm, fear evident in her eyes. 'It's alright, Lamis, I'll only be a few minutes.' The nurse repeated my words and I watched her being gently led down the corridor, the slight curvature of her spine and lobsided walk so evident from behind. Oh, Lamis, I thought, why is life so cruel?

An envelope was lodged in the door of my locker and I pulled it free. Recognising Frances's handwriting I quickly read the contents.

Morning, Mac,

I've just received your letter posted in Delhi. Jim and I will be arriving at the Corstorphine Hotel on Saturday 28th so we hope to see you on the Sunday. Let me know where and when.

As for Lamis's education, I think I have a plan, and we can discuss it once I get to Simla.

Now, there is the little matter of your Irish ex-lover. Jim tells me that they met in Bombay last Thursday for drinks and during the evening Duncan mentioned that Prince Dhawan Kapoor had been in contact with him on behalf of Vijay. Something to do with a veterinary vacancy at the Jhalanpur estate. Anyway, Duncan is hell bent on travelling up to Simla to meet Vijay personally. I'm not sure what he is hoping will come of the meeting, but after what you told me about his temporary commission with the army, you might like to ask Ruby what she knows, so you are prepared and can act accordingly.

Looking forward to getting together shortly, and 'Trotter' sends her love.

Frances

x

'Blast.' I shoved the letter into my pocket and muttered all the way to the clinic, recalling Vijay enquiring where Duncan was lecturing and realised that I had inadvertently brought them together. Well, I decided, scrubbing my hands in the examination room sink, there was nothing I could do about it now, so there was no point in worrying.

Lamis was standing in the doorway, her slight frame pressed against the door jam.

'Over here, Lamis,' I said, tapping the examination bed, spread with a clean white sheet.

She lay on top, pulling her sari up over her colostomy bag and I looked deep into her eyes and smiled, teardrops threatening to wet my cheeks. 'Close your eyes and relax,' I pressed my own lids down to mimic what I wanted. Her lids fluttered then remained still, blocking out the light and I spent the next few minutes checking her colostomy wound to be sure that there was no infection or unnecessary discharge. Agnes had done an excellent job looping the colon and suturing it to the abdominal wall and I was relieved to see healthy pink skin around the stoma, attached to the colostomy bag, with liquid excrement flowing unimpeded into the detachable pouch.

Lamis's anus, however, was still a mass of mangled, traumatised skin, but here again, there were no sign of infection and as her bowel was temporarily out of action, the severe bruising and inflammation around the area had decreased substantially which had helped with the level of pain and Lamis's ability to move and sit.

I removed the bag and replaced it, checked her for signs of anaemia and gave her more painkillers to counter the effects of the train journey. I was just finishing when Agnes found me.

'Happy?'

'Very. The stoma is working a treat and her back passage is certainly improving. She has also put on weight and her colour is excellent.'

'I've been doing some research since you left Delhi, Elizabeth, and I'm going to prescribe regular daily salt baths to accelerate the healing.'

I nodded.

'She's on a very strict, high protein diet of eggs, dairy, soups, fish and tender meat, plus mashed fruit and vegetables and lots of water.'

'It appears to be working.' I lifted the used colostomy bag, the contents resembling a brownish porridge.

'What she needs now is some gentle exercise to build her skeletal muscles, and I'm hoping the beauty of this area will be mentally stimulating, which should improve her general well-being after spending the whole of her life in Old Delhi.'

'I wish I could talk to her in Urdu. It's so frustrating to have this barrier between us when she so obviously wants to tell me how she is feeling.'

'I know, Elizabeth, but be kind to yourself. Your Hindi is coming on leaps and bounds and you've had a lot on your plate in the past few months.'

'I know, but I long to give her some loving support and tell her that her future is going to be so much brighter than her past.' Frances's words replayed in my head and I crossed my fingers hoping she had found a way to help improve this young girl's life chances.

'How's the Prince's mental state?' asked Agnes.

'Much better. He's less frustrated now he can be moved about. His portable bathchair has proved to be a Godsend.'

'You should publish the design in some medical journals. You never know, you might make some money from it.'

'I doubt it. Queen Victoria had one of sorts, so we are not the first to come up with the design.'

'Oh, I don't know. A portable bathchair for the infirm might become all the rage in the spa towns of Europe and could give you a nice little nest-egg for your old age.'

'Like the Maharaja of Panajab's yellow diamond which you thought about selling,' I quipped.

'Now, Elizabeth, I thought we agreed to let bygones be bygones.' She checked Lamis's chest with her stethoscope, appeared satisfied and went on her way, leaving me wishing I could relate the Maharaja of Panajab's story to my patient to cheer her up. Ma always said laughter was the best tonic in life, and Lamis needed a tonic as much as a farmer needed rain.

Any idea of commandeering Lady Edith's help in lobbying her father to operate on Lamis went straight out of the window when I joined her at Wildflower Hall Hotel for tiffin. She and her female friends turned out to be typical upper-class snobs who believed that a woman's duty was to marry well, bear children, delegate them to their nannies then spend their days in pursuit of personal pleasure both inside and outside of their marriages. Unless you had been to Cheltenham Ladies College, or a Swiss finishing school, you weren't worth cultivating, and as I certainly didn't fit into either category, I was obviously a bitter disappointment.

Edith's plum-in-the-mouth accent, lily-white skin, elongated nose, weak chin, and pompous opinions screamed English aristocracy, and it was not hard to see why Vijay had rejected her advances. Any attempt to bring the conversation around to obstetrics was met with derision, salacious gossip being the group's only topic of interest, so I sat through a long diatribe of hedonistic goings-on in Simla while swallowing some rather dry, curled-up egg-and-cress sandwiches and luke-warm Darjeeling tea. Frances would have been horrified, I thought, as I listened to Edith annihilating Lady somebody or other's character with wicked intent, and it was not hard to see why Cynthia Postlethwaite had turned out to be a spoilt, undisciplined, unruly brat of a daughter with ideas above her station.

I mentally crossed Edith and her friends off my contact list, made my excuses as soon as I could and left. Passing a large oil painting of Lord Kitchener hanging in the hotel lobby on my way out, I backtracked to read the plaque. It transpired that the Field Marshall had also been a resident of Wildflower Hall, and I rather wished that he still was as I saluted the old man, wondering how he would have handled the last two hours.

Better than me, I thought, as I made my way back to Mallards, angry that my afternoon had been an utter waste of time. 'Edith wouldn't know the first thing about sodomy,' I chuntered, plucking a pink rose from a bush hanging over a wicket fence and pricking my finger into the bargain. 'She's probably never even seen her husband naked.' Agnes was not going to be pleased with my lack of success.

Ruby was flying down the stairs carrying a blood stained towel when I entered the hall and immediately let rip when she saw me.

'I'll kill him, Mac. I swear, I'll kill him.'

'What's Vijay done now?'

'He decided to get out of the bath-chair when no one was looking, slid on the marble tiles and went flat on his face. His nose is bleeding, he's banged his head and he's complaining that his left ankle is hurting. He's a bloody disaster . . .'

I tore passed Ruby, all thoughts of Edith gone from my mind and found Vijay propped against the wall on the bedroom floor, his head back and his shirt spattered with bright red stains.

'You bloody idiot,' I yelled, frustration from my afternoon adding to my anger.

'That's what Ruby said.'

'And she was right.' I rubbed my thumb across his forehead.

'Ow!'

'Don't "Ow" me. You'll have a bump the size of a goose-egg there tomorrow, to say nothing of a broken nose.' I pulled his hand and bloodied handkerchief away and wiggled his nasal septum while calling out for an ice pack. 'Does that hurt?'

His eyes watered and blood dripped onto his lap.

'Jesus and Mary, why the hell can't you do as you're told?'

'I needed the lavatory, and I couldn't make anyone hear me.'

'Then I'd better get you a bedpan.' I patted him down from shoulder to thigh, but he seemed to be intact, although his plaster cast had spider cracks across the knee. 'Are you feeling dizzy?'

'No.'

'Do you feel sick?'

'No.'

'And your ankle?'

'It hurts.' His eyes were firmly shut.

'Can you move your toes?' I had everything crossed and my heart was in my mouth as I waited to see some movement, but nothing happened. 'Where the hell is the ice-pack?' I screamed.

'It's here, Mac.' Ruby rushed across the room and placed it on Vijay's forehead.

'Hold it there,' I instructed. 'Now Vijay, try again. Move your foot.'

'I'm trying, damn it.' He pushed himself upright, opened his eyes and stared at his toes. 'Are they moving?'

'Look for yourself.'

'I am, Mac, but I can't see anything.'

'Nor can I, so keep trying.'

'No, I mean I can't see, Mac. I can't see my feet. I can't see you. I can't see Ruby. I can't see anything.'

Ruby grabbed her throat and rushed for the bathroom as I froze.

Chapter Twenty-Six

T he ophthalmologist quietly closed the bedroom door and
sighed. 'I don't know what to tell you Doctor Stuart-
MacKenzie. As you well know, the eyes are very fragile organs
and any trauma to the head can affect vision. Two traumas will
make this situation far worse, and we have to face the
possibility that the Prince may suffer complete loss of sight in
one or both eyes.'

'God forbid,' I groaned.

'Right now, he must be kept quiet, with both eyes covered.
All we can hope is that the optic nerves are not damaged. Is an
orthopaedic surgeon coming to assess the damage to his left
leg?'

'He came this morning.' I led the way to the ground floor.
'The plaster cast was cracked and is being removed tomorrow
so the surgeon can examine the fracture site. Although the
Prince doesn't seem to have any movement in his ankle, he
does have feeling in the sole of his foot, so it may be that the
swelling is restricting his movement.'

'Let us hope so. Being blind is one thing, being blind and
disabled is quite another.'

I felt blood rush from my capillaries and needed to sit
down.

'I'm sorry, my dear, that was a bit harsh. One must stay
positive in these circumstances. I'll call again tomorrow.
Meanwhile, make sure the Prince is not left alone and if
anything should happen during the night, call me immediately.'

He handed me his card, shook my hand and left. Ruby was waiting in the lounge, looking as bad as I felt.

'What's the verdict?'

'He could recover in days or be blind for life.'

I collapsed on the sofa and buried my head in my hands. 'Why, Ruby? He was doing so well. Why was he left alone?'

Ruby's voice shattered into a thousand pieces. 'I don't know, Mac . . . I simply don't know . . . We all failed him. Ghalib was out at the garage washing the limousine, Sanjay had gone to the pharmacy in the Mall, and I was in the kitchen talking to cook. No one heard Vijay's cries.'

'Where the hell was the bell?'

Her pause seemed to stretch forever. 'On his bedside table. I forgot to move it.'

We sat in silence, each with our own thoughts until I could delay no longer. Someone had to tell Vijay what the eye-specialist had said, and that someone had to be me. I dragged myself back up the stairs and hesitated at the bedroom door, remembering the time I had told Ma and Pa that my little sister had lost her fight against smallpox. I was no good at giving bad news then, and I was not going to be any better now. I knocked and entered.

'Vijay, are you awake?' He nodded, his eyes hidden behind a padded head bandage. Tears described tramlines on my cheeks, and I swallowed hard, trying to keep my voice even. 'The ophthalmologist will call to see you again tomorrow.' I cringed at my choice of words and quickly moved on. 'You'll need to keep your eyes covered for the time being.'

'Will I lose my sight?' His question, though relevant, cut like a knife. I took a deep breath, crossed my fingers and tried to be objective. I was a doctor, and telling the truth was the only sensible thing to do even though it would crucify him. 'We don't know, Vijay. Your prognosis is not good after two major traumas to the head, but the body is an amazing instrument, and you have youth on your side.'

'I'm thirty-five years old, Mac.'

'And in good condition for your age, at least you were. Your sight may recover fully or partially, or you may go blind. There are no guarantees.'

'I'd rather die than go blind. I'll be no use to anyone if I can't see.' His head rotated, following the sound of my footsteps, sensing me rather than seeing me.

Anger simmered in the pit of my stomach. Comparing Vijay's prognosis to Lamis's was like comparing caviar to pork scratchings. What she had suffered in her short life had been forced on her, not self-inflicted, and her future as a low-caste Indian was unimaginable in contrast to anything Vijay was about to face, yet she was surviving. I couldn't help it, my MacKenzie hackles were rising, and I gave him both barrels.

'That's a ridiculous statement, and you know it. I won't allow you to wallow in self-pity. Millions of people live their lives with far greater disabilities than blindness and they cope, as you will.' My voice held little sympathy. 'From now on, someone will be with you at all times, and until the orthopaedic surgeon confirms that your femur has not been compromised by the fall, you'll be using a bedpan, is that understood?' I sounded like a dispassionate matron.

Vijay banged his fist on the coverlet. 'If you've got nothing more positive to say, GET OUT!'

'NO! You can shout all you like, Vijay, but I'm not listening. You brought this on yourself and you will take your medicine like everyone else has to. I also think it is high-time we let your father know what is going on?'

'DON'T YOU DARE!' He could be heard in Kalka.

'Stop shouting.'

He snorted but obeyed. 'My father is not a well man and the knowledge that I am disabled will kill him. My mistress, my physician, my chaprassi and my chauffeur are all sworn to secrecy and if you want to continue being part of this household, so are you.'

I stared at a clenched jaw and a mass of white bandage, Vijay's words ringing in my ears and chilling me to the bone. This was a royal Prince exerting his authority, instantly putting me in my place.

'Now, if you must stay here, sit quietly in the corner and read a book. I need to think.'

I decided retreat was the better option and used the time to write to Duncan at the Veterinary College. There was little point in him visiting Vijay under the circumstances, and delaying his arrival suited me just fine. Frances also needed to be appraised of the situation, so I cycled to the telegraph office on the Mall to send her a cable.

The days dragged by as I filled my hours attending to my patients at the maternity wing, working clinics in the mountain villages and sitting with Vijay for hours on end. Initially, the atmosphere between us was strained, but gradually he began taking an interest in my work, questioning me extensively on the causes of osteomalacia, dysentery or pneumonia, and my views on sanitation, hygiene and essential record keeping of indigenous births and deaths. I found myself enjoying these bedside discussions, telling him about stone-babies, the effects of venereal disease on embryos and the common use of opium by *Dais*. He was shocked, and by the time the ophthalmologist was ready to remove his bandages, Vijay was fully conversant with the vagaries of Indian obstetrics and determined to improve the lives of his own female subjects once he became the Maharaja of Jhalanpur.

The eye-surgeon closed the bedroom curtains, while I stood at the end of the bed, my fingernails digging into my palms and my bottom lip anchored between my teeth.

'Your Highness,' he said, his voice strong and self-assured, 'please don't expect immediate results when I remove the bandage today. Your eyes will take time to focus and, if they don't, this is not proof that you are blind. Now, please close your eyes.'

I could sense Ruby sitting on the velvet chaise-longue by the window, every sinew strained.

'Are you ready?' Vijay caught his breath and nodded.

'Very well.' The surgeon untied the bandage holding the eye-pads in place and gently lifted them away. I looked down at Vijay's right leg, now heavily bandaged from thigh to calf, thankful that the fall had not compromised his fracture or re-opened the wound. One down, two to go, I thought, and concentrated on Vijay's face.

'Your Highness, you may now open your eyes.'

Time seemed to stand still as Vijay's eyeballs slowly tracked from left to right, willing them to show him something, anything in the dimmed light. His throat muscles were as taut as violin strings, but he appeared to search in vain. 'I can't see anything.'

I heard Ruby's intake of breath and saw the clinician nod towards the dresser. I walked over and lit the wick of a candle, the flame gently flickering, casting shadows on the ceiling, then turned and held the heavy brass candlestick at arms-length. Vijay frowned, blinked three times, and stared in my direction.

'Your Highness,' asked the clinician. 'What do you see?'

'I'm . . . I'm not sure, everything looks black.'

A pad was placed over Vijay's right eye. 'Concentrate on your left eye.'

'Anything now?'

'No, nothing.'

'Let's try with the right eye.'

I had an image of the heir to the Jhalanpur fortune spending the rest of his life in a black void and felt my throat constrict.

'Take your time,' said the ophthalmologist, 'and don't strain your eye, just relax and let it work on its own.' He stepped back giving Vijay a clear view of the flame.

'I tell you, Doctor, there's nothing there.' He was beginning to sound hysterical; my arm-muscle was aching, and I was about to give up when his tentative voice broke the tension. 'No, wait . . . Yes, yes I can see something yellow in the darkness.' Suddenly he was shouting, 'Ruby, it's moving. I don't know what it is, but it's definitely moving.'

There was a deep collective sigh, and I grabbed my hand trying to stop it shaking.

'Good. We will continue to concentrate on this eye for the moment. Now try to focus on the object you thought you saw before.'

Vijay stared at the space between us. 'I can make out a small column of light. It's flickering and yellow in colour. Is it a candle?'

'Yes, that is exactly what it is. Now close your eye to rest it.' The clinician silently tipped his head towards the window and I moved to where Ruby was sitting and gave her the candlestick.

'Try again?'

'But it's gone.' Vijay's voice had risen by two octaves.

'Calm yourself. Doctor Stuart-MacKenzie has moved the candle. Now try and find the flame again.'

His dilated iris frantically scanned the darkness, his head jutting out from his neck trying to help his eyeball function. 'YES, I CAN SEE IT!' His relief was palpable. 'It's over to my right, and something is glistening below it. Something gold?'

Ruby lifted her arm and exposed her wide, solid gold bangle encircling her wrist. 'You're looking at my gold bracelet, Vijay, reflected in the candlelight. The one you bought me in Marseille.'

'Bring it closer.' He grabbed her arm like a desperate man drowning and peered into the illuminated gold surface. 'I can make out my face, Ruby. I can see your hand. I can see you!'

'Well done, Your Highness.' The ophthalmologist eased Ruby out of the way and slowly moved the candle flame backwards and forwards in front of Vijay's face. He then uncovered the left eye and repeated the test. Finally, he spoke.

'Doctor Stuart-MacKenzie, I can say with some confidence that our patient's right eye will make a full recover.'

'Two down, one to go,' I muttered under my breath, waiting for the surgeon's next words.

'The left eye is more problematic, but the iris is contracting and dilating which is a good sign. That's enough for today. We will try again tomorrow. Until then, His Highness must keep his eyes completely covered to stop daylight reversing the gains we've made so far.' He wound the padded bandage back around Vijay's head and blew out the candle.

'I can assure you, Doctor, your instructions will be followed to the letter,' said Ruby, brooking no argument, and opening the curtains.

'Then I'll bid you all good-day and be on my way.'

'I have to return to the Lady Reading for my evening surgery,' I added, feeling drained, 'so I'll see you out.'

'Mac.' I hovered, halfway to the door.

'Yes, Vijay.'

'When can I get rid of the bedpan?'

The tranquillity of my mountain surroundings was a balm to the continued chaos of my private life. Duncan had replied to my letter, refusing to delay his arrival in Simla, gushing with desire to be back at my side and promising all manner of romantic nights under the stars. Trying to get him to accept that I was having second thoughts was like trying to hold back Niagara Falls with a hockey stick and his salacious suggestions were affecting my dreams which were becoming more erotic by the night.

Logically, Duncan's supposed desire for my body had an underlying egocentric ulterior motive. He coveted the post of veterinary surgeon to the Jhalanpur Royal Family and saw me as an entrée into their world. The post would be very impressive on Duncan's curriculum vitae and it didn't take a genius to recognise that he would be a great asset to Vijay, particularly if the Prince did suffer from limited vision or reduced mobility.

I had learned over the weeks that the Jhalanpur stables were full of hunters, polo-ponies and racehorses, while the highly respected equine stud was the Maharaja's pride and joy. Elephants, camels and hunting dogs, used for durbars, racing and tiger shoots, all added variety to the work, making the position highly sort after, challenging and full of variety. Duncan would be the perfect choice and he had no intention of letting it slip by.

There was no way I could stop him arriving anyway, and his charismatic Celtic charm was guaranteed to make him the hit of the season with the ladies of the Shires, who would take great delight in gossiping about every minutiae of his life, including me, and I shuddered at the very thought of being the central topic of conversation in every colonial drawing-room in Simla.

'Oh, damnation,' I cursed, as I headed over to the Corstorphine Hotel, where Frances and Jim were waiting for me in the dining-room.

'Sorry I'm late, my ward round took longer than expected.'

Jim stood and held out a chair. 'Relax, Mac, we have only just arrived ourselves.'

'Why, where have you been?'

'On a day trek to Churdhar.'

'Was it worth it?'

'Definitely,' enthused Frances. 'The views from up there are stunning, Mac, and Churdhar Peak is where George Everest made his many astronomical readings and sightings of the Himalayan mountains in 1834.'

'Good for him.' My response sounded churlish but after a month in Simla, all I had managed was a visit to the Jakhu Temple, a mile away. I was about to mention this fact when raucous laughter, coming from a table of men across the dining-room, drowned me out.

'Who are they?' I asked Jim, peering over his shoulder.

'I've no idea.' He beckoned to the waiter.

'Sir Charles Ponsonby-Pritchard and his party, Sahib. They have dinner and play the poker here every week.'

'Really. Which is Sir Charles?' I asked, keeping my voice low.

'The gentleman by fireplace, Memsahib. The one with big moustache.'

So, this is the Surgeon-General, I thought, taking in his balding head, nicotine-stained facial hair and pronounced nose. He pulled a monocle from his top pocket and signed the dinner chit.

'Why are you so interested?' asked Frances.

I explained, giving her chapter and verse on Lady Edith and my boring afternoon having tiffin.

'Good Lord, is Cynthia here as well?'

I watched Sir Charles and his male guests leave the room and shook my head. 'No, she's been sent to a finishing school in Geneva.'

Frances tutted. 'I hope they have more luck controlling her than I did.'

'Fran, if you couldn't control her, I'm sure no-one else can,' commented Jim, signing our dinner chit. 'Shall we?' He led us through to the lounge and ordered coffee.

'After meeting her self-opinionated mother, I'm not surprised you had problems with the daughter, Frances. No doubt you will see that for yourself when we all gather at some social function in the coming weeks.'

'Jim, make sure I stay well out of that woman's way,' said Frances. 'She complained to Beaky Beckinsale about my reprimand of Cynthia after the Aga Khan Palace incident, which my Deputy Head then delighted in embellishing to the school's Board of Governors.'

'Perhaps the father is less bellicose than his daughter,' I suggested, wondering if I should leave a note for the Surgeon-General in reception, requesting a meeting about Lamis's sphincteroplasty operation.

Jim seemed to read my mind. 'Unlikely, Mac.' He cut the end of his cigar and lit it. 'I'd leave the Surgeon-General to your boss. She wouldn't thank you for interfering if the matter is as delicate as you say.'

'Perhaps you're right, but I so want to help Lamis. One day I'll show you the photographs I took of her injuries.'

'We can imagine, Mac, and I agree wholeheartedly, which is why I want to help her get an education.' Frances settled into her wing-backed chair, coffee cup in hand. 'Actually, I've already met Lamis.'

'Really?' I was astonished.

'Yes, I introduced myself to Doctor Scott as soon as we arrived and explained what I had in mind and asked for her support. She was delighted to help and gave permission for me to give Lamis English language lessons each day in the hospital.'

'You're kidding me?' I felt like a Northumbrian navvy having won a fortune on the football pools.

'No, Mac, I'm not. For the past three weeks, Lamis and I have been getting along splendidly and I have to say, she's turned out to be very bright.'

'I didn't know you spoke Urdu.'

'I don't, but I'm learning. By the time we leave Simla, Lamis will have learned the rudiments of our language with about six-hundred words under her belt and I'll be able to reprimand our Muslim gardener at St Saviours for being dilatory, lazy and frankly totally useless.'

'What do you mean, we?' I was having difficulty taking it all in.

'Mac, on your WMS salary you simply couldn't afford to pay for Lamis's education in a decent girl's school, so I have decided to employ her as my maid, and I will educate her in my spare time, until she is old enough to join the Lady Hardinge College as a medical student. Doctor Scott thinks it's a splendid idea.'

I almost floated back to Mallards, trying to absorb what I had just heard. While I had been immersed in Vijay's problems and my work, Agnes and Frances had taken my idea and were now turning it into reality. I couldn't wait to discuss it all with my boss and longed for the day when Lamis and I could have a conversation without the need for a translator. She was right to call me *Umi*, I thought. I was like a mother hen protecting her chick, and I loved it.

Ruby took me to one side as I walked in and told me she had received a phone-call that morning from Captain Duncan Fitzpatrick who wanted to pass on his best wishes to Vijay and to say that he would be in Simla in three day's time and wondered if he could call.

'What did you say?'

'That I would need to discuss this with His Highness and asked him to ring again once he was here.'

'Damn!'

'Is that all you've got to say on the matter, or would you like to elaborate?'

I sighed. 'Duncan Fitzpatrick is nothing if not persistent, Ruby, and I'm sure Vijay will want to find out exactly what injuries his thoroughbred sustained on the polo-field before it was shot. Has Vijay mentioned Duncan to you at all?'

'No. All he talks about is his sight and when he can get up.'

'What time is the ophthalmologist arriving today?'

'Two o'clock.'

'OK, I'll try to get back for it. Meanwhile don't say anything to Vijay about the call. With luck, Duncan may never turn up.'

Chapter Twenty-Seven

My porridge, doused in honey, tasted wonderful. I was sitting on the terrace at Mallards enjoying a late breakfast, knowing that I didn't have to be on duty until mid-afternoon and revelling in a few short peaceful hours of solitude and contentment. Staring across the garden's manicured lawns to the snow-capped Himalayan peaks in the distance, I heard male voices coming from the hall and assumed it was the eye-surgeon. I eased myself off the swing-chair intent on greeting him, then stopped dead in my tracks.

'I'm here to see Prince Vijay Kumar Singh II and have an appointment. My name is Captain Duncan Fitzpatrick.'

'I go and see His Highness,' replied Sanjay. 'Please, Captain Sahib, you take a seat in there. I not long.'

I leant against the terrace wall, my peaceful morning ruined, and closed my eyes, feeling the girlish excitement in the pit of my stomach and a sudden shortness of breath.

'Oh, for goodness' sake, Mac, grow up,' I nagged, as I took the backstairs two-at-a-time and retreated into my room.

'If Mohammed won't go to the mountain, Elizabeth, then the mountain must come to Mohammed.'

'You're in fine form, this morning, Karr.'

'Just pointing out the obvious, dear. The man may be an opportunist, but he must be good for the odd dinner or two, and I'd lay odds that he has you in his sights for dessert.'

'Do I have any say in this matter?'

'Not if your libido has anything to do with it, dear.'

'Great. Then I'll just be a lamb to the slaughter, shall I?'

'*Good Lord, no. You're always bleating on about not being a wilting violet, so give him a bit of his own medicine.*'

'How would I do that, then?'

'*Oh, for goodness' sake, dear. You now know what he is and what he's capable of, so use him the way he used you. In short, love him and leave him.*'

'Who do you think I am, Marlene Dietrich?'

'*Hardly. Elizabeth, you can't sing. But you did give a very good impression of Mata Hari on your last night with Tom Wallace.*'

'Yes, and look where that got me?'

'*Oh, not that old chestnut. Most people learn by their mistakes, Elizabeth. Perhaps you should too.*'

'Fine, I'll call at the dispensary on my way in to work and purloin the odd condom or three.'

'*Excellent idea. Can I go now?*'

Agnes was checking on a mother suffering from dysentery and suspected malaria when I found her on Ward B, and we were discussing the case when Iris interrupted us to say that Lord Irwin's equerry was in reception and wanted to speak to her.

'Now what's all this about?' said Agnes, heading for her office with me in tow.

The equerry, in full ICS uniform, was standing waiting for us as we rounded the corner.

'Doctor Agnes Scott?' He looked down at an addressed white, heavily embossed envelope.

'Correct,' answered Agnes, taking the missive from his hand. I noted the gold edging and was impressed.

'And are you Doctor Elizabeth Stuart-MacKenzie?'

You could have knocked me down with a feather. 'The very same,' I replied, and felt the quality of the stationery between my fingers as I looked vacantly into his face.

'Ladies. It has been a pleasure to meet you.' He bowed, spun on the balls of his feet, and marched away down the stairs.

'Well, I never,' muttered Agnes, opening her office door. 'I suggest we find out what these are all about over a pot of tea.

The tea arrived and Agnes gingerly opened her envelope and eased the gold-edged invitation from inside.

'Well, I'll be!' she exclaimed, taking her half-moon reading glasses off her nose. 'I've been awarded an OBE in the King's birthday honours list and I'm to be presented with the Officer of the Order of the British Empire medal at Lord and Lady Irwin's Garden Party.'

'Agnes, that's wonderful and justly deserved if you don't mind me saying so.'

'I bet this is Lady Irwin's doing.' She put her glasses back on and read it once more. 'What does yours say?'

In the excitement I hadn't yet opened my invitation. I peeled back the envelope flap and reached inside.

George V, King of the United Kingdom and the British Dominions, and Emperor of India, has pleasure in awarding you the Medal of the Most Excellent Order of the British Empire for Gallantry.

You are invited to attend Viceregal Lodge on Saturday 23rd August 1930 at 3 o'clock, to be presented with the Empire Gallantry Medal by Lord Irwin, Earl of Halifax, Viceroy and Governor General of India at His Majesty's Birthday Honours investiture in India.

I handed the invitation over to Agnes to read and recalled George Philpott's rather drunken words to me in the Officers' Mess at Landi Kotal on the night I received my Afghan Rifle.

'I have a liddle secret, Mac, though you dirn't hear it from me. Pendleton has written to Lord Irwin in despatches, recommendin' an EGM for your mantlepiece. Empire Gallantry Medal. The King's gong for bravery. You're not supposed to know about it until King George V signs on the dotted line, but it's in the bag.'

Agnes placed both invitations on the desk and chuckled. 'Tea seems a little tame, under the circumstances, wouldn't you say, Elizabeth?'

I had difficulty saying anything. My throat had completely seized.

Duncan was waiting for me in reception when I came off shift.

'Evening, Mac. I thought I would surprise you.'

In for a penny, in for a pound, I thought, and turned on the charm. 'Duncan, what a surprise. When did you get here?'

'Late last night. I've got a room at the Corstorphine Hotel. Jim Hamilton recommended it.'

'Really. When are you leaving? . . . I mean, how long are you here for?'

'I'm not sure. Perhaps we could have dinner tomorrow night and I can fill you in on what's been happening to me since you left Bombay.'

As if I didn't know. 'Well, there's a rather nice restaurant on the outskirts of town overlooking the valley which I've been meaning to try. It's called the Yellow Jasmine. Shall we give it a go?'

'Sounds perfect. I'll make a reservation in the morning. Would seven-thirty suit you?'

'Yes. I'm working in the local community clinics tomorrow, so I'll be back in plenty of time.'

'Great. Now, how about a nightcap at the Corstorphine Hotel before I see you back to the Jhalanpur residence?'

Soft music was playing as we sat on the restaurant's wooden veranda in candlelight, enjoying the last of a bottle of claret.

'Have I told you, Mac, that you're a sight for sore eyes?'

'Not that I can recall, Duncan, but my memory is a bit blurred after three glasses of wine, so say it again.' He picked up my hand and brushed his lips across my knuckles.

'You're beautiful, intelligent, and have a mind of your own, unlike the bevy of brainless beauties from England's top-drawer who I keep coming across. I tell you, Mac, I've missed your feisty character over the years.'

I dipped my forefinger into my claret and rubbed it across his lips.

'You're a Jezebel, so you are, Missy, and a right handful, that's for sure.'

'The question is, Duncan, can you handle a Jezebel?' I wondered again if he was married and whether he had any children.

'Just give me the chance?' His wink took me straight back to the White Hart pub in Edinburgh where we first met, and a shudder slithered down my spine.

'Let's get out of here,' I suggested, looking around for the waiter. 'It's a warm night and I know a bridle path back to your hotel through the forest. So much nicer than hiring a rickshaw.'

Duncan was on his feet immediately, lust driving him on. 'I'll go and pay.'

'And I'll find the powder-room to freshen up. See you at the entrance in five minutes.'

I brushed my cropped locks, added more lipstick and pouted into the powder-room mirror. 'Right, Mata Hari,' I whispered, 'do your worst.'

I knew just where I was going as I led Duncan down a gentle slope into a coppice of tall trees, the full moon casting shadows across the mossy ground. The air was fresh and aromatic, the undergrowth soft and spongy, the trees filled with the sound of cicadas, buzzing furiously with their high-pitched whine.

Duncan slid his hand across my shoulders in a protective, brotherly sort of way and we moved on, neither saying a word as the path wound deeper into the hillside. Ten years earlier, my innocent self would have believed that all this was for real, but a decade on, cynicism had set in and my head was firmly in control.

'Would you be knowing where we're going, Cailin?'

'Oh, yes, I've been this way many times . . . during the day, of course. I hold clinics in the villages around the valley and this is a short cut.'

The track levelled out and grew wider, finally curving to the left and ending at the edge of a large natural pool nestling between granite rocks. Flickering stars and pearled moonlight reflected off the still surface of the water as an owl hooted in the distance.

'Isn't this beautiful?'

Duncan wrapped his arms around my waist and brushed his warm lips against my neck as we stood in silence, the warmth of his body permeating heat through the back of my dress. I leant my head against his chest and sighed deeply.

'Do you fancy a swim?' I asked, sending shock waves through his composure.

'Christ, Mac, what happened to the innocent girl I left in Edinburgh?'

'She grew up, Duncan.' I moved across to the nearest rock and removed my shoes. 'So, what's it to be? Do we head back to Simla, or should we dampen our ardour in the cool waters of the Himalayas?' My dress slipped from my shoulders and I let it fall.

Goosebumps peppered my skin as I eased my naked body into the pool's depths and languidly swam to the centre, rippling waves cutting the glassy surface in my wake. Turning and treading water, I watched Duncan's athletic torso sink below the surface and move like a sleek torpedo towards me. He brushed against my legs and rose to the surface, his lips finding mine in a long, lingering kiss.

I wound my legs around his hips and allowed my breasts to massage his copper-red chest, while my fingers rippled across his shoulder blades and my heels gently rubbed against his buttocks.

It felt wonderful, like coming home after a long cold journey and finding a blazing fire and a crystal brandy bowl of amber liquid waiting to warm my insides, but it was Tom who filled my senses, not Duncan.

'Christ, Mac, I've missed feeling you.'

Duncan's Irish accent snapped me back to reality. 'Well, I'm here now, so make the most of me.'

My right leg slipped from his hip and my knee rubbed against his shrunken penis, feeling the wrinkled appendage against my skin. 'Finding the water a tad cold, are we, Captain?'

He took my right nipple between his fingers and rubbed it with his thumb. 'Even Veterinary Surgeons are prone to sudden drops in temperature, Doctor, unlike Northumbrian GPs.' My nipple was rock hard, and the sensation caused me to whimper with delight.

'Would the riverbank be more to your liking, Duncan?'

His hand traced a line down my abdomen and settled between my legs, his fingers gently rubbing my clitoris. 'Whatever the lady desires.'

I detached myself from his embrace and swam to the pool's edge, lying back on a grassy knoll, water dripping from my hair. Stretching for his jacket, I searched the pockets for his wallet and opened the back-flap, pulling out a sheath.

'I thought you said you were having a problem with your memory?' commented Duncan, as his legs straddled my pelvis.

I stared into his deep emerald eyes as he took the condom and tore the packet with his teeth.

'Some memories are difficult to forget, Sire.'

'And much better for the repeating, Madam.'

I closed my eyes and concentrated on my own pleasure, willing my body to follow Duncan into a maelstrom of wild abandon, desperate for the sensation of climaxing during the act of intercourse after so many celibate months. I tensed, holding my breath, expectation rising as I felt the build.

Duncan's features suddenly twisted into a contorted expression of ecstatic pain, his body shook, and a raw, guttural groan rent the air. Seconds later, it was all over and I had tensed in vain.

He collapsed on top of me, all thirteen stone of him, and I held him there, listening to his rapid breathing, until he rolled onto the moss, sated, empty, and with not a care in the world.

'Mac, that was incredible,' he muttered, then drifted into a post-coital nap.

As he quietly snored, I rose and returned to the pool, letting the cool water soothe my burning skin and wash away the perspiration, feeling physically frustrated, but knowing that I had finally broken the spell that was Duncan Fitzpatrick. I was free of his charms, free of being celibate and free to love again one day.

I floated on my back, letting my fingers do what Duncan had failed to do, and relived my erotic nights in Bombay. My memory had not failed me. Duncan was not Tom, and he never would be.

I smiled as the owl made a low-level pass over my head and winged its way towards the valley.

'How was it?' asked Karr, invading my thoughts.

'Liberating, Karr,' I whispered.

'Told you so, dear. Now, wake him up and send him on his way.'

Chapter Twenty-Eight

W e walked into Viceregal Lodge, Duncan's silver-grey morning suit complementing my russet cashmere, calf-length, day-dress with its wide single revere, buttoned side-panelling and cuffed sleeves, and were greeted by a uniformed official.

Using a dangerous looking hatpin, Ruby had attached my deep chestnut and cream broad-brimmed hat at a jaunty angle on my cropped hair, and I had to admit, it looked rather fetching.

Matching cream-capped, high-heeled shoes completed my ensemble and as I was led into an anti-room of the Grand Ballroom, I felt proud to be British, and honoured to be participating in such a ceremonial investiture.

'Doctor Elizabeth Stuart-MacKenzie,' called out the equerry.

'Here,' I said, and went to join a short line of people all dressed in their finery. Agnes was four places ahead of me and turned at the sound of my voice and smiled.

If only my family could have been here to witness this, I thought, as I scanned the audience sitting, theatre-style, in front of the podium. Duncan was just taking his seat at the back and I could see Vijay, upright on an aisle seat in the front row, a black eye-patch over his left eye and his left leg stretched out in front of him, his bandaged thigh hidden by his deep green Angarkha jacket and broad white trousers which tapered at the ankle, his crutches laid at his feet. He looked regal in his dark green pagri turban with its diamond-encrusted aigrette of white feathers and his long strings of pearls emphasising his wealth and status. This was the second time I had seen him dressed in such finery. The first was in Aden when we left the ss Narkunda to visit the British Resident, Sir George Stewart-Symes. Vijay was there to pay his respects to His Majesty, King George V's appointed representative in the colony on behalf of the Princes of India. I was there to accompany Princess Darshwanabai and her aunt to a lunch hosted by Geraldine Stewart-Symes, where the Princess could spend a few peaceful hours away from the heat, the fetid air and constant noise of the commercial port. I wondered what I would have done differently on that day I had known what the future held.

It had been too easy to forget Vijay's superiority over the past weeks and I mentally admonished myself for showing him such a lack of respect. Ruby, sitting some way back for diplomacy, looked equally ravishing in one of her haute-couture outfits of sapphire-blue and gold silk, her face half-hidden behind a sapphire-blue net veil attached to another of her cloche hats, and I wondered how she felt having to remain apart at official functions and could never be introduced to the Viceroy or Vicereine. The whole charade seemed ridiculous to me and my heart went out to her.

Suddenly there was a trumpet fanfare which made me jump and Lord Irwin appeared from the opposite side of the ballroom in full dress-uniform, his ceremonial sword hanging at his side and flanked by two uniformed officers of the British Indian Army. His equerry stood at his right shoulder and nodded to the Chamberlain by the anti-room door, who banged his white staff on the marble floor to announce the start of proceedings.

The day was a blur, Lord Irwin's few words as he pinned the medal to my dress lost in a whirl of faces, drinks, canapes, introductions, congratulations, social chit-chat and never-ending rotations around the grounds, all with Duncan at my arm, showing me off like a prize bullock at the Berwick-on-Tweed live-stock auction.

Agnes walked over and told me that Lady Irwin was keen to talk about my report, so I left Duncan on his own and crossed to where she was sitting, surrounded by a group of colonial wives. She appeared relieved to be interrupted as I approached.

'There you are, Elizabeth, let's stroll over to the tennis courts.' She nodded to various dignitaries as we crossed the lawn and I couldn't help noticing Duncan surrounded by a bevy of young 'Fishing Fleet' women, all looking for a suitable husband.

'Now, my dear, Doctor Scott tells me your young Muslim patient is here in Simla. I must say I found your report of her injuries both graphic and rather harrowing.'

'Indeed, she is, Lady Irwin, and I'm sorry if the photographs upset you.'

She flicked the apology away with her closed lace fan. 'Doctor Scott thought the mountain air would help in her recovery and I'm pleased to hear that it appears to be working. I understand you are arranging for her to receive private tutoring in Poona after her convalescence.'

'Yes, the headmistress at St Saviours School for Girls in Poona is a close friend and has agreed to take Lamis under her wing.

'Is she here? I would like to thank her personally.'

'Sadly not, but I will let her know that you are aware of Lamis's case and her future.'

'Will the child make a complete recovery?' The Vicereine was genuinely interested.

'I hope so, but she will always have a slight curvature of the spine due to osteomalacia after so many years of neglect and I doubt she will ever be able to have children.'

'The poor child. Is there anything I can do to help? My husband and I are coming to the end of our tour here in India and before I hand over the reins of the Countess of Dufferin's Fund to my successor, I would like to be sure I have done everything possible to advance the work of the WMS.'

'Then perhaps you could arrange for a donation to be given to St Saviours School. A Lady Irwin science laboratory would give the students the ability to study biology and chemistry. After spending time with me, the fifth and sixth formers are all keen to get into medicine.'

'Well, I never. Leave it to me Elizabeth. I'll see what I can do.'

We re-joined the throng of guests, and I went in search of Duncan.

'How are your feet bearing up?' asked Ruby, as I was on my second walk past.

'Killing me. When can we leave?'

'When Vijay has finished speaking with the Viceroy.' She pointed in the direction of the terrace. 'Duncan's over there, getting up close and personal with Lady Crawford.'

I watched the woman laugh at some quip Duncan was making, as his hand slowly slid down her spine.

'You and I need to talk,' said Ruby, eyeing me through her veil. 'Alone.'

I ignored her and smiled at Vijay as he slowly approached on his crutches. 'You look absolutely exhausted, Vijay. I think it's time you rested that leg.'

'I agree, Mac, but I had no intention of missing being here to watch you being honoured by the great and good of British India. That medal looks just perfect on your left chest.'

'Thank-you, Your Highness. Now, let's quietly make our way to the exit.'

Duncan saw us moving towards the Lodge, whispered into Lady Crawford's ear, bowed in an exaggerated fashion, and met us by the door.

'Will we be leaving, Cailin?'

'We are, Duncan.' Ruby caught my eye and raised her eyebrows but didn't comment. 'Perhaps you would go ahead and call for the car.'

It was when we adjourned to my bedroom, leaving Vijay and Duncan to do some male bonding on the terrace, that I found out what Ruby wanted to discuss.

'Vijay is about to offer Duncan the post of Veterinary Surgeon to the House of Jhalanpur.'

I removed my heeled shoes and wiggled my toes. 'I'm not surprised, Ruby. I've always suspected that Duncan's presence here in Simla was purely for that one opportunity, and to be fair, he'll make an excellent addition to Vijay's staff. I just wish he'd concentrate more on his professional skills and less on massaging his own ego. Did you see the way the women flocked around him like bees around a honeypot at the Garden Party?'

'You were certainly envied by most of them, that's for sure.'

'Pity they don't know what he is really like. Who's Lady Crawford?'

'The wife of Lord Irwin's Political Agent and she can put Catherine the Great in the shade when it comes to lovers.' Ruby removed her cloche hat and threw it on the bed. 'I think, your ex-boyfriend is being lined-up to be her next sexual liaison.'

'Then it will be a long-distance one if he is to remain in Jhalanpur.' I removed my hat and ran my fingers through my cropped hair.

'I must confess, Mac, he's by far the best-looking man in Simla, and if I fancied a bit on the side, Lady Crawford would find herself with a rival.'

'RUBY! Don't even think it in jest. Duncan would love cuckolding Vijay, it would boost his ego no end. Take it from me, he's not worth it. Behind his charismatic Gaelic charm and impeccable manners, there's a narcissist who's only interest is in himself.' I hung my cashmere dress on the wardrobe door. 'And I don't think you would be impressed with his sexual prowess either.'

'Talking from experience, are we?'

'Let's just say, Tom Wallace could teach him a thing or two about giving a girl a good time.' I carefully unpinned my medal and placed it on the dressing table.

'Elizabeth Stuart-MacKenzie, you shock me.'

'As Frances always said, Ruby, still waters run deep.' I stared across the lawn thinking back to our night in the forest. 'Take it from me, Duncan won't hang around to be anyone's liaison. Once the ink is dry on his contract, he'll be off to Jhalanpur without even bothering to thank me for the introduction.' I crossed my fingers and prayed that Princess Darshwanabai would remain hidden behind the walls of her zenana.

'If you feel that strongly, why did you invite him to accompany you to the investiture?'

If Ruby only knew I thought. 'Because it was either him or Lamis Abbas. I don't know anyone else who is single.' I peeled cream satin, lace garters and seamed stockings from my legs and dropped them into the laundry basket by the bathroom door. 'Oh, that's better.'

'Sometimes, Mac, I find your lack of social contacts depressing. If I didn't know you better, I'd call you a hermit.'

'May I remind you, Miss Tavener, I have to work for a living, and it's little wonder I haven't any male suitors when I spend most of my time either on a train, in a hospital or staring down the ocular lens of a microscope.' I slipped into a cool, satin kaftan.

'You know the expression, Mac. All work and no play . . .' She looked at her Cartier watch. 'I'll see you downstairs in fifteen minutes, and, Mac?'

My head popped through the neck of the kaftan. 'What?'

'Don't mark that expensive material, piercing it with your gong.'

Duncan proved to be true to form. Later that evening he left me at the entrance to Mallards with a passionate kiss, a backward wave, and a promise to write. I couldn't help experiencing a touch of déjà vu as he walked away, but was thankful that, this time, it didn't hurt one bit. At least, I thought, as I made my way back inside, my status amongst Simla's colonial females had risen by leaps and bounds, and not because of my Empire Gallantry Medal.

Agnes waved a handwritten note under my nose the next morning as I was checking the contents of my medical bag before attending a baby-clinic in the outlying village of Kufri.

'This has just come from the Surgeon General's secretary,' she said. 'Sir Charles has agreed to lead on Lamis's rectal reconstruction operation but needs a full resume of her injuries. Can you deal with it?'

I read the contents and nodded. 'Of course. I'll make a copy of my original report to you and Lady Irwin as soon as I get back this afternoon. When are you doing the operation?'

'Next week, all being well.'

'Right, I'd better get going or I'll be late.'

Not knowing where the Surgeon-General's office was in Viceroy Lodge and remembering that Vijay said he lived along the ridge from Mallards, I slipped the report and a set of photographs into an envelope, intent on handing it to Ghalib, and asking him to deliver it to the Ponsonby-Pritchard residence before the day was out. This was the first sphincteroplasty that I had ever witnessed and I needed to refresh my memory on the procedure, so I made my way to the hospital library to read the most up-to-date research on the subject. I found Lamis sitting there, alone, practising her English alphabet.

'*As-Salam-u-Alaikim*, Lamis.'

'Hello, Mother Mac.' My spirits rose as I heard her tentative voice speak to me in English.

'How are you today?'

'I well, thank-you.'

Without a second's thought, I hugged her tightly, then knelt by her side. 'Lamis, one day you will study medicine.' I took my stethoscope from my laboratory coat pocket and placed it around her neck. She fingered the instrument, bit her lip then nodded.

'I be like you, Mother Mac.'

'Maybe.'

'I pleased.'

'Doctor Lamis Abbas. It sounds good, doesn't it?'

Her forehead wrinkled as the library door opened and Frances walked in. 'Evening, Mac, how is my student doing?'

'Really well, Frances. She just told me she wants to be a doctor.'

'Like her adopted mother?'

'I guess.' I took back the stethoscope and stretched my back as I rose.

'Long day?'

'Yes. An early start at out-station clinics then Sir Ponsonby-Pritchard wanted a report on Lamis's case history,' I replied, inspecting a row of medical books.

'Sounds promising.'

'It is, and if the operation is successful, this young lady will no longer need her colostomy bag.' I pointed to Lamis's dress where the bag was located and looked into her eyes. 'Better soon.'

'Yes, Mother Mac,' she said, her lips quivering, 'I better soon, *Insh' Allah.*'

'Then I had better make sure everything goes to plan.' I pulled a large medical tome from the library shelf. 'Has Jim left for Bombay yet?'

'Yes, this morning. He'll be gone for a month.'

I wondered if he was sharing a railway carriage with Duncan. 'Then how about an early dinner on the Mall. Just the two of us.'

'Great idea. I'll meet you in the entrance at seven o'clock.'

'OK.' I raised the medical compendium and groaned. 'If I don't turn up you will find me in the common-room, fast asleep over J.P Lockhart-Mummery's 1923 research papers on rectal reconstruction.

Chapter Twenty-Nine

The tension had been growing all day. Lamis's operation was scheduled to take place in the evening when Sir Charles was free from Government business. Agnes had checked and double checked the cleanliness of the operating theatre and all the instruments and equipment, while I examined Lamis, weighed her, swabbed and sanitised her rectum, and made sure she didn't eat anything for some hours before going under anaesthetic.

With Sir Charles leading, Agnes was going to act as his Assistant Surgeon, I would be the anaesthetist, while Iris and a small team of nurses would provide theatre backup.

We were ready and sitting in Agnes's office twiddling our thumbs, waiting for the Surgeon-General to make an appearance, and the wait was making me nervous. Minutes ticked by. When Agnes could stand it no longer, she sent a runner to find out where Sir Charles had got to and he returned with a note from the secretary. Apparently, Sir Charles had been called away on a matter of urgency and would not be back in time, so we were to postpone the operation until another day.

'He must be joking,' I declared, pacing the floor.

Agnes's expression resembled Ma's when it poured with rain on washday, and when she finally spoke, her tone of voice was cold, hard-headed, and full of animosity.

'We will not postpone the operation, despite the Surgeon-General. Lamis is already prepared and has waited long enough.

I will take the lead, you will assist me, Elizabeth, and Iris will take over the anaesthetics.'

I shot round from looking out of the window. 'But I've never done a reconstruction of the anal sphincter before.'

'You may not, but I have. Well, something similar anyway.' I had never seen Agnes so determined. 'The experience will be invaluable to you, Elizabeth, and you have already read everything there is to know about the operation.'

'Yes, but . . .'

'No buts, Elizabeth, it may be a bit more complicated on this child as she is so small, but the principles are the same. We already know that the internal and external sphincter muscles are severed and need re-stitching, which means we must be extremely careful when cutting into the perineum and locating the torn ends. Damaging the anoderm or vaginal mucosa must be avoided at all costs.'

I wasn't sure if Agnes was reciting the dangers to me or to herself.

'Iris, I need you to give me a running commentary on Lamis's respiration, pulse and eye movement throughout the procedure. Elizabeth, we can't use clamps to keep the sides of the incision open because there is nowhere to anchor them. Instead, you will keep them apart using suture threads. Two at each end should be sufficient.'

'Yes, of course.' The Lockhart-Mummery diagram of this technique sprang into my mind.

'Very well. Do either of you have any questions or can we get on with it before our patient suffers a heart attack out of sheer panic?'

Iris sighed deeply and shook her head. I was already opening the office door and as Agnes led the way to Theatre B, my head filled with all the dire warnings on what could go wrong. Killing Lamis from too much ether was obvious, and with little room to work in this area of her body, accidentally slicing into the vagina wall and damaging the mucosal lining, or not being able to find the torn ends of the sphincter muscles were serious possibilities.

I checked my pulse while I waited for Agnes to finish washing her hands. It was through the roof. I stretched out my hands and watched as they shook wildly. Agnes turned, and knocked them down with her elbow.

'Elizabeth, look at me. You're frightened because you are emotionally involved with Lamis, and right now, that is not helpful. You are a first-class doctor, a very capable physician and I could not think of anyone better to assist me right now.'

I filled my lungs and expelled carbon-dioxide slowly.

'That's right. Now, close your mind to who the patient is and concentrate on the matter at hand. We can do this, dear, and we will do it, despite Sir Charles Ponsonby-Pritchard.' Her words were full of venom and her obvious anger strengthened my resolve and filled me with courage.

We eased Lamis onto the operating table and stood back while Iris dripped ether onto the gauze pad inside the Schlimmerbusch metal mask and placed it over her nose and mouth. Induction began immediately as she breathed ether vapour and atmospheric air into her lungs, but it seemed to take forever for her to go into a deep sleep. Eventually her breathing altered, becoming deep and regular. Iris lifted an

eyelid and brushed a cotton thread across the cornea. The
eyeball didn't react.

'Ready, Doctor Scott.'

'Excellent. Now keep her there.'

I placed sterile pillows under Lamis's buttocks, spread her
legs wide and exposed the narrow perineum bridge between her
vagina and back passage.

We had waited months to repair the damage done by
Lamis's sexually demanding, vicious, and violent husband and a
calmness settled over the operating-room. Agnes wiped her
forehead, looked at Iris who nodded, then sliced along the skin
with a scalpel.

After one hour attaching the internal sphincter muscle, Agnes
stretched her spine and sighed.

'Is all well at your end, Iris?'

'Yes, Doctor Scott, her breathing is good, pulse steady and
there's no reflex action.'

'Very well, Elizabeth, let's continue with the exterior
sphincter muscle.'

We were just suturing the muscle ends together when Iris
broke the silence.

'Lamis's eyelids are twitching, Doctor Scott!'

'Don't move, Elizabeth,' I froze. 'More ether.'

Iris was ahead of her, dripping liquid from the dropper onto
the gauze pad.

I shuddered at the thought of Lamis waking in excruciating
pain or dying from an overdose of ether and it took all my
concentration to stop my hands from shaking once more.

The theatre nurse, standing alongside Agnes, had her eyes closed in prayer, her fingers crossed above the tray of sterilized instruments while my heart thumped against my chest in time to the theatre wall-clock as it ticked off the seconds. I was beginning to feel faint when Iris spoke again.

'She's responding, Doctor Scott. Her reflexes are non-existent, but her pulse and breathing are steady. Please continue.'

I could have hugged her.

'Thank the Lord,' muttered Agnes, as our eyes met across the operating table and we nodded in unison.

Lamis had been under anaesthetic for over two-and-a-quarter hours when Agnes finally dropped the suture needle into the kidney bowl and examined her handiwork. The sphincter muscles were securely reconnected, a drain had been temporarily inserted into the wound and the incision was sterilised and stitched. We checked her anus for signs of fistulas. Thankfully, there were none.

'An excellent job done, Elizabeth,' said my boss as I covered the surgical wound with a padded sterile bandage and stood back. 'I doubt Sir Charles could have done any better. All we need now is for Lamis to make a complete recovery, and I think we can put ourselves forward for another medal.'

'I don't have sufficient room on my chest, Agnes' I quipped, euphoria spreading through me like a strong opioid.

'Well, I do, especially if the Surgeon-General has to pin it on me.'

Agnes was obviously not going to let this matter drop, I thought, and turned to Iris who was still monitoring Lamis's vital signs. She looked up and raised both her thumbs.

'Let's get this young lady into the recovery room and go and have some dinner, girls. I don't know about you, but I'm starving.'

We found Frances waiting in the corridor reading a book.

'I couldn't rest until I knew that Lamis was alright.'

'So far, so good,' I said, crossing my fingers. 'Agnes did an amazing job. Have you eaten?'

'Not yet. I couldn't face dining alone at the hotel. I guess I'm missing Jim more than I want to admit.'

'Then join us,' suggested Agnes, pulling off her theatre gown and dumping it in a bin. 'We're about to eat here in the hospital canteen.'

'Then, if it's not an imposition, I'd love to.'

The canteen was quiet as we settled at a table by the window, the view of the dark wooded hillside, dotted with pinpricks of light from verandas, contrasting sharply with the bright lights above our heads. I was ravenous after missing lunch and hoped Iris wouldn't be long.

She arrived minutes later with good news. 'Lamis is awake and back on the Intensive Care Ward with Sister Panajee in charge,' she informed us, settling onto a chair across from me.

'Any vomiting?' asked Agnes, showing concern for the first time that day.

'Not so far. She's only had water and some more pain relief since waking, and I've suggested that she is left to sleep for a while before ingesting any warm soup.'

'Then there is nothing more we can do for the moment other than eat.'

Frances remained quiet as we discussed the operation over our curry, her occasional interruption only necessary when our discussion became too technical.

'I thought the Surgeon-General was to lead on the operation,' she said, when Agnes made some caustic comment about him. 'Are you telling me he wasn't there?'

I waited for Agnes to respond but she chose to remain silent.

'I'm afraid so,' I interjected. 'He was called away on urgent business at the last minute and wouldn't be back in time, so Agnes took the unilateral decision to proceed without him.'

'But that can't be right,' countered Frances.

We all looked at her as if she were mad.

'He was at the Corstorphine Hotel when I left, about to have dinner with his friends.' Agnes was busy fiddling with her napkin. 'It's Thursday night you see. He always has a poker game on a Thurs . . .'

The metal legs of my chair scrapped across the tiled floor, my napkin, screwed into a ball, bounced off the table-top, and I was moving at the speed of light across the canteen to the door.

'What did I say?' asked Frances.

'Elizabeth, don't,' shouted Agnes in my wake.

'ELIZABETH, NO!'

I snatched my camera from my medical bag and left the hospital as if my feet were on fire, hailed a rickshaw and arrived at the hotel minutes later. The reception was empty, so I walked into the bar, trembling with anger and with murder on my mind.

'Where do I find the poker game?'

A cocktail shaker clattered to the floor as a nervous barman pointed to the stairs. 'Room 4, Memsahib.'

I didn't bother knocking. The door bounced on its hinges from impact with my shoulder and my camera hid my face as five men's heads turned in unison at the sudden commotion.

'Sir Charles,' I demanded, spitting bullets. 'Smile.'

The flashbulb lit up the room as the camera recorded the image of the poker game for posterity, and Ponsonby-Pritchard's words followed me out of the room.

'Who the devil was that?'

'You'll find out,' I muttered, taking the stairs two at a time and striding out into the night. I jumped back into the rickshaw. 'Mallards,' I said, 'as fast as you can.'

Chapter Thirty

Surgeon-General of the IMS is caught playing poker instead of operating on a young Muslim girl in a critical operation!

Photographer unknown

The Muslim League are up in arms today at the news that Sir Charles Ponsonby-Pritchard, Surgeon-General of the India Medical Service, informed his medical staff at the Lady Reading Hospital, Simla, that he had been called away on urgent business and could not attend as the Lead Surgeon in a complicated sphincteroplasty operation last Thursday night when, in truth, he was caught on camera playing poker at the Corstorphine Hotel.

His patient, thirteen-year-old Lamis Abbas, a Muslim child from Old Delhi, was already prepared for surgery, so the female physicians assisting in the operation, decided to proceed without him.

A source at the hospital said, "It was a complicated procedure on such a small child, but the patient is now

recovering in Intensive Care, and we have every confidence
that she will make a complete recovery."

The Head of the Muslim League is today demanding an
official enquiry into the matter and Sir Charles is now
considering his position . . .

The phone was ringing as I sat eating my breakfast at Mallards,
three days later, the Delhi Times lead article spread out before
me.

'It's a Doctor Chakramachari from the Calcutta School of
Tropical Medicine, Mac, asking for you.'

I reluctantly rose and took the phone from Ruby's hand.

'Good morning, Doctor Chakramachari, I trust you are
well?' I gripped the edge of the telephone table.

'Doctor Stuart-MacKenzie, I have been instructed by the
Board of Governors to inform you that your Ph.D. funding
from the India Research Fund has been withdrawn with
immediate effect. A letter is being sent to you today with a copy
to Doctor Agnes Scott in her capacity as Secretary of the
Countess of Dufferin's Fund.'

'And why have the Board seen fit to take this action?' I
enquired through gritted teeth, feeling my MacKenzie spirit
rising.

'Because they have no wish to be associated with someone
who has castigated Sir Charles Ponsonby-Pritchard in the
national press for what can only be described as a minor
misdemeanour.'

'A MINOR MISDEMEANOUR?' I couldn't believe what I
was hearing.

'Yes, Madam. The Board are unanimous in their condemnation of your action. You have deliberately blackened the name of our highly-respected Surgeon-General and damaged the reputation of the IMS.'

A red mist formed before my eyes. 'What I have done is highlight the injustices in this country caused by pompous, patronising bullies with too much hubris,' I yelled, but the line had already gone dead.

'What's happened?' asked Ruby, looking up from reading the article.

'I've been fired.'

'Christ! Mac. Because of this?' She stabbed the front page with her finger.

'Yes. The Board of Governors are outraged at my audacity and have cancelled my funding.'

'But surely Agnes Scott will come to your defence? Attitudes in India are beginning to change, and the likes of Ponsonby-Pritchard would do well to remember that.'

'Sadly, Ruby, Agnes has no more sway with our insufferable IMS officials than I have, and it will take a revolution to change the attitudes of men like Ponsonby-Pritchard.' I dropped into my chair and buried my head in my hands.

'So, what will you do now?'

I shook my head realising that I was fighting a losing battle. 'I've absolutely no idea.'

A movement behind me made me sit up as Ruby's eyes shifted to the hall door. I turned to see Vijay standing there, leaning on his crutches, his face ghostly white, a cable hanging limply from his fingers.

'Vijay?'

'It's my father, Ruby. He had a massive heart attack yesterday while out riding.'

She leapt from her chair, but I stopped her with my hand. 'Did he survive?' I asked, already knowing the answer.

'No, Mac, the attack killed him outright.'

Ruby's hand shot to her mouth. 'But that means you are now the . . .'

'Yes, Ruby, I am, and I must leave immediately for Jhalanpur.

I moved to Ruby's side and felt her body trembling with fear. Obviously, I thought, as I took her hand in mine, I was not the only one facing an uncertain future . . .

END

Acknowledgements

Alexandra Allden gets my sincere gratitude for her talented, patient and creative input as my graphics designer and Jenny Crickmore-Thompson, who professionally edited the first draft of the novel and whose critique helped move the story along.

To my close family and friends, whose reader critiques leading up to publication were invaluable, thank-you all for your input and support, it means a great deal. As for my husband, David, who argued his point of view with vigour and sound common sense and put up with my many moods whilst undertaking the extensive research, I can only reiterate, 'Like my previous novels, without you, this novel would never have seen the light of day!'

Finally, I pay tribute to the many long-suffering and doggedly determined female doctors, nurses and midwives throughout India whose dedication to their profession improved the plight of women and infants throughout this sub-continent and brought western obstetric knowledge and education to a country rife with female and infant mortality. They were the medical pioneers of their time and are owed a huge debt of gratitude. Your gender salutes you.

About the Author

Susie Baggaley was born in Nottingham in 1948 and by the age of nineteen had become an executive air-stewardess before starting her own successful company managing residential property for private owners working overseas.

Her passion for sailing became a lifestyle when, after twenty-three years, she sold her company, and went ocean-cruising with her husband, David, crossing the Atlantic Ocean four times and covering over 50,000 nautical miles on their private yacht. During the long hours at sea, Susie wrote articles for the sailing press and regular blogs for family and friends. Writing fiction was a natural progression beginning with her first novel, DEAD RECKONING, under her maiden name of Su Garcia, in 2015.

Susie continues writing from both the current family yacht based in the Mediterranean, and from her home in Devon.

After a lifetime of travel, her wealth of experiences forms the basis for her intricate plots and characters. MAC'S INDIA, - In the Face of Resistance, is the author's latest novel to be published.

Review this Novel

If you have enjoyed reading the second novel in the 'Mac' series, and have purchased it on a digital book website, such as Amazon Kindle or Barnes & Noble, I would be most grateful if you could spread the word by uploading a review onto the relevant site for the benefit of others considering purchasing the novel for themselves, family or friends.

MAC's India – In the Face of Resistance

Thank you
Susie Baggaley

If you have not yet read Book 1
Call Me Mac, Port Out
it is available on digital websites in both ebook and paperback and through many High Street bookshops.

Author's Books

Fiction

The 'Mac' series of novels
Call Me Mac – (Book 1)
Mac's India – (Book 2)
(by Susie Baggaley)

Dead Reckoning
Rum Punch
(by Su Garcia)

Non-Fiction

Islas Baleares Pilot Book
by David & Susie Baggaley

(published by IMRAY / RCCPF)

Baggatelle Publishers Ltd
www.baggatellepublishers.com

Printed in Great Britain
by Amazon

15156172R00234